**Praise for *Marry in Haste*
and *Francesca's Rake***

"Ms. Kerstan utterly charms us with a sinfully delicious hero, scathingly wicked repartee, and heart-melting romance.   —*Romantic Times*

"A nicely crafted Regency. Readers will enjoy the exceptionally nice use of language, well-written dialog, and good sexual tension."   —*Library Journal*

"Lynn Kerstan combines historical reality with a fascinating hero and heroine. The romance sizzles! A fun read!"   —*The Literary Times*

"Delicious fun . . . most charming."
                              —*Romance Forever*

"A delightful and charming easy-to-read story with an irresistible hero and heroine . . . a lighthearted romance that entertains."   —*Rendezvous*

"Wry and wonderful. Lynn Kerstan deserves praise not only for a delightfully convoluted tale but for her imaginative plot. . . . Ms. Kerstan's name [should be] up there with other contemporary luminaries . . . an extraordinary storyteller."
                —The Romance Reader's Connection

REGENCY ROMANCE
COMING IN JANUARY 2006

Rake's Ransom and *A Loyal Companion*
by Barbara Metzger

Together for the first time, two stories of passion from one of Regency's biggest stars.

0-451-21793-4

Lord Ryburn's Apprentice
by Laurie Bishop

After years of bad luck, Georgiana Marland strikes gold when a rich relative takes her in. Unaccustomed to the norms of the ton, however, Georgiana finds herself in need of instruction—and infatuated with her tutor.

0-451-21731-4

The Ruby Ghost
by June Calvin

Penelope recognizes the home of her new employers—a castle from an eerie recurring dream. Other bothers include ghosts and a rakish family relation who rubs her the wrong way. That is, until he determines to show her his true colors—and protect her at all costs.

0-451-21011-5

Available wherever books are sold or at penguin.com

Marry in Haste

AND

Francesca's Rake

Lynn Kerstan

A SIGNET BOOK

SIGNET
Published by New American Library, a division of
Penguin Group (USA) Inc., 375 Hudson Street,
New York, New York 10014, USA
Penguin Group (Canada), 90 Eglinton Avenue East, Suite 700, Toronto,
Ontario M4P 2Y3, Canada (a division of Pearson Penguin Canada Inc.)
Penguin Books Ltd., 80 Strand, London WC2R 0RL, England
Penguin Ireland, 25 St. Stephen's Green, Dublin 2,
Ireland (a division of Penguin Books Ltd.)
Penguin Group (Australia), 250 Camberwell Road, Camberwell, Victoria 3124,
Australia (a division of Pearson Australia Group Pty. Ltd.)
Penguin Books India Pvt. Ltd., 11 Community Centre, Panchsheel Park,
New Delhi - 110 017, India
Penguin Group (NZ), cnr Airborne and Rosedale Roads, Albany,
Auckland 1310, New Zealand (a division of Pearson New Zealand Ltd.)
Penguin Books (South Africa) (Pty.) Ltd., 24 Sturdee Avenue,
Rosebank, Johannesburg 2196, South Africa

Penguin Books Ltd., Registered Offices:
80 Strand, London WC2R 0RL, England

Published by Signet, an imprint of New American Library, a division of Penguin Group (USA) Inc. *Marry in Haste* and *Francesca's Rake* were previously published by the Ballantine Publishing Group, a divison of Random House, Inc., New York.

First Signet Printing, December 2005
10 9 8 7 6 5 4 3 2 1

Marry in Haste copyright © Lynn Kerstan Horobetz, 1998
Francesca's Rake copyright © Lynn Kerstan Horobetz, 1997
All rights reserved

 REGISTERED TRADEMARK—MARCA REGISTRADA

Marry in Haste

For Marian Jones, teacher and friend

Chapter 1

Diana dreamed of a spider made of glass.

She tossed in a restless half sleep, tears burning her eyes as she watched it creep toward her.

She had dreamed this dream before, and the ending was always the same. The spider—

A crack of thunder made her shoot upright on the bed. Heart pounding, she pushed away the lingering nightmare and drew in a long, steadying breath.

All around her, the old house shuddered against the fierce spring storm. Wind moaned over the chimney pots and howled past the windows, most of them badly fitted in their casements. As Lord Kendal had informed her, Lakeview was in a sorry state.

But it would do for now. She sank back against the pillows and pulled the thick goose-down coverlet over her head. For a few more hours she could conceal herself and pretend she was someone else, doing all the things she had once thought Diana Evangeline Whitney would do.

A thudding noise, louder than all the others, penetrated even the thick coverlet. She sat up again, attending closely.

It came one more time, from the direction of the front door. Could someone be knocking for admittance?

Springing from the bed, she dug her feet into a pair of fleece-lined slippers and pulled a dressing gown over her night rail. In the drafty room, the taper on her night table had gone dead. She relit it from the sputtering hearth fire and sped into the passageway.

As she approached the bedchamber nearest the stairs, she heard Miss Wigglesworth's rumbling snore. Ought she to rouse her? But an elderly woman would be of little help, she decided, continuing past the room and down the stairs to the entrance hall.

Windblown snow blasted over her when she opened the door, immediately snuffing her candle. There was no one there. She took a step outside and looked around.

"Hullo?" she called. "Where are you?"

No answer. Well, she had to have a look, didn't she? She tussled with the door, fighting the wind to pull it closed, and finally stood shivering in the dark foyer with her arms clutched around her waist.

For a time she considered making herself a cup of chocolate before returning to bed. But she didn't know how to brew chocolate, and Mrs. Cleese would be displeased if she made a mess in the kitchen. The cook would not return before late afternoon, though, giving her plenty of time to put the kitchen to rights again. And she did know how to make tea, which would be a much safer proposition than chocolate.

But the uneasy feeling of being virtually alone in the house persuaded her that a hot drink would be more trouble than it was worth. Carefully picking her way across the dark entrance hall, she found the splintery banister and started up the stairs.

Thud.

She froze. There was no mistaking *that*.

It came from the kitchen, she thought, or thereabouts. Sound was distorted by Lakeview's stone walls and high ceilings, so the noise may have been the one she'd heard before—a tree slapping against the house, perhaps, or a wooden shutter come loose. The footman had done his best to repair the kitchen shutters after Mrs. Cleese complained about them, but he was no better a carpenter than Diana, who had insisted on helping him. It would be little wonder if the shutters had failed to hold.

At least she now knew where to find a hammer and nails, and she would certainly get no more sleep this night. Tea and carpentry, she resolved, turning back in the direction of the kitchen. As she came near the end of the passageway, it occurred to her that a loose shutter really ought to be banging with more . . . well, consistency. But then, what did she know of such things? Still, she proceeded cautiously to the kitchen door and stole a look inside.

The banked fire cast an eerie glow over the room. Across the way, the door to the garden was closed and barred. Wind rattled the shutters at the three windows, but they appeared to be intact. She moved to them for a closer examination, aware that her knees were trembling. Strange sounds in a strange house, that was all. Noises were to be expected in a gusty storm.

And of late, there was no denying, she took fright at the least little thing. A bird suddenly erupting from a tree caused her to jump. A stranger pausing on the road to look up at the house set her heart to thumping. One afternoon while she was walking in the hills above Lakeview, a sheep came up behind her and nuzzled at her skirts. She had actually screamed, sending the poor ewe scampering away in terror.

Feeling foolish for chasing stray sounds all over the house, she went to the hearth and held out her hands to warm them. If she really wanted tea, she would have to fire up the stove, which she had seen done. Or she could unbank the hearth fire and hang the kettle over it. Or—she could simply go back to bed. More and more, that seemed the better choice.

With a sigh, she looked at the pots and pans suspended from hooks on either side of the fireplace. She couldn't have said what half of them were used for. In all her life she had never so much as boiled an egg, and if she wanted an egg at this moment, she had no idea where they were kept. She ought to—

A noise, one she could never mistake, sent her to her knees on the flagstones.

Splintering glass. From close by. The next room over. Someone was breaking into the house!

Jumping to her feet, she seized a cast-iron skillet from the wall and crept to the door that led from the kitchen to the breakfast room. Little light reached from the hearth, and she was able to distinguish only the outlines of chairs, the dining table, and a bulky sideboard.

She looked to her left, to the window at the far end of the room, and saw a large shape loom up against the background of falling snow. With only seconds to make a decision, she wavered between flight and attack. Every instinct clamored for

3

her to run, but where could she hide? Who would protect Miss Wigglesworth? And what if it was only a refugee from the storm in search of shelter?

Even as the questions roiled in her head, she edged in the direction of the window until she was standing with her back against the wall, skillet raised to strike.

The intruder swiped at shards of glass protruding from the windowpane, using something that looked very much like a rifle butt. It might have been only a length of wood, but she was taking no chances.

Well, perhaps *one* chance. How could she assault someone who might be perfectly harmless? She was about to demand that the man identify himself when he lunged inside.

Of its own accord, her arm swung the skillet at his head.

He must have sensed the attack coming, but he spun away too late. The skillet struck a glancing blow, and he dropped at her feet like a stone.

For a long moment, she stood frozen in horror at what she had done. The man lay on his stomach, arms bent at the elbow and stretched over his head. A dark greatcoat was twisted around his body and legs. The muzzle of his rifle had landed atop her right foot.

She sucked in several deep breaths before gathering sufficient wits to pick up the gun. Darting back into the kitchen, she hid the rifle in the pantry and lit one of the storm lanterns set alongside the hearth. Skillet in one hand and lantern in the other, she stole again to the morning room and lowered herself to one knee beside the fallen man.

A knit woolen cap had been knocked askew by her blow, revealing strands of overlong black hair. His face was shadowed by a dark beard about half an inch long. She had never before seen a ruffian, but she supposed this was how a ruffian would look. He was very large, at least six feet tall if he were standing, and the leg protruding from his greatcoat was heavily muscled.

Heart racing, she set down the lantern and pressed her fingers to his throat. His flesh was cold, and she detected no pulse. Had she *killed* him?

The skillet fell from her hand, clattering against the oakwood floor.

At the sound, he stirred. The one eye she could see flickered open as he raised his head to look at her. "Who the devil are you?" he asked blearily.

She slid her hand under his chin just before it fell again. Alive, thank heavens. Now unconscious—possibly. He might be dissembling.

Despite the icy wind whistling through the broken window, perspiration streaked her brow and the back of her neck. Lucy would know what to do, of course, but Lucy wasn't here.

The man's bristled cheek lay against her hand, warming from the heat of her body. She pulled off the knit cap and ran the fingers of her other hand across his forehead until she encountered a swollen lump. Blood trickled down his temple. Gently she lowered his head to the floor and stood, gazing down at him while panic swept over her.

She held her ground until it subsided. And when the panic was gone, she was left cold and oddly detached. He seemed a long distance away now, less a man than a problem to be dealt with. All to the good. So long as she felt nothing, she found herself able to think.

Miss Wigglesworth first. With a last look at the prone, motionless figure on the floor, she turned and sped out of the breakfast room and down the passageway and up the stairs.

Wilberta Wigglesworth slept like the dead. Diana had to shake her to get any response, and then the elderly woman jolted up with a start and gazed around in confusion. When her eyes focused on Diana's face, she came immediately alert. "What is it, my dear?"

"Come with me," Diana said, tugging a blanket from the bed. "Wrap this over your shoulders. I'll tell you what happened on the way."

The man was sitting up when they came into the breakfast room, clutching his arms around his sides against the cold.

He looked dazed, Diana thought, but no less dangerous. He was large, clearly strong, and he had been carrying a gun. She mustn't forget that in her relief to see him still alive and capable of pulling himself this far from the floor.

Miss Wigglesworth made a clucking sound and hurried to

drape her blanket over him. "Lost in the storm, were you? Bad night to be out. You should have known better."

He raised his head, blood already thickly caked on his cheek. "What hit me?"

Diana stepped forward. "I did."

He put a hand against the lump above his temple. "A *child* brought me down?"

"A frying pan, sir. Why were you breaking into our house?"

He swayed forward.

Miss Wigglesworth dropped to her knees and held him up. "Water and a towel, Diana."

When she returned with a basin of cold water and several clean towels, the man was stretched on his back with his head on Miss Wigglesworth's lap.

He gave Diana an unfocused look. "If you want me alive, Madam Fury, why the deuce did you try to kill me?"

She knelt beside him and began to dab a wet cloth at the blood on his cheek. "I'm not altogether sure I want you alive, sir. You are proving to be a dratted nuisance. And I never tried to kill you. I meant only to stop you." She turned worried eyes to Miss Wigglesworth.

"Scalp wounds bleed more than most," Miss Wigglesworth assured her. "You can't have hit him terribly hard, or he'd not be awake and talking nonsense."

His teeth began to chatter, and soon he was shivering uncontrollably.

"I believe we should see him warm before tending to his head," Diana said, setting aside the towel. "Are you able to crawl into the kitchen, sir? It's only a short distance."

"C-crawl?" His eyes flashed. "I think not. Help me to my feet."

"It would be best," Miss Wigglesworth said, "to get him upstairs. The kitchen fire can be built up, of course, but the stone floor is prodigiously cold."

"I'll make a pallet on the table," Diana suggested. "He can climb up there."

"Stop t-talking about me as if I wasn't here!" He sat up, reached for one of the wooden chairs, and used it to pull himself to his knees. A few moments later, he managed to stagger to his feet. "Where the devil are we going?"

Even in the flickering lantern light, his face was ominously white. He swayed, and looked about to topple over.

Diana rose swiftly and slipped her arm around his waist. "If you care to try, sir, I'll help you to one of the bedchambers. Or you can—"

"Let's get on with it then." He steadied, one hand propped on the chairback for support. "Don't attempt to support my weight, madam. Should I fall, I'd bring you down with me."

"I won't let you fall," she told him, not at all sure she could keep that promise. "And it would be no more than I deserve if you were to land atop me."

"A not unpleasant prospect," he said with a flash of white teeth.

"Come along," Miss Wigglesworth said briskly, taking the lantern and leading them into the passageway.

Diana kept hold of his waist, more to secure his balance than to keep him upright. He was wet clear through to the skin, and cold as a block of ice. She sensed the effort it was costing him to continue moving, step by slow step, but he never faltered. He was definitely weakening, though, and she began to wonder if he could make it up the long flight of stairs.

He did, using the banister to pull himself up. Once his foot caught on a step and he nearly tumbled over backward. She held on to him with all her strength until he righted himself, and then they went on.

"In here," Miss Wigglesworth said when they reached the landing. "We'll put him in my bed."

"It's far too small," Diana objected. "His feet would hang over the end."

"Never mind his feet. Your room is at the far end of the house. He won't make it."

"Dammit," he swore, breathing heavily. "This is one hell of a time for a debate."

"Come, sir." Diana towed him along the passageway.

He made it to her bedchamber, but not by much, and fell onto the bed face-first with a groan. At least he had stopped shivering, Diana thought. The exertion had gone a long way to warming him up. But his strength had run out, and it was all she could do to strip off his soaked greatcoat while Miss Wigglesworth helped her lift his arms and roll him from side to side. There was no point trying to remove his boots, she decided. He was virtually a deadweight now, and would simply have to stay in his wet clothes.

After a considerable struggle, they got him onto his back with his head on the pillows and piled blankets and the down coverlet on top of him. By then he was unconscious or asleep—she didn't know which—but his pulse was strong and he was breathing easily. She allowed herself to hope he would survive the attack, even if he had come to the house bent on robbing it and murdering the inhabitants.

While Miss Wigglesworth built the fire to a roaring blaze, Diana examined the wound on his head. It had stopped bleeding, thank heavens, but dried blood covered the right side of his face. Fearing that she would reopen the cut if she tried to clean him up, she left him be.

"You have got wet from holding him," Miss Wigglesworth said, touching her on the arm. "Change into dry nightclothes, my dear, and go to bed in my room. I'll sit up with him."

"I will change," Diana agreed, "but it would be impossible to sleep. Could I persuade you to make some tea, Miss Wigglesworth? I'm feeling a bit shaky at the moment. Then you can return to your bed."

"I'll bring up the tea, yes, and we'll keep watch together." On her way out of the room, Miss Wigglesworth paused for a moment to study the man's face. "He has a familiar look about him, although I am quite certain I have never seen him before. I wonder who he could be."

Chapter 2

Pale light crept over the sky as Diana made her way down the sweeping hill to the road. Like the countryside, it was still covered with pristine, ankle-deep snow. No one had passed this way since the storm, which had blown out three hours earlier. A light breeze ruffled the fur lining of her hood.

Just beyond the road, Coniston Water lay smooth as glass, its color a deep pewter gray. On the hills behind the house, bare tree branches were mantled with snow. Everything was still. Hushed. The vapor of her breath wafted like white smoke in the cold air.

Mr. Beadle would be along soon. Whatever the weather, he never failed to pass by shortly after dawn. She had met him soon after taking up residence at Lakeview. Word of her arrival had spread quickly, and visitors avid to meet the new tenants soon began to call. Mrs. Alcorn, wife of the local squire, had fluttered and clucked to see the shabby condition of the parlor.

"Is all the house in such decay, Miss Whitney? I declare, two gentlewomen such as yourself and Miss Wigglesworth must not be permitted to live in such a fashion!"

Helpless under the assault of so formidable a woman, Diana found herself giving Mrs. Alcorn a tour from attics to cellar. There was no hiding the smoky chimneys, the peeling wall coverings, the drafty windows.

"Mr. Beadle is the man you need," Mrs. Alcorn had declared with authority. "He is a man of many trades, and whatever you require, he will provide it for a remarkably small fee. Mind you, he does not speak. Some say he cannot speak, but I heard from Mrs. Corbel, whose uncle was at school with him, that he'd a terrible stammer as a boy and was so bedeviled for it that one

9

day he simply stopped speaking and has never spoken since. I shall have him call on you first thing tomorrow."

And so he had done. Diana, expecting a strapping young fellow, was surprised to see on her doorstep a short, narrow-faced man of at least threescore years. Everything about him was scruffy, from his worn boots to his droopy felt hat. She soon discovered he invariably wore that hat, indoors and out.

Mr. Beadle handed her a piece of paper where he had inscribed his offer and the terms. He would spend two entire days on the most urgent repairs, and thereafter come by three afternoons a week until his services were no longer needed. He asked a painfully small fee, reimbursement for supplies, freedom to keep any leftover materials, and one meal a day.

Unable to imagine what such an unimposing little man could accomplish, she had agreed to employ him. And she very quickly learned that Mr. Beadle's small body concealed wiry strength and remarkable endurance. He was, moreover, a gentle, comforting presence around the house. She felt less lonely simply knowing he was there.

Diana stomped about in the snow to stay warm. If not for the townsfolk who continued to drop in uninvited, she might have considered staying at Lakeview until her birthday. But Lord Kendal would never permit it, she supposed. He was displeased with her as it was, and would sweep her back to his estate when his houseguests took their leave.

A dark splotch appeared in the distance, moving slowly along the road, and soon Diana could make out the familiar shape of Mr. Beadle's pony cart. When he reined the gray nag to a halt directly in front of her, she rushed to his side.

"Good morning, Mr. Beadle. Forgive me for being abrupt, but I must beg a favor of you. A stranger became lost in the storm last night and sought refuge at the house. He has sustained an injury to his head. Will you stop by Mr. Crackett's house and ask him to come here as soon as may be?"

Mr. Beadle's weathered face scrunched into a worried frown. He sketched a question mark in the air with a knit-gloved forefinger.

She had learned to read some of his own peculiar language, made up of posture, facial expressions, and hand gestures. "The

10

gentleman does not appear badly hurt," Diana assured him with more confidence than she felt. "But Mr. Crackett will be a better judge."

Mr. Beadle nodded and made a sign that meant *quickly*.

"Yes. Thank you. And I brought you some bread and ham." She handed him the small parcel. "The gentleman arrived on horseback, but we've no hay. Will you secure some, and oats as well, and deliver them here on your way back? Here's money for the purchase."

He accepted the coins and raised a brow.

"No, nothing more. Unless you think of something I've forgot. And do tell Mr. Crackett to hurry."

Touching the brim of his hat in a salute, Mr. Beadle snapped the reins against Old Molly's backside. The nag swerved her head to give him a look of astonishment before proceeding with unaccustomed briskness along the snowy road to Coniston.

Thank heavens for Mr. Beadle, Diana thought as she made her way back up the hill. He asked no useless questions and simply did what had to be done. She had not been altogether honest with him, but there was no reason to mention that the gentleman had tossed and turned in bed, mumbling indistinguishable words in the throes of what she expected were terrible nightmares. She had sat with him until shortly before dawn, when she left to dress herself and come down to the road.

Guilt continued to rake at her conscience. Had he not jerked away in time, he'd have required a coroner instead of an apothecary. What had possessed her to attack him in such a way? In general, she could not bring herself to swat a fly.

She still didn't know if the stranger was a housebreaker or a perfectly innocent man caught by the storm. She had studied his face while she sat beside the bed, the shadows marking out the hollows in his cheeks and the small lines at the corners of his eyes.

In his restless sleep, he appeared more exhausted than wicked. His nightmares had roused her sympathy, for she rarely passed a night without bad dreams. And then his startling good looks, which she had scarcely noticed until her toes started to curl for no apparent reason, drew her attention and held it for longer than was proper.

Even handsome men can be villains, she reminded herself.

She felt his presence the moment she stepped into the house. And sure enough, she soon spotted his tall straight figure at the head of the stairs, his hand wrapped around the newel post.

"Sir! You should be in your bed."

"Nonsense." He set out, not rapidly, down the steps. "And you needn't dash for cover, madam. I am perfectly harmless."

She forced herself to hold her ground. "Where is Miss Wigglesworth?"

"When I left, asleep in a chair. She snores like a sailor." He stopped a short distance away, towering a head above her, his shaggy hair and whiskers giving him a decidedly menacing appearance. "Is there coffee to be had?"

"Only tea, I'm afraid." Her voice squeaked perceptibly. "Do you mind taking it in the kitchen?"

He followed her down the passageway, going directly to the trestle table when they reached the kitchen. Atop it was a large cast-iron skillet. He eyed it sharply. "Is this what you clubbed me with last night?"

She nodded.

Hefting it in his hand, he whistled softly.

She turned her back to him, concealing her trembling hands, and removed her cloak. "I am most frightfully sorry, sir."

"And well you should be. When you take up a weapon, madam, have the bottom to use it properly. I might have been a cutthroat."

"I supposed that you were." She glanced over her shoulder. "And how do I know that you are not?"

"You don't. Two more muttonheaded females I have yet to meet. One thinks nothing of taking a snooze when she is supposed to be standing the watch, and the other waltzes me into the kitchen and all but puts her own weapon of choice into my hands."

Flushing hotly, Diana went to the stove. "If you mean to throttle me, sir, please get on about it. Otherwise, I shall brew the tea." She heard a sharp crack of laughter and looked up in time to see him wince.

"I've the devil of a headache," he confessed, "and a lump the

12

size of a pineapple. Providentially, the men in my family have skulls of steel."

"I'm sorry for striking you," she said, misery knotting her stomach. "I ought to have asked beforehand why you were breaking into the house."

"Oh, by all means. Do clarify whether a housebreaker is bent on robbing you, ravishing you, or murdering you in your bed before deciding whether or not to bludgeon him. You require a keeper, madam. Is there no man in residence?"

"Only you, at the moment."

"Excellent." He scowled. "Reassure me that I can get on about my nefarious business unimpeded. Are you an absolute goose-wit, young woman?"

"It would seem so." She went to the pantry and returned with a canister, rather expecting him to renew his lecture. But he sat quietly, one elbow propped on the table and his chin buried in his hand, watching her every move.

Unnerved by his steady gaze, she fumbled with the spoon and dropped as many tea leaves on the floor as made it into the pot. Then she lost count and was forced to dump the leaves back into the canister and begin measuring again. One. Two. Three. The pulse pounded in her ears.

He appeared at her shoulder, holding the steaming kettle. "You're shaking," he said. "Stand aside." He poured hot water into the teapot and returned the kettle to the stove.

For such a large man, he moved like fog. "Th-thank you," she said.

He made a noise that sounded like disgust and went back to sit at the table.

She tried to pretend he wasn't there, but she could as easily have ignored a panther. He terrified her, but she didn't precisely fear him. If he meant to do her harm, he would surely have got on about it by now. She laid out cups, saucers, spoons, and a cone of sugar while he continued to stare at her, so intently he might as well have been touching her.

He was, of course, looking at the scar. What else could hold his attention to such a degree?

The scar was the only thing people ever looked at, before turning their eyes away and deliberately *not* looking at it. But their gazes inevitably strayed back. He at least had the grace to regard her openly. Not once had his eyes shifted, as others' eyes so often did, vacillating between curiosity and repugnance.

"Before coming through the window," he said, "I pounded on the front door."

"That was what brought me downstairs. But there was no one there, so I decided I had been mistaken. Then I heard glass breaking, so I grabbed up the skillet and . . . well, you know the rest. I'm sorry."

"If you say that to me one more time, madam, I may yet throttle you. There will be no more apologies. Understood?"

"Yes, sir." She busied herself straining tea into the cups.

"At the time," he said, scraping sugar from the cone, "I thought this to be *my* house. Last I heard, it was standing empty. But I haven't set foot in this area for half a dozen years, and with snow blinding me, I could not be certain. Still, there were no lights at any of the windows, and when no one came to the door, I was sure I had the right place."

"I see. Well, as to the dark windows, we keep fires only in the kitchen and in our bedchambers." She brought a tin of almond biscuits to the table. "This house is in need of repair, I'm afraid. Most of the rooms are drafty, so we purchased exceptionally heavy curtains for the few rooms we are using."

He waved a hand. "Do sit, madam, and drink your tea."

She perched on the edge of the bench across from him, wishing he would stop looking at her in such a way. If only she'd thought to put on one of her veiled bonnets before going outside, she would be wearing it now.

"I left a horse in the stable," he said after an eternally long silence.

"Yes." She felt relief to have something to say. "We'll see he is cared for."

"Unfortunate nag. A job horse I hired in Liverpool, not at all suited for this terrain. He must be wondering how he got himself assigned to the Forlorn Hope."

"Whatever is that?"

"The name given to troops at the head of a charge, or the first to be thrown at the wall of a city under attack. Most all of them die."

"Oh." She tasted the words on her tongue without speaking them aloud. *Forlorn Hope.*

"Earlier," he said, "I told you I had come to the wrong house. That was, indeed, my first impression. But this one is laid out just as I remember."

She dropped the spoon she had been holding. Oh, please, don't let it be *him*!

"Why does that trouble you?" He leaned forward, frowning. "Are you not supposed to be here?"

Heart in her throat, she had to push the words out. "C-Colonel Valliant?"

His dark eyebrows flew up. "The same. So this *is* my house. Well, I have retained a few of my wits, it seems. Are you a new tenant?"

"Oh dear."

"Young woman, I assure you this changes nothing, except that I won't be forced to wander about Coniston Water this morning in search of my residence. And if you are concerned that I mean to evict you, rest easy. I came here for no very good reason and can as swiftly remove myself. The terms of your lease will be honored."

Diana was barely heeding his words. The horror of what she'd done, or nearly done, assailed her. Paralyzed with remorse, she could only gaze helplessly at her teacup.

"Well? Have you gone mute?"

"I almost killed you," she murmured.

"That subject, I believe, was closed several minutes ago. For the last time, you did what you had to do, and you did it badly."

"Thank God. If I'd d-done it better, you would be dead."

"People have been trying to kill me for years, madam. I do not take it as a personal offense. May I know your name?"

"Diana Whitney. My companion is Miss Wilberta Wigglesworth. And we are not, strictly speaking, tenants. It was our intention to stay here only a few weeks. Naturally we shall make immediate arrangements to depart."

"That won't be necessary." He reached for a biscuit. "I planned to go directly to Candale, but when I chanced to learn that my brother had a houseful of guests, I thought to wait here until they departed."

15

In hiding from those very same guests, she wondered why Colonel Valliant wished to avoid them as well. But she dared not ask, of course, nor could she have located the words. She felt numb from her scalp to her toenails.

"I have been long gone from England, Miss Whitney. Let me see. I was seventeen when I bought a commission in the army, and I am rising five-and-thirty now. In all that time, I came home perhaps six or seven times, never for long. So you see how it is. When I meet my brothers again after so many years, I'd prefer we not be surrounded by strangers."

Her gaze lifted to meet his. "They will take their leave within a fortnight, sir. The strangers, I mean."

"Ah." He drained his teacup and pushed it toward her for a refill. "I had been thinking you'd moved into an unoccupied house to avoid paying rent. Apparently that was a misapprehension."

She took her time straining tea into his cup. "I cannot pay rent, for at present I have no money. But Miss Wigglesworth and I are not squatters. We are here with Lord Kendal's approval, and I mean to repay him every penny spent on my behalf while I remain under his protection."

The colonel's eyes narrowed. "Under his *protection*? I had thought him to be recently married."

"Nearly three years ago, in fact. Before I made his acquaintance."

Colonel Valliant looked so disapproving that her composure fled again. What had Lord Kendal's marriage to do with her presence in this house?

"I appear to have stumbled into murky territory," he said, mauling his hair with one hand. "It's none of my business."

She had no idea what he was talking about.

"Don't tell Kendal," he said. "However innocent the circumstances, I expect he won't like to know I slept in your bed last night. That *was* your bed, I presume?"

"Such a question, young man!" Wilberta Wigglesworth bustled into the room, shaking a finger in his direction. "Mind your manners when addressing a lady."

Cheeks burning, Diana lifted a worried gaze to Colonel Valliant's face. He looked amused.

"Yes, ma'am," he said humbly.

Miss Wigglesworth advanced on him. "And the next time you exit a room where a lady is present, you will first have the kindness to wake her up and inform her of your intentions."

His lips were twitching, as if he wanted to laugh. "My most profound apologies, ma'am. I ought to have done so."

"Well, and I ought not to have dozed off when I was charged with your care. But I am six-and-seventy, so there is some excuse for me. I would have expected more sense from a man of your age. You ought to have known better than to leave your bed at all. You are pale as candle wax. And far too thin for one of your height, I am persuaded."

"Sea travel does not agree with me," he said. "I was too many months on ship from Lima to Liverpool."

"You have come all the way from Peru?" Miss Wigglesworth looked impressed. "Such an adventure. I declare myself envious."

"Unless you've a taste for weevil-ridden hardtack, I cannot think why you would."

Diana took hold of Miss Wigglesworth's sleeve. "This is Colonel Alexander Valliant, you should know. Lord Kendal's brother."

"Ah!" Miss Wigglesworth examined him more closely. "Yes, there is a resemblance. But your eyes are much darker."

"I am darker in every way, ma'am. Hair. Skin. Eyes." There was a short pause. "Temperament."

"Well, if you are who you say you are, it's as well Diana failed to dispatch you. That would have been difficult to explain. Mind you, had I been wielding the skillet, you would be presenting yourself at the Pearly Gates."

"I've no doubt of that," he agreed amiably. "But I'm fairly sure they'd not have opened for me."

"Then it seems you've been given a second chance to redeem yourself." Miss Wigglesworth glanced at Diana, who was frozen in place. "I shall deal with you later, missie. For now, Colonel Valliant, I suggest you take yourself upstairs and have a restorative sleep while we brew up a hearty soup for your luncheon."

Diana expected him to object, but he only nodded. He *did*

look ashen, despite his sun-bronzed skin, and there was pain in his eyes.

"As you say, ma'am." He stood, propping both hands on the table for several moments before letting go the support. "Damn. My head is spinning like a misfired rocket. Will one of you show me the way?"

Miss Wigglesworth looked a question at Diana.

"I'll make the soup," she said in a plaintive voice.

The fact that Diana could not so much as toast bread was not lost on Miss Wigglesworth. Clicking her tongue, she took Colonel Valliant's arm and led him from the kitchen.

When he was gone, air filled the room again. Diana felt exactly as she did after falling from her horse, all the breath knocked out of her.

Forlorn Hope.

The phrase curled in her mind like a serpent.

The least she could do was peel potatoes for the soup, she thought, rousing herself to invade the pantry. By the time Miss Wigglesworth returned, she had produced a bowl of tiny peeled potatoes and a large pile of skins with most of the potato still attached.

"Interesting man," Miss Wigglesworth said briskly. "I shouldn't like to cross him. And what did you think of him, Diana?"

She sucked at the cuts on her thumb and forefinger. "How can I say? He is . . . forceful."

"To be sure. He was uninclined to go off to sleep and quizzed me quite unmercifully. Well, no surprise he wished to know about his brothers. He'd not heard that Kit was married, or that Lord Kendal's wife is expecting her second babe." Miss Wigglesworth filled the soup kettle with water. "He was exceptionally curious about you, I must say."

Diana's heart sank. "And what did you tell him?"

"Nothing of significance. Better he get his answers from the source."

As if she could untangle her tongue to speak with him directly. The very thought he might put questions to her made her shiver. "I've got the potatoes ready," she said. "What shall I do next?"

18

Before Miss Wigglesworth could respond, a loud knocking at the front door sent Diana hurrying into the passageway. Oh, heavens! It could only be Mr. Crackett. She'd forgot all about him.

Chapter 3

Mr. Crackett, tight-lipped and scarlet-faced, descended the stairs very shortly after ascending them. He set his case on the vestibule floor and extended his hand, palm up.

"Colonel Valliant refused to see you?" Diana guessed.

"Oh, aye. Swore at me, he did, and sounded right healthy while he were about it. I'll be paid anyway, Miss Whitney, for m'trouble."

"Yes, of course. I do apologize for the unpleasantness, which was entirely my fault. I neglected to inform the colonel that I had summoned an apothecary, you see, and I expect your sudden appearance startled him from a deep sleep."

"Happen it did." Mr. Crackett thawed sufficiently to pick up his case and proceed to the door. "I'll not charge you this one time, Miss Whitney. But if there is need to call me back on the gentleman's behalf, I'll be asking double."

"Certainly you will be paid for coming here through the snow," she insisted, following him outside. "Won't you stay for a cup of tea while I persuade the colonel to let himself be examined? I am certain that he ought to be, for he took a fearful blow to the head."

"Yes, yes, you have told me all that. But I know a lost cause when it bites me, Miss Whitney. He won't have me look at the wound. And if he's gone addled, there be nothing I can do for him anyway."

Helplessly she watched the offended apothecary shuffle down the hill, untether his horse, and climb into the gig. He was well on his way before she directed her leaden feet to the kitchen.

Miss Wigglesworth, just tossing a pinch of something into

the soup pot, looked up with a frown. "That took an exceptionally brief time."

"Mr. Crackett's services were refused, I'm afraid. He is quite displeased. And by his report, Colonel Valliant is in a frightful temper."

"I expect he does not take well to being an invalid. You must not worry over him, my dear. Sit yourself down and let us discuss how next to proceed."

Diana sank gratefully onto the trestle bench. "Do you realize how very odd this is? Only . . ." She counted on her fingers. "Only eight months ago, I met Kit Valliant in remarkably similar fashion. He had been shot, and when Lucy came upon him, we found ourselves in a remote place with a wounded man to care for. There were all the same problems as well. Ought we send for a physician? How could either of us tend to his personal needs? Of course, you and I needn't disguise ourselves, or worry that our patient will betray us. But the coincidence is most strange, don't you think?"

"To a degree." Miss Wigglesworth stirred the soup with exceptional vigor. "The Valliant men appear to have a knack for getting themselves into trouble, and it has been your fortune—or your misfortune—to be on hand for two such incidents. But the business with Kit worked itself out to advantage, did it not? I believe that will be the case here as well, so long as you have a bit of faith."

Diana sipped the remains of the long-cold tea in her cup, thinking of how the colonel had looked an hour earlier, sitting across from her at this very table. "Faith in *what*, Miss Wigglesworth?"

"Destiny. There is providence in the fall of a sparrow, you know, and what appears to be purely chance is the manifestation of a greater plan." She waved the dripping spoon. "You may fancy I am speaking rubbish, child, but I've lived nigh four years to your one. And I *wish* you would cease addressing me as Miss Wigglesworth. It is a dreadful mouthful of a name. Call me Bertie, will you? Or Wilberta, if you must."

It wasn't the first time she'd asked, but Diana had been taught the proper way to address her seniors. Moreover, there was a kind of safety in polite manners. "If you insist, Miss— Wilberta," she murmured uneasily. "But however can we plan what to do with Colonel Valliant? Unless I very much mistake his character, he will assuredly decide for himself."

"In which case, my dear, fretting will gain you nothing. Most likely he will take himself off as soon as he can mount his horse. We have only to go about our business."

But I have no business to go about, Diana thought immediately. The one decision she had taken for herself—sending for the apothecary—had resulted in a mild disaster.

"We shall let him sleep for so long as he can," Miss Wigglesworth said. "Then we'll feed him some soup. In the meantime, I suggest you light a fire in the parlor. We'll soon be having guests, I shouldn't wonder, what with word gone out that we are harboring Colonel Valliant."

"Mr. Crackett would spread gossip about a patient he was summoned to attend? Oh, surely not."

"Do you not recognize an old busybody when you meet one? He'll give the tale to Mrs. Crackett, who will swan through every parlor in Coniston with the news. Very shortly, I promise you, the ladies will descend upon us with noses to the wind, sniffing for scandal."

"But . . ." Diana's voice faded off as she began to understand. She had been so concerned for Colonel Valliant's health that she had failed to heed the consequences of his presence in this house. In her bedchamber. In her very bed.

But why must there be any such complications? Once the circumstances were explained, no rational person could fail to understand. "There has been no scandal," she protested. "You have been here all along as chaperone. Besides, he had been knocked senseless. What harm could he possibly do?"

"Fact and perception are quite different things, as I suspect you are about to learn." Miss Wigglesworth tasted the soup and added a sprinkle of salt. "Perhaps I am wrong. I hope that is the case. But prepare yourself, young woman."

Before the morning was out, half a dozen female members of the local gentry had appeared at the door, come to inquire after the health of the unfortunate gentleman. Diana had little choice but to invite them in, and once they were settled in the parlor, they could not be budged. She feared they meant to take root there until they had clapped eyes on Colonel Valliant.

Clustered around the fireplace, they drank tea and nibbled at the biscuits Miss Wigglesworth provided, all the while casting speculative looks in Diana's direction. For her part, Diana fended off their tart questions with vague replies. Only the habit of good manners held her temper in check. Until this particular ordeal, she hadn't realized that she *possessed* a temper, but it was at full boil beneath her polite demeanor.

Unfortunately, she had not thought to put on her veiled bonnet. Well, she had, but it was in the room where Colonel Valliant lay sleeping, and the last thing she wanted to do was wake him up. Perhaps it was just as well. The tabbies had only to look at her face to realize that no man would engage in improper behavior with the likes of her.

"Perhaps you should tell us more about your Miss Wigglesworth," Mrs. Alcorn said when she had run short of questions about the colonel. "She is your . . . er, companion, is she not? Who are her people?"

"Naturally," Miss Alice Yoodle put in, "we are certain she is everything she ought to be."

Miss Gladys Yoodle fluttered her fan. "But of course she is. How could she be otherwise?"

Diana turned her attention from the sharp-faced squire's wife to the Yoodle spinsters. Lilac powder, applied in liberal doses, puffed in little clouds from their clothing whenever they moved.

"Take no offense at my questions," Mrs. Alcorn said sharply. She did not like to be interrupted. "But standards do differ from one place to another. What is regarded as acceptable in, shall we say, Westmoreland might well be disapproved of here in Lancashire."

"Then there can be no misunderstandings among us," Diana said with a forced smile. "Miss Wigglesworth and I are Lancashire born and bred."

"You are not from Westmoreland?" Mrs. Alcorn's eyebrows rose to her scalp. "But I had understood you to be the ward of the Earl of Kendal."

Reluctant to confide in this meddlesome woman, Diana merely nodded.

She should have remembered that nothing would deter Mrs. Alcorn, who had the tenacity of a barnacle.

"How did that come about, Miss Whitney? You will pardon me if I ask what all of us are most eager to learn. Now that you have become part of our small community, we naturally wish to become better acquainted."

"And who the devil are *you*?" said a deep voice.

Like the others, Diana looked over to see Colonel Valliant standing in the doorway, one shoulder propped negligently against the jamb. Black-bearded, scruffy-haired, and altogether menacing, he gazed back at them from cold blue eyes.

"Are you speaking to me?" Mrs. Alcorn said, puffing her chest.

"Not particularly. I only wondered why the lot of you are here. If it is to inquire after my health, you can see for yourselves that I am fully recovered."

"We are so very glad of it," Alice Yoodle simpered.

Gladys Yoodle emitted a giggle. "Oh yes. So very glad."

The colonel rolled his eyes.

"Nevertheless," Mrs. Alcorn said sternly, "our primary concern is for the welfare of Miss Whitney. I am certain you take my meaning, sir."

"Are you?" He spoke in chips of ice. "You are quite wrong, madam. I cannot think what you could possibly mean."

Sensing disaster, Diana scraped up the courage to stand. "Our guests were just about to take their leave, Colonel. How fortunate that you were able to assure them of your recovery before they departed. And now, if you will excuse me, I shall help the ladies gather their cloaks and return to their carriages."

"Do that," he said curtly, striding off in the direction of the kitchen.

It took several minutes for Diana to rid the house of six decidedly reluctant ladies, even with the help of Wilberta Wigglesworth. Colonel Valliant must have sent her to the rescue, because she appeared shortly after his departure.

Just before mounting the steps into her coach, Mrs. Alcorn

fired a parting shot. "I much fear for you, Miss Whitney," she said with a knowing smile. "Truly I do."

"What do you suppose she meant by that?" Diana asked Miss Wigglesworth as they returned to the house. "It sounded rather like a threat."

"Of course it was a threat. She resents you, my dear. What is a mere squire's wife when compared with the daughter of a baron, especially one who also happens to be the ward of an earl? She is accustomed to playing the grand lady hereabouts, and now you have come to steal her thunder."

"But that is purest nonsense. I wish only to live quietly, as well you know. Mrs. Alcorn is welcome to queen it as she has always done."

"I expect she is not convinced of that," Miss Wigglesworth said dryly. "Take yourself off to the kitchen, my dear. The colonel wishes to speak privately with you."

Worse and worse, Diana brooded as she made her way slowly down the passageway. After her ordeal with the Coniston Inquisition, a private conversation with the intimidating Colonel Valliant was the very last thing she felt up to confronting. And to think that she had come to this out-of-the-way lakeside house for a few weeks of quiet reflection!

Colonel Valliant was at the stove, ladling soup into a bowl. "My third helping, I'm afraid. If you expect to have soup for lunch, I suggest you claim a portion before I devour the entire potful."

"You are most welcome to it, sir." She edged into the room. "I'm not the least bit hungry."

"That tangle of vipers would put a saint off her appetite," he said in a remarkably pleasant tone of voice.

Too pleasant. More than ever on her guard, she went to a tall three-legged stool and perched atop it, welcoming the additional height. The colonel filled every room he entered, she could not help but notice, and even the large kitchen felt crowded with only the two of them present.

Instead of taking a seat at the trestle table, he went to the hearth and stood with his back to the fire, fixing her with his gaze as he spooned soup into his mouth.

She looked at her hands, tightly folded on her lap, and willed them to stop trembling. He didn't speak, and she could think of nothing to say. After a while, the longcase clock in the passageway chimed twelve times. Only noon? It seemed much later to her.

Finally he put his soup bowl on the mantelpiece. She heard the sound and looked up briefly. He was standing tall and straight, his legs slightly apart as if he were planting himself against attack. From behind, the firelight outlined the shape of him, the taut muscles and rigid stance, casting shadows on his cheeks and glazing his dark hair with a reddish halo.

"I suppose we may as well go about the thing properly," he said. "Will you, Miss Whitney, do me the honor of becoming my wife?"

Stunned, Diana was distantly aware that her mouth had dropped open.

"Come now," he said. "You must have been expecting this. In point of fact, I'm not altogether sure you didn't set out to arrange it. But I can assure you that if you did, you will soon be very sorry for it."

She made herself look directly into his eyes. It was a mistake. She could read nothing there, but he met her gaze and held it with such force that she could not look away again. From a dry mouth, she summoned the only words that she could put together. "I don't know what you mean, sir."

"No? Well, perhaps I have misjudged you. But when that quack showed up, followed not long after by a flock of hens, I assumed you to be responsible for bringing them here."

"I did send for the apothecary, sir. And I apologize for not mentioning it to you this morning, but I plainly forgot. You may be sure I did not mean him to inform the entire population of Coniston that you were here, although he appears to have made a good start at it within a very short time."

"And the battle-ax with the pointed chin will doubtless cry the news from here to Hawkshead. But never mind how it came about. The deed is done, and we must deal with the consequences. Your reputation has been compromised, through my own fault, and I stand ready to salvage it as best I can. Mind you, marrying a man of my less-than-sterling character will not stand to your credit, but you've little choice in the matter now."

That skillet upside his head must have done more damage than any of them realized, she thought. "But of course I do. How can the misjudgment of a few old gossips signify? I assure you, they mean nothing to me."

"But then, yours is not the only reputation to be considered."

"Oh. I hadn't thought of that." She studied his face. "Do you put store in their opinion of you, sir?"

"By no means. I refer to my family, of course. You are, I have been informed, my brother's ward. As such, the regard in which you are held must reflect on him."

She lowered her head. "I would not have it so."

"Nevertheless, that is the way the world goes, madam. And in this particular situation, Kendal has brought trouble upon himself by permitting you to live in this remote house with only an elderly woman for company. He has clearly neglected his responsibilities."

Outraged, Diana sprang immediately to Lord Kendal's defense. "He has done nothing of the sort. Coming here was entirely my idea, and you may be sure he disliked the plan enormously. You should know, sir, that the role of guardian was all but thrust upon him several months ago. He had never even met me. And when we did meet, he promised that I would be his ward for legal purposes only. Mind you, I'm not at all sure this arrangement *is* legal. But he said that he would not be meddlesome, and that I could do as I wished. So when I wished to spend a few weeks in the country, he could hardly go back on his word."

Frowning, Colonel Valliant lowered himself onto the settle and rested his elbows on his knees. "If he'd dreamed you might do something so bird-witted, I expect he'd not have given his word in the first place."

"To be sure. But as I said, he does not know me well."

He quelled her with a stern look. "However much you wish to absolve him of responsibility, the fact remains that Lord Kendal's ward has been caught in a compromising situation with his brother. There is no walking away from *that*, madam."

"I've no intention of walking away," she informed him woodenly. "Nor will I be stampeded into Parson's Mousetrap." She hesitated. "Unless Lord Kendal insists, of course."

The colonel gave a bark of mirthless laughter. "You would marry me on my brother's command?"

"I am greatly indebted to him, sir."

"But not so much that you would oblige him by remaining at Candale, out of harm's way."

"No. Well, yes." She took a steadying breath. "The thing is, who could have imagined any harm would come to me here? Two servants are generally in residence with us, but the footman has gone to care for his father, who is ill, and the housekeeper always stays with her family on Wednesday nights. She will return this evening."

"I chose a particularly awkward time to break into the house," he said wryly.

"Yes indeed." She sighed. "In all our planning, sir, we did not allow for you."

He laced his fingers behind his head and leaned back against the settle, regarding her with a rueful expression. "Nothing is ever simple, is it? So what are we to do next, Miss Whitney? I take it that my proposal of marriage has been rejected."

He didn't sound the least bit sorry for it. "Yes, sir. Lord Kendal is regrettably saddled with me for another year, but I'll not subject his brother to a lifetime tenure."

His laugh sounded almost genuine. "You are trying to *protect* me, madam?"

"I expect you can take good care of yourself," she fired back, astonished at her own temerity. But really, men found amusement in the oddest things. "As it happens, I first went into hiding to escape a marriage my uncle had arranged for me. I'll not be forced into *any* marriage, sir, unless compelled to pay the debt of honor I owe to Lord Kendal."

"He would not call in such a debt. Of that, you may be sure. Much has changed since I saw him last, but his character cannot have greatly altered."

"No indeed. He is a man of uncommon integrity. I am persuaded, Colonel Valliant, that you ought to go home and reacquaint yourself with your brother."

"I mean to. Had I gone there directly, you'd not be embroiled in a scandal." He rubbed the bridge of his nose. "Under the circumstances you will, of course, depart for Candale immediately."

"No." Diana rose and straightened her skirts. "I am done with running away, and it is past time I stopped relying on others to take care of me. Soon enough I shall be entirely on my own, and no matter where I decide to live, there will be the likes of Mrs. Alcorn and her comrades to deal with. I mean to face them down. Or ignore them, or perhaps win them over. Coping with this predicament is certain to be . . . educational."

He smiled then, the first true smile she had seen from him. White teeth flashed, and the tiny lines at his temples and the corners of his mouth crinkled.

It was, she quickly discovered, a breathtaking smile. Feeling suddenly dizzy, she reached behind her and held on to the stool for support.

"As you wish, Miss Whitney." The smile vanished. "But you might as well spare yourself further trouble and come with me now. When he hears of this, Kendal will almost certainly pluck you back to Candale."

"Must he? Hear of it, I mean. He never comes to Lakeview, and even if he did, he'd not mingle with Mrs. Alcorn's set." Her nails dug into the wooden stool. "Unless you tell him, sir, he needn't ever know."

The colonel raised a dark brow. "You would have me lie to him?"

"Not . . . precisely. It is more a matter of withholding the truth, which is not at all the same thing as telling a direct lie. And what is the point, really, of calling this incident to Lord Kendal's attention? It is over and done with."

"You astonish me, madam. I'd have pegged you as a female of strict conscience, but you are squirming around the truth like a politician."

"Yes. I am ashamed of it. I shall do penance for it." She studied the toes of her slippers. "Nonetheless, Colonel Valliant, I beg you to keep silent about what happened here."

"And so I shall. Unless I am compelled to do otherwise, of course, for gossip is rarely contained for very long. The story may reach Candale before I do. But we can hope, Miss Whitney. It's worth a try."

"You are very good, sir."

"I am nothing of the sort. I am abandoning a young woman to the jackals instead of wedding her, which is clearly my duty. I am not even trying to persuade her to accept my offer. What's more, I am about to deceive my brother, whom I've not set eyes on these last several years. And his wife, whom I've never met."

"You heap coals of fire upon my head," she murmured. "Tell him, then. I'll not spoil your homecoming any more than I already have."

"You have certainly made it interesting," he said, crossing to where she stood. "Buck up, my dear. We'll muddle through. And now, I must be on my way if I am to reach Candale before dark."

She regarded his haggard face with concern. "Do you feel up to traveling, sir?"

"Oddly enough, Wellington never asked me that when we were marching through Spain." He put his hands on her shoulders. "I'm an old trooper, you know. And I'm not about to admit that a wisp of a female brought me down with a frying pan. So yes, I am perfectly well enough to ride."

Even through the heavy kerseymere dress, his touch burned into her shoulders. And this close to him, she saw that his eyes were so deep a blue as to be almost violet. The stool she was still clinging to suddenly toppled over, hitting the floor with a loud thump.

He released her immediately. "Will you mind retrieving my coat and gloves while I saddle the horse?"

"Certainly, sir. And your rifle as well."

"Keep it," he said shortly. "And learn how to use it, in case someone else decides to come through your window one of these nights."

And then he was gone, out the kitchen door.

She stood for several moments, willing her heart to start beating again, before rushing upstairs.

Miss Wigglesworth met her in the passageway. "He is leaving, I gather."

"Yes. And so far as Lord Kendal is to know, he has never been here." It occurred to her that Miss Wigglesworth would be caught up in the deception as well. Oh dear. What a tangled web she had set out to weave. "Do you mind very much?"

"Not in the least, child. If you did not look quite so miserable, I would enjoy being part of a conspiracy. Simply tell me what story we are giving out, lest I trip you up."

"Thank you." Bless Wilberta Wigglesworth! "When the colonel is gone, we shall get ourselves in order."

By the time Diana arrived at the stable, her arms full of coat and hat and gloves, he was leading his mount into the courtyard.

Unaccountably reluctant to see the last of him, she watched him shrug into his coat and pull on his gloves. "What shall I tell Mrs. Alcorn about your departure?" she asked, if only to prolong his stay. "She is bound to quiz me."

"Whatever you like," he said curtly. "But I advise you to stick to the truth. The bare bones of it, mind you. Offer no details, and explain nothing. I came to my house, thinking it to be empty. Lacking a key, I broke in through a window. You heard noises, assumed I was a burglar, and ambushed me. When you learned my identity, you put me in one of the two rooms that had a fire and sent for the apothecary. It's simple enough."

He swung into the saddle. "One lie only. You were never alone in my company. Not for a moment. Miss Wigglesworth was with us beginning to end."

She gave him the knitted cap and stepped out of the way. "I understand, sir. And I wish you a happy reunion with your family."

"Naturally, I cannot give them your regards." His lips curved. "May I say, Miss Whitney, that except for the blow to my head, I am glad to have made your acquaintance. We shall meet again, of course, and pretend it is for the first time. But for now, Godspeed."

Touching his forehead in a salute, he turned his horse and made his way down the snow-covered hill to the road.

Diana waited until he was out of sight before trudging back to the house.

I could have *married* him, she thought.

He would have despised her for it, to be sure. He would have been legshackled to a bride he never wanted, and all on account of a stupid coincidence. An accident.

31

But still, what if she'd said yes to his offer? What would it have been like to be his wife?

Well, she would never know. And it would not do to refine on what would never be.

Kicking a pebble out of her path, she resolved to put him from her mind altogether.

Chapter 4

Two days had passed since Colonel Valliant's departure, and Diana had nearly succeeded in putting him from her mind. But when he was gone from her thoughts, she had nothing of interest to think about. Nothing, in any event, that did not lower her spirits.

The swarm of Coniston ladies had diminished, although Mrs. Alcorn buzzed in every morning with a few of her cronies to make her disapproval excruciatingly clear. A gentleman would have done the decent thing, she declared. And if he failed to offer marriage, a decent woman would have found a way to compel him.

Diana painted on a smile and recited the lines Colonel Valliant had given her to say. As much as she disliked their visits, the Coniston Cats allowed her to play hostess, one of the few things she did well. Above all things, she required something to *do*. Reading, embroidering, and walking occupied too few hours of the day. Miss Wigglesworth had begun restoring the kitchen garden, which had been devoured by weeds after the previous tenants moved away, and Diana enjoyed giving her a hand. But although Miss Wigglesworth would never have said so, Diana knew that she was more of a nuisance than a help.

Resolving to find new ways to occupy her time, she decided to take inventory of her talents and skills. As soon as Mrs. Alcorn had taken regal leave, she closed herself in her bedchamber and seated herself at her writing desk.

It would not be a difficult task, she was persuaded. After nearly a score of years on this earth, she had surely accumulated a considerable number of skills. And not a one of them must be excluded, however unsuitable they might be for the life she would be leading in the future.

At first the words flowed swiftly. *Embroider. Paint with watercolors. Fluent in French, passable in Italian. Converse politely in society. Dance. Excellent penmanship. Well versed in all forms of proper correspondence. Preside over a tea tray. Play the pianoforte and sing.*

She scratched out *sing.* Her voice was melodious, but too soft for drawing-room entertainment.

Turning to household matters, she began with the general heading *Manage a Gracious House* and listed everything from planning menus to cataloging the silver and linens. When she was done she examined the entries, which had carried her to a second sheet of paper, with considerable pride. Unlike the frivolous accomplishments that headed her tally, some of these would prove useful when she set up her own household. The residence of a reclusive spinster would not be precisely "gracious," but neither did she intend to live beneath her station.

Unaccountably, tears welled into her eyes. Rubbing them away with the back of her hand, she set even more fiercely to work.

Thus far she had discovered only what she already knew. Miss Diana Whitney, bred to marry well and be a charming ornament to society, was well suited to the kind of life that had been snatched from her and wholly unsuited for any other.

Spanking rider! she wrote in capital letters. *Perhaps raise horses?* she added in parentheses.

Mr. Beadle was teaching her the rudiments of carpentry—sawing, hammering, planing, and the like. She listed those with a question mark after each one.

Mrs. Cleese, the cook, was reluctantly allowing Diana to help prepare the meals. "Peeling, chopping, measuring, and stirring" got written down.

Her inscriptions grew more labored, more infrequent, and more humdrum. Recalling the short time she'd spent on a pig farm, she noted mucking out sties, feeding poultry, gathering eggs, and churning.

She remembered that she could skate. Drive a gig. Arrange flowers.

Although she'd no prior experience with infants, Lady Kendal had trusted her to hold Master Christopher Alexander. But she discounted that and did not write it down. Everyone at Candale had gone to great lengths to make her feel useful and important, when she was nothing of the sort.

The ghost of Colonel Valliant rose up again, and she ordered him to go away. Once met, he was not a man easily dismissed from one's mind.

Sharpening her pen, she tried desperately to think of something else to write. She'd have done better to list all the skills that she lacked. Years could be spent on such a list as that.

After long consideration she wrote in a shaky hand, *Won't give up.*

It wasn't precisely a skill, but at the end of the day, it was perhaps her greatest asset. Not that it came easily to her. She surrendered constantly. She collapsed under the slightest pressure. But she always scrambled up again. She pulled herself erect and continued forward.

What she needed now was somewhere to go.

Her next task was to find a goal. Discouragement washed through her as she read over her list from top to bottom. So little there. So few things she could do. No hint of anything she *wanted* to do, except for that notion of breeding horses sometime in the future.

"Diana?" Miss Wigglesworth stepped into the room. "Forgive me for disturbing you, my dear. I did knock, but you failed to respond."

"I beg your pardon." Gathering up the sheets of paper, Diana shoved them into the drawer. "I was wool-gathering."

"Thomas Carver has arrived from Candale and brought with him a maidservant. I expect you'll wish to speak with him."

The Candale underbutler, no more than five years her senior, was waiting in the entrance hall beside a pert, curly-haired girl. He bowed, his freckled cheeks flushed red under a thatch of carrot-colored hair.

"Good morning, Miss Whitney. Lord and Lady Kendal convey their warmest regards. And . . . ah . . . Lord Kendal requests that you return to Candale. We have come to escort you."

She went cold with dread. "Has there been trouble regarding my uncle?"

"Not that I am aware, ma'am. But several of the guests have gone into Scotland—for the fishing, I believe—and the house is no longer filled to the rafters. Lord Kendal suggests that you will be more comfortable at Candale than here."

"I see." She could not restrain a small sigh. "Then I suppose I have no choice."

"As to that, ma'am, his lordship also said that if you preferred to remain at Lakeview, which was more than likely, I was to stay and be of service to you." He gestured to the maid. "Betsy as well."

"I do indeed prefer to stay here," she said, elated. "And the two of you are most welcome, although I'm not sure where to put you. We'll have to open up two more rooms." And what of the colonel? she wanted desperately to ask. Servants always knew the latest gossip.

Carver drew a small parcel from his coat. "Lady Kendal asked me to give you these letters. And you will wish to know that Lord Kendal's brother, Colonel Valliant, has returned from South America."

"Indeed?" she said too brightly. "He has been gone a very long time, or so I understand. Lord Kendal must be pleased to have him home again. Although now that I think on it, Lakeview belongs to Colonel Valliant, does it not?"

"I cannot say, ma'am. I have not heard that he means to come here, if that is what concerns you. Perhaps Lady Kendal's letter will provide more information."

Butlers were annoyingly discreet, she thought, knowing she'd get no more from Thomas Carver. And ladies, after all, ought not to be interrogating the servants. "Well, we must get you settled in. Go along to the kitchen for a cup of tea while Miss Wigglesworth and I choose the most suitable rooms."

Carver bowed again. "One more thing, Miss Whitney. Lady Kendal thought you might like to have your mare. I've put her in the stable."

"Oh, but that is *wonderful*!" She clapped her hands. "I have so missed riding. I shall take her out this very afternoon."

"As you wish, but Lord Kendal has given me strict instructions in that regard. I am to accompany you whenever you ride, and for that matter, whenever you leave Lakeview for any reason."

"A good thing, too," Miss Wigglesworth put in, slicing her a knowing look. Diana Whitney's reputation was already in shreds, it said plain as day. There would be no haring about the countryside on her own.

She concealed her disappointment with a smile. "In that case, I shall have to postpone my ride. But we shall go exploring tomorrow, Carver. Be ready first thing after breakfast."

It had rained during the night, and Diana feared her ride would have to be delayed yet again. But the sun was breaking through the clouds when she set out, Carver in tow, to see what lay beyond the grounds of Lakeview. Since arriving, she had not left the small estate, not even to walk the two miles into Coniston.

A crisp morning breeze played with the veil on her blue felt bonnet. By now, she supposed, everyone for miles around knew precisely what was to be seen beneath the veil. The Coniston Cats had doubtless spread the word, and she could well imagine how they spoke of her.

Oh, yes, they would say. They had seen it with their own eyes, and a dreadful sight it was. Miss Whitney bore the mark of the devil on her face. Wicked Miss Whitney, who had taken at least one man into her bedchamber. They had seen the man, unshaven and thoroughly disreputable. And rude. He had ordered them from the house. Oh dear, oh dear. What was this world coming to?

She wanted not to care what they thought of her. She had quite made up her mind not to care. And to prove it, she would no longer keep herself prisoner at Lakeview. Today, she was making a start at getting along in the world. She was striking out on her own for the first time since, well . . . for the first time.

What a lowering thought, and so dizzyingly true. Miss Diana Whitney, spoiled child of doting parents, had never taken a decision for herself. No one had expected her to. She willingly obeyed the wishes of her mother and father. At school she obeyed her teachers. She was a good, obedient girl.

And she hadn't minded in the least, because everyone took pains to make life pleasant for her. When she was at home, a maid laid out what she was to wear. Cook prepared her favorite foods. She was given puppies and kittens to cosset and ponies to ride. When she was sent off to Miss Wetherwood's Academy for Young Ladies, she had a room of her own, unlike most of the other girls, and she always got good marks in her classes. She excelled at music and drawing and dancing. She did what she was told. Always she was a good, a *very* good girl.

There was no reason to be otherwise. She knew that she was being prepared to make the one and only important decision of her life. When she was ten-and-seven her parents would take her to London for the Season. She would be presented at court, and go to balls and routs and to Almack's, the Marriage Mart, where she would be an Incomparable. She had been assured that she would be an Incomparable. She never doubted it.

Young men would flock to her. She never doubted that, either. Her father, wiser than she, would turn away the scoundrels and fortune hunters. The others, all of them titled and eligible and rich, would be laid out before her like a banquet. They would be madly in love with her, of course. They would woo her. Send her flowers. Write poems in praise of her beauty. Steal kisses in garden arbors and hold her a trifle too closely when they danced the scandalous waltz.

And finally, feted and courted and made much of, she would choose from among all these men the one who would be her husband. That decision was to be hers alone, her parents had promised. Their greatest wish for her had been that she would marry for love, as they had done. And with their happiness as a model for the life she wanted for herself, she'd been certain that she would make the right choice. After that, of course, she would do her husband's bidding. And live happily ever after.

With a grim laugh, Diana wrenched her thoughts from dreamland. It only pained her to dwell on what she had lost.

For the first hour she kept to the road that ran alongside Coniston Water, following it all the way to where it narrowed into the River Crake. Then she turned off and wound her way back along a narrow track set against the hills, following the route Mr. Beadle had suggested. She'd gone down to meet him just after dawn, when he passed Lakeview as he always did, and asked him to direct her to where the country folk lived.

She was looking for something. That was all she knew. It would help greatly, though, if she had some notion what it was that she sought. Should she chance to stumble upon it, she hoped that it would have the kindness to pop up and identify itself.

Directly ahead, a swift-flowing beck emerged from the fold between two low hills, rattling over worn rocks and pebbles before vanishing into a stand of beeches. She let Sparkles enjoy a drink before guiding the mare carefully over the narrow footbridge, which was no more than a few planks tied together with cord. Just the other side, she saw a lane cutting through the trees and decided to see where it led.

When she came out of the spinney, she was startled to find herself in a forest of fluttering linens. Sheets, towels, duvets, pillow casings, and all manner of clothing were suspended from a dozen lines attached to poles driven into the ground. Sparkles shied, spooked by the flapping linens, and Diana quickly steered her to open ground. There, alongside the beck, she saw an enormous metal vat on props above a fire. Beside it, a tall woman with graying hair was stirring its contents with a wooden paddle. She looked up when Diana appeared from behind the screen of sheets.

"Good morning," Diana said, wondering why the woman was glowering at her. Then she realized the glare was directed to a point behind her, where Carver had got himself tangled in the clotheslines. His face red as holly berries, he extricated himself and mumbled an apology to the laundress.

"Well, that's all right then," she said, letting go her paddle and wiping her hands on her apron. "If you be lookin' for Annie Jellicoe, you found 'er. But I be takin' no more customers, never mind the money would come welcome. Got all I c'n manage now and a bit more."

Diana glanced back at the waving rows of laundry. "I should say that you do! Is there no one to assist you?"

"Assist?" She laughed heartily. "And where would I be findin' such a creature? You don't hail from these parts, I warrant. Be you on a tour of the lakes?"

"Actually, I am in residence within a few miles of here, although it's true that I've only recently arrived." Passing Sparkles's reins to Carver, Diana slid from the saddle and looked about with interest. Firewood was stacked against a small tin-roofed shed that was used, she guessed, to store supplies. There was a rough-hewn table covered with oilcloth, and beside it, a number of large willow baskets. Some were piled with folded laundry.

"Ah, then you be the lady what is stayin' at the big gray house. The lady what the old Alcorn goat keeps yammerin' about."

"Diana Whitney," she said with a sinking heart. "Mrs. Alcorn does not approve of me, I'm afraid."

"That be a feather in your cap, to my way o' thinkin'. 'Tis a pleasure to meet you, Miss Whitney. Call me Annie if you like, or Mrs. Jellicoe if that suits you better." She took up her paddle and went back to stirring the soapy contents of the vat. "Be there somethin' I c'n do fer you, so long as it's nowt to do with laundry?"

"In fact, Mrs. Jellicoe, I was trying to learn something about this area. I am given to understand by a gentleman of my acquaintance, Mr. Beadle, that many of the residents are unable to find work."

"Oh, aye. We all know Mr. Beadle. He built that shed and planted the poles for my lines, so I do 'is washin' for free. Not that there's very much of it. He's right about the jobs. None to be found. I be Yorkshire born, but I married a Lancashire man and we come to live here so as he could work in the copper mine. But it closed, and he couldn't get no other work, so he went inter the army and got 'imself killed." She wiped her forehead with her sleeve. "It were much the same for 'alf the women in these hills. You ride around and 'ave a look, Miss Whitney. You won't be seein' many men."

"They were lost in the war?"

"A good number of them. Others be gone south to work in the factories. Some be rascals and just took off, leavin' their families high 'n dry. That be what 'appened to Meggie Doyle, who lives just yonder. You c'n see the smoke from 'er chimney.

40

In the cottage past that is Dora Fellson, what be a widow. Same for Jane Renfrew, down the way a bit."

"But however do they survive?"

"On the parish," Mrs. Jellicoe said grimly. "They scrape by what ways they can. Dora has three milk cows, and Jane keeps chickens. Meggie's scrap of land is good for plantin', not like most around here, but she's got nobody to work it. 'Tis all she can do to keep after her youngsters."

"Do you think they'd mind if I called on them?" Diana asked hesitantly.

"They would if you came offerin' charity. It's shame enough bein' on the parish dole. And bein' poor don't mean they ain't proud."

"Thank you for telling me. I should not wish to offend them. Perhaps I will ride in that direction, though, and make their acquaintance. And may I visit you again, Mrs. Jellicoe?"

"When the sun be shining, I be here. If there's rain, come on down to the cottage and I'll make a pot of tea." She smiled, revealing surprisingly white teeth. "Should you be goin' by Meggie's place, mebbe your man there could take up a basket and give it to her. She'll be needin' the nappies, I warrant."

"It will be our pleasure." Diana beckoned to Carver, who helped her onto the saddle. "I shall come again very soon, Mrs. Jellicoe."

When Carver was mounted, the laundress passed him a round willow basket. "If the others don't be welcomin'," she called as they rode away, "take no mind of it. They don't be used to minglin' with the gentry."

That became painfully clear as Diana went from one cottage to the next. The women, two of them with children clutching at their skirts, mumbled a greeting when she introduced herself and then stared fixedly at the ground. Realizing that her presence made them uncomfortable, Diana promptly bid them farewell and rode on.

Only Mrs. Doyle spoke audibly. After passing the infant in her arms to a little girl, no more than five or six, she took the basket from Carver's hands and turned to Diana. "Thank you, m'lady," she said in a shy voice. Then she fled into the cottage, followed by all but one of the children.

A too thin freckled boy stayed behind, gaping up at Diana. "Why you got that thing in front o' yer face?" he piped.

She was fumbling for a response when Mrs. Doyle stuck her head out the door. "Come in here this instant, Willie!"

"B-but she looks funny, Mama."

"Now!"

He scampered into the cottage and the door closed firmly behind him.

Diana saw his face at the window as she rode past. Not sure if she ought, she raised a hand and waved at him. To her delight, he grinned and waved back.

All the way home she thought about what she had seen and heard. And by the time she arrived at Lakeview, the glimmer of an idea had begun to take form. She rushed past a surprised Miss Wigglesworth, who had come down to greet her, and closed herself in her room.

Miss Wigglesworth was not to be denied, though. She knocked just as Diana was pulling off her riding habit and entered before she could be told not to. "Has something happened, my dear?" he asked, her face creased with worry.

"Oh, I have had *such* a day!" Diana smiled. "It has given me so much to think about. Please excuse me for being rude, but I wish to be alone for a while. Perhaps the rest of the day, and probably the evening as well. May I have supper on a tray, Miss Wigglesworth? And a pot of tea now, with some biscuits and a slice of Mrs. Cleese's apple cake, if there's any left."

"I'll see to it. But you *will* tell me if I can be of assistance?"

"Yes indeed." Diana sat on the bed to remove her half boots. "It's far too soon to say at the moment, but I rather expect you will find yourself being a great deal of help. More than you can imagine."

"My, my. Well, be mysterious if you must, so long as that lovely light remains in your eyes."

When Miss Wigglesworth was gone, Diana put a hand over her scar and went to the mirror. There *was* a glow in her eyes, she thought before turning quickly away. Fancy that! And she felt exhilarated, the way she used to when she had something good to look forward to.

Now if only she could pull together the tumble of ideas in her head and make some sense of them!

When she was comfortable in her eiderdown dressing gown and slippers, she went to the writing table where she had begun the day. Gracious, it seemed ages ago that she inscribed her paltry list of talents and skills. Once again she stacked clean sheets of paper atop the desk, removed the stopper from the inkwell, and sharpened her pen.

Then she paused, bowing her head. "Please, dear Lord, help me find what I am seeking," she begged. "Show me how to do what needs to be done. And if You don't mind, could You tell me precisely what that is?"

Chapter 5

Alex was pleased to see his brother after so long a time and to meet the new Lady Kendal, who was in every way an improvement over the previous countess. He'd a new nephew as well, and the heir, now a robust ten-year-old, was brought up from Harrow to renew acquaintance with his uncle.

For the first few days, family and Kendal's houseguests provided distraction from his dour thoughts. But when the guests departed and Charley had returned to school, the house seemed to close in around him. All that domestic bliss began to cloy, and feeling an outsider in the only home he had ever known, he took to spending his days walking the fells. Sometimes, if the night was clear, he would remain in the high country and sleep under the stars.

He knew that at some point he must separate himself from the army, and resigning ought to be a simple enough matter. He still had the letter excusing him from duty on his own recognizance, although Ross could hardly have expected him to vanish for two years. But the general had been killed shortly after penning the orders, and following Bonaparte's escape from Elba, no one had cared what was transpiring in the American War.

Alex Valliant was a paper soldier now, an unpleasant reminder of a conflict everyone would prefer to forget—no one more than he. But somewhere in an office at Horse Guards he still held his commission, and the habit of military discipline would not permit him to leave loose ends to dangle, however painful the tying off of them.

There was no reason to keep putting it aside, he supposed. In

the month he'd been at Candale, he had succeeded only in reac-
quainting himself with the lakelands and disrupting his family.
Celia had done her best to make him welcome, to be sure, and
gone so far as to take him under her wing. She deliberately
sought his company in the evenings and chattered away, fully at
ease, while he struggled to think of something to say. Fortunately, she never seemed to mind his abrupt, chilling responses.

"You are the quiet one," she informed him, as if he didn't
know that already. "James and Kit probably never let you get a
word in when you were growing up together."

That wasn't the case, although he allowed her to go on
thinking so. Unlike his brothers, both of them articulate and
witty, he had always been solitary by nature. A throwback
to some stolid, unimaginative distant ancestor, he expected,
since his parents were reputed to have been as charming as
his brothers.

As befitted the second son of an earl, he had dutifully taken
up a career in the military and found himself surprisingly suited
for it. In retrospect, he supposed it lucky for him that he'd been
driven into the army before finishing his studies at Cambridge.
The only commission he could buy on sudden notice was in the
44th Foot, not the glamorous cavalry regiment he had hoped to
join, but with less competition from influential fellow officers,
promotions came rapidly. He was a major at age twenty-seven
and a lieutenant colonel not long after.

He was doing it again, he thought as the Candale gatehouse
came into view. Dwelling on the past. And in light of its inglo-
rious end, his military career was the last thing he ought to be
calling to mind.

Better to concentrate on his new horse, a large, temperamental bay that suited him exactly. The search had taken him all
the way to Doncaster, and with an excess of time on his hands,
he had remained at the breeding farm for several days, putting
the steed through his paces and enjoying long rides on the open
moorlands.

At least he was returning to Candale in a better mood than
when he departed, which Kendal and Celia would doubtless appreciate. Having a brooding, bad-tempered relation hanging

about, even one who spent little time at the house, could not have been a great pleasure for them.

Timmy darted from the stable as Alex reined in and dismounted. "Ooo, he's a good 'un, sir. Best I seen since I been workin' here."

"I'm glad you approve," Alex said dryly, handing over the reins. "Give him a rubdown, will you?"

"Yes, sir. I'll be takin' good care of this 'un. What's 'is name?"

Alex tossed a coin to the impertinent stableboy, who flashed him a grin of thanks. "The breeding farm listed him as Number Seven out of Courageous and Miss Buttercup. Any ideas what I should call him?"

"I never got to name a horse before." The narrow face wrinkled in thought. " 'Ows about Thunder?"

Alex removed the saddle pack and slung it over his shoulder. "Thunder it is."

He had grown fond of the boy, Alex was thinking as he walked up the path from the stable to the front door of the house. Timmy had aspirations to be a jockey if he continued small, or a trainer if he grew as his five brothers had done.

A flashing thought—Alex Valliant as the owner of a horse-breeding farm—stopped him in his tracks. Yes. Possibly. He'd no money to finance such an enterprise, of course, but if he sold the house at Coniston Water, he could make a small beginning. And his commission might be worth something, although he expected that adjustments had been made to the system after the war. What with scores of officers wanting to sell out, colors must be going a-begging.

Well, it was worth considering, the horse farm. Nothing else had the slightest appeal to him, and he felt an unaccustomed spark of enthusiasm at the prospect. If it was not soon extinguished, perhaps he'd swallow his pride and ask Kendal for a loan.

Alex let himself into the house, surprised to see two men waiting in the entrance hall. One, a portly fellow with a red face and a receding hairline, was slumped on a bench with his arms dangling between splayed knees.

The other was pacing the black-and-white-tiled hall, hands clasped behind his back. Tall, lean, and hawk-faced, he spun around as Alex closed the door and fixed him with a belligerent glare.

"Are you a servant in this household?" he inquired sharply.

Clothed as he was, with a saddle pack thrown over his shoulder, Alex supposed he could be mistaken for one. Then again, a servant would hardly be using the front entrance. "No," he said coolly. "Do you require one?"

"I most certainly do. The butler left us here like common tradesmen nearly an hour ago, and I have pulled the bell rope a dozen times thereafter. Why has he failed to respond?"

"I have no idea. Why are you here?"

The man's slate-gray eyes narrowed unpleasantly. "We have come to speak with Lord Kendal on a matter of importance."

"Indeed. Well, I've no doubt that Geeson has informed him of your presence." Alex felt the man's glare prong him in the back as he mounted the stairs. At the top he turned in the direction of the study, where Kendal was generally to be found at this time of day.

The earl was seated at his desk with a number of documents spread out across the blotter in front of him. "Ah, good," he said when Alex came into the room. "I'd hoped you would be here in time for the fireworks display."

Alex dropped his saddle pack on the floor. "You refer to the pair of idiots bivouacked in the entrance hall?"

"I'm afraid so. The tall one, Sir Basil Crawley, is a particularly repellent mushroom. The other is Lord Whitney, uncle to the young lady now in residence at Lakeview. You may recall that I mentioned her to you some weeks ago?"

"Vaguely. She is your ward, I believe."

"That is, in fact, open to some question. My arrangement with Lord Whitney was more in the nature of a gentleman's agreement than a strictly legal transfer of guardianship. There was always the chance he'd take up the matter with Chancery Court, and it appears that he has done so." Kendal thumbed through the sheaf of documents. "Amid all this lawyerly blather, two things are abundantly clear. The court, which means to take up the case, has ordered the concerned parties to make themselves available in London. Moreover, until a judgment is rendered and in accordance with the terms of her father's will, Miss Whitney is to be returned to Lord Whitney's custody. The gentlemen waiting downstairs have come, I would imagine, to collect her."

"You don't mean to hand her over to them?"

"Well, she's not here, is she? But the authorities will have every right to seek her out and seize her, should Whitney demand that the magistrate enforce the pronouncement of the court. I expect that he will."

Alex went to the sideboard. "And what has Crawley to do with all this?"

"I'll have a brandy, so long as you are pouring." Kendal leaned back in his chair. "Left to his own devices, Whitney is a drunken, witless boor with debts up to his eyebrows. Not coincidentally, most are owed to Sir Basil, who made a point of buying up his gaming vouchers." He accepted the glass Alex handed him and took a drink. "Since I mean to keep them waiting as long as possible, would you care to hear about the events leading up to this confrontation?"

Damn right he would. He had developed a proprietary interest in Miss Whitney's affairs, if only because she was the only female he had ever proposed to. She was certainly the only female who'd ever whacked him with a skillet. "If you wish to tell me," he said with studied indifference.

Kendal glanced over at the clock on the mantelpiece. "A summary, then. Only Kit knows the whole of it, since I did not become involved until near the end. And for some reason, no one is willing to give me the details of her rescue."

"If Kit was involved, I can well imagine why."

"Where our little brother is concerned," Kendal said with a smile, "there are a great many things I'd rather not know. But to the subject at hand. When Miss Whitney's parents died of typhus a bit more than a year ago, the title passed to Lord Whitney's brother. The new baron was living in London at the time, trading on his expectations and apparently unaware that he was to receive none of the family's considerable fortune. Only the land and the house are his, and being entailed, he can neither sell nor mortgage them."

Alex paced the room. "I take it that Crawley means to wed the heiress?"

"He has offered for her, but not, as you might expect, to get his hands on her money. It is her birth and breeding that prompt him, for she is descended from a line dating back to the Conquest. Moreover, her family has always lived in Lancashire, where most of Crawley's business interests are centered."

"But if she refused him, which I assume she did, is not that an end to it? Whitney cannot force her to marry against her will."

"No. But he can make her life devilish miserable, which he has already done." Kendal steepled his hands beneath his chin. "Crawley offered to forgive his debts and provide a hefty marriage settlement, but if Whitney failed to produce her, he would be ruined. One evening, blind drunk, he roared into her bedchamber and demanded that she accept Crawley's proposal. When she continued to defy him, he struck her. It was the first and only time, she has always insisted, but the consequences were . . . appalling. By ill luck, she fell against a fragile glass dish that shattered against her face and left a prominent scar."

Alex took a long drink of brandy, remembering the spider-web of scars on her cheek. After the first look, he had paid them little mind. A soldier soon grew accustomed to scars, his own and those of his fellows, and held them to be badges of honor.

His vision clouded. He thought of the brutal uncle slumped on a bench downstairs, only a short distance from the reach of his fists. He thought of pounding those fists into that pudgy red face until it burst like a melon.

Kendal's voice reached him when he had one hand on the door latch. "Don't, Alex."

"Why the devil not? He deserves no less."

"Unquestionably. But punishing him will not help the young lady, whose welfare is our primary concern. If we behave as brutally as we claim Lord Whitney to have done, it will only give him more credence with the courts. Besides, Crawley is our real problem."

"Then I'll put him out of commission, too." But Alex knew

better than to rush into action while fury was driving him. With a muttered oath, he let go the latch and turned, propping his shoulders against the oak door. "I cannot credit that a cit and a drunkard baron have got the better of you, James. Tell me that you have a plan to scotch them."

"Would that I did. But I confess to underestimating Crawley. Once Whitney had signed his niece into my custody, I frankly assumed the business to be settled."

"Then why isn't it? If Crawley requires a wife with aristocratic connections, there must be scores of them to choose from. Why must he have this one in particular?"

"Because she was denied to him, I suppose. He is not a man to accept defeat, most especially at the hands of a family like ours. We have, by simple right of birth, what he most covets. And I have sharpened his resentment, I'm afraid, by conducting an investigation into his business practices. I'd not have meddled further with him, you understand, had he not purchased an estate nearby and set about taking control of several canals and turnpike roads. I've a responsibility to the citizens of this county, and have already thrown a spanner into more than one of his pet projects. Indeed, I am resolved to drive him from Westmoreland if I possibly can. Or that was my intention, until he presented me with these documents."

Kendal looked grim. "Plainly I should have waited until Miss Whitney came of age, but I failed to anticipate the level to which he would sink. Kit might have expected it, being better acquainted with the fellow. But off he went on his wedding trip, I falsely assumed Miss Whitney safe in my custody, and now— as Celia would say—we are in the soup. I can tell you that I do not look forward to giving her the news. She will have my head on a platter."

"Much as I'd like to see that," Alex said, "we'll do better to extricate ourselves from the soup pot. Let's hear from the enemy, shall we?"

"You're nearest the bell rope."

Alex rang for the butler, who must have been anticipating the summons. Despite his arthritic knees, Geeson arrived quickly to get his orders and soon returned with Lord Whitney and Sir Basil Crawley in tow. Alex had barely refilled his brandy glass and settled on a wingback chair when they were announced.

Crawley immediately launched the attack. "You kept us waiting overlong, Lord Kendal. I would have expected more courtesy."

"Indeed?" Kendal raised a brow. "I cannot think why, since you appeared on my doorstep without notice. And naturally I required time to read through the considerable mass of documents you have delivered to me."

Lord Whitney backed himself into a shadowed corner. This is all Crawley's doing, his expression said apprehensively.

Kendal was more than a match for Sir Basil, of course. While they exchanged veiled insults, Alex sat back and quietly took Crawley's measure.

He had seen his sort before—clever, ruthless, and occasionally petty. Much like the French-loyalist mayor of a Spanish town Alex's regiment had once occupied, who gave orders that every sheep, goat, pig, and chicken be incinerated to prevent the British invaders from making a supper of them. Never mind that, unlike the French, Wellington's troops did not live off the land, or that the town's citizens would starve when the soldiers had moved on to their next objective. For vanity's sake alone, Señor Viscaya asserted his power, and others suffered because of it.

"Miss Whitney will return with us to her home," Crawley was saying.

"Not today," Kendal said mildly. "You will pardon my lamentable unfamiliarity with Chancery statutes and edicts. Naturally my solicitors must examine the documents and advise me what steps are to be taken."

"The court's directions are perfectly clear," Crawley said. "Lord Whitney intends to see them enforced by whatever means you compel him to use. But we are civilized men, sir. This matter should be resolved in a civilized manner. Or do you prefer that the young lady be hauled away by officers of the law? I assure you that if you refuse to turn Miss Whitney over to her rightful guardian immediately, you may expect constables and Bow Street Runners on your doorstep before tomorrow noon."

"I see. Well, you have made yourself clear, Sir Basil. Now take yourself off my estate before I summon a few exceptionally large footmen to throw you off."

With a discernible moan, Whitney shuffled to the door and let himself out.

Crawley watched him go, a look of disgust on his face, before turning back to Kendal. "You have interfered in matters that do not concern you, my lord. Perhaps you imagine that your rank puts you above the law. But even those not born into a privileged class have the right to conduct business without being trampled on by arrogant aristocrats. One day, someone with the determination and the means will contrive to bring you down."

"How very melodramatic. Should your other enterprises fail, Sir Basil, which I expect they will, might I suggest you consider a career on the stage?"

Alex saw the color leach from Crawley's face, but there was no mistaking the fury in his eyes. With a curt bow, he turned on his heel and strode decisively from the room.

"Well," Kendal said when he was gone, "what do you think?"

"Were he a gentleman, I'd call him out."

"Not very helpful, Alex. Do concentrate. You may be sure that in the long term, I have the means to render Crawley harmless. But where Miss Whitney's immediate fate is concerned, he holds the trump cards. We can expect a search of the estate tomorrow, and when she is not discovered, he will cast his net over all the properties belonging to the family."

"In his place," Alex said thoughtfully, "I wouldn't limit tomorrow's search to Candale. I'd have a constable at Lakeview first thing in the morning, and another at Kit's cottage in Hawkhurst. I'd also set guards on the road just beyond the gatehouse, in case we tried to make a run for it tonight." Alex rubbed the back of his neck. "If he is so clever, why doesn't he know that Miss Whitney is not in residence here?"

"Because he has only just returned from London with this damnable court order, I presume. In any case, if an enemy never made a mistake, he would be invincible. Let's agree that we've a few hours of grace to devise a plan. Should we spirit her away to Scotland?"

Alex's blood ran cold. The family owned an estate in the Highlands, but none of the Valliant brothers had ever set foot there. On one of their annual visits, his parents were caught in a snowstorm on Rannock Moor and perished, along with the servants and the horses. He was nine years old then, and remembered when the news was brought to Candale. James, only twelve, was suddenly Earl of Kendal. Kit had been too young to understand what had transpired.

Caretakers managed the Highland estate now, and he supposed Miss Whitney might be concealed there for a time. But an enterprising Bow Street Runner would eventually track her down, and Crawley was perfectly capable of going there himself and dragging her back across the border.

"That won't do," Alex said finally. "We can't hide her. Crawley will harry her until she is run to ground. She has to be put beyond the control of her guardian, and of the courts as well."

"A lovely idea, to be sure. But how are we to accomplish such a feat?"

Alex took a deep breath. "I shall marry her."

For the first time in his life, he saw his elegant, invariably composed brother gape with openmouthed astonishment.

Kendal picked up his glass and swallowed the last of his brandy in a single gulp. "N-no," he managed to say on a cough. "Impossible."

"How so?" Alex warmed to the idea with startling speed. "Your mention of Scotland gave me the idea. A speedy wedding at Gretna Green will turn the trick, so long as we can get her across the border before Crawley puts his hands on her. It's the obvious solution, James. The *only* solution."

His composure recovered, Kendal propped his chin atop steepled fingers and regarded his brother with cool blue eyes. "It's madness. She will never agree to it. And what in blazes has put such a notion into your head? I've no doubt you are a gallant fellow, but you needn't throw yourself on your sword to save a young woman you have never even clapped eyes on."

Alex leaned back against the chair, making a few swift

calculations. He had made promises to Miss Whitney, but under the circumstances, they would have to be broken. James had to hear the truth or he'd not agree to cooperate with a plan that was suddenly—inexplicably—a plan that Alex had taken to heart. He didn't want to explore the reasons. He had no good reasons. He wanted only to do the thing and deal with the consequences later.

"As a matter of fact," he said, not meeting his brother's intent gaze, "Miss Whitney and I are acquainted. What's more, I have already made her an offer of marriage. She refused me, understandably, but perhaps I'll have better luck on my second attempt."

"I think you had better explain, Alex."

"Very well, although I'd prefer to get on with the business at hand. While I was in Liverpool arranging for my luggage to be sent north, a clerk mentioned that he had made similar provisions in the weeks just past. Lord Kendal was hosting a house party, he said. So far he knew of a duke, two earls, and several lesser members of the Quality gone to Candale, not to mention their families and servants. Naturally I chose not to descend on you while you were preoccupied with your guests."

"Damn the lot of them. If I'd any notion you were on the way home—"

"It doesn't matter, James. Truth be told, I was somewhat unsettled about seeing you again after so many years, and Coniston seemed a good place to wait until the coast was clear. I expected the house to be empty, of course. But I'd no sooner arrived than I fell ill—nothing of consequence—and an apothecary was summoned. One way or another, the news spread through the neighborhood and a few of the local gossips transformed an insignificant incident into a scandal."

"I see. Was not Miss Wigglesworth in residence at the time?"

"Certainly. As I said, the uproar was out of all proportion to the circumstances. Nevertheless, I considered myself bound in honor to make a proposal, which was summarily declined."

"And there was some reason you chose not to mention this before now?"

"Bloody hell, James, what was the point?"

"Until the court snatches her away, I am charged with Diana's welfare."

"And a damnable job you've made of it, permitting her to reside in a decrepit country house with an old woman her sole protection. Miss Whitney has no more worldly sense than a kitten. Make that a mouse. She trembles at a puff of wind."

Kendal fixed his cool, blue-eyed gaze on Alex's face. "Were that the case, you would be crying the banns even now. She had the strength of will to refuse your proposal, just as she refused Sir Basil's—"

"The two offers of marriage are hardly to be compared!"

"I know she looks as if she'd melt under a harsh word," Kendal continued more gently. "She often behaves like a frightened rabbit. Kitten. Mouse. Whatever small creature comes to your mind. But I assure you that Miss Whitney has a will of iron. I also suspect she is unaware of it, even when she quietly defies my wishes and most charmingly goes about having her own way."

"She cannot have it when she is wrong. Would you permit her to jump off a cliff if she insisted on doing so?"

"I might have held her here at Candale, under duress," Kendal said in a level voice. "But she has suffered much at the hands of less benevolent men who were charged with her care. At the time, I was persuaded that she would do better to try her wings in what I considered to be a safe environment. And unless I am much mistaken, Alex, she was doing well enough until you paid an unannounced call."

He should have known better than to debate his diplomat brother on points of logic. Not that logic had much to do with any of this. He had resolved, for reasons that did not bear close scrutiny, to marry her. And so far as he was concerned, that was that. "We are wasting valuable time, my lord earl. Do you mean to help me or not?"

Kendal regarded him in silence for what seemed a very long time. Then he released a sigh. "No good can come of us working at cross-purposes, that is certain. But before you go haring off to Lakeview, let us contrive a plan. Do you really believe that you can persuade Miss Whitney to marry you?"

"Yes!" Alex said immediately. And untruthfully, he was

forced to acknowledge, although not aloud. "At the least, I can bring her into Scotland. We shall assume the best and prepare for what is to happen when we get there."

Chapter 6

Alex arrived at Lakeview in the early afternoon, surprised to find two pony carts, a gig, and a battered carriage drawn up in the stable yard. A grizzled postilion, snoozing under a tree, opened one eye and closed it again.

Bloody damn. Whoever they were, the people belonging to those vehicles, he had to get rid of them without alarming Miss Whitney.

Carver directed him to the kitchen, which struck him as a devilish odd place to be entertaining guests. He heard her voice as he came to the end of the passageway, stopping just short of the open door where he could look inside without being observed.

Wearing a stained apron over a brown dress, Miss Whitney was standing at a butcher's block with bowls, cutlery, and small jars spread out in front of her. Tendrils of hair, come loose from the knot atop her head, dangled at her nape and over her ears. She was addressing an audience of eight females seated around the trestle table directly across from her.

"I wish to thank Miss Gladys Yoodle for donating the perfume," she said, "and Mrs. Pottle for allowing us to borrow her earthenware pipkin. Our first batch of Paste of Palermo appears to be successful, but in the next week you must all test its effectiveness. Be sure to take a jar with you, and apply the concoction each day without fail."

"I'll be takin' a double helping," said a worn-looking female, holding out her hands and wriggling her fingers.

The others laughed.

"An excellent suggestion, Mrs. Jellicoe. There can be no better trial than the hands of a laundress. Now, as all of you know, we shall meet again Thursday next, and for our project I have selected Eau de Veau. If you are able to provide one of the ingredients, please raise your hand." She picked up a piece of paper and read from it. "Two calves' feet."

Calves' feet? Alex wondered if he'd stumbled into a coven of witches.

"No? Well, I'll procure those, along with the rice. A loaf of white bread? Thank you, Mrs. Jellicoe. A gallon of milk? Mrs. Fellson. Ten fresh eggs? Mrs. Renfrew. Two pounds of fresh butter? Mrs. Fellson again. Thank heavens for your cows, ma'am. Mr. Beadle will procure camphor and alum from the apothecary, and then we shall be ready to proceed."

"Be we testin' the odevo?" The Jellicoe woman frowned. "It don't sound so nice as the paste with the perfume in it."

"No, it certainly does not," Miss Whitney agreed. "But according to the receipt, Eau de Veau serves much the same purpose as Paste of Palermo, which is rather expensive to make because of the perfume. If it works as well as the paste, we'll simply give it a fancy new name."

"Better not tell folks what be in it," Mrs. Jellicoe advised laconically.

"Dear me no. How we do what we do will be entirely our secret. Now, are there any questions or suggestions before we close the lesson? No? Very well, then. I shall inform Carver that you are ready to depart. Mrs. Renfrew, don't forget to take an extra jar for Mrs. Phelps, and tell her we hope she will soon be feeling more the thing."

Alex quickly made his way to the entrance hall. "I've only just arrived," he told the startled butler. "Please inform Miss Whitney that I am waiting in the parlor."

She appeared at the door not long after, a worried look in her eyes. "Colonel Valliant?"

He bowed. "Pardon me for intruding while you have guests, Miss Whitney, but I must speak with you on a matter of some urgency."

"Of course." She closed the door. "What is it, sir?"

She was putting a brave front on it, but her face was ashen and her hands gripped at her skirts. Suddenly the well-ordered

58

speech he'd planned to deliver went completely from his mind. "Perhaps you would like to be seated," he said after a moment.

That frightened her all the more, he could tell, but she shook her head. "Pray go on, Colonel. I shan't swoon, I promise you. Has this to do with my uncle?"

"I'm afraid so. He has made application to Chancery Court, which has agreed to consider the matter. You are summoned to London, along with the other parties concerned, and pending a ruling, his rights as legal guardian have been reaffirmed. Kendal is ordered to return you to his custody."

"I see." Her hands dropped to her sides. "Then I must go to him at once. Will tomorrow morning be acceptable, do you suppose? I should like to pack a few things. But I can be ready to depart within the hour, if you have come to escort me back."

"It's not so simple as that."

She cast him a reproachful look. "Believe me, sir, I find the prospect of returning to my home—my uncle's home— anything but *simple*."

"No. Of course it is not." Alex fumbled for words, but they slithered away. "I meant . . . something else."

"What, then? I am perfectly resigned to the circumstances, however much I regret them. 'Tis only for eleven months, and Lord Whitney would not dare to do me harm while he is under the scrutiny of the court."

"On his own account, no. But if ever he had a will of his own, it has long since been drowned in hock. Whitney is Sir Basil's creature now, and I suspect he will do as he is told."

"Perhaps he will try. But since he cannot compel me to marry Sir Basil, which is the only thing either of them wants of me, there is no reason for concern."

"I fear this has gone far beyond Crawley's intention to have you to wife, madam. Kendal's interference has set him on something of a vendetta against the family, and we believe that Crawley means to use you as the instrument of his revenge."

"Dear heavens." She leaned her back against the door for support. "After all that Lord Kendal has done for me, to have it come to this. I am so dreadfully sorry. What can I do to spare him further difficulties on my behalf? Will Sir Basil call it off if I wed him, do you think?"

She would give herself to that blackguard in hopes of protecting Kendal? Alex had seen men sacrifice themselves on the battlefield to save their fellows, but never expected to find that sort of courage in a young girl. "There can be no question of you marrying Crawley," he said gruffly. "Before permitting such an abomination, I would dispose of him."

She blanched. "You would do me no kindness, sir, to put a man's death on my conscience."

"I expect it won't come to that. But you are to forget any notion of returning to your uncle's custody. Kendal is resolved that you shall not, as am I, and you cannot stand against us both."

"But if Lord Kendal has been instructed by the court to hand me over, what will happen if he fails to obey?"

"He'll not be chained up in the Tower of London, if that is what you are imagining. I assure you that Kendal is well able to deal with the consequences, whatever they may be, of defying the Lord Chancellor's order. You are not to concern yourself with him. Understood?"

She wanted to object, that was evident. But she lowered her head, her gaze fixed on the threadbare carpet. "Am I to go into hiding, then? If Lord Kendal will advance me the funds, I could travel south and hire a cottage in some out-of-the-way village. Perhaps in Devon or Cornwall—"

"That can be arranged, of course. But it's not a good idea. Crawley has employed Bow Street Runners to hunt you down."

She gave a small shrug. "He did so before, you know. And the Runner found where Kit had concealed me. But in the end, nothing came of it."

"Indeed? Well, I know little of your prior experiences, but the next time you may not be so fortunate."

"Perhaps." She raised her head, a smile wavering on her lips. "You won't allow me to marry Sir Basil, nor may I return to my uncle. What other choice have I, then, but to hide from them?"

And now, finally, they were come to the point. Cold perspiration formed at his neck and trickled into his collar. How to say it? He was astounded to realize how important it was for her to agree. How very much he wanted her to agree, although he could not have said why.

She was regarding him quizzically, still with that gallant little smile on her lips. Were he in possession of a heart, he thought, it would have cracked in the presence of that smile. As it was, his chest felt wrapped about with knotted ropes. Bracing himself, he snatched a shallow breath of air and said softly, "You could marry *me*."

Her eyes went wide. Plainly that was the last thing on earth she had expected to hear. Shock and bewilderment and something he could not put a name to—fear, most like—washed over her face.

"I—no. You *mustn't*. Why would you even suggest it? Well, you did so once before, to be sure. But there is no more reason now than then. You keep trying to save me by marrying me, sir, but what would become of you if you did? It is most kind to make such an offer, of course. Thank you. Terribly kind. No."

Is the thought so repellent to you? he wanted to ask, as if she hadn't just said so as politely as she could. I am not kind, he wanted to say, but she already knew that.

All the way to Lakeview he had tried to convince himself that she had no choice but to accept his offer. The poor child was backed into a corner. As he had told his brother, what else could she do but marry him?

Now he'd found out. She could say no.

He pulled together what remained of his pride. "I cannot blame you for refusing, Miss Whitney. You do not know me. And if you did, you would be all the more unwilling to endure my company. But the fact remains that you have been dealt poor cards, and now you must play them as best you can. With our help, to be sure. Content yourself to be in our hands, madam, at least until we have got you away from Lakeview. There will be time later for a discussion of what we are to do next."

She stood away from the door. "May I ask where you mean to take me?"

"North, into Scotland. We'll go on horseback as far as you are able and hire a post chaise from there. Kendal and Celia are already on their way. We'll join up with them just across the border at Gretna Green."

The significance of their destination wasn't lost on her. "If they are expecting to witness our marriage, sir, they will be disappointed."

"So it seems." But not nearly so disappointed as the rejected groom, he thought, even as he wondered why he thought it. Wedding Diana Whitney would be, after all, something on the order of adopting a stray kitten. And he rather suspected that this particular kitten, if roused, could unsheathe a formidable set of claws. A smart man would stay clear of them.

He was well free of her. Of course he was. But though he meant to tell her to change into warm clothing and prepare herself for a long ride, he heard himself saying something quite different. "I'll not exhort you to accept my offer, madam. I suspect that it would distress you if I spoke of it again. But it remains open nonetheless, and as we ride to Gretna, I would ask you to give it further consideration."

Her gaze slid away. "What is to be done with me, sir, if there is no marriage?"

"I don't know," he said frankly. "Perhaps Kendal will have devised a plan. My task is to get you there, and we must depart at once. Make yourself ready now and dress warmly, for we'll be traveling well into the night. Meantime I shall explain the circumstances to Miss Wigglesworth and see your horse saddled."

"Yes, sir." She curtsied and turned to the door, pausing with her hand on the latch. Her head was inclined, and he wondered for a moment if she was weeping. But she soon straightened, and let herself into the passageway without a backward look.

Chapter 7

"Welcome to Gretna Hall, sir. Madam." The slender gentleman bowed with grave courtesy and ushered them inside. "How may I be of service?"

"Colonel Alexander Valliant," came the curt reply.

"Ah, yes. You are expected. Follow me, please."

Diana gazed around her as he led them across the reception hall and through an arched doorway, surprised to find herself in such a large, impressive establishment. She had expected something quite different, although she could not have said what. A blacksmith's shop, perhaps. Were not Gretna marriages said to be conducted over an anvil?

"Lord and Lady Kendal await you in the Green Parlor," the gentleman said, pausing before a carved oak door. After knocking lightly, he opened it and stepped aside to let them enter.

Kendal had been embracing his wife, Diana saw at once. Although he rose from the sofa with his usual dignity and bowed to her, color was high on his cheeks. Behind him, Lady Kendal combed her fingers through disarrayed blond curls.

Kendal crossed to shake his brother's hand. "You made excellent time, I must say. We didn't expect you until well after midnight."

"Miss Whitney is a superb rider," the colonel said with one of his almost-smiles. "I was hard put to keep up with her."

"Since we'd no idea when you would arrive, it was naturally impossible to make arrangements for the ceremony. But Mr. Lang has promised to come whenever we send for him, no matter the hour." Kendal gave the colonel a steady look. "It would do well, I believe, to proceed immediately."

Ghosting behind the words, Diana sensed, was a private communication between them. But . . . *immediately*?

She felt light-headed. Nothing must happen immediately! She plucked at Colonel Valliant's sleeve.

He sliced a brief glance at her. "Not right away, James. After the long journey, Miss Whitney will require time to catch her breath. I certainly do."

Looking mildly displeased, Kendal nodded. "In that case, perhaps the ladies should withdraw upstairs."

No! She desperately summoned the will to protest, but it declined to respond.

Lady Kendal appeared at her side. "Come, my dear. I expect these gentlemen mean to apply themselves to a bottle of brandy, and you must be longing for a cup of tea. Please have a tray sent to us, James."

All in a fog, Diana was swept from the parlor, up the stairs, and into a large bedchamber. Every ounce of the energy that had carried her this far suddenly flooded out of her. She stood, limp as rags, while the countess removed her cloak and bonnet and gloves. When told to be seated, she went on legs of jelly to a chair by the fireplace and sank down with a sigh.

Dear heavens, what was she to *do*? Evidently Lord and Lady Kendal assumed she had come here to marry Colonel Valliant, and for some unspoken reason, the earl was in a great hurry to get on with it.

This is what it must be like, she thought, to be caught up in a whirlwind. One word from her—a firm *no*—would put a stop to this. But she couldn't bring herself to say it, any more than she could produce the *yes* that sometimes trembled, unwelcome, on her lips.

For hours and hours, for all the miles up the steep winding road over Kirkstone Pass and down again, along narrow tracks and across fields as they proceeded to Scotland without ever venturing onto the Great North Road, she had prayed for an answer to be given her. The smallest sign would do. If she saw a falling star before she counted to a hundred, she would wed the colonel.

She counted and watched the sky, but no stars fell. So she made another deal, offering Heaven a bit more latitude this time. If a rabbit ran across the road *or* a star fell, she would say yes. And this time she'd count to a thousand.

Next it was two thousand, and she threw in catching sight of a cow or a deer. By the time she increased the count to five thousand, she was willing to settle for a sheep. Surely she would see one miserable sheep!

When that failed, she tried turning her bargain the other way around. She would count again to five thousand, and promised at first sight of rabbit, falling star, cow, deer, or sheep to irrevocably decline the colonel's offer.

But there were no signs from Heaven, no miracles to be had. No answers. Nothing but the man riding beside her, more silent and remote than the stars.

Lady Kendal tugged a leather ottoman across the carpet and sat beside Diana's knee. "This must be a great trial for you," she said. "I am so very sorry for it. We had thought you to be safe, but I fear that is no longer the case. Kendal will not tell you this, because men have the addled notion that women wish to be spared hard truths, but our carriage was twice stopped and searched on the way here. I think the constable suspected we were hiding you under the floorboards, or perhaps in one of the portmanteaus, for he was quite thorough."

"But *why*, Lady Kendal?" Those were the first words Diana had spoken for several hours, and they came out in a froggy croak. "My uncle can do no more harm to me than he's already done. I'm sure he would never dare to beat me, and even if he did, I would refuse to marry Sir Basil until my dying breath."

"Well, it won't come to that, I assure you. And I quite enjoyed our little adventure on the journey to Gretna. A Bow Street Runner followed us across the border, you know. Not Mr. Pugg, unfortunately. Sir Basil has employed a less kindly man this time. Kendal reasoned he would track us until convinced we truly meant to visit the Highland estate, so we kept on going right past Gretna and all the way to Moffet before he finally gave up. When we were sure he had turned back, we waited a few hours at an inn before retracing our way to Gretna Hall."

"Where is he now, do you suppose?"

"Possibly he has gone back to look for you at Candale, or

Lakeview, or any other place you might be found. But Kendal is fairly certain he is still lurking about Gretna. Sir Basil and his Runner must realize that we are plotting your escape, for it cannot be a coincidence that we set out for Scotland so soon after learning of the court's ruling. When they failed to find you in our company, they surely mounted guards near the border. Indeed, I thought the Runner would plant himself directly center of the bridge to waylay you. But you crossed without difficulty, so it seems we have thrown him off the scent."

"Colonel Valliant thought it too dangerous to use the bridge," Diana said. "We followed the river until we found a place shallow enough to ford."

"Oh, well done! Naturally Alex would anticipate a trap. But the Runner may think to check here again, and should he find you before you are securely wed, he has the authority to snatch you away. I expect you noticed that Kendal is in something of a hurry to proceed with the ceremony."

"Yes." If there was to be a wedding at all. Why were they not considering other possibilities, such as taking her deeper into Scotland or dispatching her to Cornwall? Or even casting her off to fend for herself? Colonel Valliant had said they would discuss it further, the question of their marriage, when they reached Gretna. But nobody was discussing anything. Not with her, at any rate. Everybody was assuming she'd go to the altar or the anvil or wherever she was led and do what she was told to do.

And most likely she would.

Why could she not turn him away? In all good conscience, that was the reasonable—the *decent*—choice. It was her moral obligation, was it not, to save the colonel from this act of folly? But while a servant bustled into the room with a tray and laid out cups and saucers and the teapot and the rest, she gazed up at the plaster ceiling and hoped for a shooting star.

Lady Kendal pressed a warm cup into her hands. "Drink this, my dear. And then we must get you dressed. I knew you would be traveling without luggage, so I packed several of the gowns you had left at Candale and brought them along. Three have been pressed, and of course, you must choose whichever you prefer. But I quite favor the pale moss green. It looks so well with your hair."

She remembered the gown, one of a large number already made up for her London Season before her parents died. All were two years out of fashion, of course, and far better suited for a carefree young girl eagerly looking forward to her come-out. The girl she had been.

She felt a great deal older tonight. Aeons older. But very little wiser, alas. While they lived, her parents had made every significant decision for her. Now strangers ordered her life while she sipped tea and dithered.

Lady Kendal placed a reassuring hand on her knee. "All will work out for the best, you know."

Diana set down her cup, sloshing tea into the saucer. "You mean well," she said in a raw voice. "All of you mean well, and I'm ever so grateful. But I cannot marry Colonel Valliant."

"Ah." The countess tapped a manicured nail against her chin. "You dislike him, then?"

"By no means. Not . . . precisely. I confess that I find him more than a little . . . well, formidable. But the fault is all mine. He has always been exceedingly kind."

"In an abrupt, military sort of way." Lady Kendal smiled. "Alex is another of those obstinate I-know-what's-best-so-do-as-I-tell-you men who will run roughshod over you should you permit him to. Kendal is much the same. I vow that sometimes he makes my teeth ache! And Kit is no better. It must be a family trait, this penchant for issuing orders and expecting them to be obeyed without question. But one soon learns how to deal with excessively strong-minded husbands. It's rather amusing to let them imagine they are having their own way while all along, you are having yours."

"But it's not the same with me, Lady Kendal. You and Lucy had far more experience of life when you were wed. You are possessed of stronger characters than I shall ever have. And you married for love, while Colonel Valliant is—oh, I don't know *what* he is doing! Sacrificing himself at the altar, I suppose, for the sake of his brother's not-quite-legal ward. And if I permit him to do so, he'll be stuck with me *forever*! He is certain to regret it. We don't know the least little thing about each other. I have met him only twice, under difficult circumstances, and—"

"And both times he proposed marriage." Lady Kendal stirred honey into her tea. "Is that not extraordinary, Diana? Bringing a man to scratch once is strenuous enough. Twice is a marvel. It's perfectly obvious that Alex wishes to be *stuck* with you."

"I believe, Lady Kendal, that you are mistaken. He is impelled by a misguided sense of honor, or duty, or whatever causes gentlemen to behave in so irrational a manner. I haven't the slightest notion what he is thinking. Not ever. All the way here he said practically nothing to me. Whenever we stopped to rest the horses, he wandered off by himself." Her voice faltered. "As if he could not bear my company."

"Oh, I assure you that is not the case. He behaved in very much the same way at Candale. We rarely saw him, and he seldom spoke unless asked a direct question. It was my feeling—only guesswork, you understand—that something deeply troubles him. Perhaps you will be able to discover what it is, if indeed it be anything at all. Kendal says that Alex has always been reserved, so you must not imagine that he suddenly fell silent on your account."

Diana mustered a faint smile. "We would have a quiet household, then. Colonel Valliant has no inclination to engage in conversation, and I dare not say a word to him. Perhaps that is why he is willing to enter into a marriage of convenience. He has found himself a wife who will leave him in peace."

"Give me leave to doubt that," Lady Kendal said, laughing as she rose from the ottoman. "And so, my dear, will it be the green dress?"

Much to Diana's embarrassment, Lady Kendal cheerfully played lady's maid, helping her pull on silk stockings and the veriest wisp of a chemise. She had been concerned about the green muslin dress, a summer frock with embroidered cap sleeves and a band of dark green ribbon tied under her breasts, but it still fit her even without the corset Lady Kendal had forgot to pack. She'd forgot to bring the long kidskin gloves as well, the ones dyed to match the ribbon, so Diana's arms and hands would have to go bare. At least she was relatively clean, after sponging herself from scalp to toe with lukewarm water from a basin, and she'd washed her hair that very morning.

While Lady Kendal was arranging her tangled locks, she slumped dejectedly on the chair in front of the dressing table, making sure never to glance up at the mirror. "Why are we taking such trouble to rig me out for a slapdash Gretna wedding?" she asked. "Especially with Lord Kendal in so great a hurry to get on with it?"

"Ah, my dear, this is perhaps the most significant event of your life. Don't you think it merits a bit of trouble? And Kendal has always been rather formal when it comes to—well, to just about anything. Certainly a wedding in the family requires a proper ceremony, as best we can manage under the circumstances. He brought along something for Alex to wear, I believe, so you needn't fear that your bridegroom will be standing there in all his dirt."

When Lady Kendal finished pinning up Diana's hair in what she described as a style of "relaxed elegance," she handed her a small bouquet of tulips. "I picked these in the garden this afternoon," she said, brushing a kiss against her cold cheek. "Are you ready to go downstairs?"

No. No. No.

"Yes," she replied, her heart plunging to somewhere in the vicinity of her ankles. "But how can it be that I seem to have come to a decision without ever making up my mind?"

"Put it down to instinct," Lady Kendal advised. "I knew that I wanted Kendal the very first moment I saw him, which happened to be on the day of his wedding to another woman. I was ten-and-seven and married to another man. Nine years passed before I saw him again, at which time I made his acquaintance in the most humiliating way, and from there the tale becomes even more unconventional."

"Is this meant to reassure me?" Diana murmured into her bouquet.

"Well, it might if we'd time for you to hear the entire story. The point is, you have seen us as we are now, despite the unpromising beginning we made. It may well be the same for you. Wilberta Wigglesworth once told me something that I knew by

69

experience but had failed to comprehend. One can fall in love in the space between heartbeats."

"But I'm not the least bit in love with Colonel Valliant!"

"She didn't specify *which* heartbeats, my dear." Lady Kendal took her arm and led her from the room. "Have you read *Hamlet*?"

Startled, Diana could only nod.

"Then remember, 'If it is not now, yet it will come. The readiness is all.' "

Her bad luck then, for she was not at all ready. Indeed, she'd not have objected overmuch if Sir Basil's Bow Street Runner put a stop to the wedding and swept her off to some less terrifying fate. But only a footman appeared, to escort them to the reception hall. And when she stepped inside, her heart bounded to her throat.

Colonel Valliant was standing directly across the room, a tall impressive figure in scarlet coat, white breeches, and high black boots. One white-gloved hand rested on the hilt of his sword, and his other arm was folded behind his back.

In his regimentals, the colonel was positively dazzling. Light from the chandelier directly overhead gleamed off silver epaulets, silver buttons, the silver braid across the front of his coat, and the yellow and silver braided sash at his waist. Most striking of all, it shone on the bright silver sword at his left hip. He stood as rigidly as the high stand-up collar he wore, his face without expression, his eyes watchful.

Suddenly aware that she had been gawping at him like a schoolgirl, Diana wrenched her gaze to Lord Kendal. Beside him stood a gray-haired man dressed in a black frock coat and loosely knotted cravat.

Kendal smiled. "You look lovely, my dear. May I present Mr. David Lang, the . . . er—"

"Priest," Lang supplied. "I'm no cleric, but 'priests' is what we be called."

"I am pleased to make your acquaintance," Diana murmured, wondering how she was supposed to conduct herself in these excessively odd circumstances.

Lang pulled a thin, tattered book from an inside pocket. "Are you here of your own consent, miss?"

Surprised by the abrupt question, she managed to nod.

"Be there impediments to this marriage?"

Not sure what those might consist of, she said, "None that I know of, sir."

"Shall we proceed, then?" He flipped open the small book and waited expectantly.

Colonel Valliant moved to stand beside her, his gazed focused directly forward. The top of her head was no more than an inch higher than his shoulder, and this close to him, she was more conscious than ever that he was, by nature and experience, a warrior.

Mr. Lang had begun to speak, but his voice seemed to be coming from a vast distance. The colonel spoke as well, in a soft baritone, and as he did, something brushed lightly against her. She slid a glance to where his sleeve touched her arm from elbow to wrist, scarlet wool against pale, goose-pimply skin. It was warm, the sleeve, and slightly scratchy. It entranced her. Not a speck of lint on it, she thought in wonder. When it pressed more firmly against her arm, she liked the feel of it and of the muscles swelling inside it as his hand drew into a fist.

Her gaze dropped to the white knit glove stretched tautly over his knuckles.

"Well?" Mr. Lang said, his voice sharp. "Will you or won't you?"

She looked up at him blankly. Was he speaking to her? Then she saw Lady Kendal, who was standing a little way behind him, nodding vigorously.

"Yes," the countess mouthed silently.

"Y-yes," Diana said.

"Very well, then," said Mr. Lang. "Have you a ring, sir?"

Turning slightly, Colonel Valliant raised her left hand and slid a gold band onto her finger, repeating very softly the words Mr. Lang gave him to say.

When he was done, he turned again to face the priest. But he kept hold of her hand, which felt impossibly small encased in his.

"You being sworn to each other," Mr. Lang intoned, "I declare you rightly married by the form of the Kirk of Scotland and agreeable to the Church of England." He snapped his book

71

closed and returned it to his pocket. "Now if ye'll sign the register and the papers, I can go back to me bed."

Colonel Valliant led her to a small table strewn with documents and let go her hand to take the pen offered him by the innkeeper.

Had he been here all this time? Diana accepted his good wishes with a distracted smile, watching her husband—her *husband*!—inscribe his name in bold letters. Alexander Rutherford Valliant. He wrote it thrice more before giving her the pen and stepping aside.

"Directly under his," the innkeeper said when she hesitated, wanting to read what was written on the papers she was signing. But everyone was looking at her, waiting for her, so she hastily scrawled her name where she'd been told.

Mr. Lang added his signature, a rough scribble, and the innkeeper applied a wax seal at the bottom of each page.

"All right and tight," he said with satisfaction, handing the documents to Lord Kendal. "Now if you'll pardon me, I shall see to the other arrangements." With a bow he left the room, followed by Mr. Lang.

What other arrangements? Diana thought, feeling more like a footstool than a bride as everyone carried on as if she weren't there. Kendal drew the colonel aside, where they spoke in voices too low for her to make out what they were saying. She saw Kendal give over one of the papers and slip the others inside his coat.

"For a moment," Lady Kendal said, coming to stand beside her, "I thought you meant to bring a halt to the wedding."

"My mind wandered, is all." She sighed. "It happened so quickly. I was scarcely aware we had begun, and then in a flash it was finished." Lifting her hand, she gazed bemusedly at her wedding ring. It was of chased gold set with a teardrop-shaped emerald. "I *am* married now, I suppose."

"Oh, yes. The ring belonged to Alex's grandmother. It's lovely, don't you think?"

"Indeed." She shivered. The room had gone frightfully cold. "But what is to happen now, Lady Kendal?" She gestured to the men, whose backs were now turned to her as they conversed.

"Whatever can they be talking about that I am not permitted to hear?"

"Of course you are permitted, and I assure you there is nothing confidential about what they are saying. But when gentlemen are discussing business, they've a lamentable tendency to forget that we exist. Shall we go over there and remind them?"

Gazing at Colonel Valliant's wide shoulders, the dark hair brushing against his stiff collar, the long legs planted slightly apart, she felt safer keeping her distance. "No, Lady Kendal. I shouldn't care to interrupt them."

"As you wish. They are merely deciding the most expedient way to notify your trustees, your uncle, the magistrate, Chancery Court, and anyone else who ought to learn of the marriage. For that very purpose, Kendal had the proprietor supply several copies of the marriage lines. And I expect they have a few loose ends to tie as well, for Kendal and I shall be departing within a few minutes. Our luggage is being put onto the carriage even now."

"But why?" Diana's voice was shrill with panic. "Surely you cannot mean to travel at night? And how can we go with you? Our horses won't bear another long journey so soon."

"Kendal thinks it best we return immediately with proof of the marriage, lest the constables descend on Candale with a warrant to search the house. I shouldn't like to imagine them barging about, especially in the nursery, before we can arrive to stop them. You will remain here with Alex, of course. A light supper is being laid out in your room, and the things I packed for you have already been taken there."

The whirlwind caught her up again. She hadn't thought what would happen after the wedding. Heavens, she still had not decided to marry him—never mind that she'd already done so.

The innkeeper swept through the door, all smiles and courtly grace as he bowed to the earl.

"He has been well paid for his services," Lady Kendal whispered, drawing Diana across the room to join the men. "Ask of him anything you require while you remain at Gretna Hall."

Lord Kendal turned to greet them. "The carriage is ready to depart, Celia, and a servant is waiting in the foyer with your cloak and bonnet. I shall join you in a moment."

The countess pulled Diana into a warm embrace. "Now we are sisters, you know, and I am so very glad of it. Perhaps at long last you will consent to address me as Celia!"

Heart sinking, Diana watched her sole ally disappear through the door. *Please* take me with you, she begged silently. Don't leave me here alone with *him.*

Lord Kendal took hold of her limp hand and held it between his. "I hope you will be very happy, my dear. And it is my conviction that Alex could not have chosen better if he'd searched a thousand years. Military men, it seems, have a talent for recognizing a desirable objective."

"They sometimes make mistakes, my lord."

"Even the best of them," Kendal agreed mildly. "We are pleased to welcome you into the family, Diana Valliant, but we shall save the speeches and toasts until you arrive at Candale." With a bow, he took his leave.

"I'll walk out with you," Alex said, passing directly by Diana as if she were a doorstop.

She must have been glaring at him, because her expression appeared to startle the maid who entered the room a moment later.

The girl dipped a curtsy, color blazing on her cheeks. "I come to take you upstairs, ma'am. To the Bridal Chamber."

Chapter 8

Diana had seen larger beds, she supposed, but none that dominated a room in such a way as the one in the Bridal Chamber. She kept her distance, hovering against the opposite wall and deliberately not looking at it.

Instead, she inventoried the rest of the furnishings. In two vases atop the mantelpiece, spring flowers were somewhat wilted from the fire blazing just beneath them. A lacquered screen in the Chinese style was folded in one corner. Candles flickered from a pair of wall sconces and a silver brace on the marble-topped dressing table. The maid had opened the armoire to show her that her dresses were there, and her stockings, underthings, and a night rail were folded in a stand of drawers.

Had she been left here alone to change into that decidedly flimsy night rail? Like the dresses, it was part of her London wardrobe and had never been worn. Nor did she wish to wear it tonight, not unless all the lights had been extinguished.

The supper Lady Kendal had spoken of was laid out on a small round table near the center of the room. Beside it were two graceful wooden chairs and a tripod that held a silver pail filled with ice chips and a bottle of champagne. As she gazed at the basket of pastries, the lobster patties and sliced meats, the open syllabub tart and wedges of cheese, her stomach roiled.

There was a sharp rap at the door. Without waiting for a response, Colonel Valliant strode in, closed the door behind him, and gave her a perfunctory bow. "Is everything to your satisfaction, madam?"

"Y-yes indeed. The chamber is most elegant, don't you think?"

He glanced around indifferently. "It's well enough, I suppose."

Having exhausted her meager supply of polite bedroom conversation, she watched with growing apprehension as he unbuckled his sword belt. He held it in one hand for a moment, as if deciding what to do with it, and finally tossed it onto the bed.

Her gaze fixed on the sword. Silver and leather against maroon and gold brocade.

"If you are considering making a run for it," he said, a trace of amusement in his voice, "there is no need. I have secured a second bedchamber for myself."

Chagrined, she drew herself away from the wall and squared her shoulders. "I had no thought of fleeing, sir."

"Did you not?" A faint smile lifted the corners of his mouth. "You put me forcibly in mind of a raw recruit about to panic at first sight of the enemy."

Enemy? "You are quite mistaken, Colonel Valliant. I stand firmly prepared to do my duty as your wife."

The smile broadened. "I'm afraid that if you stand firmly, my dear, we shall have no little difficulty carrying through."

"You know very well what I meant, sir!" Heat flooded her cheeks. "And this is hardly the time for word games. I was never any good at them, and they accomplish nothing."

"To the contrary." He stripped off his gloves. "Until I made you angry, you were undeniably afraid."

"Well, now I am angry *and* afraid."

"So I see. One of your hands is clutching at your skirts, and the other is knotted into a fist."

She glanced down in surprise. Good heavens! Hastily, she clasped her hands behind her back.

"Better if you had made two fists," he advised her, the smile gone. "Be angry when you will, madam. But if you fear me, we shall have very rough going."

"I don't fear you!" she said immediately. "Well, not terribly much," she added in strictest honesty. "The thing is, I don't *know* you. And now, willy-nilly, I am *married* to you. I do find that fearsome, sir."

"Quite." He folded his gloves over his sash. "As a matter of fact, I had become convinced you didn't mean to go through with it. You had made it clear you'd no intention of doing so, and while I had some hope you would change your mind, I cannot say that I expected that you would." His eyes narrowed. "You were closeted with Lady Kendal for rather a long time— one hour and eighteen minutes, to be precise—before sending word that Mr. Lang was to be called. Tell me the truth, please. Did she talk you into this?"

"Not exactly." Diana tried to recall their conversation. "Did you *wish* me to refuse?"

He crossed to the ice bucket and pulled out the bottle of champagne. In silence, his expression unreadable, he removed the cork.

"You have not answered my question, sir."

"I beg your pardon. To my mind the answer was perfectly clear. I said that I *expected* you to decline my offer, not that I wished it. Were I reluctant to marry you, you may be sure the offer would never have been made."

"I don't understand. How could you possibly have wanted to marry me? You know me no better than I know you."

He filled two flutes with champagne. "We have chosen an odd time for this conversation, don't you think? Why is it, do you suppose, that we married first and only began to debate the wisdom of our decision over our wedding supper?"

"I wish I knew," she said on a long sigh. "But here we are. And neither of us seems to know why."

He looked up at her, holding her gaze. "We can come to no conclusions tonight, Diana. You are exhausted and confused. I am . . . well, very much the same. But I believe that neither of us will sleep until we have made a beginning of some sort. At the very least, shall we drink a toast to our marriage?"

When he stayed in place and held out a glass of champagne, she understood that he meant for her to come to him. The distance between them was no more than a few steps, but he seemed to her very far away and impossible to reach. Then, without knowing quite how she got there, she was standing directly in front of him and he was pressing the glass into her hand. When she looked straight ahead, she saw the silver braid on his crimson collar and the black stock at his throat.

Slowly she lifted her gaze to his chin, and to his lips, and finally to his eyes.

He touched his glass to hers. "To my reluctant bride," he said with another of his faint, enigmatic smiles. "And to her remarkable courage."

She swallowed the lump in her throat. "To my equally reluctant groom," she replied softly. "And to his noble sacrifice."

Stepping back, he frowned at her. "I'll not drink to that, madam. You are very much mistaken to think me remotely chivalrous, and I am disinclined to martyrdom. Let us not pluck that crow again." After setting his glass on the table, he pulled out a chair and gestured for her to be seated.

"I meant no insult," she murmured, sinking down under his stern glare and watching him take the chair across from her. "And it is no more than the truth."

"Have we not agreed that neither of us knows the truth?" he countered in a level voice.

"But certain things are implied, are they not? Had my uncle left me in peace, you would never have considered marrying me."

"No? I distinctly recall making you an offer before I knew of his existence. I could as easily accuse you of accepting my proposal solely to escape him. Is that the case?"

She put down her glass. "I would hate to think I had done such a cowardly thing, but it may well be that I did. How can I explain myself to you when I've no idea what sort of creature I am? You have made a bad bargain, sir. You have wed a *nothing*."

"I promise that you have drawn the shorter straw," he said with a harsh laugh. "Unlike you, I do know what I am. And while you can yet become anything you choose to be, I have already cast my lot with the devil."

"Rubbish. You *could* not!"

"Don't be so sure of that." He raised a mocking eyebrow. "It's not too late, you know. The papers are easily torn up. Mr. Lang, if I read him aright, can be bribed to forget the marriage ever took place."

"But it *is* too late. Lord Kendal is already on his way south to spread the news." She took a deep breath. "Besides, I don't wish to tear up the papers and forget what we did tonight. I simply want to know what to do next."

It might have been her imagination, but he appeared to relax. Infinitesimally, to be sure, but she supposed that soldiers never relaxed to any great extent.

"We have got off to a rocky start," he said, propping his elbows on the table and resting his chin on his folded hands. "I meant for us to find common ground tonight, but we appear to have dug ourselves into separate trenches. And as you plainly see, I have no talent for conversation, particularly with a young woman who is trying very hard not to regret becoming my wife."

"I am fairly sure I've no regrets, sir. What concerns me are *your* regrets."

"Ah. Will it help if I promise to tell you the moment I have any?"

"Dear me, no." She shuddered. "Each time you spoke to me, I'd be expecting the ax to drop. But you must always correct me when I displease you, and instruct me how to mend my character. I shan't mind that in the least."

His eyes shadowed. "I'll not be reading you any lectures, madam, save this one. Fear invariably displeases me, unless I see it on the face of an enemy. Even then I have a disgust of it, although I have been afraid more times than I can count. For that very reason I will never sit judgment over you, and if you perceive me doing so, put it down to my bad temper and pay me no mind. Is that understood?"

She made a vague gesture, still trying to imagine Colonel Valliant in fear of *anything*. It was beyond her power. She did understand, painfully, that he despised cowards, and now he had married one. Whatever was to become of them?

"Drink your champagne," he said, not unkindly. "It will help you to sleep tonight."

She obeyed, wondering if he could hear her teeth chattering against the rim of the glass. Then the bubbles went up her nose and she sneezed. Mortified, she took the handkerchief he offered her and buried her face in it. "I shall be stronger tomorrow," she mumbled. "I promise you that I will."

"And what do you wish to do tomorrow? Kendal assumes

that we will proceed directly to Candale, but when he said so, you appeared to dislike the plan."

She was astonished that he had noticed. "Would you mind very much if we returned to Lakeview instead?" she asked, peering at him over the top of the handkerchief.

"Not at all." He gave her a wry smile. "You see how easy it is? What else do you want to ask of me?"

His mood had softened, she realized, and there might never be a better time to approach the second most important thing on her mind. "Well, there is one matter I had hoped to mention, sir. I should very much like your permission to continue working on several projects that Miss Wigglesworth and I have undertaken. Oh!" She clapped one hand over her mouth. Until this moment, she had not considered that he might object to Miss Wigglesworth living with them.

"You will need to define *oh!* for me," he said when she failed to continue.

"M-may she remain at Lakeview?"

"Why not? I like her. She speaks her mind."

Taking heart to find him so unexpectedly agreeable, she plunged ahead. "And may we proceed with our venture? Of now it is little more than a seed, but I've no end of schemes to make it grow."

"Then do so." He refilled her glass. "What else, madam?"

"Nothing more, sir. Thank you. Except . . ."

She could not ask him. She wasn't even sure what it was she had to know. How were they to live together? What did he expect of her?

"Blurt it out, Diana." He looked mildly amused. "Before it chokes you."

It all but paralyzed her. "Is this to be a r-real marriage, Colonel Valliant?"

"If you mean will I bed you, the answer is yes."

"No." She waved a hand. "I mean, that is not what I meant. I always assumed that you would."

"Then what are you asking? I have every intention of keeping to the vows I made you, in case you were imagining otherwise. There is no love between us, of course, but we, too, have planted a seed. Perhaps it will grow and flourish. I must warn you, however, that it would be unwise to expect a great deal of me. I shall be faithful, yes, and protect you and honor you. More than that, I cannot promise."

It was what she had needed to know, she supposed. He was an honorable man, and she could safely depend on him to keep to every letter of the wedding vows. Well, save for the one than mentioned love. She presumed that love had been mentioned, although she had no recollection of it.

She had never considered the possibility he'd fallen in love with her, nor dared she to dream that he might come to love her sometime in the future. Really, she ought not to care that he had put into words what she already knew. But she did care.

Forlorn Hope.

He touched her hand. "I believe we will make no more progress this night, madam. Shall we start afresh tomorrow? Sleep as late as you like, and we'll head out for Coniston whenever you are ready."

"I'm an early riser, sir."

"Excellent. More common ground." He went to the bed and retrieved his sword. "It won't be so bad as you are thinking, you know. Remember, you have only to tell me what you want. Don't make me guess. I have lived in the company of men all my life, and what I know of females wouldn't fill a canteen."

"Then you are far advanced of me, sir." Standing, she brushed at her skirts with quaking hands. "What I know of men wouldn't fill a thimble."

To her astonishment, he came directly up to her and brushed the lightest of kisses on her forehead. "Then we must stumble along in harness, madam wife, and make the best we can of this marriage. For now, I hope you will sleep well."

The words bubbled to her throat of their own accord. Heaven knew she hadn't formed them in her mind, but out they came. "Stay. If you wish. If you want to . . . to . . ."

She couldn't finish. But he knew what she meant. She saw the light flash in his eyes. And then it was gone.

His smile was singularly sweet, though. She had not seen such a smile on his face before.

"I always want to, " he said. "I am a man, and men are fairly predictable in that way. But I'm not a beast, Diana, and you are not ready."

Yes I am!

But she couldn't say such a thing, and it probably wasn't true. What she wanted, emphatically, was to get it *over* with. She would not feel married until they did what married people did together, which she knew about in theory but had trouble imagining in actual practice.

It seemed so very . . . intimate. Invasive. He would put himself into her body! Perhaps he was right. When she considered what was to happen, she wasn't the slightest bit ready for it.

"Very well, sir." She forced herself to smile. "I bid you good night."

Chapter 9

Diana was on her way downstairs when her husband stalked into the house, his jaw set and a leather portfolio clutched under his arm. Pausing with one hand on the newel post, she watched him toss his hat and gloves to Carver.

He barely glanced at her. "I wish to speak with you, madam. Carver, see to it there is a decanter of brandy in the study and inform Miss Wigglesworth that we are not to be disturbed."

Crimson-faced, the butler hurried down the passageway.

Diana, greatly wishing that she could go with him, studied the wintry look on Colonel Valliant's face. He was in a black mood, that was perfectly evident, although she could not begin to think why. This day had been exactly like all the others since their marriage. He'd left the house after a breakfast taken in solitude and returned not much later than he usually did.

She never asked where he was going, or how long he'd be gone, or what he did with his time. If he wanted her to know, no doubt he would tell her. And because he expressed no interest in her affairs, she dared not meddle with his.

Clinging to the newel post for support, she waited, as he waited, for Carver to bring a decanter to the library and ignite the lamps. The colonel stood in rigid silence, his gaze fixed on the floor. At length he turned and strode with military assertiveness down the passageway, plainly expecting her to follow.

She would, yes she would, just as soon as her legs steadied under her.

There were scores of reasons, she supposed, for him to be displeased with her. He had married her on a gallant impulse, and what had he gained but a wife he didn't want and a ramshackle household overrun with the sort of people not generally admitted to aristocratic drawing rooms.

All in all, she readily admitted, he had been remarkably patient with her these last few weeks. He never interfered with her activities. He asked nothing of her, not even his rights as a husband. But she ought to have prepared herself for when his patience ran out, because it was inevitable that sooner or later he'd take control of the house. And her.

She had been careful not to think of it. She could not bear to. He engulfed her. Overwhelmed her. He filled every room when he wasn't even there. And when he was, the effect on her was cataclysmic. He was too powerful. Too intimidating. Too *male*.

Diligently she hid from him. Her days were spent among the women, who provided an effective shield, and in the evenings she closeted herself with Miss Wigglesworth. But she couldn't always escape, not altogether. Occasionally he joined them in the drawing room after dinner, settling in a chair by the fireplace to read his book.

She often glanced over to see his gaze fixed on her. She could *feel* him looking at her. Not merely sense it, but actually feel it, like a touch.

And now he was angry. Dear heavens. She would sooner face a rampaging boar than Colonel Valliant in a temper. But no rampaging boars came to her rescue, so she was forced to make the long walk down the passageway and into his study.

He was standing beside his desk, looking excessively severe. "I have been to Lancaster," he said. "Your trustees wished to consult with me regarding the disposition of your inheritance. They have provided me a detailed accounting of their stewardship and a list of your assets."

"Oh?" she said warily. The trustees had been selected by her father, and she'd always assumed them to be reliable. "Has there been some difficulty?"

"Not that I am aware. For the time being they will continue to manage your inheritance. I was prepared to make disposition of the funds then and there, but was persuaded to speak with you beforehand."

That explained why he was so out of temper, she thought, sitting when he pointed to a chair. Colonel Valliant would not appreciate lessons in conduct from his wife's solicitors. "I know nothing whatever about matters of finance," she said. "You must do as you like."

He opened the folio, withdrew a sheaf of papers, and spread them over the desk. "You are an heiress," he informed her brusquely, as if she were unaware of the fact.

"That has never been a secret, sir. Surely you were told the conditions of my father's will."

"The terms were perfectly clear. But no one saw fit to mention the *amount* in question. I certainly never expected a rural Lancashire baron with an insignificant estate to have amassed a substantial fortune."

"Well, the family has been about it for several hundred years, you know. And the estate itself was of considerable size until my great-grandfather sold the unentailed land. He preferred collecting art to farming, so now the Whitneys have very little land and a great many paintings. Excluding the contents of the house, which have not recently been appraised, I believe the total is fifty-eight thousand pounds."

"More than sixty now," he said from the oak sideboard where he was filling his brandy glass. "The funds are currently invested on the Exchange."

"You are displeased with that arrangement, sir?"

"How could I be, knowing virtually nothing about managing large sums of money? Kendal will make an evaluation when he has examined the records."

"He has already done so. But I meant displeased about the amount. One could imagine that you wished the fortune to be significantly . . . smaller."

"Of that, you may be sure." His eyes narrowed. "Had I known the truth, there would have been no question of entering into this marriage."

"Good heavens." Had he taken leave of his senses? "You are affronted because your wife turned out to be *wealthy*? But that is nonsensical. I should think you would be delighted."

"To be thought a fortune hunter? You greatly mistake my character, madam."

"Probably so," she agreed with a sigh. "I know very little about you. But why should anyone believe that you married me for my fortune? I never had such a notion, and at the time we were wed, I assumed you knew all about it."

"It never crossed your mind that I might be looking to line my pockets?" He gave her a look of patent disbelief. "Most men would wed a barn owl if it flew in with a dowry of sixty thousand pounds. Why should I prove an exception? And why the devil are you smiling? This is not in the least amusing."

"I'm sorry, but what you said put me in mind of Fidgets, who was at one time vastly in love with Kit. But Fidgets turned out to be a male, as if being a barn owl were not obstacle enough, and—"

"What in blazes are you talking about?" The colonel mauled his hair. "No. I'm quite sure I don't want to know. Let us return to the subject, if you please."

Diana shrank back on the chair. "I beg your pardon, sir."

"And *stop* that! No apologies, not even if they are due. Understood?"

"When you are looming over me, Colonel Valliant, and shouting at me, I have difficulty understanding much of anything."

"Fair enough." He dropped onto a chair behind the desk. "I'll not loom and shout. But you must confess that I warned you, Diana. I said you would have by far the worst of our bargain, and now you are learning what I meant."

That, she reflected with sudden insight, was the sort of thing *she* might have said. But she would not debate which of them was the least worthy, for the answer was perfectly clear. How achingly discouraging it was to learn that the one thing of worth she had brought to the marriage—her fortune—only displeased him. Gazing at the white-knuckled hand gripping his glass, she wondered how to deal with this stranger who was her husband.

There was one other bond they shared, she thought, astonished when the notion popped into her head. They were both angry. But he was free to show it, while she must guard her tongue. Ladies were not supposed to *have* tempers. Ladies, she had been taught, were invariably polite. If they had strong feelings or controversial opinions, no one—most particularly no gentleman—wanted to hear about them.

Even so, she had observed that Lady Kendal freely spoke her mind, and Lucy could strip paint from a wall with her tongue. Why did the rules of deportment not apply to them? Both had husbands who adored them, which must prove something. It was significant that two of the Valliant brothers had chosen to marry females who had no fear of asserting themselves.

But then, unlike his brothers, Colonel Valliant had not married for love.

"Here." He pushed the glass of brandy across the desk. "Drink the rest of this. You've gone white as chalk."

She obediently took a swallow, disliking the taste immediately, but it was deliciously warm as it slid down her throat and settled inside her. Dangerous stuff, brandy. She set the glass on the floor. "The fortune will not go away simply because you wish it did not exist, Colonel. And it wasn't as if I had a choice in the matter. The money passed from my father to my trustees, and from there to you. I have never touched a shilling of it. Nor can I put a hand on one now, unless you give it me."

"The lot is yours to dispose of as you will." He lifted his gaze, meeting hers. "With one key restriction. For so long as you elect to live with me, I shall provide for you from my own pocket. Which is all but empty, you should be aware, and like to stay that way for a considerable time. What funds I can muster will be directed primarily to the development of the land. Eventually the house will be repaired, although we'll see to the most urgent problems immediately. There will be nothing to spare. No luxuries. Neither of us will have access to the fortune, which will be held in trust for our children. Assuming you ever mean to get about producing any, of course. Am I making myself clear?"

"Oh, perfectly. We are to live in poverty. You imagine that I have embraced chastity. It is certain I have taken a vow to obey you. Lakeview appears to have become something of a monastery, sir." She put aside the remark about children, which hurt far more than she could bear. "Am I permitted to express an objection to your terms?"

He looked startled. "Yes indeed. Say whatever you like. But for practical purposes, the subject is closed."

"And why is that, sir? Because you are too proud to spend my money, even if I wish you to? Am I to do without an abigail? Pin money? Will the chimneys be permitted to smoke and the masonry to crash about our ears for the sake of your *pride*?"

Color stained his high cheekbones. "Naturally I shall make every effort to provide clear chimneys, an abigail, and a reasonable level of comfort. That is my duty, madam wife."

A neat evasion, she acknowledged, of the question relating to his pride. A question he'd no intention of answering. Which meant the answer was *yes*, of course, and that he knew it was *yes* and that he could not in honor deny the truth of what she'd said.

It was enough for now. To push her small advantage would be to lose it, she understood, observing his taut lips and the lines between his drawn-together brows. But if she proceeded cautiously and chose her goals carefully, perhaps he would someday agree to a more flexible arrangement regarding her inheritance.

"I expect you'll want an allowance," he said, propping his elbow on the desk and cupping his chin in his hand. "I am prepared to be reasonable. So long as you do not touch the principle, you may draw a reasonable sum every quarter from the interest. Not a penny, mind you, is to be used for household expenses. Buy fripperies, or spend the money on those women you have apparently adopted. I've no doubt that you will. They have already laid claim to virtually all of your time."

Gracious. Unless she was much mistaken, his tone had been decidedly petulant. Her uncle had sounded very much the same when bemoaning his ill luck at the gaming tables.

Was Colonel Valliant *jealous* of the hours she devoted to her ladies and their welfare? Surely not. The idea was so improbable that she nearly dismissed it out of hand.

But he raised the subject again. "I can't walk five steps

without tripping over one female or another. They cringe into corners when I pass and curl into knots if I chance to enter a room where they have gathered. What the devil are you *doing* with them, Diana? More to the point, why are they always *here*?"

"You gave me permission to invite them," she reminded him nervously. "We discussed this on our w-wedding night."

"Probably. But since my thoughts were decidedly elsewhere at the time, I cannot recall what you said. Did you tell me *why* they would be trooping in and out every damn morning, or why you ride off every afternoon and stay gone the rest of the day?"

How could he know that? *He* was the one who stayed gone the entire day, and she could not imagine him quizzing the servants. "You didn't seem interested, sir. You said I could do as I wished. Have you changed your mind?"

He shrugged. "Even if I had, I'd not dishonor my word. You may go on as you have done, certainly. But if you've no objection, I would very much like to know what it is you are about."

"Gladly." She folded her hands in her lap, searching for the best way to explain. A military man was bound to find her vague, disorganized schemes entirely unacceptable. She knew very well that she was always guessing what she ought to do, and speeding ahead because if she stopped, everything might collapse around her.

"You needn't frown, Diana," he said, his gaze intense. "Nothing will change unless you wish it. I ask no more than an explanation."

"Very well, sir." Brief and to the point, she told herself, before he loses patience. Seizing a deep breath, she began speaking at a rapid pace, taking care not to look at him.

"When first I rode out to explore the countryside, I could not help but see the difficult circumstances under which so many of the people are forced to live. Primarily the women, most of them widowed by the war or left to care for the children while their husbands are elsewhere looking for work. There is none to be found here, so they go to Manchester or Birmingham. And some appear to forget they have families, for they send no money home."

She warmed to her story, which was at the heart of everything she dared to let herself care about. "Each woman you have seen here has a different tale to tell, but the endings are very much the same. They have been abandoned. They are without funds. The parish cannot support them all, and few have anywhere else to go. So you see, I have set about helping them find ways to provide for themselves. Which is really quite absurd, when you think of it. Of the lot of us, I am the least capable."

"I rather doubt that," he observed mildly. "But go on. How do you mean to accomplish these marvels?"

"*They* will do the accomplishing, sir. I am merely the one who brings them together. And since I've little idea what ought to be done from one day to the next, we stagger along as best we can."

"Have you not mapped out a plan? There's no use gathering an army and launching an assault without a clear objective."

"Well, we do have a goal of sorts. We are producing merchandise to be sold at the Michaelmas Fair in Kendal. But we got off to a late start, and with only a few months to prepare, we are forced to select our products carefully. So far we are mostly experimenting with items we can manufacture quickly and with minimal expense. There is little seed money for our endeavors, I'm afraid. And the ladies, many of them, have children to tend to. They can spare no more than a few hours a week learning to make hand creams and the like."

"Hand creams?"

"Among other things," she said quickly. "I am always looking out for ideas that offer more stability and better income than selling goods at a fair. Small enterprises, if you will, that permit the ladies to work independently. The Michaelmas Fair is our most immediate objective, but we have many others."

"And are like to achieve none of them," he observed, "without coordination of time, effort, and resources. Am I mistaken to think you currently lack organization, madam?"

"Oh, no. You are quite on the mark. Consider that I am the one leading this endeavor, sir, and I scarcely know my left foot from my right. There is a good chance I'll lead the lot of us over a cliff."

He fell silent for a prodigiously long time, looking past her at the wall.

She could not read his expression. Did he mean to tell her to give it up? She squirmed on the chair, wishing he would say something. *Anything*, just so it put an end to this awful suspense.

Would she fight him if he ordered her to abandon her women? She hoped that she would. But the brief fire of anger that had propelled her when they quarreled about her inheritance had long since burned out. She waited with cold dread for his verdict.

"It happens," he said slowly, "that I have a degree of talent for organization. It runs more to marshaling troops than . . . er, matters relating to hand creams, but it is possible I could be of some assistance. If you have any interest in what advice I might offer you, of course. I don't mean to interfere." His gaze went from the wall to the top of the desk, never meeting hers. "Feel free to tell me to go to the devil."

She could scarcely believe her ears. He hadn't ordered her to put an end to her projects. He had offered to help! What was more amazing, she had the distinct impression that he *wanted* to help.

She regarded him with astonishment. Color tinged his cheekbones and his gaze remained firmly planted on the desk, as if . . . but no. It couldn't be. Not Colonel Valliant.

He could not be *shy*.

Were she looking at anyone else, though, that is exactly what she'd have thought.

"*Would* you advise us, sir?" she asked, still unable to credit that he meant what he'd said. "We would be so very grateful. The ladies pretend that they have faith in me, but I know they wonder if this is all a foolish caprice on my part and a waste of time on theirs. Were you in charge, they would have a great deal more confidence."

"*They* mean nothing to me." He still refused to look at her. "How do *you* feel about it?"

"Deliriously pleased," she replied honestly. "Profoundly relieved. Terrified you'll take back your offer because I fail to say the right thing. We need you, sir. *I* need you."

He cleared his throat. "Advice only, mind you. I'll not usurp your authority, nor do I wish to take on your responsibilities."

"Oh, no. I'll do all the work. Really. You needn't put yourself out."

"Well, then." He gathered up the papers on his desk and stuffed them back into the leather folder. "Pull your chair next to mine, madam, and let us begin."

Chapter 10

Diana settled herself to his left, a little sideways on her chair because of the desk drawers directly in front of her, and smoothed her blue skirts over her knees.

She was, Alex realized, closer to him than she had been at any time since their wedding. He sucked in a deep breath, burningly aware of the soft, feminine scents hovering around her and the heat pulsing from her body. His bride. His wife.

What would she do, he wondered, if he pulled her onto his lap and kissed her? He had been unable to think of anything else for the last several minutes, while she nattered on about hand creams and private industries and Michaelmas Fairs.

She looked over at him expectantly. "Well, sir, how are we to proceed?"

Quite evidently *her* mind was entirely on the business at hand. Resigning himself, he arranged paper, pens, and ink in front of them. "Since I know no other way to go about it, we shall approach this as a military exercise. You have already chosen a target and recruited the soldiers, so let's begin by aligning them for battle."

At the top of a sheet of paper he wrote, in large letters, *Diana's Regiment.*

She laughed, the sound clear and musical. Like wind chimes in a Spanish courtyard, he thought, immediately distracted again. Had he ever heard her laugh before? Not in such a fashion, he was sure. He had given her few enough reasons to do so.

"I am to command a whole *regiment*? Does that make me a general, sir?"

"A mere colonel, I'm sorry to say." He regathered his wits.

"The first thing you must do is look over your troops and select those qualified to become officers." He drew a series of boxes. "We'll not assign ranks as yet, or set up a chain of command. For now, we shall list only their names and their skills."

"Now? But I cannot simply choose the leaders off the top of my head. I must think on it."

"To be sure. I mean only to show you how to begin. Later, when you have taken a decision about someone, go to this chart and fill in a box."

"I see." Her brow knitted. "Then we should start with Miss Wigglesworth, I suppose."

He wrote her name in the topmost box. "And what can she do, Colonel?"

She laughed again. "I shall have difficulty answering to that, especially when it comes from you."

"It will *only* come from me, unless you inform the ladies that they have enlisted in an army. I'm not persuaded they would be pleased to know it. Keep in mind that this chart is no more than a device to help you become better organized. Later, when you have mentally divided your regiment into battalions and companies, you will know who to put in charge. Understood? Now tell me about Miss Wigglesworth."

Diana propped her elbows on the desk. "Well, she is an excellent gardener. Mostly flowers, but she also grows herbs for the kitchen. She embroiders. She is an expert in the stillroom. She has a talent for nursing. Oh, she can do a great many things."

He had stopped writing after *embroiders*. "This is all too vague. What specifically qualifies her as an officer?"

"Hmm. Primarily, she lives here. She is always close to hand, and we deal well together. Moreover, she is practical by nature, which I am not. She sees when something must be accomplished long before I do. And she fears no one, while I fear anything that moves. Quite simply, I need her."

In the box he inscribed, *Colonel's Prop.*

As she leaned forward to read the words, her long hair brushed his sleeve and trailed over his wrist. He felt the touch resonate throughout his body.

"Infamous!" she exclaimed. "*Prop* indeed."

"That is what you just described to me. Mind you, half of what you said was twaddle. If necessary, you would get on perfectly well without her. But she has the experience of many years for you to draw upon, and you would be a fool not to take advantage of it." He scratched out *Prop* and wrote *Adviser.* "How's that?"

"Better." She gave him an impudent grin. "And I've thought of another reason to promote her. She is a gentlewoman, which sets her apart from the others. They defer to her. And they respect her as well, for more significant reasons than her birth. Whenever one of them is creating a problem, and I'm sorry to say there are more than a few troublemakers in the ranks, Miss Wigglesworth quickly sets the miscreant in order again."

Second-in-Command, he penned. "I'll leave you to fill in the rest. Decide how best she can serve, and be precise. Otherwise you are like to waste her time and talents."

She nibbled at her lower lip. "This isn't easy, is it?"

"You don't know the half of it," he murmured, wrenching his gaze from her mouth. The full, beautifully shaped lips. The— What the devil were they called? Small. White and even.

Teeth!

Damn. He couldn't think straight. His body, mounting an insurrection of its own, was drawing all the blood from his head and dispatching it in a southerly direction.

"I think I get the point," she said, her whole attention focused on the chart. "But I need more practice. Can we do another?"

"Another what?"

"Another officer, of course." She drummed her fingers on the blotter. "But you don't know the regiment ladies. Drat. You won't be able to tell if I get it wrong."

Alex chose a box near the bottom on the page and scribbled *Sergeant Alexander Valliant.* "We'll do me," he said.

She leaned closer to see. "Sergeant? *You?* Surely not!"

"Ah, but the sergeants are the ones who know everything, Colonel Diana. We gentlemen buy colors and swoop in, more ignorant than dishrags, good at riding and shooting and not very much else. The sergeants endure us, and teach us about war, and eventually we learn enough to lead them. I have always aspired to be a sergeant. In your regiment, it is the only rank I'll accept."

"Oh, very well, since this is purely an exercise. But I've no idea what the duties of a sergeant can be. What do we write in your box, sir?"

He had a sudden, intense desire to know what she expected of him. What she wanted him to do. She wouldn't write what he longed to hear, that was certain. But for a few minutes she would be thinking about him, which was more attention that he'd got from her since Gretna Green.

"Here." He gave her a blank sheet of paper and handed her his pen. "You put down what you think I can do to help. If in doubt, put down what you *hope* I can do. I'll write my own evaluation, and then we'll compare notes. Agreed?"

Her brow wrinkled. "I am to devise a list of your duties?"

"Precisely. And remember, sergeants are remarkably versatile. Use me however you will."

She bent over her paper with the concentration of a child trying to inscribe her name for the first time. Her knuckles were white as she clutched the pen tightly, the feather brushing at her chin the way his fingers wanted to do. Finally she wrote something.

He tried to see what it was.

"Oh no," she said, making a barrier with her shoulder and a curtain of her hair. "No fair peeking until I'm done."

Locating another pen, he dipped it in the inkwell and swiftly scrawled a few words. Then he leaned against the arm of his chair, pretending to be thinking, and simply gazed at her.

In the candlelight, her heavy auburn hair was molten copper. Unable to see her face, he traced the shape of her arm resting on the table. The shadows at the curl of her elbow and wrist became dark, seductive caves. The fine texture of her milky skin, so different from his own tanned and weathered body, entranced him. The pale golden hairs on her forearm were a forest he longed to roam for hours. Months. Years.

Even his too-long-banked sexual urgency melted in the softer heat of his desire to explore, with something close to worship, the seductive mystery of this woman. Sweet Diana. Brave and fearful Diana, who had no idea the power she wielded over him. She had only to look at him to bring him to his knees. And at the same time he knew that she was far too young and gentle for a rough-and-tumble soldier like Alex Valliant.

But he wanted her anyway. His very toenails ached from wanting her. He had restless dreams about her at night and erotic fantasies about her when awake. She was his wife. With a word or a gesture, he could have her. He was entitled.

Wasn't he? Why then could he not bring himself to say the words? Make the gesture? Did he fear to take a woman so precious as Diana to his bed?

Lost in thought, she brushed a shock of hair behind her ear. For once she had forgot to keep him to her left side, where he could not look too closely at the spiderweb scar on her right cheek. Now, the ridges of it etched out by candlelight, he could see clearly what she always tried to conceal.

She thought the scar made her ugly, he knew. Most probably it was the first thing anyone noticed when meeting her. She would be aware of that, and watchful for any sign of repulsion.

He wondered how she would react, could she see *his* scars. But they were invisible, thank the Lord, except to him, and he could not fail to be aware of them at every moment. They never stopped bleeding. They existed, he often thought, to keep him in mind of what he most wanted to forget.

He must make sure that Diana never saw them.

"I'm done," she announced, setting down her pen. "And were Sergeant Valliant to actually take up all these duties, he would be a busy man indeed."

Alex snapped to attention, curious to know what she would have him do. "Well, let me hear what they are, Colonel Diana. I hope they do not involve the testing of hand creams."

Her gaze went immediately to his hands. "Eau de Veau might do those calluses some good, I must say. But no, that is not on my list." She raised her sheet of paper and began to read. "Seek out suppliers of necessary materials and negotiate their purchase at favorable rates. Coordinate distribution of same to the respective manufacturers. Assist Mr. Beadle with construction and engineering. Arrange transportation for the troops, especially in bad weather, when they are required to attend classes or engage in group projects. Take note of particular abilities and recommend privates for promotion. Put down quarrels—a stern look will generally suffice. Be alert to profitable enterprises no one else has thought of."

She lowered the paper and smiled at him. "Above all else, advise hapless colonel how to go on."

Her smile caught at his heart, a piece of him he had thought long since turned to stone. "A formidable list indeed, madam," he said evenly. "Can you clarify 'construction and engineering'?"

"Not very well," she replied after some thought. "The soldiers, many of them, are billeted in unsuitable quarters. Am I using the correct terms? Anyway, Mr. Beadle has taken it on himself to repair leaky roofs, shore up disintegrating walls, and hammer down loose floorboards. The farm animals require decent lodging as well. And if we restore a few old boats fallen out of use, fish can be caught to supplement the army's rations. Also, much land that would otherwise be planted is too often flooded by runoff from the hills. If we found a way to divert the water—"

She threw up her hands. "Oh, I don't know what I'm talking about. I see the problems, but I've no idea how to solve them."

Awestruck, he regarded her with considerable respect. And annoyance, because she was so naive as to credit that miracles could be worked by a few country women and old Mr. Beadle and a weary, disillusioned soldier. She would do well to confine her ambitions to perfumed creams and small-town fairs.

But he'd no more squelch her enthusiasm than snuff out the last candle in a world already too dark by far. "One problem at a time, madam. It's well to have great dreams, but wise to build up to them in small ways. As you have already determined, I am sure. The Michaelmas Fair is a good beginning, but channeling water from the fells will have to wait."

"Yes." She sank back on her chair with a sigh. "I do get carried away. Half the regiment thinks me Bedlam-bait when I rattle on about grandiose schemes and impossible goals while they worry about feeding their children."

"If they are penniless, how the devil are you financing the projects you've already begun?"

"Oh, they give what they can—milk and eggs and wool, that sort of thing. For the rest, I've been selling a few bracelets and rings and earbobs. I've no need of them, after all. But the regiment mustn't know of it. The ladies do not wish for charity, I promise you, nor would they learn independence if they thought I would always be there to support them. You needn't think I'll come asking you for funds, sir, on my account or on theirs."

She was referring to their quarrel about her inheritance, of course, which he would as soon forget ever happened. He'd behaved like the backside of a mule. He had never considered her wishes and feelings. Females came equipped with a damnable lot of feelings, he was discovering, and he had not the least notion how to deal with them.

"You haven't showed me *your* list," she said, reaching for the sheet of paper on his side of the desk.

He took hold of her hand. "Leave it be. There's nothing on it."

"No fair, sir. We had an agreement. Let me see what you wrote."

Releasing her, he watched her turn the paper over and scan the five words he had scribbled there. *Whatever is asked of me.*

"I don't understand," she said, frowning at him. "What does this mean?"

"What it says," he replied tersely. "I was to list what I was willing to do, or capable of doing, for the regiment. There is my answer."

"Oh."

"Mind you, I'd no idea you had it in mind to divert rivers." He mustered a smile. "But I should have guessed. You are a remarkable young woman, Diana. You never fail to astonish me."

"Oh," she said again. She seemed unable to say anything else, but tears had gathered in her lovely hazel eyes.

He regarded them with something close to fear. "Colonels do not weep," he informed her sternly. "Nothing will be accomplished if you indulge your female sensibilities."

She wiped her eyes with the back of her hand. "That is your opinion, sir, but I cannot agree. All good things come from caring enough to make them happen. And men have sensibilities as well, even if they are not accompanied by tears. You have a devotion to honor and duty, do you not? And how does that differ from my own desire to be honorable and to make myself useful?"

It differed, he was sure. How, he could not say, but if females were so much like males, he would be able to understand them. Stood to reason.

She folded the paper where he had inscribed his commitment to the regiment and slipped it into her pocket. "You needn't answer, sir, but I hope you will think on it. And you may be certain that I shall call on you for help, if you truly meant what you wrote. No engineering projects, though. I shall confine my requests to reasonable duties."

"And I shall try not to disappoint you," he said, his mouth dry. *If* he meant what he wrote? How could she doubt it? He watched her stand, shake out her skirts, and move to the door. She was leaving, and he wanted to stop her, but his tongue was stuck behind his teeth.

She turned, with the grace of motion that never failed to entrance him. "I am most grateful, Alex. I know you do not care to hear words of apology or of gratitude, but sometimes they must be said. I'll not rabbit on about it, but I trust you know what is in my heart."

He nodded.

"Well then. I'll leave you in peace. You must be hungry, though," she added, her hand now on the door latch. "Shall I send a supper tray to you here, or would you prefer to eat in the dining room?"

He stood, willing his tongue loose, not sure he dared to say what he wanted. But he wanted it too much not to say it. "Come to bed with me, Diana."

Her hand dropped to her side. For the barest moment she held in place, her head bowed, and then she turned to face him again.

"Certainly," she said.

He felt as if a blanket of snow had fallen over him. *Certainly?* She'd have given the same answer if he'd said he preferred to take supper in the dining room. Asked her to pour him a glass of brandy. Pass him the saltcellar.

For an infinite time they gazed at each other in silence. Her face, which had been so bright with enthusiasm when she spoke of her plans to save half the world—or at least the part of it immediately surrounding Coniston Water—was totally without expression now.

Well, perhaps not quite. He would not have called it resignation. He would definitely not term it repugnance, or reluctance, or anything approaching an unwillingness to do his bidding. A maelstrom of female sensibilities was concealed by her passive acceptance. He'd have bet on it. But he was certain of only one thing, and it froze him past his rampaging desire to make love to her.

She would go to his bed because she was grateful to him. She would lay herself down under him because he had promised to help her, and she reckoned he was due some form of repayment for his efforts on her behalf. Oh, he doubted that was her conscious intention—he'd learned more respect for her than that—but it was true nonetheless.

"Shall we go, sir?" she asked quietly.

He shook his head. "*You* go, Diana. I spoke on impulse. It has been a long day, what with the journey to Lancaster, and I am somewhat tired."

"Are you certain? If you imagine I do not wish to—that is, I am not at all unwilling."

"I know," he said, the arid taste of dry sand on his tongue. "But now is not the time."

"As you wish," she said at length, turning back to the door. As she moved into the passageway, she cast him a look over her shoulder. "May I ask if there will ever *be* a time, Alex?"

He longed to ask if she would ever *want* him. If she ever felt the slightest spark of sexual desire for him. But he had discovered that she was painfully honest, and what would he do if she said "no"?

"Soon enough," he said more harshly than he intended. "Good night, Diana."

Chapter 11

Diana scratched item seven from her task list and moved on to number eight, which took her from the root cellar to the kitchen. She had it to herself, because on Wednesdays Mrs. Cleese always visited her sister.

Miss Wigglesworth and five of the regiment ladies were gathered in the parlor, assembling the openwork squares each had embroidered into a tablecloth. Since Diana believed that the completion of a project ought to be celebrated, a tray of cakes and sweets was waiting for them in the larder.

On that thought she put down her spoon and went to filch a macaroon for herself. Then she dragged the heavy ceramic pot from beneath an iron plate warmer, raised the lid, and set to work.

Her list of tasks grew longer by the day, but she took pride every time she could mark one of them accomplished. Indeed, she had never felt such a sense of purpose, and no longer minded very much when one of her efforts went awry.

"Here you are." Alex came through the door, his arms wrapped around a good-sized box. He set it on the pinewood kitchen table and gave her one of his faint half smiles. "I am pleased to report a large discount for buying in quantity, and the glazier has agreed to accept the return of unused merchandise."

He looked rather pleased with himself, she thought, putting down her spoon and crossing to where he stood. Alex had taken up his regimental duties as purchase officer with astounding diligence. She expected that merchants were somewhat intimidated by his commanding presence, but he was also willing to ride great distances in search of better materials and better prices.

"It will be a fortnight before the small jars are ready," he said, "but Mr. Dodd has adjusted his bill to reflect the delay."

"But we don't even require them yet, Alex. Seven or eight weeks would be soon enough."

"Nevertheless, he has failed to honor his contract. In future, when you require prompt delivery, he will be careful to provide it."

Laughing, Diana gestured to the box. "May I see what you've brought?"

He pried the lid from the box, brushed aside the packing straw, and handed her a square bottle about eight inches high. "The others are of similar shape, some larger and some smaller. Ten boxes in all. Will they do?"

"Oh, very well indeed. I'm so glad you suggested the square bottles, Alex. They will attract far more attention than the usual sort. Miss Gladys Yoodle is persuaded that we ought to tie colorful ribbons around the necks. What do you think?"

"I have no opinion on the subject of ribbons, madam, but every penny spent on packaging cuts into your profits. The bottles were not inexpensive, and we've yet to purchase the corks."

"Well, no ribbons then. We shall rely on the hand-painted labels, which the Yoodle sisters are producing for us."

His brow knitted. "Perhaps I am mistaken, but were not the Yoodle females in company with Mrs. Alcorn and her scandalmongers?"

"I fear so. They are gently born and would naturally prefer to move in the highest level of Coniston society, but they're also poor as church mice. When they asked to join us, I hadn't the heart to refuse them, and I must say that their labels are quite splendid. Come have a look."

She went to a cupboard and drew out a small stack of cards. "These are only samples, because we don't yet know how many we'll need of each one. Oh. Remind me to ask you about glue. And you see, they have inscribed the names of the different wines and painted a picture of what each is made from." She handed him the labels one by one. "So far we have rhubarb wine, cowslip wine, rose hip wine, elderberry wine, nettle wine, burnet wine, parsnip wine, dandeli—"

"Parsnip?"

"Parsnip wine, or so Mrs. Pottle informs me, will grow hair on an egg. She also says that it is delicious, but I shall have to take her word for that. In addition to our wines, we have orgeat, ratafia, and several varieties of cordial."

"What is that brew you were stirring when I arrived?"

"Ratafia." She led him to the ceramic pot. "It must be stirred every day."

He leaned over and took a sniff. "Good Lord, Diana. What the devil is in there?"

"Well, brandy for the most part, along with almonds, spices, and grated rind from lemons and oranges."

"That doesn't sound too bad—for a ladies' drink. May I taste it?"

"Not yet, I'm afraid. In another three weeks I'll add melted sugar, and then it will be ready to sample. Mind you, this is my first try at making ratafia, and the ingredients were frightfully expensive." She gave him a sideways glance. "Should I end up with a disaster, which is not at all unlikely, I shall feel responsible to pay for them myself."

"That is your decision, of course. But has the regiment become a guild of tapsters? I cannot help but notice that you are primarily engaged in the production of spirits."

"Oh, indeed we are. I have great confidence in the selling power of spirits, especially when they are sold in pretty bottles to give them a bit of cachet. Ladies will flock to them, Miss Wigglesworth assures me, and gentlemen can always be persuaded to buy intoxicants."

When he chuckled she rushed ahead, hoping the subject would hold him in the room a few more minutes. "The wines cost very little to produce, you know. The primary ingredients—rhubarb, dandelions, nettle tops, and the like—are available in our gardens or can be gathered in the fields. We have only to add water, sugar, yeast, and sometimes a bit of lemon juice. What's more, a number of the ladies already know how to make wines and cordials. They have their own special receipts and mean to show up all the others."

"Rivalries provide an excellent incentive, I agree." Seeming to lose interest, he gave her back the labels and headed for the door. "I am neglecting Mr. Beadle and Carver, who are waiting for instructions. Where do you wish the boxes to be stowed?"

"In the breakfast room, I suppose, stacked in a corner." She followed him down the passageway, digging into herself for a paring of courage. "Alex?"

He stopped immediately and turned to face her. "Yes?"

"Have you made plans for this afternoon?"

"None of importance." He clasped his hands behind his back, regarding her with a wary expression. "I had thought to help Mr. Beadle repair Mrs. Hinshaw's roof, but I'd more likely be in his way. Have you another errand for me?"

She hesitated. He did not look at all forthcoming, and perhaps this was not the best time to ask him. But with Alex, there never seemed to be a best time. "N-not precisely an errand," she ventured in a meek voice. "You see, this is the first free afternoon I've had in a long while, and I'd like very much to visit a farm where I once stayed for a few weeks. While there I learned a great deal, but I've many questions to ask the lady who took me in."

In the dim passageway, his eyes were an impenetrable midnight blue. She had no idea what he was thinking—not that she ever did. When he made no effort to enlighten her, there was nothing for it but to plunge ahead. "It's rather a long ride from here, sir. The farm, I mean. I had hoped you might be willing to accompany me."

"Certainly. When do you wish to leave?"

The immediate capitulation rocked her back on her heels. "Well . . . ah, right away, if you don't mind. First I must make sandwiches for Mr. Beadle and put on my riding habit. But I'll hurry."

She fled to the kitchen before he could change his mind.

An entire afternoon with Alex! Diana unwrapped cheese-cloth from a joint of cold roast beef and took up a knife.

In the last three weeks, ever since the night he appointed himself her sergeant-of-all-purposes, she had rarely set eyes on him. When he wasn't gone to Kendal or Lancaster to procure supplies, he spent most of his time with Mr. Beadle, the only other male member of the regiment. More often than not they were employed elsewhere, after which they took supper together at one of the local pub houses. She often heard Alex return to Lakeview long after she'd retired to bed, his gait unsteady and his hand fumbling on the door latch of the adjoining room.

She could never sleep until he was come home. She listened for his arrival and for every sound he made until he went silent. And always she tossed and turned for an hour more, wondering what would have happened if she'd plucked up the courage to go to the connecting door, and open it, and go through it to his bed.

She wondered, but it never occurred to her to actually do so. By the end of a day spent teaching and putting down squabbles and making decisions when she hadn't the fuzziest notion what she was about, her allotment of courage was all used up. There was none to spare for her husband. None for their decidedly unconventional marriage. Not so much as a grain for her own unfathomable longings.

He knew perfectly well that he could bed her anytime he wished. She had taken vows to that effect. Gracious, she had twice offered herself in the most straightforward way she could—only to be rejected.

She hacked through a loaf of bread. What did he *want* of her, for pity's sake? When she said she was willing, he didn't believe her. Or she wasn't willing *enough*, by some incomprehensible standard of his own. Exactly how willing was she supposed to be?

It was plain as a pikestaff that *he* was the one with reservations. A man who wouldn't take "yes" for an answer must have been hoping for a "no." She understood his reluctance well enough—how could she not?—and would never blame him for it. But after all, they could consummate their marriage in the dark. It wasn't as if he'd have to *look* at her.

She slapped slices of beef between slabs of bread, added two cucumber pickles and several hard-boiled eggs, and wrapped the lot in a length of brown paper.

Leaving the parcel in the breakfast room for Mr. Beadle to find, she sped upstairs to change into the hunter-green riding habit she had worn on the journey to Gretna. Perhaps it would remind Alex what had happened when they got there. Colonel Valliant had taken himself—for better or worse—a wife.

He was waiting for her in front of the house, wearing a dark blue riding coat and a wide-brimmed beaver hat. "It looks to rain this afternoon, I'm sorry to say. Do you still wish to make the journey?"

"Oh, indeed. It rains most every day. Haven't you noticed?" She lifted her veil to glance up at the dark clouds scudding across a sky that had been clear only a few minutes earlier. "Never say you mind getting a bit wet, Colonel?"

Grinning, he tossed her onto the saddle and slipped her foot in the stirrup. "Where are we off to?"

"South, to the Rusland Valley." She watched him mount his restive horse with practiced ease. "When we get to the road, shall we have a run?"

He touched his hat. "After you, madam."

The rain set in as they were picking their way single file along a grass-floored track that led through holly groves and stands of silver beeches. Wind shuddered through the leaves, and fat drops of rain splatted on her bonnet and shoulders.

Alex pulled up to ride beside her. "Within a few minutes we are in for a deluge. Is there shelter close to hand?"

"None that I know of, but I've come this way only once before. I believe the farm to be no more than three miles from here, though, and the nearest village is Colton, which we passed some time ago." She gave him a hopeful smile. "We might as well go on, don't you think?"

With a shrug he dropped back, and they proceeded at a slow pace over the marshy ground. The storm blew in not long after, announcing itself with a crack of thunder that bounced off the surrounding hills. Rain hissed through the trees. When they emerged from the woodlands to open ground, they were pelted in earnest. The rain quickly soaked through Diana's riding habit and streamed down into her half boots. She could scarcely see through the sodden veil, but when she tossed it over the brim of her bonnet, the wind soon carried it down again.

The landscape became a patchwork of hillside pastures fenced in by low graystone walls. Inside them, sheep and cattle huddled with their backsides to the fierce wind.

"Over there!" Alex shouted, moving past her. "Wait here."

Confused, she reined in and saw him wrestle open a low wooden gate just ahead and to her right.

"Come now," he called.

She guided Sparkles through the narrow opening onto a rock-strewn field. The path, if there was one, could not be distinguished in the downpour. She waited for Alex, who seemed to know where he was going, and a few moments later he took the reins from her hands and led her up an increasingly steep hill.

At the top, on a ledge about thirty feet wide, a wattle-and-daub hut nestled against the cliff that rose straight up behind it. Rained poured down the sloping slate roof and puddled around the building, very much like a moat. There was a thatched canopy jutting out to one side of the hut, supported by wooden posts, and Alex drew the horses underneath it.

Diana slid from her saddle and splashed through the ankle-deep water to the door of the hut. It was unlatched, and she soon found herself inside what looked to be a storage shed for hay. Bales were stacked to the low ceiling against three of the walls, leaving only a small space where a herdsman had stashed a few tools and a rolled-up pallet. Two square blocks of hay, hip-high and likely used as a makeshift bed, made up the only furniture.

She removed her limp bonnet and gloves and shook her drenched skirts. So much for her lovely afternoon with Alex, she thought sourly, wrenching pins from her dripping wet hair and combing it out with her fingers.

But on the other hand, perhaps this was an unexpected opportunity, one she had scarcely dared to hope for. Until the storm subsided, she would have him alone in a confined space. A very dim space as well, for the only light came through the door she had left cracked open for him.

108

If he couldn't see her, she wouldn't be so terribly self-conscious. Well, not so much as usual. At least she would not be blisteringly aware of his height and his strength and his splendid good looks, which generally rendered her tongue-tied.

Perhaps, just perhaps, they could have a real conversation. Not one concerning the regiment's business, which was the only thing they ever seemed to discuss, but a conversation about them. More specifically, about *him*. She knew virtually nothing about the man she'd married, and thought it long past time he told her what he'd been doing for the four-and-thirty years before they met.

He appeared in the doorway, filling it as he stomped his feet and brushed water from his hat. "A snug enough cubbyhole. Have you got yourself oriented, madam? Unless I close this door, the hut will soon be as wet as we are."

She sank down on one of the blocks of hay and waved a hand. "Do come in, Alex."

He pulled the door shut, sealing off the light, and she heard the creak of wood. He was leaning against the door now, she guessed. When her eyes adjusted to the dark, she affirmed that he was. The barest trace of light, slicing through a narrow crack between the bottom of the door and the floorboards, was broken at the two spots where his boots were planted. She imagined him standing as he so often did, arms folded across his chest, watching and waiting.

If only she'd had time to prepare for this opportunity. Here they were, and she could not think of a single way to inaugurate a conversation. The silence grew like an inflated balloon. He would be content to wait forever, she expected, before saying a word.

"The storm will pass quickly," she said too brightly. "Don't you think?"

"In my experience, lakeland storms rise swiftly at this time of the year and soon blow through. With any luck, we can be on our way within the hour."

Again silence enveloped them. So much for the weather as a topic of conversation. And as she had resolved not to mention the regiment, what remained? Her toes curled inside her half boots, making a squishy sound.

It dawned on her that he was angry. He had not said so, but of course, he wouldn't. Nor could he be pleased to spend his afternoon in a pitch-black hay shed on her account. Possibly it would clear the air if she addressed the subject.

"I'm sorry for bringing you out in the rain," she said, taking care that her voice did not squeak. "When you indicated that we ought to stay at home, I should have heeded your advice."

He made a low noise in his throat. "I gave no advice. I simply asked a question. It occurs to me, madam, that I ought to levy a fine for each time you torment me with one of your needless apologies. Have I not made it clear that I don't want to hear them?"

"Perfectly clear, sir." Heat rose up the back of her neck. Why must he behave in such an off-putting manner? He was no wetter than she, and they'd soon be dry again. He could have said no when she asked him to ride out with her, but he had accepted straightaway. And what was the good of her sitting here on a bale of hay and him standing there against the door without a word passing between them? If he was angry with her for no good reason, she might as well give him a *real* reason.

Even though he could not see her, she deliberately sat straighter on the hay bale. "I believe, sir, that this would be an excellent time for us to come to know each other somewhat better than we do. We have been married for seven weeks now, but we remain strangers in almost every way." She took a deep breath and went on before he could stop her. "Naturally I'd be glad to tell you what little there is to know about me, although it would make a tedious story for a rainy day. The interesting bits, what few there are, you have already heard. They are, after all, the reasons you married me. For the rest, you cannot wish to hear about life at Miss Wetherwood's Academy for Young Ladies, nor how I went on as a pampered only child in my parents' home before being sent off to school."

"To the contrary," he said while she was seizing her next quick breath. "I would very much like for you to tell me

110

about yourself. I would be interested even were I not a captive audience."

She let the faint joke pass her by. Another time she might have given him what he said he wanted, but she knew it was only an evasion, his wish to listen to a schoolgirl's stories. And she was too fired up to let him have his way, as he always did simply because she never dared to defy him.

Not until now.

Before her patched-together courage fractured, she closed her eyes and clenched her hands and jumped into deep waters.

"I wish to hear about *you*, Alex. It's my turn now. You have lived nearly twice as long as I, and you have gone to war, and you have seen and done a thousand things to my every one. Tell me of—oh, I don't know. What it was like to be in Spain."

"Hot."

"That is hardly a sufficient response, sir."

"Hot and dusty, then. I've no intention of discussing the war with you, madam. There is nothing of it that I care to recall."

This was much like drawing teeth, she supposed, never having seen it done. But she would keep pulling and wrenching, because she meant to have at least one tooth from him before the day was out. "Were you ever wounded?"

He made a low noise in his throat, rather like a snarl. "No. Not to any degree. Few soldiers escape the odd scratch. Now leave it be, Diana. I won't be subjected to an inquisition."

"We are having a *conversation*, sir. That requires you to participate. And since you have spent the better part of your life in the army, I cannot help wishing to hear about it. Surely you were not always engaged in combat. There must have been times that were not so very unpleasant. Can you not speak to me of those?"

"They would be incomprehensible to a female," he said after a lengthy hesitation. "We found ways to amuse ourselves, of course. Sports, wagering, drinking—the usual pastimes of men in the company of other men. For the rest, you may imagine long days of tedium and routine, broken occasionally by short periods of extreme horror. We marched a great deal. When encamped, the companies spent most of their time in training, preparing themselves to form squares against a cavalry charge, load quickly and fire, use bayonets to advantage, that sort of thing. They must learn to react automatically, because in the noise and smoke and chaos of a battle, there is no opportunity to stop and think what to do."

"Did you train with them?" she asked, wondering what he meant by forming squares.

"At times I supervised, but the sergeant majors were primarily reponsible for drilling the troops. The Forty-fourth is a foot regiment, but like most superior officers, I went into combat on horseback. Officers ride as much to be seen as for any other reason, I have always thought, but there were occasions when I was in the thick of it and fought from the saddle. When horses were shot from under me—three at Salamanca alone—I had occasion to wield my saber from the ground."

"*Three?* But when you lose one, where does another horse come from? Do you have spares?"

"I traveled with a string of horses, yes. But they were never to hand when most I needed them. If grounded, one waits for a riderless horse to come by, and leaps on its back, and gets on with the fighting."

"Oh my."

"And that, madam, is all I have to say about the war." His voice was hard as granite. "I have done as you asked. I have *participated.* You must content yourself with what you have already heard."

Very little that signified, she realized, although she had been fascinated nevertheless. But he'd told her nothing about *himself.* Nothing that helped her to know him, certainly. She would have to leave the subject of the war now, if she hoped to make any progress, but what else was there? His childhood was too remote, although one day she meant to quiz him about it. She wanted desperately to know about the women in his life, for there must have been some, but even the rush of courage that had brought her this far would not permit her to broach such a dangerous topic.

What of his travels after the war? She remembered how anxiously Lord Kendal had watched for one of his brother's rare letters in the post. Months went by between them, and in the interim, no one could be sure where Alex was or if he was still alive.

"No more conversation about the war," she agreed. For now, she added silently. "But I should like to hear about what you did when it was over. You traveled extensively, I am told, all the way to South America. That must have been quite an adventure. But I've wondered why you went there instead of coming home."

"That is none of your concern, madam. And you needn't pry any further, because I'll not address the subject now or in the future. Understood?"

"No," she replied, clutching the bale of hay with both hands. He had never before spoken to her in precisely that tone. She could not have explained it, but in the darkness, she imagined ghosts hovering in the air. There was the faintest odor of blood, and the sound of iron walls dropping between them. "I *don't* understand, Alex. Why can you not speak of it?"

"Are you altogether certain you wish to know? Perhaps I have done unspeakable things."

"Rubbish!" she fired back immediately. "You could no more be wicked or dishonorable than I could fly to the moon. But I do believe you are troubled by something that happened in Spain, or possibly in the American War It haunts you even yet, does it not? I can feel its presence here and now, Alex. You wear it around you like a shroud."

"Bloody hell, woman! You have no idea what you are talking about. All soldiers are haunted by what they have seen and done. It comes with the profession. And you may be sure that the last thing they want is to revisit the past and reopen old wounds to satisfy the pernicious curiosity of a green girl."

"I am not being fanciful," she said as calmly as she could manage. "As well you are aware. Nor am I the only one to recognize that you bear the weight of—well, whatever it is you are keeping to yourself. When I knew you even less well than I know you now, Lady Kendal advised me that—"

Something, probably his fist, slammed into the door. "You *dare* to discuss my affairs with members of my family? That is betrayal of the highest order, madam. Do so again and I cannot answer for what I will do in return. Meantime, we are finished here. Rain or no rain, we proceed now or return to Lakeview. And whichever direction we take, I'll hear not another word from you about matters that are none of your damn business!"

With that, he flung open the door and was gone.

Chapter 12

She was taking him to a bloody damned pig farm!

There was no mistaking the odor that hung thickly in the damp air as they came through a narrow fold in the hills. He had smelled it often enough in Portugal and Spain, a noxious brew of wet bristles, offal, and mud.

Diana was riding a considerable distance ahead, her posture straight as a rifle barrel, never looking back to see if he was still following her. Perhaps she hoped that he was not. Since leaving the cottage, she had spoken only once, a cool "Thank you" when he helped her mount, and she'd ridden off at a fast clip before he'd managed to swing onto his horse.

How was this quarrel *his* fault? he wanted to know. And who the devil was that prying, prodding female he'd been marooned with in the hut? Not his sweet-natured wife. Not shy, couldn't-say-boo-to-a-goose Diana, who melted into a puddle if he looked at her the wrong way.

What had possessed her to confront him all of a sudden? Demand that he tell her things she had no business knowing? He'd thought he had safely married a woman who would leave him be.

Well, she'd certainly done *that*.

Leave the *past* be, he meant. Take him as he was and never question how he got that way. How the devil could he answer her, even if he were willing to try? He'd spent more than two aimless years roaming the Americas in search of—well, he couldn't have said what, but all he'd got for his pains was a bout of dysentery that almost did him in.

As he'd told Diana, what did any of it matter now? Knowing why things had fallen out as they had, or what he could have

115

done differently, changed nothing. He wanted only to forget. He never would, he was all but certain, but dear God, he wanted to. Moving on would help, he kept hoping. A purpose in life would help. Diana in his bed would definitely help.

But from out of nowhere she'd asserted herself, as she had never before done with him in such a fashion. He supposed that no harm had come of it. She had learned nothing, and he had set her right. It would be a long time before she tried such a thing again, and if she did, he was now firmly on his guard. Hell, it took only a raised eyebrow to set her shivering in her slippers. Oh yes, she would behave.

So why did he have the distinct feeling that this battle had only just begun?

The musky odor of wet animals grew keener. Directly ahead he saw smoke wafting from the chimney of a neat, two-story stone cottage set a little apart from half a dozen low farm buildings and a good-sized barn.

Diana was already off her horse and embracing a tall, full-bosomed woman of about his own years. She wore a mobcap over lush chestnut hair, a homespun gray dress with the skirt tied into a knot about her knees, and rubber work boots. A rake lay fallen at her feet, close by a repellent heap of straw and dung.

As he rode up, an ugly mongrel, all teeth and wet fur standing on end, rushed from the barn to bark at Thunder and spring about his hooves in a doggy game of tag.

Swearing under his breath, Alex quickly dismounted and planted himself between the dog and his horse.

"Alicia! *Come!*"

Bowing its head, the dog slunk to the farm woman's side and nosed repentantly at her boot. She scratched behind the floppy ears. "Good girl."

To Alex's profound disgust, Diana dropped to one knee in the mud and opened her arms. Yipping deliriously, the dog flung itself at her, licking her face and wagging a stubby tail so hard it ought to have broken off.

The woman approached him with open friendliness, a wide smile on her lips, one hand outstretched. With little choice he took it, meaning to bring it to his lips in a formal salute, but she grasped his hand in a firm grip and shook it vigorously.

"You are Kit's brother," she said. "The military one. He told me about you. And I am Helen Pratt, but I answer only to Nell." She made a sweeping gesture. "Welcome to Pratt's Piggery, sir, a thriving little establishment if I do say so myself."

"Honored to meet you," he said, somewhat taken aback.

"You must be uncomfortable in those wet clothes. Remove your coat, Colonel, and I'll hang it to dry." When he hesitated, she clicked her tongue. "Surely we needn't stand on ceremony in a barnyard."

"No. I suppose not." He peeled off his sodden riding coat and passed it to her. It wouldn't dry anytime soon, but perhaps the sun, just breaking through the clouds, would have some effect on his shirt. The soaked cambric adhered to his flesh like a second skin.

Nell regarded his shoulders and chest with a look of unconcealed admiration. "My, my. Diana did very well for herself, I must say. But then, the same could be said about you. She's as good-hearted as they come. In the short time she stayed here, I grew extremely fond of her."

Alex glanced over his shoulder at Diana, who was now surrounded by ducks and geese, all of them clamoring for her attention. She was *petting* them, by Jupiter. The dog, shunted aside by the aggressive birds, crouched at the perimeter of the circle and whimpered forlornly.

He knew precisely how that dog felt.

Nell cleared her throat. "Colonel, where I mean to hang your coat is t'other side of the house. Will you you join me for a few moments? There is something I wish to ask you."

"Certainly." He followed her to where a length of thin rope was suspended between two birches. "How may I be of service?"

"Well, sir, it happens that my Eddie was in the army as well. He died at Fuentes de Onoro." She carefully stretched his coat over the rope line. "Were you there?"

"I was."

She turned to him with an assessing gaze. "This will strike you as an odd request, I am sure, but I have always wanted to know what it was like. You see, Eddie took the king's shilling only a year after we were wed, and I saw him no more than a handful of times after that. He wrote nearly every day, though. Packets of his long letters would arrive twenty and thirty at a time, and in them he shared with me even the most insignificant of his experiences. I marched with him and fought with him and scavenged meals with him all the way to Fuentes de Onoro. And then I had only one letter, from his colonel in the Fifty-second, informing me that he had died heroically in battle."

Alex reflected on the scores of letters he had written under similar circumstances. Instant death. No pain. The fallen soldier had sacrificed himself to save his comrades. Would live in memory as one of England's finest and all that rot, when the poor sod was probably shredded by grapeshot without knowing what had hit him.

"I am acquainted with many officers of the Fifty-second," he said in a guarded tone. "Indeed, they are my particular friends. Whichever of them sent you the letter was doubtless giving no more than the plain truth of it. Eddie Pratt died a hero, although that can be little consolation now. Nor can I think how I might add to what you already know. In my experience it is always a mistake to dwell on the past, especially when it concerns matters of war and death."

She gave him an understanding smile. "I am sure of it, Colonel. Nevertheless, I want you to describe what happened there. Not the gruesome parts, of course. I'd not dream of asking you to call them again to mind. But I need to see all the rest. The countryside. The town. Where Eddie would have been and what he'd have been doing in the hours before battle. It's important to me, Colonel Valliant. I was with him nearly all the way to Fuentes de Onoro, and then he vanished. I lost him too soon. But if you will sketch for me his last few days and hours, I will then be able to join him there in spirit."

He must have been scowling, because she looked suddenly apologetic. "Although this seems exceedingly peculiar, I assure you that I am quite sound of mind. But I live my days and nights on a pig farm, sir, with only my memories for company. And the one memory I most long to have is the one you can supply me."

After all the battles that followed Fuentes de Onoro, he could scarcely recall details of the engagement with Massena save that it had lasted four interminable days. He remembered well enough the maze of cottages and alleys that swept down from a high plateau to the River Dos Casos, and the courtyard where he'd been pinned under his fallen horse for several hours, and—

She put a work-roughened hand on his forearm. "Never you mind. It was wrong of me to presume on you when I've no more than the briefest acquaintance with your wife. And Kit, of course, although I know him somewhat better. He is wed now as well, I understand. I've not met his Lucy, but Diana informs me that she is just the one to bring him to respectability."

"I cannot say," he said, wildly uneasy in the presence of a female so quick to share confidences with a stranger. He liked Nell, certainly. One could scarcely help liking her. But why was it that women were so prodigiously bent on cutting up a man's peace? He'd been too long in the company of men to have any knack for dealing with females. Somewhere along the way he'd picked up a notion of what they were supposed to be like, but the ones he'd met since returning to England defied his every expectation.

"I confess I'll miss the rogue," Nell said, leading him back to the farmyard. "He'd sometimes go to ground here when the excisemen were on his trail, and he never arrived without several bottles of excellent French wine. We had quite the time of it, we did."

They came around the corner, and Alex was stunned to see Diana whirling in a sort of dance and flapping her skirts up and down. She stopped the moment she saw them, but not before he'd got a comprehensive look at her shapely calves and creamy thighs.

Blushing furiously, she smoothed her wet skirt with both hands. "I was trying to dry out," she explained weakly.

"Come inside, love, and change into one of my dresses." Nell led Diana toward the house, flashing Alex a knowing look over her shoulder.

When they were gone, Alex let out the air he'd been holding. In those few seconds, he had seen more of his wife than in all the forty-eight days since the wedding. His reaction was predictably immediate and uncontrollable.

Nell had been aware of it, that was evident, but he couldn't be sure about Diana. Probably not, though. She never appeared to notice anything about him, save how he could be of use to the regiment. Where she was concerned, he might as well have been a packhorse.

Oh, she would come to his bed if he gave the order or made the request. She had said so often enough, in that calm, bloodless, I'll-do-my-duty tone of voice. And while he was heaving on top of her, she'd no doubt be calculating how many bottle labels would be required for the parsnip wine. Her detached resignation slapped cold water on his desire whenever it heated him to the point of asking. It stopped him short when he was all but ready to beg. He wanted her, by God, but not unless she wanted him as well.

Nell bustled from the house, a notebook and pencil in one hand and a cup in the other. She pressed the heavy ceramic mug into his hand. "Tea. It's left over from breakfast, I'm afraid, but it will warm you up. Diana will be out shortly. I told her to dry her hair by the kitchen fire." She cast him a sly look. "I understand, Colonel Valliant, that you are about to go into the pig business."

He choked on a swallow of tea.

"First you've heard of it, I expect," she said with a grin. "Or perhaps I mistook Diana's meaning. But she intends to learn all there is to know about raising pigs—within the next hour, it seems—and during the fortnight she was here, she did develop an inordinate fondness for the beasts. Mind you, that is not the proper state of mind for a swine seller. Pigs are well enough, I suppose, and they are certainly profitable, but it's a mistake to feel affection for any creature you mean to sell for slaughter."

He went cold, remembering how it was to give an order dispatching men to almost certain death. To lead them there and escape untouched, as he invariably did, while his fellows were cut down all around him. He almost never let himself recall those events. But she had spoken of Fuentes de Onoro, and asked him to think back on it, and now he couldn't stop himself. Nothing out of the ordinary had happened there, not to him, but

120

now that the floodgates were open, battle after battle began to replay in his head.

"To be sure," Nell said, "she'd barely escaped a Bow Street Runner, and she'd been hiding for weeks with nothing whatever to do because it was far too dangerous for her to venture outside. When Kit brought her here, the poor child was boiling over with energy. She fed all the animals, mucked out the sties, and left me practically nothing to do. First holiday I'd had in years. For Diana, working on a pig farm was far better entertainment than hunkering down in a cave with constables and Runners poking about overhead."

That got his attention. "She was living in a bloody *cave*?"

Nell tilted her head, regarding him with curious eyes. "Diana has told you nothing of this? My, my. You should ask her about her adventures, Colonel. She has quite a tale to tell."

He produced a noncommittal grunt just as Diana emerged from the house.

She was wearing a woolen dress the color of wheat, far too large for her and shapeless as a sack. But he had seen something of what lay underneath, and thought of her legs, and was forced to turn his back to her.

She paid him no mind, to his great relief. And even greater regret, were he to be perfectly honest about it.

Nell and Diana had vanished into the barn before he rallied himself. For the next hour he trailed behind them, ignored, while they prattled about pig houses and farrowing rails and mast, whatever the devil *that* was. He learned what pigs ate, which was apparently everything, how fast they grew, and the best treatments for various porcine ailments.

All the while, he watched Diana. He had never before seen her eyes so bright. She laughed when Nell told her that pigs were fond of drinking spirits, and her mouth dropped when she discovered they were excellent swimmers. She asked scores of questions and took meticulous notes, her body practically vibrating with unmistakable passion.

For pigs.

She was all on fire—just as he'd always wanted her to be—for bloody damned *pigs*!

Next came herding techniques. After releasing several swine

from their stalls, Nell gave Diana a small sack of beans and showed her how to recognize the Leader Pig. That was an easy task, since a formidable-looking porker immediately began nosing at her skirts in search of food.

Diana headed for the barn door, dropping beans one by one in front of the Leader. It gobbled them up posthaste, but the others trotted along as well, evidently hoping for a stray bean to come their way. Very soon Diana had got them all to the court-yard, where she was quickly surrounded by eager pigs.

"What am I to do now?" she asked, giggling like a schoolgirl.

"A handful of beans directly center," Nell instructed. "Then extricate yourself."

Diana did as she was told, clambering over the pigs when they circled, snouts to the beans and curly-tailed rumps sticking out like spokes on a wheel.

"They will remain in that position for quite some time," Nell said. "Long after the beans are gone, they refuse to stray from the last place they found food."

"But why?" Diana regarded the ring of swine with a frown. "I thought pigs were supposed to be smart."

"So they are, but at times they think with their stomachs." Nell tossed a grin at Alex. "Creatures often do their thinking with irrational bits of their anatomies. You must learn, Diana, to exploit that particular weakness whenever you come upon it."

Alex gritted his teeth.

"One final lesson," Nell said, reaching into her pocket for a length of twine. "When you cannot get a stubborn pig to go in the direction you wish, you persuade it that you are aiming in the opposite direction." She expertly separated one pig from the circle, tied the string around a hind leg, and gave the other end to Diana. "Return him to the barn, my dear."

Looking puzzled, Diana moved to the front of the pig and tugged on the string. The pig speedily backed up, went off bal-ance, and plopped onto the ground.

"Remember what I said," Nell advised. "You want to lead him into the barn, so that is precisely what you are trying to do. It won't work, I promise you."

"Oh!" Laughing, Diana made her way to the pig's backside. "I take your point." This time she pulled the string directly away from where she wanted to go, and the pig lumbered to its trotters, heading forward. To the barn, as Nell had predicted, and intent on getting there in a hurry. Diana, towed helplessly behind, vanished through the doors.

"She learns quickly," Nell said with a sly wink.

He nodded curtly, rather sure Nell Pratt had been educating his wife in matters that had nothing to do with pigs.

Diana soon emerged from the barn, beaming with satisfaction. "Right into the stall he went, bless his heart. I can't remember when I've had so much fun. Did you see that, Alex? Who would have thought pigs to be so biddable?"

"Biddable?" He gave her a black look. "You employed treachery, madam."

"It was wonderfully effective, though, and I've no objection to treachery in a good cause. Kit used it to advantage against my uncle, and now I have used it against a pig. Although come to think of it, my uncle *is* a pig."

Her eyes had gone bleak of a sudden, reminding Alex that his resourceful wife bore the scars of her uncle's fury. Never conscious of her scar until she put him in mind of it, he sometimes forgot that she was unceasingly in mind of it. Casting about for something to say, he found only a terse, "Some pigs are better than others."

But her face lit up again, and she came to him and gazed hopefully into his eyes. "Might we choose one of the better ones, Alex, and take it home with us?"

"Now? *Today?*"

"Oh, yes. We ought to get started right away, don't you think? And if we don't select a pig while we are here, we'll only have to come all the way back to get one."

After seeing her brightness snuffed, even for that brief moment while she was thinking of her uncle, he could not say no to her. Not to anything she asked of him. "Are we to tie a string around its leg," he said with a forced smile, "and pull it backward the whole distance to Lakeview?"

"That won't be necessary," Nell said, visibly enjoying his discomfiture. "Why don't you retrieve your coat, Colonel Valliant, while Diana decides which pig she prefers? And if you take your time about it, I'll have everything ready to go when you return."

He understood well enough that the ladies wanted to exchange confidences out of his earshot, and he was acutely aware that they would likely be talking about him. "As you say, ma'am," he agreed with a stiff bow before retreating in the direction of the clothesline.

He paced for twenty minutes behind the house, pocket watch in hand to check the time. Twenty minutes was all he was willing to allot for pig selection and the dissection of his character, which was doubtless their prime order of business.

Nell was attaching an oval-shaped wicker cage to his horse when he returned to the barnyard. Inside the openwork container was a wriggling, squealing piglet.

"I trust you can mount in spite of this," Nell said, fastening the last tie and tugging at the cage to make sure it was firmly affixed behind the saddle.

He gave her a sour look.

Diana finished rolling her wet clothes into a bundle. "If you don't mean to wear your coat, sir, I'll add it to this lot."

He passed it over, and when she had stuffed the clothing into a sack and secured it to her mare, he helped her onto the saddle. "You will be chilled on the ride home, madam. We'll not reach Lakeview before dark."

"Nell has gone to fetch me a woolen cloak," she said, "and you are to have a blanket. But what think you of our pig, sir? Is he not a handsome fellow?"

He was spared having to answer by Nell, who tossed a blanket over his shoulders. "Diana chose well," she said. "Now off with you both while the light holds."

Mounting effortlessly, still mildly insulted she had implied that he couldn't, Alex looked down into her gold-specked brown eyes. Quite a woman, Nell Pratt. And she had sheltered Diana, befriending her when most she needed a friend.

"Regarding the matter we discussed earlier," he said in a stilted voice, "I have had a change of mind. If you still wish it, and when time permits, I'll call on you again."

Nell's smile all but knocked him off the horse. "Thank

you, Colonel Valliant. I knew I could not have mistaken your character."

He could not help but smile back. "It will be my pleasure, ma'am. And it will be soon, I promise you."

"Excellent. But for now, sir, your wife is leaving without you."

He looked up to see Diana disappearing around a curve some distance away. And without so much as a good-bye to Nell, which was unlike her, or a sign to him that she was going. What in blazes had set her off *this* time?

Not wanting to appear in a great hurry, he guided Thunder along the path at an easy trot. Trotting, he quickly discovered, did not agree with the pig, which expressed its displeasure in no uncertain terms. Alex supposed it could not be comfortable, trapped in a cage and bouncing about atop Thunder's flanks, but he wished to hell it would shut up.

He slowed and the level of noise decreased, but that meant it was half an hour before he caught up with Diana. She had put on her soggy bonnet and lowered the veil.

They rode side by side for a time, not speaking, and the silence was so tense that even the pig joined in.

Finally Diana looked over at him. "I know that you dislike it, sir, but I feel that I must apologize to you for my behavior in the hay shed. I had no right to quiz you in such a fashion, let alone continue to do so when you told me quite plainly to stop."

She must have been rehearsing that little speech, he thought. It clipped along like hoofbeats on a flagstone courtyard. And unlike her usual meek apologies, it had sounded not in the least repentant.

"The incident is forgot," he assured her. "You mustn't refine on it. I was out of temper."

Nodding, she picked up her pace and rode ahead of him for what seemed an eternity. They were leaving Nell's house, he thought, the same way they got there—at odds. Diana, javelin-straight in the saddle, was leading the way while he straggled behind, wanting to close the distance between them and unable to think how to do it. Telling her things she had no right to know was not an option, even if he wanted to take her into his confidence.

Sometimes, primarily when he'd had overmuch to drink, he wanted to do precisely that. He'd spent too many long nights in the taproom of the Black Bull with only Mr. Beadle for company, staggering home in the wee hours several sheets to the wind. He'd stumbled to his empty bed and collapsed there, wondering if he ought to have gone instead to the room next to his where Diana lay. But there'd been little he could do in his inebriated state, even if she'd welcomed him with open arms, and he soon fell fast asleep.

Nevertheless, he had actually considered telling her. That was progress of a sort.

The track widened, and she dropped back again to ride alongside him, her veil fluttering in the late-afternoon breeze. "I have to know, Alex," she said. "You have every right, I'm sure, and I'll not make any objections. But she *is* my friend, and you must see how difficult this will be."

"How difficult *what* will be?" Damn, but he hated that veil. He could not see her eyes. "I've no idea what you mean."

"Of course you do. I may be a virgin, sir—well, I *am* one— but that doesn't make me altogether stupid. If you intend to take Nell as your mistress, just say so."

"As my—?" He reached over and snatched the hat from her head. "What in bloody blazes gave you such a ridiculous idea?"

She was white as milk, but she raised her chin and regarded him with disdain. "What you said to her. 'If you wish it.' 'I'll call on you.' " She gulped. " 'It will be my pleasure.' "

If she weren't trembling so, he'd have broken down in laughter. From her perspective, his conversation with Nell must have sounded decidedly odd. Even provocative, come to think of it. Dear Lord.

He schooled his voice to a calm tone. "Do you really imagine, Diana, that I'd have arranged an assignation with another woman in your presence? You have a poor opinion of me, I must say."

"Well, I'm not sure I really thought it." Her hands clenched on the pommel of the sidesaddle. "But then I couldn't stop thinking *about* it, so I made up my mind to ask you straight out."

He knew her well enough by now to understand what it had

cost her, that direct question. And he was astonishingly pleased that she cared he might take a mistress, although he certainly never would.

"I regret the misunderstanding," he said slowly, casting about for an explanation that would reassure her. "Nell had asked me to tell her about the battle at Fuentes de Onoro, where her husband died. And as you might expect, I declined. But when we were about to depart, I heard myself agree to do so, and because I hadn't intended to say any such thing, my words were not well chosen. It was all perfectly harmless."

Color flamed on Diana's cheeks. "Oh, my. Oh, do forgive me, Alex. How foolish of me to—"

"*Stop* that!"

She froze in alarm.

"I was talking to the pig," he said between clenched teeth. "Sorry. But what the devil is he *doing* back there?"

"Well, he's got his front trotters through the openings in his cage, and they are having at your . . . your—" She erupted in laughter.

He scrunched forward on the saddle, to no avail. "I have tried to cooperate, madam, and if you insist on turning Lakeview into a pig farm, I'll not prevent you. But in future, you will import your stock without my direct assistance. Understood?"

"C-certainly," she replied, still laughing. "But only this one pig, I promise you, is destined for Lakeview. If there are to be any pig farms, they will be established elsewhere. I am hoping that a few members of the regiment, those with little productive land, will take up the profession, but Nell was of the opinion that the very idea of raising pigs would meet with resistance unless you and I showed the others how easy it is."

"How can we raise pigs with just one? Even swine require a pair for mating purposes."

"Yes." She blushed again. "We will only demonstrate the care and feeding of a weaner. Most anyone can rear a weaner. Indeed, I want every member of the regiment not living in town to have one."

"And you believe they will follow our example?" he asked dubiously.

"Oh, yes. And just imagine, Alex. Come winter, we shall have a lovely supply of ham and bacon and sausages."

Winter, he thought as the pig squealed and prodded, could not come soon enough.

"And he'll find most of his own food," Diana continued blithely. "He's a clever little thing, our piglet, with a spirited nature and remarkable vigor."

Oh, indeed. A pattern-card of pighood. The absolute cynosure of swinedom.

"I think he should have a name, Alex. What shall we call him?"

He cast her a dark look. "Dinner."

Chapter 13

Dinner, Alex couldn't help but notice, seemed to spend most of his time in the house.

Mr. Beadle had constructed a pen behind the stable to lodge him, but the determined young pig was not so easily contained. Every night he contrived to escape and take up a position by the front door, waiting for someone to open it. Then he shot inside like a bullet, aiming directly for the kitchen.

There was little point trying to catch him, Alex had learned after several attempts. And since no one else was keen to evict him, he'd resigned himself to a piglet running tame in his house.

The regiment ladies took special delight in the pig's company, slipping him morsels from the refreshment trays or bringing him treats from their own kitchens. When there was no food in the offing, the pig trotted briskly behind Diana as she went about her tasks, grunting with pleasure whenever she paused to scratch the top of his head. In the evenings, while she worked at the writing table or sat reading a book, Dinner was invited to stretch out on her lap for a snooze.

This particular weaner would never live up to his name, Alex was certain. If Diana had her way about it, Dinner would enjoy a long and pampered life as a member of the Valliant household.

Not unexpectedly, he had joined Alex that morning for breakfast, poised beside the chair like an alert puppy, his bright piggy eyes focused expectantly on the fork as it moved from the plate to Alex's mouth. Now and again the flat disk of his snout nudged Alex's boot, reminding him—as if he could fail to be aware of it—that a poor starving pig waited expectantly for a handout.

Trying to eat in the face of such intense regard grew increasingly irksome. Alex finally abandoned the effort, set his plate on the floor, and left the room, taking his cup of coffee with him to drink in peace.

He wandered in the direction of the entrance hall, where Diana was greeting the ladies who were arriving for a lesson in pencil making. That was one of her favorite projects, and she had high hopes for its success. A fortnight ago he'd accompanied her to Keswick, where the graphite was mined, and on the way he had learned considerably more than a man really needed to know about pencils.

Much of the assembly work, Diana informed him, was contracted out to independent laborers. They required little space, which meant that her ladies could set up shop in their own homes. But first they must be taught the skills, so she planned to hire an instructor and hoped that Alex wouldn't mind if he stayed at Lakeview while the classes were in progress.

Having accepted a pig into his home, he could scarcely object to a pencil maker. Bemused, he had followed her through the streets of Keswick as she popped in and out of shops and small factories, asking questions, collecting names and information, and evaluating suppliers of cedarwood, blacklead, and glue.

None of those encounters began well. Without exception the men in the shops and factories listened politely to what she said, and then promptly turned to him. Business was not the province of females, their expressions said clearly, and when it came to actual discussion of terms, she must naturally step aside.

His heart ached for her. He wanted to step in, take over, and spare her the humiliation. But she would resent him if he seized command, so he pasted a look of profound stupidity on his face and pretended to be a servant. When someone addressed him, he mumbled, "Dunno what you be talkin' about," and slumped off to the nearest corner.

Left a mere female to deal with, the shopkeepers and manufacturers dismissed her out of hand. All the air seemed to go out of her then. But she straightened her spine, turned on her heel, and flounced away with Alex slouching after her, his hands itching to pummel the louts. When they reached the pavement she marched to the next shop and tried again.

As the day wore on, he suffered for her until he could scarcely draw breath. Unused to playing a passive role, he had to force himself minute by minute to hold back, look stupid, and bank his rage. She was unaware of his presence, he suspected, all her energy and will concentrated on the task at hand. Like a racehorse or a soldier in the heat of battle, she permitted nothing to distract her.

Only once, as they emerged from the office of Keswick's most prominent pencil wholesaler, did she speak to him. "I should very much like," she said solemnly, "to carve out the entrails of that pompous windbag and feed them to Dinner."

"No discriminating pig would have them," he replied, pleased to hear her laugh from under that damnable veil. She had kept it pinned back on the ride to Keswick, but the moment they came in sight of the town, down it came and down it stayed.

In every other way she was uncommonly brave that day, and eventually her persistence won out. When they finally set out for home, she had found her teacher, struck bargains for the necessary materials, and negotiated a contract with a wholesaler for several thousand pencils to be supplied by her regiment within six months. All on her own.

He was so proud of her that his tongue twisted into knots. And just as well, for she never stopped chattering all the way back to Lakeview. With an acerbic wit he'd not seen in her before, Diana skewered the pretentious merchants with devastating accuracy. Success had freed her of her inhibitions, and she glowed with triumph.

He fell in love with her that day in Keswick. Or he admitted to himself that he had loved her for a considerable time, assuming love consisted of respect, desire, and a red-hot cannonball lodged in his chest.

The classes had been going on for the better part of a week now, and Mr. Filbert, a shy, thin man with gold-rimmed spectacles balanced precariously on his narrow nose, reported that all five students were making excellent progress.

Hoping for a word with Diana if he could catch her alone,

Alex waited in the shadows, aware that his presence always made the ladies uncomfortable. Gradually they filtered into the parlor where their tools and supplies were laid out, and soon after, Dinner trotted by. Alex watched the upturned comma of his tail vanish around the doorframe, and heard the women greet him with enthusiasm.

Mr. Beadle came through the door just then and immediately began speaking to Diana with unusually rapid gestures. Whatever he was saying appeared to distress her.

Alex set his cup on a pier table and went to join them. "Is something amiss, my dear?"

"Mrs. Derwent isn't coming to class today," she said in a worried voice. "When Mr. Beadle stopped by to give her a lift, Mr. Derwent said that his wife was needed at home."

Mr. Beadle made another series of agitated gestures, from which Alex divined that Mrs. Derwent would not be returning at all, by order of her husband.

"But she has done so well!" Diana exclaimed. "Better than any of the others. And Mr. Filbert says that the final two lessons are the most important. She mustn't miss them."

"It's unfortunate, certainly. But if Mr. Derwent refuses to let her continue, there is nothing to be done about it."

"Rubbish. I shall go directly there and speak with him. Will you be so kind as to accompany me, Mr. Beadle?"

Shaking his head, Mr. Beadle pulled a stubby pencil and a scrap of paper from his pocket, went to the pier table, and scrawled a few words.

Diana leaned over to read them. "Oh dear God." She clutched at the table for support.

Grim-faced, Mr. Beadle handed the note to Alex.

Window. Saw her face. Beaten.

Alex crushed the paper in his fist and crossed to the door. "I'll deal with this. Mr. Beadle, come with me to the stable, if you will. I require directions to the cottage."

Diana hurried after them. "I'm coming with you."

He turned and placed his hands on her shoulders. "Indeed you are not, madam. I'll hear no discussion on the subject."

"But what if I'm needed? She could be badly hurt."

"You may safely rely on me to do whatever is necessary.

Now, go back to the house, and carry on as if nothing has occurred."

She released a long sigh. "Oh, very well. I'm sure you are right. But, Alex, please take care. I know that you mean to punish him—I can see it in your eyes—but he will almost certainly take it out on her."

"Understood." He brushed a kiss against her hair. "She will come to no further harm."

While his horse was being saddled, Alex memorized the rough map Mr. Beadle scratched for him in the dirt with a stick. And the journey, taken at a gallop, put him within minutes at the narrow track that led from the road to the Derwents' cottage. A low, white-walled building with a slate roof, it was set at the base of a sloping hill patched with spinneys of oak and hazel. Just beyond a small, scraggly garden, one thin brown and white cow stood dejectedly in a crude paddock.

Alex dismounted and went the rest of the way on foot, leading his horse and making no great hurry of it. The curtains were drawn shut, he saw as he drew nearer the cottage. Except for the raspy call of rooks in the trees, the landscape was eerily silent and motionless, as if it were holding its breath.

The door opened and a man emerged, slamming it behind him. Not overly tall, with beefy arms and a barrel-shaped torso, he had a ruddy face under a thick shock of salt-and-pepper hair. Standing with his arms folded across his chest, he looked strong, angry, and defiant.

"Go away," he shouted when Alex continued moving in his direction. "This is my land. You're not welcome here."

"I didn't expect to be." Without halting, he looped the reins over a bush.

Derwent visibly dug in his heels, his hands clenching and unclenching. Sweat beaded on his forehead. "That's far enough."

Alex stopped precisely ten feet away, an unthreatening distance but close enough to read his opponent's face. He regarded Derwent steadily, unsurprised to see the man's eyes shift away. In his experience, most bullies were cowards at heart. "I am Colonel Alexander Valliant," he said evenly. "I wish to speak with your wife."

"Can't. She's sick."

"So I understand. Nevertheless, I *will* speak with her."

"You got no right! I say who comes into m'house. You try it and I'll set the constable on you."

"Do that. I'm sure he'll be interested to see what it is you are hiding in there."

"Ain't hiding nuthing." Derwent glanced over his shoulder at the door. "M'wife be sick, that's all. She don't want to see nobody. Told me so."

Alex closed the distance between them, wondering if this oaf had any idea how close he was to being soundly thrashed. "Move aside, Derwent."

For several tense moments Derwent stood his ground. Alex had begun to hope he'd be forced to go through him when he sidled out of the way, leaving clear the path to the door.

The room Alex entered was low-ceilinged and sparsely furnished, lit only by a pair of candles set above the hearth. A thin shaft of sunlight sliced through a gap in the curtains to his right, and he moved to it, making sure that his face was illuminated. "Mrs. Derwent?"

"Over here, sir," came a faltering voice from the farthest corner. She was huddled on a low wooden chair, arms clutched around her waist. "You had best go away, sir. Mr. Derwent won't like it that you be talking to me."

"He has already said so." Alex gentled his voice, which sounded harsh and strained even to his own ears. Lord knew what she must be thinking to hear it. "You needn't worry, ma'am. All will be well."

A choked sound, wordless and agonized, carried to his ears.

Her fear—of him and of what might happen when he was gone—curled around him like acrid smoke. He was far out of his depth here. Perhaps he should have brought Diana with him after all. She would know what to say, and how to comfort and reassure this woman. It had been a mistake to come here alone.

"I'm a soldier," he said, fumbling ahead as best he could. "Most of my life has been spent among men very much like myself, more given to action than to words. If I am blunt, ma'am, it's not because I mean to be unkind. I know no other way to proceed."

"I understand," she said after a moment. "But you cannot help me, sir. Nor should you try. We are nothing to you."

"To the contrary. You mean a great deal to my wife, which makes you my concern. May I see your face, Mrs. Derwent?"

The figure on the chair shuddered, and he thought she would deny him. But to his astonishment, she came to her feet and crossed slowly to the hearth. Taking a candle, she clutched it between both hands and held it so that the flame danced just below her chin.

He moved closer, careful to maintain an impassive expression. Pity was the last thing any wounded creature so brave as this one would accept. Even so, his knees went weak when he saw the bruises on her face. One eye was nearly swollen shut. Her lips, puffed and cracked, trembled as he gazed at her. Light brown hair streaked with gray hung in tangled damp strings around her shoulders.

"Has he beaten you before?" Alex asked softly. "Tell me the truth."

"No. Not like this. Not so bad."

"But he's struck you?"

"Yes. A slap, sometimes. The back of his hand sometimes. He never used his fists afore."

Alex took the candle and returned it to the hearth. "He'll never do so again, I promise you."

"He's not a bad man," she said urgently. "We did well enough for more'n twenty years, when he was working at the slate quarry. But a load of rock fell on his leg and broke it in three places. He was fit enough when it healed, saving for a limp, but they wouldn't hire him back. Things went hard for him after that. There be no jobs hereabouts except at the quarry, and mining slate is all he knows how to do."

"I see." Alex rubbed his chin. Plainly Derwent objected to his wife taking up a job while he remained unemployed. "What do you do for money, Mrs. Derwent?"

"We have none," she said simply. "Everything we could sell is long gone. The parish helps, and sometimes Mr. Derwent finds a bit of work mending fences or the like. He never stops looking for work. He's a proud man, sir. He wants to make his own way."

135

That struck home. She might have been talking about him, Alex thought, except that Derwent was a desperate man while Alex Valliant had the safe cushion of his aristocratic family to fall back on. Not to mention a wealthy wife, whose fortune he had already spurned. Would he turn it away with such disdain, he wondered, should his own efforts come to nothing?

In any event, there was no excuse, not *any*, for what Derwent had done to his wife. It was unforgivable. But it would be forgiven, he knew, gazing at Mrs. Derwent with better understanding than he'd brought with him into the cottage.

"My wife tells me, ma'am, that you are by far the best pencil maker in Mr. Filbert's class. She also says that you can't afford to miss the final two lessons, although today's class is half the way through by now. But someone will catch you up tomorrow. I'll instruct Mr. Beadle to come by an hour before the usual time."

"I—" She plucked at her apron. "Mr. Derwent will never permit it."

"Leave him to me. And pardon me, for I should have asked this beforehand. Do you feel well enough to attend the class?"

Her hand went to her swollen cheek. "I doubt that I can do the work, sir, with only one eye to see with."

"But you can observe the others, and hear Mr. Filbert explain the procedures. Would you like me to have the apothecary stop in?"

"Oh, sir, don't you understand? The shame of it. I don't want anyone to see my face. I don't want anyone to *know*."

Damn. How could he have failed to consider that? He nodded. "Perhaps other arrangements can be made. I'll ask Mr. Filbert to remain at Lakeview another day or two, and Mr. Beadle can bring him here to give you private lessons. Would that be acceptable?"

Hope lit her battered face. "Do you think he might?"

"Yes, indeed." Alex would pay him whatever he asked. "No one need hear of this, Mrs. Derwent. But Mrs. Valliant will insist on dispatching a servant with food and whatever else she reckons you might need, so I beg you to indulge her. She'll also wish to come herself, perhaps tomorrow if you've no objection."

136

"Whatever you say, sir." Mrs. Derwent sank onto a ladder-back chair, looking overwhelmed. "You are very kind. It's no wonder Mrs. Valliant thinks you put the moon in the sky. But I don't know how we are ever to repay you."

Diana thought *what*? He returned his attention to Mrs. Derwent, who was regarding him curiously.

"Repay? Ah, yes. What say you give me the first pencil from your workshop, and one every month after that for so long as you continue to produce them. A man is always in need of a good pencil. And now, if you will excuse me, I require a few words with Mr. Derwent." Taking her hand, he bowed and touched his lips to her wrist. "Never fear. We shall come to a peaceful understanding."

He left the cottage, blinking against the bright midmorning sunshine and looking around for Derwent. He was slatting stones at one of the paddock fence posts. Splinters flew as a rock slammed into the post and bounced away. When he saw Alex striding in his direction, he picked up another stone, this one large and sharp-edged, and planted his worn boots some distance apart.

Battle stance, Alex thought, coming directly up to him. "I will say this only once, Derwent. Raise a hand to your wife again, and you will answer to me. Is that understood?"

Scarred knuckles whitened as Derwent clenched the jagged rock. "I don't got to do what you tell me. Even a plain man knows his rights. If my wife don't obey me, I can make her. It's the law. And you can't stop me."

"I can," Alex said, holding his gaze. "I will."

For several tense moments, he thought he might actually have to fight the man. And for all his promises to Diana and Mrs. Derwent, he was looking forward to it with considerable pleasure.

But Derwent's bravado soon crumpled. Indeed, he appeared to sink into the ground. His gaze fell, and the ruddy color in his cheeks leached away. The rock dropped from his hand.

Alex almost felt sorry for him. Derwent was far from the only man who had done a great wrong, never expecting to, surprised to find that he had. In that way, if in no other, they were meeting on level ground. They had each betrayed the trust of those who depended on them. It was a bond of sorts—a bond of shame and regret. He would not strike a fellow sinner.

"If you imagine the law gives you the right to brutalize your wife," he said evenly, "you are very much mistaken. But we'll let that pass. You will not make the same mistake again."

Derwent wiped his nose with his sleeve. "I never meant it. All to a sudden I was fistin' her, but it was like sommat else doin' it, not me. I dunno who I come to be now. We was always bacon and eggs, me 'n Molly, afore I lost m' job. Even when the babies died we stuck together. She had three boys 'n a girl, but they was sickly. John made it all the way to seven years, but then the fever got 'im."

"And now it's only the two of you," Alex said, his stomach knotting up. Four children buried. Dear God.

"Since twenty years ago. We've 'ad cross words, but we always made it up. Then Mrs. Valliant come and took her away. Suddenlike, Molly were never to home. All the time goin' off to the fancy house 'n comin' back with fancy things like I don't got the money to buy for 'er." He scuffed his toe in the dust. "I thought if she got work makin' perfumes and pencils, she'd go away and not never come back. Mebbe she oughter go. She'd be well rid of me."

"So far as I can tell, she would not agree," Alex said. "It was always her intention to work here at the cottage, once she had learned a trade."

"Women wasn't meant to take up a trade. Don't matter where, they oughtn't be doin' it. Ain't natural for a wife to do the providin' for a family."

"It's somewhat unusual, to be sure. Before making the acquaintance of my own wife, I thought much as you do about what females were meant to be in this world. But the world is changing, Derwent. At the least, it is rarely as we wish it to be. I think you ought to give your wife permission to make her pencils. It is what she wants, and after what you did to her, you have an obligation to make amends. Don't you agree?"

"Rather do it some other way," he grumbled. "But she can go on about the pencils if that's what pleases her. I won't make no more trouble about it."

"Had you considered the possibility of helping her? She could show you how it's done."

Derwent held out his gnarled, stubby-fingered hands, bent nearly shapeless after punishing years in the slate quarry.

"I see," Alex said, embarrassed for failing to notice earlier. "Well, pencil making is clearly out of the question. Shall we take a walk together?" He clasped his hands behind his back and set out for the hill that rose up behind the cottage. "Do you own this property?"

"From here down to the lake, and more'n half a mile t'other direction, but that's all hills 'n trees. No good for sheep. Narrow, too, mebbe three hunert yards across at widest point. Water runs off them hills and goes to the lake, leaving nuthin' but mud in between. Can't grow a crop in mud. It's no use to anybody."

"As it happens, mud is practically a requirement for the scheme I have in mind," Alex said, giving him a wry smile. "Tell me, Mr. Derwent. What do you know about pigs?"

Chapter 14

Alex was eating his breakfast in company with a fat and greedy Dinner when Diana came into the room.

"Mr. Beadle is nowhere to be found," she said, her voice edged with concern. "He didn't pass by this morning at his usual time, and he failed to pick up Mrs. Truscott and bring her to the embroidery class."

"More than likely his pony has gone lame," Alex said. "Or his cart suffered a broken wheel. Such things happen, my dear."

"They've never happened before. You are the one who spends time with him. Have you any idea where he lives?"

He put aside his fork and set the plate on the floor for Dinner to clean. "I've seen where he turns off the main road when we leave the pub house. You want me to go in search of him, I gather?"

She did, and she meant to accompany him. Half an hour later they made the turn onto a narrow track that led through a series of increasingly high hills. They followed it for a considerable time, into a part of the country Alex had never seen before. They were going the right direction, he was certain, because the ground was worn into two grooves that matched the wheels on Mr. Beadle's cart. But when they had passed through a copse of ragged oaks, he saw that the ground was now unbroken.

Telling Diana to wait, he went back through the trees to a spot where the terrain was exceptionally rocky and made a careful search. After a considerable time he detected a break in the woods, all but invisible unless one happened to be looking for it. Low-hanging branches shadowed the path, and he was forced to duck as he followed it a short distance. When the trees and undergrowth thinned, he was startled to come upon a tall wrought-iron gate set between a narrow gap with steep cliffs rising on both sides of it.

"What in heaven's name is *that*?" Diana asked, drawing up beside him.

He should have known she would follow. "It's not locked," he said, bending from the saddle to raise the crossbar. "Mr. Beadle appears ready to welcome visitors, if they can find him."

They rode side by side for another quarter mile, passing a small tarn that gathered water from a stream flowing down from the hills. Alongside it the track widened, and once again they saw the imprint of the wagon wheels. The high cliffs cut off most of the early morning light, and Alex felt as if they had entered a tunnel. It twisted and turned as they moved deeper into the fells above Coniston Water, the beat of the horses' hooves on marshy turf and water rushing over pebbles the only sounds to be heard.

"This is positively eerie," Diana whispered. "Can he really live in such a place?"

"Look there," Alex said as they came around a sharp curve. The cliffs melted into soft hills, still steep but now covered with grass, and one more turn carried them into a lush dale several hundred yards wide. The stream hugged one side of it, and at the other to their right, an enormous building rose up like something from a dream.

Diana gasped.

They both reined in, equally stunned.

It was part castle, with towers and turrets and arrow slits set high in the walls. Part church as well, with spires and Gothic arches and stained glass in some of the windows scattered helter-skelter as if put there on impulse. Tiled mosaics decorated otherwise bare stretches of stone and mortar. Fantastical figures, animals and human faces and cherubs, were molded at every corner, and there were many corners. Seashells and carved wood had been fitted into the walls. Every kind of ornament was to be found. Finials protruded from the parapets. Ceramic gutter spouts shaped like open mouths hung wherever water might gather. And directly in front of them, set in a stone arch, two thick oak doors stood wide open.

Alex had seen many wonders on his travels—palaces and

Inca temples and great cathedrals—but nothing quite like this. He dismounted, tethered both horses to a small marble obelisk near the doors, and helped Diana from the saddle.

Her eyes were round with astonishment. "What in heaven's name have we come upon, Alex?"

"Mr. Beadle's cottage, I expect." He felt as amazed as she looked. "Shall we see if he's to home?"

They knocked at the open doors, calling his name, but no one responded. No lights were to be seen. A cavern lay straight ahead, unbroken by windows.

Diana tugged him inside, and he soon saw that all the beauty was to be found on the exterior. A short wide passageway quickly came to an end, and beyond was a seemingly endless series of rooms, most of them tiny, connected to one another at random.

They found themselves in a labyrinth. Whichever path they followed, opening doors to go from one room to another, they eventually came to a dead end. It was pitch-dark when they wound themselves near the center of the edifice, and brightly lit when they stumbled upon a room that boasted windows.

Now and again, fanciful carvings were etched into the walls and doors. Other times they passed bare stone and openings that had no doors set in them. Once they found themselves back where they had started, sunlight pouring through the wide arch of the main entrance.

"We went to the right before," Alex said. "Let's try the left this time."

They came through a number of rooms they'd been in before, or so he believed. They all looked pretty much alike. But by turning left whenever possible, they eventually arrived at a tall, narrow oak door inset with bits of colored glass. On either side, like sentries, two brightly painted plaster angels had been affixed to the walls.

Alex, sensing they had come to where they were supposed to be, rapped on the door.

Again there was no response.

He raised the wooden latch, which was carved in the shape of a serpent, and stepped inside an enormous room with a vaulted ceiling. On the opposite wall were a number of small windows, zigzagging high and low. The morning sun had yet to reach them, so the room was a patchwork of pale light and shadows. It was bare of furniture, he saw, save for a narrow bed with a brass-work headboard. It was nearly center of the room, resting on a colorful handwoven carpet.

On the bed, unaware of them, Mr. Beadle lay on his back with a blanket covering him to his waist.

Diana grasped Alex's arm. "Oh dear God. What—?"

"Wait here." He went to the bed and looked down at two closed, sunken eyes and an ashen face. Mr. Beadle was struggling to breathe, wincing with each raspy gulp of air. Alex pulled off his gloves and put two fingers against Mr. Beadle's bony wrist. His skin was clammy. His pulse was irregular and weak.

Diana came to Alex's side. "Is he very bad?" she asked in a whisper.

Mr. Beadle's eyes flickered open. For a few moments he gazed blankly at the stone ceiling, his breath more labored than before.

"It will help if we raise him up," Alex said. "See if you can find pillows or blankets to put at his back."

"I'll hold him." She brushed the sparse, damp hair from Mr. Beadle's forehead. "Lift him for a moment, please."

While Alex held Mr. Beadle, Diana slipped onto the bed and wrapped her arms around him so that he was sitting with his back against her breasts. After only a short time, his breathing grew noticeably easier. Traces of color appeared on his cheeks and lips, and he gave a choked cough.

Alex passed Diana his handkerchief. "I'll see if there is water to be had. Will you be all right for a few minutes?"

She nodded, her attention focused on Mr. Beadle's face.

There was no distinct order in the house; as he had already learned. Alex wandered through a score of empty rooms before locating the primitive kitchen. It was sparsely equipped with a water pump, a scatter of dishes and pots on a small table, and a banked fire in the hearth. He filled a kettle with water, took the lone cup from the table, and made his way through the tangle of rooms in what he hoped was the right direction.

The chill of death hung in the air. He felt it as he had countless times before, that hushed twilight when flesh and spirit cling fiercely to life while death wrestles with them to claim its own.

His heart clenched. In the few weeks since they met, the peculiar old man had become a friend of sorts. They'd spent considerable time together, working in companionable silence, sometimes sharing a meal and tankers of ale at the Black Bull. It was a relaxing, undemanding comradeship between two men with nothing to say to each other, although Alex had always sensed that Mr. Beadle understood far more than he let on.

Recognizing a gargoyle he'd passed on the way to the kitchen, he took only one more wrong turn before arriving where he'd left Diana. She looked up with a faint smile when he entered the room.

"I think he's feeling better, Alex. Perhaps he can swallow a little water."

Dropping to one knee beside the cot, Alex filled the cup and raised it to Mr. Beadle's lips. This is futile, he was thinking just as a pair of faded brown eyes flickered open.

They took several moments to focus. Then, holding Alex's gaze steadily, Mr. Beadle sipped the water. When he was done, he sagged back against Diana's hold with a sigh.

"Th-thank you," he murmured.

Astonished, Alex nearly dropped the cup.

Mr. Beadle's white lips curved with amusement. "I d-didn't mean to startle you. B-but there's so little time. How does it go? I must s-speak now, or forever hold my peace."

Diana's eyes were round as dinner plates. "What can we do to help you, sir? Should Alex go for a physician, or—"

"No need. No n-need. This has happened before, you s-see, only not so bad. But I've been told what to expect, and here it is. Weak heart, I'm afraid. N-nothing to be done now."

When Diana looked poised to object, Alex shook his head in warning. He had seen it before, this last surge of energy and coherence before the body closed down. He'd sat with dying men and listened to them—sometimes for hours—because they must be allowed to say what they needed to say.

"Do you l-like my castle?" Mr. Beadle asked, a secret smile

in his eyes. "I hoped you would c-come here one day and see it. No one else ever has, you know."

"It is altogether splendid," Diana said. "I cannot imagine how you built such a wonder all by yourself."

Good girl, Alex thought.

"And you want to know why," Mr. Beadle said, resting his head against her shoulder. "There's no sense to it, most folk would say. N-not you, though. I saw it first time we met, the ambition to make something beautiful. 'Tis better your way, to do so with people, but I could work only with mortar and stones."

"But that's not at all the case, sir. You have helped us enormously."

"I have tried. Think of me when the regiment goes to the Michaelmas Fair. God willing, I shall contrive to be there with you in spirit." He coughed, and Alex gave him another drink of water. "Forgive me. You must look to the future, but my thoughts carry me into the past. And have you observed that my stammer has all but left me now? 'Tis proof that I have one foot in heaven. Or my tongue, at the very least. When a boy, I could not put three words together before everyone around me lost patience, and who could blame them? Often I became stuck on a single syllable, unable to leave it however much I tried. Had I addressed you then, you'd have heard Mrs. Va-Va-Va-Va-Va until I fled in shame."

"I'd have followed you, sir, to hear what you wished to say."

"I am sure of it. But my schoolfellows were less k-kind, in the way of boys who mock anyone chancing to be different. On my tenth birthday I resolved never to speak again in company, and I have kept to that vow these four-and-fifty years. That same day I left school, and my family as well, and apprenticed myself to a carpenter."

He fell silent then, and Diana shot Alex an anxious look.

"Will you tell us about your castle?" he asked softly.

"What?" Mr. Beadle murmured, as if awakened from a deep slumber. His brow furrowed with concentration. "Ah, yes. You see, one of the bullies—worse than all the others—lived in a large house that I passed each day on my way to school. It was unjust, I thought, for the likes of him to live in such a fine house, so I resolved to build an even finer one for myself. It was not

145

long after that I came upon this dale, and for many years I scavenged stones and t-tools and hid them here, awaiting the time I had saved enough money to purchase the land. When it was mine, I moved here and began to build. The castle will never be finished, of course. It was never meant to be. Were I to live a thousand years, I'd continue building, because it gives me pleasure." He smiled. "I call it Beadle's Folly."

A tear streaked down Diana's cheek. "I am sure it is the finest house in all of Lancashire," she said.

"There can be no other like it, that is true. As I laid stone upon stone I spoke to each one, telling it precisely where it fit and how important it was—even if it was a very little piece of rock in a p-place where it would never be seen. The stones were patient. They didn't mind that I stammered. And over the years, what with p-practicing every night, I learned to talk in almost a normal fashion."

His voice was growing perceptibly weaker, and his skin had taken on a faint bluish tone. Alex, keeping a close watch, reckoned it would not be much longer now. He wondered if Diana had been misled by what had taken place in the last few minutes. There was no hope, none at all. She ought to be warned, and prepared for what was to come. But how could he tell her while Mr. Beadle remained conscious to hear him?

"Why did you never speak with us?" she asked gently.

Mr. Beadle raised a trembling hand to cover her hand, the one that rested over his failing heart. "I had t-taken a vow. 'Twas only a foolish promise to myself, but I was ever a p-proud and stubborn man." He gave a ragged sigh. "If you will forgive me, perhaps God will grant His mercy as well."

"You may be sure of it." She brushed a kiss against his temple. "I love you dearly, Mr. Beadle. And I shall never forget you, or what you have taught me today."

"S-sleepy," he murmured, his eyes drifting closed. "But all is well. Ready." He raised his hand, making a vague gesture. "In th-there."

His hand fell onto his lap. He slumped against Diana, his head on her shoulder, his face turned in to her neck like a child gone to sleep in the arms of his mother. He still breathed, Alex saw, but he would not wake again.

Diana looked up, a question in her shimmering eyes.

"I don't know," he said, coming to his feet. "A few minutes, perhaps, but it could as easily be hours. You cannot remain any longer in that cramped position, Diana. Let us lower him onto the bed."

"No, please. He can stay as he is. I'm perfectly fine."

Alex rubbed his forehead. "He won't know the difference, my dear."

"You can't be sure of that. How can any of us guess what he knows and what he feels at such a time as this? He is *dying*, Alex. And he has had little enough of love in this world. Before he leaves it, I mean to give him all the love that I can."

Alex managed to nod before turning away, his eyes burning. This young girl, holding an old man in her arms and waiting for Death to take him from her, rendered him mute. He went to one of the windows, a small square with cast-off fragments of glass leaded together into a pane, and leaned his shoulder against the casement.

Bright morning sunshine poured over the grassy hillside and danced on the swiftly flowing stream that sliced through the narrow valley. Mosses and wildflowers huddled among the stones alongside the beck, and in the distance he saw a pair of small roe deer pick their way down the steep hill for a drink.

Diana had begun to sing. Soft and clear, the words of an old hymn floated in the air, and then another hymn, and another. She sang ballads, too, about knights and princesses in their castles, long intricate tales of honor and love—and death. She sang of it fearlessly, unafraid to draw it into the room.

After a while, Alex turned to look at her.

Still cradling the old man in her arms, she stroked the back of his head and gazed down at him with loving attentiveness, as if they were the only two people left in the world. From a score of arrow-slit windows set high in the walls, thin shafts of golden light poured over them from all directions, transforming the shabby brown blanket wrapped around Mr. Beadle to molten bronze. Diana's hair shone like a torch.

This was, Alex thought, the way every man would choose to die. He could ask no more than to be wrapped in the arms of a comforting woman, his last sight that of her beautiful face, her soft skin the last touch he feels, her fragrance in his nostrils, her soothing voice singing him to sleep.

An intruder in their intimate communion, he put his back to them and gazed out the window, seeing nothing. Mindless and empty of soul, he waited—as they all waited—for the arrival of one last visitor to Mr. Beadle's castle.

At some point, minutes or hours later, he became aware that Diana was no longer singing. The room was achingly still. He turned. She was looking at him, tears streaming down her face.

"I think he's gone, Alex."

He went to the cot. Mr. Beadle's brown eyes, open and fixed, stared past him into eternity.

Taking hold of his shoulders, Alex held him while Diana stood, staggering as blood rushed into her cramped legs. She grabbed Alex's forearm for a moment, using it to steady herself, and then moved out of the way.

He lowered Mr. Beadle's head onto the flat pillow and straightened the blanket over his lean body. "Good night, sweet prince," he murmured, using his thumbs to press the eyelids closed.

Diana came to stand beside him, wordless with grief. He opened his arms and she fell into them, burying her head against his shoulder and weeping soundlessly while he rubbed her back. It must surely pain her after so long a time supporting Mr. Beadle's weight.

Finally she gazed up at him from swollen eyes. "I've never seen anyone die before."

"And I've seen a great many. He felt no pain, my dear. You may be sure of it."

"I scarcely knew when it happened. He grew colder and colder, and after a while the sound of his breathing became a whisper, like feathers brushing together, and then I couldn't hear it at all."

Lifting her chin with the back of his hand, he gazed into her luminous eyes. "Because you came when most he needed you, he was able to tell you his story. He was proud that you had seen his castle and marveled at it. You gave him joy, Diana. Remember only that."

"Yes, I know he would not wish us to grieve for him. But I

can't help being a little weepy. He was such a loyal, generous friend. All the regiment ladies will miss him enormously. Well, perhaps not Mrs. Myrtle. For some reason, they never scratched along together."

"Is Mrs. Myrtle the one with saggy jowls? Looks like a basset hound and never stops talking?"

"Indeed she is. I'd have cashiered the old battle-ax long since, but we needed her horse and wagon to carry all the things that wouldn't fit into Mr. Beadle's pony cart. Besides, she makes the best jams and jellies in Lancashire." Diana chuckled. "This is a sorry discussion to be having, Alex."

"But one Mr. Beadle would appreciate." He drew her away from the cot. "I think we should be going now. The authorities will have to be notified, and there are arrangements to be made for his burial."

"I've been thinking on that. What do you suppose he meant at the end? He said, 'All is well. Ready.' Then he pointed—I could not tell where—and said, 'In there.' It must have meant something."

"Only that he was ready to die, I expect." Alex started for the door. "Come along now. We've much to do."

She held back, looking around the room. "He was trying to tell us . . . oh, I don't know what. But it was important. I'm sure of it."

Swallowing his impatience, Alex watched her go to one of several doors set into the walls of Mr. Beadle's bedchamber. It must have led to the privy, because she quickly pulled it closed again, her nose wrinkling as if she'd smelled an unpleasant odor, and went to a door set in the opposite wall.

"Come see this, Alex!"

He halted just inside the small room, looking around in amazement. The first thing he saw, directly center, was a plain wooden coffin with a shovel laid across the top. The coffin was recently constructed, he could tell by the tools and shavings and sawed-off planks piled at its side. Mr. Beadle, always precise in his habits, must have been too weak to clean up the mess.

Near the room's only window, he saw a chair and a small table with a number of items strewn across the top. Diana was standing next to it, holding a sheet of paper to the light, her head tilted as she read what was inscribed on it.

"He wrote a will, Alex. It's barely legible, though. Can you make out what he was trying to say?"

Alex took the paper and scanned the short paragraphs, scrawled in pencil by a shaky hand. It was a will, sure enough, and the provisions were few and simple. He translated them for Diana.

The parcel of land, the castle, the pony and cart, all his tools, and any other property of value were given to the regiment, to be sold or used however would best profit the new owners. His pocket watch, handed down through several generations of Beadles, was for Colonel Valliant. Mrs. Valliant was to have his mother's lace handkerchief and wedding ring. The hand-carved birds on the desk went to Miss Wigglesworth. There were several other tokens designated for regiment ladies he held in special regard.

His signature, unlike the rest, was written in bold, steady letters.

And there was a postscript, which made Alex laugh. The large cork on the desk, the one carved into the shape of a snarling dog, was Mr. Beadle's gift to Mrs. Myrtle. He hoped that some kindly soul would stuff it in her mouth.

"Oh my," Diana said when Alex was finished. Then, like him, she dissolved in laughter.

"A gallant gentleman, Mr. Beadle," Alex said when he recovered his voice. "He took his leave with one final jest. To be sure, he has been playing his games with us all along, pretending to be mute and forcing us to communicate with him by means of finger signs and gestures. When we tried to speak his language, *we* were the ones who stammered. He must have enjoyed that."

"Yes, indeed. How we underestimated him, though." Her expression grew sad again. "I should very much like to have known him better, Alex. If he had known I cared about him, if I had made the effort to convince him that I did, perhaps—"

"Hush, Diana. This serves no purpose. You were acquainted with Mr. Beadle for—what? Two or three months? Do you truly imagine you could have changed his life in so short a time? He

150

was thrice your age and more, long set in his ways, with no apparent wish to alter them. Would he be glad to think his legacy to you is one of regret? Honor his memory, my dear, but let him go in peace."

"You are right, I suppose." She emitted a grudging sigh. "And we did arrive in time. He was not left to die all alone."

Alex folded the will and put it in his pocket. "I'm not sure what is likely to become of his property, given that the will was not witnessed, but we shall make every effort to see his wishes carried out. Kendal will be the best judge how to proceed. For now, madam, please let us go."

"You go," she said. "Do whatever has to be done and fetch whoever has to be fetched. I'll wait with Mr. Beadle until they come."

Recognizing that mutinous glint in her eyes, he braced himself for battle. "You cannot stay here alone, Diana. I'll not permit it."

"And I won't leave him here by himself. It's out of the question. Animals might come down from the hills and get at him."

He reminded himself that she was overset and mourning a friend. "We'll secure the doors," he said in a calm voice, "and check all the windows before we leave."

"Well and good. But this is an odd sort of dwelling. He built rooms and left them empty when he moved on to build others. What if there are rats? Can you say there are none? And I've seen any number of spiders already."

The man is *dead*, Alex thought, his frustration mounting. Worms would be at Mr. Beadle soon enough. Visions of twisted bodies scattered across the arid Spanish landscape rushed by him. Bodies piled high in the breach at Badajoz. Bodies tossed into a common pit with lime shoveled over them, left behind as the army marched to the next deadly objective. Sweat broke out on his forehead. He closed his eyes, willing the ghosts away.

"This once," he said, forcing the words past a clogged throat, "you must obey me."

"I'm sorry, sir." She wrapped her arms around her waist, looking only a little more determined than frightened. "Even if it makes you angry, I will not go."

"How then if we put him on the pony cart and take him out with us?"

"We'd only have to bring him back again. Don't you see? He wanted to be buried here, on his own land. He left the coffin." She went to it and picked up the spade. "He left this as well, and we are meant to use it. What could be more clear?"

"You think we ought to plant him now and be done with it? Confound it, Diana, there are laws regarding the disposition of bodies. It's possible an inquest will be required."

"I care nothing for any of that. Mr. Beadle's last request must surely take precedence." Shovel in hand, she marched to the door. "If you won't dig his grave, Alex, *I* will."

No longer surprised to find himself outmatched, he snatched the shovel away and ordered her to select a burial site.

As if by instinct, she went directly to a spot overlooking the castle, a small piece of nearly level ground where a low hill folded into a steeper one. They'd have the devil of a time carting Mr. Beadle such a distance, Alex thought, but he peeled off his coat and set to work.

It was damnably *hot* work under the noonday sun. The rocky ground resisted him at every dig of the spade, but he carefully set aside the rocks he dug up. Later, he would pile them atop the grave to keep it free of predators.

Diana had returned to the castle. To defend Mr. Beadle from the rats, he presumed, driving into the soil with a too familiar motion. Even colonels dug their share of graves when the army was on the move. He had done so, at any rate, rather than leave a single man of the 44th to the scavengers.

When the hole was chest high, he struck a shelf of limestone and knew he could go no deeper. Another few minutes of work leveled the grave, and by the time he climbed out, he had devised a plan to bring Mr. Beadle up the hill.

Two long poles were located near the scaffolding on the other side of the castle where Mr. Beadle had been constructing a round tower. Alex attached a blanket to them. With Diana's help, he lifted Mr. Beadle into the coffin, nailed it shut, and set it on the blanket. He'd thought to use the pony, but it proved impossible to secure the poles to the animal without causing it discomfort. In the end, he took hold of one pole while Diana grappled the other, and together they towed the coffin from the castle, along the narrow track alongside the beck, and finally up the steep slope to where the grave lay open.

Carefully they tilted the poles, and the coffin slid down into the shallow grave, the sound of it like a long sweet sigh in the still afternoon.

Stooping, Diana took a handful of dirt and sprinkled it over the coffin. "Good-bye, Mr. Beadle," she whispered. "And thank you. You have taught me that all things are possible."

Chapter 15

When Alex had broached the idea of a picnic with Mrs. Jellicoe, one of the few regiment ladies who did not walk in fear of him, she had leapt on it immediately. A celebration was certainly in order, she'd informed him. Only a handful of women would be going to the Michaelmas Fair, which had left the others feeling a bit let down.

They planned a gala event to include the regiment, any menfolk still in residence with their families, and a great number of children. Alex had been given little to do, practically speaking. He'd provided barrels of ice for lemonade, kegs of ale, and brought in ponies for the children to ride. The ladies had supplied enough food to feed three regiments, and the Yoodle sisters had been charged with creating a gift for Diana.

That had been his idea as well. He had even sketched out the design, and naturally he purchased the materials. Shortly before the picnic had got under way, Alice Yoodle, fluttering with excitement, had showed him the results. It was, he'd assured her sincerely, a masterpiece.

Alex asked only for the sight he was now gazing upon—Diana, moving from group to group, *not* wearing her veiled bonnet and clearly enjoying herself. He was standing apart from the others, leaning against an oak tree about halfway up a grassy hillside. It was a good spot from which to observe the grand presentation, which looked about to begin.

Mr. Pottle, who had lost an arm at Waterloo, blew a discordant tattoo on his battered cornet. The picnickers gathered around, and Mrs. Jellicoe led Diana to a knoll where everyone could see her.

"I won't make no speeches," Mrs. Jellicoe shouted.

The crowd cheered its approval.

"Oh, stubble it, you lot! We've all of us worked hard, and day after tomorrow, we'll finally get paid for what we done."

More cheers and a few catcalls. Alex began to regret supplying such a large quantity of ale.

"Most of us got regular work now," Mrs. Jellicoe persisted. "Some is raising pigs and some is making pencils and some is doin' other things. But we'd all be in the same dark place we was if Mrs. Valliant hadn't put her spurs to us. She don't want our thanks, but we mean to give it anyway. Come up here, Yoodles, and show what you made for her."

The Yoodle sisters, rigged out in all their finery, made a procession of it as they mounted the knoll. The crowd fell silent as Gladys Yoodle, her arms full of something shiny and colorful, curtsied to Diana and put something into her hand. It was the end of a thin rope, Alex thought, not expecting this development. Slowly Miss Yoodle retreated down the hill, and as she did, the rope unraveled to disclose dozens of fluttering triangular flags—red and yellow and green—attached to it.

"These will wave atop our booth at the fair," Mrs. Jellicoe announced to oohs and aahs from the crowd. "And from every booth at every fair we go to from here on out."

Alice Yoodle stepped forward then, her face more crimson than the scarlet flags rippling from her sister's rope. Gently, she set the folded bundle she carried into Diana's arms.

Alex suddenly wanted to be standing closer, where he could better see his wife's face as Mrs. Jellicoe helped her unfold the banner. Together they held it up. A hush fell over the crowd.

Against a background of white satin, a golden bolt of lightning streaked from corner to corner, cutting the banner into two triangles. In the upper triangle was a blue castle—a tribute to Mr. Beadle—and in the lower triangle, by Alex's command, a green bow and arrow, the symbol of Diana the Huntress. At the very bottom corner, invisible unless one came very close, Alice Yoodle had embroidered a small pink piglet.

"The Regimental Colors," Mrs. Jellicoe announced with evident pride.

The audience broke into wild applause, giving three cheers for Diana and three more for themselves. Then a fiddler struck up a tune and people began to dance, mothers with children or with their husbands, children with other children, and spinster ladies with whoever was to hand.

Alex turned away and wiped his sleeve over his eyes, which had unaccountably watered at the sight. He wished Diana were with him now. Wished she did not belong more to these people than to him. It was a selfish wish, but dammit, he needed her more than they did.

When he looked back again, done with his repugnant bout of self-pity, he saw that someone had tied the rope of pennants between two trees. Someone else had mounted the banner atop a tall pole, which someone had thought to provide. All these splendid people, doing wonderful things while he stood alone and useless.

Perhaps he wasn't fully recovered after all. But when was it he had started feeling sorry for himself? It was so out of character, at least out of the character he'd always assumed he possessed, that he could not begin to explain it. Still, he was most assuredly envious of the regiment ladies who absorbed so much of Diana's attention. And were he perfectly honest with himself, he'd sometimes been jealous of Dinner. A *pig*, for pity's sake. How low could a man sink?

Diana had separated herself from the others and was making her way up the hill to where he stood, her face flushed with pleasure. "You arranged all this," she said. "I knew it the moment I saw the pig on the banner."

He shrugged. "I made a few suggestions, no more than that. The ladies did all the work."

"Very well, sir, have it your way. But we both know better, don't we?" She came to his side and gazed down at the rollicking dancers. "I still cannot believe that we've done it. Look at them, Alex. They have accomplished so much in only a few months. I am so very proud of them."

"Reserve more than a little of that pride for yourself, madam. This was all very much your doing."

"I regret to inform you, sir, that I am *insufferably* proud of myself. True, I ruined two entire batches of ratafia, created rosewater that smells like vinegar, and produced a freckle cream that turns one's skin alarming yellow. But so long as I didn't actually *do* anything, I did very well indeed."

"Admirably." He watched her pluck a sprig of heather and thread it behind her ear. "You have a gift for leadership, Colonel Valliant."

"If you continue in this fashion," she said with a laugh, "you will make me quite full of myself. Shall we walk up to where all those wildflowers are growing? They must be the last before autumn sets in. Oh my. Harebells! How lovely."

He trailed a little behind her as she went from flower to flower, collecting a bouquet and humming along with the distant music. How graceful she was, he thought. How unutterably lovely with her green skirts flowing around her legs and her glorious hair loose about her shoulders.

She looked over at him. "Tell me something, Alex. Do you believe in Destiny?"

"Only that which we create for ourselves." He saw a tiny frown come and go on her brow. "Did you wish me to say otherwise?"

"Not at all. I only wondered what you thought on the subject. Miss Wigglesworth is persuaded that we inevitably end up with what is best for us, no matter that we may have wanted something else entirely." She paused to look down the hill again. "I can scarcely credit that in two more days it will all be over."

"How so? When Michaelmas Fair is passed, will you not begin preparations for another fair? I'd have expected you to set to work the very next day."

"*They* will, I am sure. But it is time for me to withdraw and leave them to proceed on their own. Oh, the natural leaders among them will provide direction and order, but I should not want them to become dependent upon anyone—least of all me."

"Understandable. But I fail to see why you must entirely separate yourself from their enterprises. Unless that is your wish, of course."

"It's they who wish it, Alex." She went to a patch of daisies, adding a few to her bouquet. "I know they are fond of me, and of you as well. But most of them were greatly relieved when the classes at Lakeview drew to an end. They felt out of place in the home of an aristocrat, and so they were. Surely you have been aware of their discomfort?"

He'd assumed they were only uncomfortable in *his* company. "How does it signify?" he asked. "You are perfectly at ease with them. You even left off wearing that pernicious veil in their presence."

"I fairly well had to, after all but setting it on fire a dozen times while working near the fireplace. But that is nothing to the point. The regiment will march on without me, Alex. I am firmly resolved to sell out."

"By all means, madam, if you think it best. But I cannot imagine you content to remain idly at Lakeview while others continue on with what you began."

"Nor can I," she said, her expression becoming somber. "It would be intolerable. Will you sit with me for a few minutes, sir? There is something I have long wished to discuss with you."

The blow was so unexpected that it rocked him on his heels. She meant to leave him!

What else could it be? Staying, she had said, would be *intolerable*. And he'd told her that he would not prevent her, should she ever decide to go. Not that he imagined she actually would, of course. How could the shy, naive girl he had married get on in the world by herself?

Now he knew. She would go on very well indeed. He had seen the proof of it.

She went gracefully to her knees beside him and sat back on her heels, flowers spilling over her skirts. When he continued to stand there like a post, she selected a daisy and held it out to him. "Please, Alex?"

His legs melting under him, he sagged to the ground and drew up his knees, folding his arms across them.

She put the daisy into his hand. "I have been thinking on this for a considerable time, but feared to address the subject because I expect you will disapprove. Still, I don't believe I shall ever feel braver than I do today, so I may as well leap into the fire. You see, during the last few months I have learned a number of things about myself. Not all of them to my credit, certainly, but I don't appear to be quite so helpless as I used to think I was. Well, as I *was*, actually."

Say it and be done! he thought, cold needles digging into his spine.

"The thing is," she said, "I require something useful to do. And while I've no idea as yet what that will turn out to be, I'm fairly sure I cannot do it here."

His hand fisted, crushing the flower she had given him. "You wish to leave, then."

"Well, yes." She looked surprised that he had grasped the obvious. "This is a small community, and you have met what passes for gentry in Coniston. What's more, Mrs. Alcorn has done everything in her power to set them against me. And Lakeview is a very small estate. I know you mean to develop the land, but Mr. Beadle once told me it was good only for sheep, and truly, I cannot see myself as a shepherdess. If you *want* to run sheep, then of course you must, although—"

"Enough!" The thin thread of his control had snapped. "Will you come to the point, madam?"

She paled. "Yes. I'm sorry. I invariably dither when I'm nervous. And now I'm doing it again. Oh, drat." Her hands twisted on her lap. "Alex, would you mind terribly much if we didn't remain at Lakeview? If we moved somewhere else?"

All the breath rushed out of him. We. She had said *we*! "To where?" he managed to ask, not that it mattered. So long as she stayed with him, the moon would suit him sublimely.

"I haven't thought so far ahead," she admitted. "We should make that decision together, don't you agree?"

We again. That was rapidly becoming his favorite word. "I've no objection," he said, knowing he sounded curt. Relief had clogged his brain and stiffened his tongue. "Lakeview will have to be sold, of course. And there's no telling how long it will take, given the poor condition of the house and the relative worthlessness of the land. I don't expect we'll be able to relocate for a considerable time."

"Why so?" She plucked the petals from a harebell. "We needn't remain there while it's on the market. And truly, Alex, I don't think you should sell it at all. The house was willed you by your grandmother, was it not? It ought to remain in the family.

159

Miss Wigglesworth could live there as caretaker. I know she'd like to continue working with the regiment, at least for a while."

He finally began to see where she was headed. Damn! A few moments ago, when he thought he had already lost her, he'd have severed both his legs to get her back again. The last thing in creation he wanted to do was stand against her now. But if they were to stay together, it had to be on his terms. He would not live on her money. He *could* not.

"Unless I sell Lakeview," he said, "I cannot provide you another home."

She met his gaze steadily. "You would have me always dependent on you, then?"

"Yes." He sensed the ground crumbling under his feet. "Financially, I mean."

"Might I ask to what purpose?"

"We have had this conversation before, madam. You understand well enough."

"I'm afraid that I do. But let me ask you this, Alex. Why should the fortune I brought to the marriage, the fortune you now control, sit idly in the three percents when we could make such good use of it? Why must we scrape by on an officer's half pay when we could build something together and pass it on to our children? Wouldn't you rather give them a flourishing estate or a thriving business than a bank account?"

"Business? You would have me go into *trade*?"

"I would see you occupied, sir. It matters not what you do, so long as it gives you pleasure and a sense of accomplishment. You can no more be idle than I. And as there is no war for you to fight, you must find another way to use your abilities and challenge your spirit. Taking root at Lakeview simply because you own it is no solution. You did not even buy the house yourself. You did not earn it. It was *given* you."

He was sinking rapidly, clinging to the shreds of his pride with his fingernails. And she met him with equal pride, even though her hands were trembling and she had gone alarmingly pale. Despite the strength she had discovered in herself, the confidence that had begun to grow in her, Diana remained inordinately fearful. But she defied him anyway, this astonishing young woman he had taken to wife.

At the protracted silence, her gaze lowered. "It appears that I have your answer, sir. And I must accept it, because I took a vow to obey you. But while I cannot promise I won't keep trying to change your mind, I *will* try very hard not to be a nagging wife. That's the best I can do, I'm afraid." She stood, flowers tumbling from her skirts. "Shall we return to the picnic?"

"Wait." He clambered to unsteady feet. Courage and fear were so carefully balanced in her now that he could crush her in an instant. He didn't want that much power over her. He wondered what she would do if she realized how much power she wielded over him. Hesitantly he placed a hand on her shoulder, searching for words to bridge the chasm he had opened between them. "Diana."

She gazed up at him, her beautiful eyes shimmering with tears. Sunlight washed over her face and lit her hair to fire. And he knew, there *were* no words, and bent his head to touch his lips to hers.

It was the lightest of kisses. He expected her to end it, to turn her head or step away. But she swayed into him, soft and supple and yielding, her arms at her sides and her breasts against his chest and her mouth against his mouth.

Wrapping his arms around her, he deepened the kiss. He felt her welcome it, felt his body surge with desire for her.

She raised a hand and threaded her fingers through his hair, drawing him even closer. He tasted her desire then, all the lush feminine sensuality banked inside her until this moment now suddenly ablaze. And like to incinerate them both, he thought dizzily, unless one of them put a stop to it before he carried her down onto the grass and made love to her in full view of the regiment. And the children. *Damn.*

Willing control into flesh that was all but beyond it, he lifted his head, seized a ragged breath, and gently set her away.

She gave him a stunned, heartbroken look. "D-did I do it wrong?" she asked into the shivering silence. "I've not been kissed before. I'm s-sure I could learn to do it better."

"I—" He made a vague gesture in the direction of the picnickers.

"Oh." Her face brightened. "Too many witnesses. Is that why you stopped?"

He nodded.

"Thank heavens. I have waited so long for you to kiss me. I thought you never would. Except for when I was afraid you would, and then not like it, and never want do it again."

"You needn't ever worry about that," he assured her, aching to do it again this very moment. He held her gaze. "I want to do a great deal more, Diana."

Her lips curved. "Yes, please."

Just like that. Yes. Well, she always said yes. She had said it on their wedding night. But she had never said *please*. And when he kissed her, she had opened herself to him and passion had flowed out from her. Hot waves of passion. He felt them even now, although she was standing an arm's length away and touching him only with her smile.

"Tonight, then," he said.

"Tonight." She glanced up at the sky. "Go away, sun. Will this day *never* end?"

Bewildered, he watched her scoop up handfuls of flowers and toss them over his head. A sprig of heather slid down his forehead and came to rest on his nose. He examined it cross-eyed. Was he dreaming all this? She was dancing around him, scattering flowers and laughing. Were they both gone mad?

"Cheer up, sir." She plucked the heather from his nose. "I'm the one supposed to be skittish and shy. To look at your face, one would think *you* were the virgin here."

He cleared his throat. "I had not expected you to be so . . . so eager, madam."

"Well, I am. And I have been for a good long time. I'm very much afraid that you have married a wanton, sir." She fluttered her lashes. "Will that be a problem, do you suppose?"

By Jove, she was *flirting* with him. No. *Flirting* was not the word. His shy schoolgirl bride was openly seducing him. She was a sliver away from *ravishing* him.

He must have died and gone to heaven.

She tilted her head. "Do you know, not counting when you kiss me, I like it above all things when you smile. And I wish you would not measure out your kisses and your smiles like a

162

miser, Alex. I want lots and lots of both." Laughing, she twirled away again. "Gracious, just listen to me. I cannot believe I am saying such things. I must be a good deal braver than I ever imagined."

He could not mistake the low note of fear in her voice. The vulnerability. She had daringly offered herself, all of herself, while he continued to stand like a granite monolith. And still, as always, she took care to keep her scarred cheek turned away from him. Dear God.

He must find a way to make her understand that he never saw it when he looked at her. Well, yes, he did. But it was part of her, as lovely in his eyes as all the rest of her. In a way, it had given her into his hands. Without the scar, she would have felt free to dance in London ballrooms instead of here, on this hillside, with only a tongue-tied soldier to watch her with painful longing. She would have found a better man than Alex Valliant to marry.

He treasured that scar. He wished desperately that she did not regard it with such shame, but she did. She thought herself no longer beautiful and would go on thinking so, he feared, for a very long time. His eyes burned. Catching her hand as she danced playfully by him, he drew her close for another deep, breathtaking kiss.

Tonight, he thought. Tonight he would tell her what he had known since they went together to Keswick, and what had probably been true since a long time before that. Tonight, when he made her his wife in more than name, he would tell her that he loved her.

Chapter 16

Coniston Water lay smooth and still, the color of molten brass as the setting sun hovered over the western fells. Fingers of light painted the cloud-streaked sky pink and amber and gold.

Diana's heart was singing as she rode beside Alex on the way home. Although they hadn't spoken since leaving the picnic, she felt him reaching out to her. Their silent understanding curled her toes and set the ends of her hair on fire.

The last two hours had seemed to her an eternity. They had rejoined the others, taking care to single out each member of the regiment for special attention. Although Diana never said so, she was bidding them farewell. And she had wondered, as she chatted with Annie Jellicoe and Meggie Doyle and all the loyal soldiers, if they had seen her with Alex on the hillside. If they had seen her kissing him.

Well, what if they had? He was her husband, after all, and had been so for nearly five months. They could not possibly imagine it was the first time he had ever kissed her. But she'd felt the heat of embarrassment in her cheeks, and a greater heat elsewhere in her body, as she'd sampled the homemade wines and eaten lightly from the lavish picnic baskets.

When Alex had finally taken her arm and led her to where their horses were tethered and lifted her onto the saddle, she had felt as if her life were about to begin.

"What the devil is that?" Alex said when they made the turn from the road.

She looked where he was pointing and saw a carriage drawn up in front of the Lakeview stable, the crest of the Earl of Kendal emblazoned on its lacquered doors. "Oh, dear," she said, giving him a rueful smile. "It appears that we have guests."

They had left their horses at the stable and were approaching the front door when it sprang open and Kit Valliant stepped out, his arm wrapped around his wife's slender waist.

He gave Alex a reproachful look. "Past time you ambled home, old lad. Lucy and I had about decided you were avoiding us."

"Need I point out that you were not expected?" Alex went to him and shook his hand. "It's been a long time, Kit."

"Six years, I do believe. But as you see, I'm still a handsome devil. And Kendal tells me you've had the uncommon good sense to marry yon fair lady. Hullo, Diana." He gave her an exaggerated wink. "I was of a mind to marry her myself, but Lucy wouldn't let me. Snapped a shackle on m'leg while I wasn't looking."

"Twaddle." Lucy separated herself from her incorrigible spouse and curtsied to Alex. "I am pleased to meet you, sir."

He bowed. "And I am in your debt, madam. You are responsible, I am told, for rescuing Diana from her guardian."

"Ahem." Kit looked offended. "I played no small part in that adventure."

Laughing, Diana swept them all into the downstairs parlor. Of all the days for her two best friends to drop out of the blue! But here they were, and she expected that the brothers would like some private time to become reacquainted. "Shall I make us a pot of tea?" she offered with a nod at Lucy, who took her meaning instantly.

"May I join you?" she asked, already on her way to the door.

"Uh-oh." Kit waggled his brows at Alex. "The ladies want to be alone. Think they mean to talk about us?"

"Only when we have exhausted every subject of real interest," Lucy informed him as she flounced from the room.

"I think we've been insulted, old man." Kit flopped onto a wingback chair. "Any chance the Lakeview cellar runs to a decent bottle of wine?"

"I may have just the thing," Alex said. "Diana, you know the one I mean."

She was rather afraid that she did.

Lucy was waiting for her a short distance down the passageway, her gray eyes alight with curiosity. "My heavens," she said, pulling Diana into a warm hug. "I have come home to find that we are *sisters*! Kendal told us how it all came about, of course, but I must have the story from you. Men invariably leave out the best parts."

She would be leaving them out as well, Diana was fairly certain. Not even to Lucy could she open her heart on the subject of her marriage. "Of course," she said, detaching herself before sentiment got the better of her. "I'm so glad you are home. I have missed you prodigiously."

"And I have worried about you constantly. But to no purpose, it seems. How extraordinary that Alex should return to England precisely when you found yourself in need of him."

"Yes. A remarkable coincidence, although Miss Wigglesworth insists on calling it Destiny. But never mind all that. I wish to hear about your wedding trip."

"No, no. I shall leave Kit to tell the tale. He is far more entertaining. I do have news to share, though, probably the same news he is giving Alex at this very moment." Smiling, she patted her stomach.

"Oh, Lucy!" Diana stepped back for a better look. "But are you certain? You are slim as a whippet. How can you tell?"

"The signs are unmistakable. I lose my breakfast every morning, I've missed my courses three times, and blessed be heaven, my breasts are expanding. Needless to say, Kit is especially pleased with that development. Mind you, when first I suspected, I dared not believe it for the longest time. He so wants children, and I knew how disappointed he would be if I told him and then proved to be wrong. But now a physician has confirmed the pregnancy, and Kit is strutting around like the veriest rooster."

"I'm so pleased for you both," Diana said sincerely. And more than a little envious, although she could hardly say so.

Lucy regarded her searchingly. "You asked how I could tell. Does that mean you have been experiencing—"

"Nothing of the sort! No indeed. I was merely curious. I assure you that I have experienced nothing whatever." Heat rose to her face as she realized what she had just said.

Lucy appeared to take no notice. "He is astoundingly handsome, your Alex. I was quite taken aback when I saw him."

"Yes. I feel much that way each time I see him. But to be perfectly honest, I could wish he were not so . . . well-favored. It makes it all the more difficult."

"Because of this." Lucy brushed her fingertip against Diana's scar. "Will you ever understand that it is of no consequence?"

"Understanding, I have learned, has very little to do with how I feel." She sighed. "I do try, you know. I tell myself a thousand times a day that it doesn't matter. Sometimes I can forget it ten whole minutes at a stretch. But the moment I go into company, the instant someone stares at me or makes an effort *not* to stare, I become a giant scar atop a pair of quaking legs. And if I am standing near to Alex, the effect is multiplied beyond accounting. How could so handsome a man have married such an antidote? they are thinking. I know they are. How could they not?"

"The real question," Lucy said reprovingly, "is why do you care what they think? You tie yourself in knots, Diana, worrying over the possible thoughts and impressions of people who mean absolutely nothing to you. Clearly Alex takes no mind of your scar, and surely his is the only opinion that signifies."

"You are right, of course." She had nearly spoiled their reunion by raising a subject better left alone. "Pay me no mind, Lucy. I grow braver day by day. I shall come about."

"Yes, my sweet, I am sure of it. Now, where is the kitchen?"

Mrs. Cleese threw up her hands when they appeared at the door. "What am I to do?" she exclaimed. "Guests for dinner and no one to help. I cannot prepare a meal and set the table and serve the food all by myself!"

"It was unforgivable of us to descend on you in such a fashion," Lucy said. "You must not put yourself out on our account. Cold meats, cheese, bread, whatever you can toss together will suit us perfectly well."

Diana knew she ought to take charge of her own kitchen and servant, but Mrs. Cleese had always been so temperamental. She left it to Miss Wigglesworth, and now to Lucy, to put her cook in order. Feeling chickenhearted, she busied herself measuring tea and laying out cups and saucers.

Carver and Betsy arrived just when she was about to lift the heavy kettle from the hook over the fireplace. They were arm in arm, she noticed, although Carver quickly let go of the maid to help with the kettle.

Diana turned to Betsy, who looked a trifle starry-eyed. "We have company for the night," she said. "Lay a fire in the Blue Chamber, please, and put fresh linens on the bed. Well, you know what to do. And then you may retire, for I'll not be needing you this evening." Because I'll be spending the night with my husband, she thought with a shiver of anticipation. Sooner or later, they would contrive to be alone together.

While Carver finished preparing the tea tray, she went to the pantry in search of wine, really hoping she would not find the sort Alex had in mind. But there was one last bottle, so with some reluctance she carried it, along with a bottle of brandy for Alex, to the parlor. Lucy brought glasses, and Carver followed with the tray.

"They have dissected us into little pieces," Kit told Alex mournfully as the ladies entered the room. "They have measured out our faults, plucked our imperfections to the bone, and concluded that we are worthless fellows."

"Indeed we have," Lucy affirmed. "And you may as well know, Kit, that Alex came off significantly better than you did."

"I am delighted to hear it," Alex said, taking the wine bottle from Diana's hand. "And not in the least surprised."

She watched in some dismay as he removed the cork.

"I don't suppose," Lucy said, "that you gentlemen came around to discussing your beloved wives?"

"Only to praise your charms," Kit shot back with a grin. "And you may as well know, Lucy mine, that Diana came off a great deal better than you did."

Laughing, Lucy drew up a tapestry stool and sat at his knee. "But it is so much easier for Diana to be charming, my love, for she hasn't to put up with the likes of you."

Kit ruffled her short, pearl-colored hair. "I was just about to explain to Alex how it is we are here. He is far too civil to ask, of course, even though he has given me the distinct impression that he wishes us to the devil."

"You are not so dull-witted as I have always believed," Alex said, handing his brother a glass of yellowish wine. "Since Diana and I are expected at Candale tomorrow morning, I wonder than you did not wait to greet us there."

Kit swirled the wine in his glass before taking a sniff. His nose wrinkled. He sniffed again.

Diana watched apprehensively. Kit was inordinately fond of good wine, she knew. He had been smuggling a load of French contraband across Morecambe Bay when robbers accosted him, put a bullet in his shoulder, and made off with the booty. His compatriots had fled, leaving him to bleed to death or drown. He was alive only because Lucy had seen the encounter and brought him to shore.

Destiny. A miracle. Or amazingly good luck. Who could say, except that the results were unquestionably for the best. She glanced at Alex, who looked singularly pleased when Kit raised the glass to his lips and drank.

"B-bloody hell!" he sputtered. "What in Lucifer *is* this swill?"

"Vintage parsnip," Alex said with satisfaction. "I knew you'd like it."

"*Parsnip?* Good Lord." Kit took another sip. "Not bad, really. Not what I was expecting at first taste, but it has a kick to it."

Alex chuckled. "Look to your chest, halfling. Diana assures me that parsnip wine will grow hair."

"I've hair aplenty, thank you very much." Kit drained the glass and held it out for a refill.

Lucy rolled her eyes. *Men!* her expression said.

Evidently Kit would down the entire bottle of parsnip wine before admitting he disliked it. But brothers, Diana thought, must always be rivals of a sort. She'd too little experience with men to know how they behaved on a regular basis, but these two appeared to be enjoying their squabble. She was glad of it. Alex was overly somber by nature, and Kit could wring laughter from a stone. Already he had got Alex to play something of a practical joke on him.

"As I was saying," Kit remarked pointedly, "we didn't set out to call on you. But it seemed foolish not to drop by when we were so close. Who was to guess you'd be off at a picnic?"

"We were close," Lucy explained, "because we had decided to have a look at Kit's cottage in Hawkshead and see if it would suit us. I don't wish to remain overlong at Candale."

"She's scared of Kendal," Kit said, grinning.

Diana knew precisely how she felt. Lord Kendal was invariably kind, but one always felt the need to walk on tiptoes in his presence. She certainly did. Until this very afternoon, when Alex kissed her, she had felt much the same in *his* company.

"Nonsense!" Lucy slapped Kit's knee. "Deranged creature that I am, I simply want a home of my own. The cottage is small and somewhat drafty, but it will do well enough for now."

Alex poured himself a glass of brandy. "As it happens," he said with a darting glance at Diana, "Lakeview will soon be in need of tenants. You might consider taking residence here."

Diana's heart jumped about in her chest. Gracious! Alex was telling her, in sideways fashion, that he had agreed to move elsewhere. She had forgot, when he kissed her, what they had been discussing beforehand. But he remembered, and now he was giving her his answer.

"You're not staying here?" Kit's brows shot up. "Why ever not? Where will you live?"

"Slow down, Kit. We're not gone yet." Alex smiled at Diana. "We mean to look for a house with more land attached. I have some thought to raising horses, and since I married an excellent horsewoman, it seems the logical thing to do. But no decisions have been made, except that we will move from here. You are welcome to Lakeview, rent-free, so long as you allow Miss Wigglesworth to remain if she wishes to."

"No rent? Did you hear that, Lucy? I won't have to sell you to the Gypsies after all."

Before Lucy could respond, Betsy appeared to announce that supper was laid out. They trooped to the dining room then, and later returned to the parlor for tea, Kit regaling them all the while with improbable stories about the wedding trip. There were a great many of them, since he and Lucy had traveled the better part of a year. Once the children started popping out, he explained with a grin at his wife, there would be no more gallivanting about.

Alex sat close by Diana on a sofa, not touching her, although it felt as if he were. She listened to Kit, and laughed in all the right places, but her mind was far away. Well, not too far. Only up the stairs, in Alex's bedchamber, and she could hardly wait for the rest of her to join it there.

Finally Lucy gave a pointed yawn and tugged at Kit's sleeve. "That's enough, my love. You've started telling tales about places we never even went to. And we must all make an early start of it in the morning."

"Oh, right. The fair." Kit stood, stretching broadly. "Well, we'll toddle off now. Where to?"

Diana jumped to her feet. "I'll show you the way. Alex, will you extinguish the lights? I told the servants they could retire early, since they were half asleep anyway after the picnic."

"Go along," he said, his eyes heated. "I'll join you in a few minutes."

"Lucifer! I nearly forgot. Alex, when we were in London a fortnight ago, I ran into a friend of yours." Kit looked over at Lucy. "What was his name, moonbeam?"

"Are you speaking of Lord Blair?"

"That's the fellow. It seems he's about to tie the knot, poor sod, and is relying on Colonel Valliant to stand at his side and hold him steady. The wedding is—let me think. Well, I've got it written down somewhere. I'll give you the particulars when we get to Candale. No more than a week from now, I'm fairly sure, and he said all the chaps will be there. I presume you know who he means."

"Yes," Alex said shortly. "I know."

Diana looked at him with alarm. The color had washed from his face, and he'd gone stiff as a board. The others seemed unaware of it, but she knew that something terrible had just occurred. He had gone away from them, and from her, as surely as if he'd taken himself to the far side of the moon.

Kit was already at the door, his arm around Lucy's waist. "Coming, Diana?"

"Y-yes." With one last glance at Alex, who was staring fixedly into nowhere, she led them upstairs. Miss Wigglesworth must have stolen in and gone to her bed, because her snore could be heard as they passed her room.

Kit raised an eyebrow. "I hope we're not right next door."

"No. Clear the way down." She showed Kit and Lucy to the Blue Bedchamber, assured herself that Betsy had arranged everything they required to be comfortable, and bid them good night.

Once in the passageway again, she couldn't decide where she ought to go. Downstairs, to find out from Alex what had overset him? To his bedroom, to wait for him? Or to hers, hoping he would come and get her?

Fear made her weak as she stood indecisively for several moments. She could hear Kit and Lucy bantering as they readied themselves for bed, and the distant rumble of Miss Wigglesworth's snore. Finally she went to her own room and sank down on the edge of the bed. It had all gone terribly wrong, and she had no idea why. Something to do with Lord Blair, of course, but how could an invitation to a wedding be of such grave consequence?

Wild thoughts skipped about in her head. Could Alex have once been in love with Lord Blair's wife-to-be? She had no reason to think so, but it was the only explanation that made the slightest sense. Well, unless he had some other quarrel with Blair, or with the "chaps."

After what seemed a long time, she heard a light tap on her door. He stepped inside without waiting for her to admit him, his face still shadowed and his eyes distant. He leaned against the closed door and folded his arms.

"I'm sorry, Diana," he said.

She knew what he meant, of course. Her eyes blurred with tears. "Will you tell me why?"

"No."

Well, she had expected that, too. But he had spoken gently this time, unlike the other occasions when he'd fended off her questions. "Very well, sir. I'll not ask you again."

"It has nothing to do with you, I promise. Nothing to do with *us*." He swiped his fingers through his hair. "It is not even of any great import, except that it has stirred up memories that would come between us when nothing should. I want you to have all my attention, Diana, when we make love. You would not have it tonight."

"Yes. I know." She pulled herself from the bed and went to

172

him, hearing the regret in his voice. Seeing the sorrow in his eyes just before he opened his arms to embrace her.

"Soon," he whispered, his breath soft against her cheek. "When the fair is over, when I have come to my senses again, we shall take up where we left off this afternoon. I want nothing more, I swear, than to be with you."

She lifted her gaze. "We may become lovers, Alex. I want that as well. But we will never truly be together while you keep so much of yourself hidden from me. Will it always be this way?"

"I honestly don't know," he said after a moment. "But I will try to give you what you want. Not now, certainly, and perhaps not very soon. As for tonight, I shall do far better left to myself."

He was too much alone, she thought. But neither could she force her company on him. "After the fair, then." She stood on tiptoe and brushed a kiss on his cold cheek. "When I am rid of my ladies, we shall contrive together to rid you of your ghosts."

He gave her a faint smile as he opened the door. "I have seen you work miracles, Diana. Perhaps you can work another."

Chapter 17

Late the next morning, on the very fringes of town, Diana watched the finishing touches being applied to the regiment's booth.

She had been warned not to expect a prime location, for those were reserved far in advance by merchants who made the round of markets and fairs in northern England. Local merchants were given second priority, and apparently every decent spot had long since been spoken for. Market square and all the nearby streets were filled, and as one of the last to apply for a site, she had been relegated clear the other side of the River Kent, hard by one of Kendal's arched stone bridges.

The four ladies chosen to work in the booth on fair day were gathered around her, waiting to unpack the boxes and arrange the merchandise. Alex, wearing shirt, trousers, and boots, was atop a ladder, tying the rope of triangular pennants to the roof.

"They have certainly stashed us in the back of beyond," she said, trying to keep the disappointment from her voice. "Except for that pie seller, we are the only ones this side of the river."

"It's not so bad," Mrs. Jellicoe said bracingly. "I've been watching, and there be considerable traffic over that bridge. We wasn't like to be noticed until his lordship sent over the tent, but now everybody looks in this direction."

A blue and white pavilion tent had been erected over the squat little booth that had been sitting there when first the ladies arrived. Now only the front of the booth, with its wooden counter for displaying goods, was visible. The tent covered the rest and extended a good way beyond, creating a rather striking edifice.

"Perhaps it is all for the best," Diana conceded, holding the hem of her veil between thumb and forefinger against the morning breeze. "Were we crowded in among the others on market square, we'd not make so impressive an appearance."

"And when we're done workin' this afternoon," Mrs. Pottle said, "we mean to go around spreadin' the word where we are. See?" She handed Diana a small card.

Recognizing the work of the Yoodle sisters, Diana read the words inscribed in elegant print and embellished with bright flowers. *Gifts. Wines. Cordials. Jams and Jellies. Fine Foods. Embroidered Linens. Creams. Ointments. Fragrances.*

"We have two hundred cards," Mrs. Jellicoe informed her. "When we come on a likely customer, we'll give over a card and say where our booth is. It was Meggie Doyle's idea."

"And such a fine one!" Diana exclaimed, more than a little impressed with Mrs. Doyle's transformation from bitter abandoned wife to entrepreneur.

Glancing over at the bridge, she saw Kit and Lucy coming across it arm in arm. Lucy, anticipating the new wardrobe she would soon require, had gone in search of a mantua maker, and naturally Kit had accompanied her.

"He sticks to me like a plaster," Lucy had confided shortly before they left. "Kit is under the misapprehension that because I am with child, I am consequently frail and helpless."

She certainly looked the picture of good health, cheeks glowing and a decided bounce in her step. As Kit led her to where Diana was standing, the women of the regiment silently melted away.

"Look what I found!" Kit proclaimed with a broad gesture in the direction of a short, thin man wearing baggy trousers and an oversized coat. "Mrs. Valliant, may I present Felix the Magnificent?"

With his wizened face and bright round eyes, Felix the Magnificent put Diana strongly in mind of a monkey. "How do you do?" she said politely.

"More to the point," Kit said, "*what* does he do? Show her, my good man."

Looking befuddled, Felix raised his arms and snatched at the air as if trying to catch flies. Suddenly a red ball appeared in his left hand, and then a blue one in his right. He tossed them up and snatched at the air again, producing two more balls. Green and yellow, they joined the others midair, arcing up and down as he caught them and sent them flying again. From nowhere, a fifth ball appeared, and then a sixth. He juggled them low and high, behind his back and between his legs, an expression of surprised panic on his face as if he couldn't figure out how it was all being accomplished.

Then one by one the balls disappeared. Felix stared down at his empty hands, looking sorrowful.

Diana applauded with enthusiasm, and from some distance behind her she heard the regiment ladies clapping as well. "You truly *are* magnificent," she told him. "The juggling is splendid, of course, but however do you make those balls appear and vanish?"

In reply he plucked an orange from behind her shoulder. It must have displeased him. He tried again with his other hand and came up with an egg. Then he slammed his hands together and when he opened them, the egg and the orange were gone.

Kit smiled benevolently. "I have persuaded Mr. Magnificent that his talents will not be appreciated in the center of town, where there is precious little space for him to work or attract an audience. So, Felix, what think you? Is not this the ideal spot to ply your trade?"

The juggler bounded up a good yard or more, clicking his heels together.

"I'll take that as a *yes*," Kit said, laughing. "Seven o'clock, then, and don't be late."

Four balls reappeared in his hands as Felix left, juggling all the way across the bridge.

Diana saw people point to him and follow along to watch him perform. "Kit," she said under her breath, not wanting the regiment ladies to hear, "you *hired* that man to draw a crowd."

"So what if I did?" He gave a negligent shrug. "Felix will have himself a very good day, what with wages from me and what he'll earn passing the hat. I shouldn't be at all surprised if a number of street performers play here tomorrow. They're a close-knit lot, I have discovered. We met while Lucy was being measured for her new clothes."

"Madame Gloriette tossed him out on his ear," Lucy said with a grin. "He was getting on her nerves."

"If that old fussock is French, I am Marie Antoinette. Under all those *'très biens,'* the woman had a Yorkshire accent thick as bacon fat."

"It was excessively kind of you," Diana said, putting a hand on his arm. "I'll not even tell you that you ought not have done it, because I am so very glad that you did."

"Can't let Alex be the only one of use," Kit said, a tinge of color on his cheeks. "I must say, though, that if he leans over any farther, he's going to fall directly into that tent."

Diana glanced up, horrified to see Alex balanced precariously on the ladder, tying her regimental banner to a pole he'd affixed to the top of the booth. A brisk wind had sprung up, and he was having considerable difficulty holding on to the flag while he secured the ties. Mr. Pottle stood below him, clutching the ladder with his one arm to hold it in place.

After several breathless moments of watching Alex teeter a dozen feet above ground, Diana had to close her eyes. She heard Lucy gasp and closed them even tighter. If Alex plunged to his death on account of the regiment, she didn't want to see it.

"You can look now," Kit said. "And breathe again, if you've a mind to. He's on his way down."

Alex had both feet on the ground when she dared to open her eyes. He was gazing up at the tent.

Blue and white silk billowed in the wind. Pennants of red and yellow and green fluttered in a cheerful dance. And streaming out only to snap back with a crisp sound, the regimental flag flew proudly against the clear morning sky.

Tears welled in Diana's eyes, blurring her vision. Within a few hours, everything she had worked for would come to the test. What the members of the regiment earned tomorrow would see them through the harsh Lakeland winter. The money would feed their children, buy coals for their fires, and put warm blankets on their beds. It would pay for the materials they needed to produce goods to be sold at the first spring fair. It would give them the confidence to keep working. It would give them hope.

The women bustled forward, Mrs. Jellicoe and Mrs. Pottle,

Mrs. Renfrew and Mrs. Truscott, to help unload the flatbed wagon. A few passersby had stopped to look at the tent. She heard them inquire of the women what was to be sold there and promise to return on the morrow.

One gentleman insisted on taking a bottle of burnet wine immediately. He remembered seeing his mother make burnet wine when he was a child, but had never been granted the opportunity to taste it. Mrs. Jellicoe fished out a bottle, gave it him, and rushed to Diana with the coin he'd given her in return.

"A whole sovereign!" Mrs. Jellicoe's eyes were wide as serving platters. "He never even asked the price!"

"Our first sale," Diana said, fingers curling with pleasure. "Keep this coin aside, Mrs. Jellicoe. You'll want to show it when you tell the story to all the ladies who cannot be here with us for the fair. How I wish everyone could have come. After all their hard work, it's a shame they won't get to enjoy the excitement firsthand."

"Not this time. But in future, we'll be taking turns going to the fairs. 'Tis only fair." Laughing at her own joke, Mrs. Jellicoe hurried back to the wagon.

How she would miss them all, Diana thought with a pang of regret. Wherever she went, she would always be thinking of them and wondering how they were getting on.

Alex materialized at her side, wiping his forehead with a limp handkerchief. "It looks well, don't you think?"

"Altogether splendid. Thank you for putting up the flags, Alex. Are you finished now? Will you be coming with us to Candale?"

"There's still much to be done here, and I am required for the heavy lifting." He smiled. "But I'll be along directly the work is completed. Mr. Pottle has agreed to stay in the tent tonight and keep an eye on things, and the ladies have rooms at a nearby inn. There is nothing more for you to worry about."

"Don't dawdle," Kit told him. "Celia has planned a feast for the grand reunion of the Valliant clan. It will be the first time we are all of us together, and you know that females like to make a fuss about such trifles."

"I'll be there." Alex rushed over to the wagon and seized a

wooden box from Mrs. Truscott before it brought her to her knees.

While Kit and Lucy went to the carriage, which was drawn up a few yards away, Diana took one last look at the tent and especially at the banner, thinking of Mr. Beadle when she saw the blue castle. It was the exact color of the sky. She remembered his promise to be here in spirit, and perhaps he was. But who could ever really know?

She had just turned to the carriage when half a dozen street urchins, whooping and hollering, came over the bridge and spotted the tent. Apparently wanting a closer look, they galloped past her, and as they did, the wind lifted her veil and tossed it over her bonnet.

One of the boys, thin and dirty with hair the color of straw, pulled to a halt and pointed at her face. "Cor! Lookee that. It be a dragon woman."

The others, laughing and jeering, formed a circle and danced around her as if she were a Maypole. "Dragon!" they chanted. "Dragon!"

Hot with embarrassment, she couldn't bring herself to lower the veil. She doubted she could move at all. Others had clustered about to watch the boys make fun of her, and she stood silently, pretending not to care and willing herself not to cry. It seemed to go on for years, their singsong chants and her humiliation.

But it was probably only a matter of moments, because Alex came charging at the boys like an enraged lion. They scattered in all directions, their skinny legs pumping as they fled. Alex went for the leader, who dodged around the pie stall, keeping it between himself and his assailant. Kit came up behind him then, sending him off in the direction of the bridge.

Alex was on him before he reached it. Grabbing the boy by the collar of his shabby jacket, he lifted him high into the air. The boy flailed at him with legs and fists, catching him a glancing blow on the thigh. Alex swore and looked about to cuff him soundly.

"Don't hurt him!" Diana cried, rushing in their direction.

Alex glanced at her over his shoulder, receiving another kick from the boy while he was distracted. "Keep away," he ordered Diana. "I mean it."

She stopped, and saw him set the boy on the ground and grapple him by the shoulders, turning him so that they were face-to-face. At one point, Alex shook him soundly.

Remembering to lower her veil, she waited in place. Of a sudden Lucy was by her side, taking her hand in a warm, reassuring grip. Kit was busy dispatching the curious onlookers.

And this was what it was like to go out in public, she thought. A chance gust of wind, nothing more, and she became the object of ridicule. She didn't blame the boys. Children who lived on the streets had no opportunity to learn manners. It was the whispers from the crowd she took to heart, the "Poor thing" and the "She'd be so pretty without that scar." "No wonder she wears a veil." "She oughtn't to show herself, looking like that."

But Kit had got rid of them all, and now the silence was even worse than what they had said. It gave her time to take their words to heart.

Alex came up to her, towing the ragged, red-faced urchin by one arm. He set him loose directly in front of her and stepped behind him in case he tried to scarper.

She looked down at the thatch of greasy yellow hair. The boy was staring at the ground, scuffing his worn shoes in the dirt.

"I be sorry," he said. "It were wrong of me."

"What else?" Alex demanded.

"I won't never do no such thing again. Not to nobody. Swear to God I won't."

Diana put a hand on his shoulder. "That's all right then. You can go along now."

He raised his eyes. "I really is sorry, ma'am. Really truly."

Alex stepped aside, and the boy ran off as if the devil were on his heels.

"Thank you, Alex," she said, keeping her voice steady. "I believe he has learned his lesson now." She turned to Kit. "Celia will be growing impatient. Shall we go before she comes looking for us?"

Everyone seemed to understand she wished the incident put behind her. Alex bowed, and Kit went to open the carriage door.

Lucy kept hold of her hand until she mounted the steps. But in that short time, Diana had come to a decision.

Never, not *ever* again, would she permit a stranger to see her face.

Chapter 18

Diana was dreaming of the glass spider when something woke her.

She opened her eyes and saw Alex leaning over the bed. He was wearing his dressing gown. In the flickering light of the candle he was holding, his face looked somber.

"A messenger has just arrived from town," he said. "There has been some sort of disturbance at the booth. He could give us no details, save that the constable thought we should be informed immediately."

She sat up, cold with dread. "What are we to do? Shall we go there?"

"Kendal has ordered the carriage brought around. You needn't come if you'd rather not, but I expected that you would wish to."

"Of course." She threw back the covers. "I'll dress straightaway."

"Come downstairs when you are ready, then." He brushed his fingers over her tangled hair. "And try not to worry, Diana. It may be nothing of consequence."

The sun had just appeared over the horizon, but already the road was choked with vehicles and pedestrians making their way to the fair. Alex guided his horse alongside the crested carriage and rapped on the window.

Kendal lowered the panel. "Problems ahead?"

"You'll make slow progress from here on out, I'm afraid. Kit and I are taking to the fields."

Diana's face appeared at the window. "Will you take me with you?"

He gestured to the driver, who brought the carriage to a halt. Diana bounded out and Alex scooped her onto the saddle in front of him.

She was a warm, silent presence in his arms as they rode behind Kit, following the roundabout route he had assured them was the swiftest way to town. "Don't think about it," Alex said after a time. "There's no use anticipating the worst."

"I know." She rested her head on his shoulder. "I am putting together my courage, is all. I mustn't fly to pieces in front of the others."

"You won't."

They didn't speak again until they came in sight of the tent. And then there was nothing to be said.

He heard the breath catch in her throat. For the barest moment she went limp in his arms. Then she drew herself up and raised her chin.

The tent looked as if a troop of cavalry had charged through it. One side had been trampled to the ground and the other listed at a sharp angle, a few colorful pennants fluttering bravely in the morning breeze. The wooden booth, still intact, was smeared with creams and jams. Broken glass covered the display counter.

Standing in front of it, as if they could not believe what they saw, three of the regiment ladies huddled together. A few curious fairgoers had gathered nearby, and others viewed the devastation from the bridge.

Not far from the riverbank, Mr. Pottle was sitting with his back against a tree. Beside him, Mrs. Pottle dabbed a wet handkerchief against his temple. A stocky man wearing a blue uniform appeared to be asking questions and taking notes.

The constable, Alex supposed. When he set Diana to the ground, she hurried to the women and embraced each of them in turn.

Alex tethered his horse and went to Mr. Pottle, who looked slightly dazed.

"It's me own fault," he said. "I nodded to sleep, and they was on me afore I knowed they be there."

Alex crouched next to him, noting the crimson lump just above his temple. "Can you tell me what happened?"

"Aye, the first part. I come awake when I heard a noise, and then I sees a knife cutting through the tent. *Whoosh!* it went. I were about to yell for help, but summum musta come in from behind me. Next thing, I was hit on me noggin."

"They tied him up," Mrs. Pottle said in a tight voice, "and put a gag in his mouth. Then they hauled him behind those bushes."

"I couldn't see nuthin' after that," Mr. Pottle said, "but I heared them breaking up all what was in the tent. They was laughin'. I guess I went fuzzy-headed then. Next I knowed, a man were leanin' over 'n askin' if I be hurt. Like I could answer 'im with a rag in me mouth."

"He thinks there were two of them," the constable put in. "Hooligans, I expect, out on a lark."

Alex very much doubted that. The destruction was too complete. He stood. "Lord Kendal will be here shortly, ma'am. He'll see the both of you cared for. For now, I wish to speak with the constable."

"I'm a Carlisle man, hired on for the fair," he said when Alex drew him to one side. "I'll give my report to the magistrate, but I can tell you that nothing will be done about it. Not today."

"Have you found any witnesses? This booth was not ransacked without a good deal of noise. Someone must have heard it."

"Happen so, if they were crossing the bridge just then." The constable made a sweeping gesture. "But there's nothing close by, no houses or shops. Only that pie stall, and nobody has come to open it."

"Understood. When Kendal arrives, you will take your orders from him. Meantime, station yourself by the bridge and keep the sightseers at a distance." Alex waited until the constable was in place, and then went in search of Diana.

She was standing alone amid the ruins of her dream, ankle-deep in shattered bottles and shredded tablecloths. The regimental banner—what remained of it—was clutched in her arms.

She looked up at him from wounded eyes. "Why ever would anyone do such a thing, Alex?"

He made his way across the fragments of glass and took her

in his arms. "I mean to find out," he said. "You may be sure that I will."

"They left nothing. Not one single bottle or jar. Not a scrap of lace or an embroidered napkin. They ruined *everything*. And how are we to tell all the others waiting for us to come back with our pockets full of money? I cannot bear to face them."

"There is no reason. The regiment will be paid."

"Yes. I'll pay them myself, if you will permit it. But they mustn't be told that I did. We'll pretend we caught the vandals and that they made resti . . . oh, I cannot think of the word."

"Restitution." He could scarcely breathe, the stench of wine and perfumed creams and pickled vegetables all but over-whelming. "Trust me to deal with this, Diana. And now, come away from here."

She let him lead her into the fresh air.

"Don't look back," he said, holding her close at his side. "What's done is done."

"I know." She sighed. "I shall remember the tent as I saw it yesterday, with the flags flying and all our beautiful things laid out. And Mrs. Jellicoe has the sovereign from our first sale. Our only sale, but it proves that we would have made a great success, don't you think?"

"Absolutely." Alex had never before felt so helpless. "You'll wish to have words with Mr. Pottle, I expect. He holds himself responsible for what happened."

"Gracious!" She looked at him with alarm. "How could he? Of course it's not his fault. I must speak with him directly."

She sped away, the frayed banner still clutched in her arms.

"Sir?"

Turning, Alex saw a familiar dirt-streaked face. "What is it?" he snapped.

"I saw the men what did this," the boy said in a nervous voice. "Thought you'd wanna know."

"You can be sure of it." Alex beckoned to Kit, who was standing with the women. "My brother may as well hear this at the same time. What's your name?"

"Jemmy Thacker. But it's a made-up name. I be a foundling."

"What have we here?" Kit said. "Not in trouble again, are you, lad?"

"He claims to be a witness," Alex said. "Go ahead, Jemmy. Start from the beginning."

"Well, I wuz sleepin' in there," he said, indicating the pie stall. "Weren't nobody to stop me, and it be better than the streets. Anyways, suddenlike there was noises. Woke me up, they did. I reckoned folks had got in a fight, but I were too scared to go see. Went on a long time, them noises. I could tell they wuz comin' from the tent. Then it got real quiet."

"You told me you *saw* the men."

"Don't bark at the lad, old thing." Kit put a hand on Alex's forearm. "He'll come to the point when he gets there."

Jemmy chewed at his lower lip. "I didn't see 'em *do* it. But I sneaked outside after it were quiet, and I saw 'em goin' over the bridge. There was two men, and I knows they wuz the ones 'cause they wuz carryin' some bottles. Square bottles, like I seen yesterday at the tent. Afore I said those bad things," he added, flushing.

"Never mind that. Would you recognize the men if you saw them again?"

"I 'spect so. Went after 'em to get a better look. But they took a turn, and when I come round it, they wuz gone."

Alex swallowed his disappointment. Even if he trolled Jemmy through the crowded streets for the rest of the day, there was little chance of spotting the vandals.

"I been lookin' for 'em ever since," Jemmy said. " 'Bout an hour ago I saw 'em come outer a posthouse the far side of town. Luck, it were. I wuz gonna give it up, and then there they wuz. So I followed 'em till they went inter a pub. Then I come here. Run all the way, I did."

"Excellent work, young man!" Kit clapped him on the back. "You have the makings of a Bow Street Runner. Let's go find them, shall we?"

"Hold on," Alex said. "Kendal is finally here, and we'd better tell him where we are going. Do you know the name of the pub, Jemmy?"

"Can't read," the boy muttered. "But the sign had a pitchur what looked like a cheese."

"Wait here with him, Kit."

Kendal was regarding the ruined tent with a grim expression

on his face. "It's true, then," he said. "I had hoped we were misinformed."

Alex quickly recounted what he had learned. "Kit and I are going after the two men. Will you see to Diana and the others?"

Kendal raised a brow. "I presume, Alex, that you mean only to apprehend the vandals. It would be most inadvisable to kill them."

"Not the way I see it. But I won't. You may tell that to Diana."

"Oyez, oyez, oyez!" the bailiff cried, clanging his handbell.

Above the din of the crowd, the official summons to the fair rang out from the market square. Alex and Kit, mired in a throng of fairgoers one street away, had lost sight of Jemmy.

"Where the devil is he?" Alex jumped onto the back of a stalled wagon heaped with cabbages and searched the crowd for a thatch of yellow hair. Finally he spotted Jemmy at the next corner, waving his arms.

At this rate, Alex thought as he led Kit to where he'd seen the boy, they would reach the pub house well after dark. Someone stumbled against his back, muttered an apology, and shoved past him.

". . . that no person pick any quarrel, matter, or course for any old grudge or malice," the bailiff shouted, "to make any perturbation or trouble!"

"He's charging us to keep the peace," Kit said with a short laugh. "Small chance of that, wouldn't you say?"

"None whatever. There's the brat. I think one of us had better hang on to him the rest of the way."

"Not far now," Jemmy said as Kit took his hand. "We'll go round the back where they don't be so many people."

The buildings they passed were each one shabbier than the one before as he guided them away from the market square and through a rabbit warren of narrow streets. Just the sort of place the men they were looking for would go to ground, Alex was thinking when Jemmy drew up across from a good-sized pub house.

"That be where they wuz," he said, pointing to the half-timbered building.

A weather-worn sign hung above the open door with "The Wheel of Cheese" crudely printed atop the picture of an orange cheese. To judge by the noise coming from inside, the pub was a popular gathering place. All the voices were male, and even at this early hour, most of them sounded well to let.

Alex had to dodge a pair of louts emerging from the pub as he led Jemmy inside. The taproom, its low ceiling blackened with smoke from the hearth fire, stank of ale, foul breath, and sweat. There were a few small round tables ringed with ladder-back chairs, all of them occupied, and a long wooden bar was elbow-to-elbow with roughly garbed men.

Jemmy plucked at his sleeve. "Them two," he said in a whisper. "That tall 'un near to the middle of the bar and the one next to 'im takin' a drink."

Alex saw a tankard at the mouth of a big-shouldered, barrel-shaped man with spiky black hair. To his left, a man about his own height was trying to get the barkeep's attention.

"Lucifer!" Kit indicated the black-haired man. "That's the fellow who shot me."

"Did he?" Alex regarded his brother with a frown. "When was that? And why is he not in gaol for it?"

"Long story, old lad. More to the point, the rascal works for Sir Basil Crawley. I expect we both know what that means."

"No great surprise," Alex said. "Jemmy, wait outside until we are done here."

"I wanna watch!" the boy protested, looking eager at the prospect of a fight.

"Go!"

Grumbling, Jemmy slouched away.

"This reckoning is long overdue," Kit said, striking out for the bar. "You take care of Longshanks. Blackie belongs to me."

Alex followed, halting directly behind his quarry. Kit did the same.

The men paid them no mind. They were tossing dice together, and a considerable amount of money was piled before each of them. Their pay for demolishing the tent, Alex surmised.

Kit tapped a finger on Blackie's shoulder. "Hullo there, darlin'."

"Huh?" The man turned, a scowl knitting his thick eyebrows. "Who the devil—?"

"Remember me?" Kit planted his right fist in Blackie's face, sending him halfway across the bar.

Alex seized the other man's wrist, wrenching it up behind his back, and grabbed the man's hair with his other hand. He smashed his face against the bar. "Make the slightest move," he cautioned, "and I'll break your arm."

Blackie pulled himself upright and launched himself at Kit, who ducked his swinging fist and sent a blow to his stomach. He doubled over, groaning. Chairs and tankards clattered to the floor as everyone scrambled out of the way.

"Come on, sweetheart," Kit coaxed, standing loose-limbed with his hands open at his sides. "You can do better than that."

Bellowing an oath, Blackie went at him with both fists flying. One caught Kit on the shoulder, but he grabbed hold of it and used Blackie's momentum to send him flying headfirst into the wall. He bounced off and landed on his backside.

The audience, clustered at the far side of the room, laughed and applauded.

Blood streamed from Blackie's nose and a cut over his eye.

Grinning, Kit tossed him a handkerchief. "On your feet, my good fellow. I can't hit you while you're down."

Blackie rocked to his knees, his sleeve pressed to his nostrils. " 'Nuff," he mumbled. "I'm done for."

"Pity. And here I was just getting started." With a dramatic sigh, Kit turned to Alex. "What of your little pussycat, Colonel? Any fight left in him?"

Alex looked down at the limp figure in his grasp. "None to speak of, I'm afraid. It appears we'll have to turn them over to the magistrate relatively intact."

"Knife!" someone shouted.

Kit hit the ground just before the blade could drive into his back. The blow met empty air, sending Blackie off balance and staggering forward. Kit rolled away and sprang to his feet.

The taproom grew hushed as the two men circled each other. Blackie, a malevolent sneer on his face, waved the long-bladed knife in mocking arcs. "We'll see who has the last laugh, boy."

Kit, his arms splayed and hands held shoulder-high, came

up against a fallen chair and hopped over it. Blackie used the opportunity to slash at him, but Kit darted out of reach. Again they moved in a circular pattern, face-to-face, but Blackie was slowly forcing him in the direction of the wall.

Alex knew better than to make a move. It would only break his brother's concentration. But his heart was pounding in his chest, and the man he was holding moaned as his grip tightened on the bent arm.

Still smiling, Kit came closer and closer to the wall with each turn of the circle. One more time around and he'd have no room to evade the knife. "Now or never, luvvie," he invited, drawing to a halt and beckoning with his forefinger. "Come and get me."

With a howl of rage Blackie charged at him. The knife slashed at Kit's throat.

And then it was skittering across the floor, landing against the bar where Alex was standing. He planted his foot on it and watched Kit pummel his adversary to the ground.

When Blackie lay unconscious, Kit brushed his hands together with evident satisfaction and gazed around at the stunned crowd, one brow raised. "Any of you chaps got a rope?"

The barkeep came to life. "I'll fetch one from the back room, sir."

"Make it two," Alex said, regarding his brother with some awe. "But first, pour the winner a stiff drink."

Leaning against the bar at Alex's side, Kit downed most of a large glass of whisky and poured the rest over his bruised knuckes. Wincing, he said, "And here I was thinking that the fight wouldn't get interesting."

"How the devil did you do that, Kit? I've never seen a move like it."

"A thing of beauty, what? Ran into a Chinese fellow once upon a time, me smuggling wine and him smuggling tea, both of us chased by a pair of excise cutters. Our boats were driven onto Jersey by a storm and we were stuck there for a considerable time. With nothing better to do, I taught him to deal seconds, and he taught me to fight with my feet. One quick twirl, foot lashes out, knife gone. Piece of cake."

It was nothing of the sort. Kit had been a blade's edge from a slit throat or a length of steel in his chest. And he knew it as well, however lightly he dismissed the affair.

"Oughtn't you let your sweetie come up for a bit of air?" Kit asked. "If you don't smother him, he might answer a few questions for us."

Alex had forgot he was still pressing Longshanks's face to the bar. He released the greasy hair and the thick wrist, turning the man so that his back was to the wooden railing. "You are in the employ of Sir Basil Crawley, I believe."

"Not me!" the man blubbered, pointing to the prone figure on the floor. "Him!"

The barkeep had returned with several lengths of hemp rope, and two men were cheerfully tying Blackie's hands behind his back. "Feet, too?" one of them called.

"Hobble him," Alex ordered, returning his attention to Longshanks. "What is your name?"

"Ned Tyler. The other 'un be Mick. Dunno the rest. Met 'im yesterday at the posthouse where I been stayin'. In the stable, mind ye. Couldn't pay fer a room. Come in for the fair, I did, lookin' for work. Mick said 'e'd pay me to 'elp him break up one o' the booths. Said 'is boss didn't want the folk what set it up to be sellin' their things." Sweat trickled down his battered face. "It were good money for an hour's work, so I done it."

"Otherwise," Kit said pleasantly, "you are no doubt an honest fellow with a wife and six children to feed."

"Four. An' one of 'em ailin'." He sniveled. "I'd have took an honest job, but there weren't none."

Alex, remembering the regiment ladies and their hard times, nearly tumbled to Ned's hard-luck story. Then his gaze fell on the dice the two men had been tossing, and the coins Ned was wagering between rounds of ale. Not a coin would have made it home to his family . . . assuming he had one.

Lord, he was going soft, to be so taken in. It was Diana's influence, he supposed, and the openhearted generosity he admired in her. Were she here, she'd sweep Ned under her wing and offer him a job at Lakeview, never mind that he'd probably loot the place first chance he got.

The taproom, which had erupted in noise once the fight was

over, suddenly went hushed again. Alex glanced over his shoulder and saw everyone facing the door.

Kendal turned his gaze slowly around the room. It paused a moment at the bound man laid out on the floor, moved to the barkeep standing with pieces of rope dangling from both hands, and finally settled on Kit and Alex. One brow arched in a query.

"About time you got here," Kit said. "You missed all the fun."

"Someone had to tend to business," Kendal replied, a look of resignation on his face as he moved past Mick and saw the damage Kit had done to him. "I've brought along a pair of constables, if you are quite finished beating up on the prisoners. May I presume they can be taken away now?"

Alex shoved Ned in the direction of the two men trailing behind Kendal. "They're all yours."

Mick, still dead to the world, had to be hauled out. Kit tossed coins to three fellows eager to do the job, and within a short time the taproom was virtually empty. Kendal's arrival appeared to have put a damper on things, because most of the patrons wandered off in search of another place to bend an elbow. The barkeep, looking distinctly unhappy, poured whiskey into three glasses at Alex's order before retreating to the back room.

"You *do* know how to nip a party," Kit said.

"And you continue to find unorthodox ways of entertaining yourself. What will your wife make of those battered knuckles, I wonder?"

"Oh, she'll kiss them and make them all better," Kit said with a laugh. "You don't know her. After my first encounter with Mick, she ordered me to chase him down and wring his neck. Bloodthirsty wench, my moonbeam."

Kendal shook his head. "This 'Mick' was the prone gentleman recently dragged away, I assume. How came you to know him?"

"Our paths crossed once or twice," Kit said negligently. "Three times, to be precise. The first is irrelevant. The second and third, he was in company with Basil Crawley."

"Ah. I'd assumed he was responsible for the destruction of the tent, but it's well to have proof. Can his thugs be persuaded to testify against him?"

"Mick went after Kit with a knife in front of a score of witnesses," Alex said. "He'll talk in exchange for deportment instead of the hanging he deserves."

"Thank you," Kit said sourly. "Jimmie wasn't supposed to hear of that."

"Sorry. I lack your talent for deception." Alex turned to Kendal. "The penalty for hiring vandals to demolish a booth cannot be of any account."

"Oh, I have a bit more than that to discuss with him. Not to put too fine a point on it, his business practices have not stood up to close scrutiny. I shall advise him of certain information in my possession and suggest that he depart Westmoreland with all possible speed."

"You'll let him go *free*?" Kit erupted. "I think not, Jimmie."

"I wish him gone," Kendal said coolly. "But he'll not escape punishment, you may be sure. Now, shall we drink up, gentlemen, and be on our way? Before the morning is out, I mean to pay a call on Sir Basil."

Alex picked up his glass. "Have you magically divined where he can be found?"

"Oh, at home, I should imagine. Perhaps Mick, if he has come to his senses, will enlighten us. And I must hire a mount, assuming that one is to be found in this hubbub. The carriage has taken Diana and the other ladies back to Candale."

"We'll go with you, of course."

"Not you, Alex. I'll take Kit along, but you would do better to see to your wife. She is putting a brave front on it, but I fear she has taken this incident rather hard."

"Yes." Alex thought of her standing in the ruined tent, her banner held tightly in her arms, trying not to weep. "I'll leave Crawley to you. But see to it he makes full restitution, James. Return with cash or the equivalent so that we can put it into Diana's hands."

"She will have it by this evening." Kendal raised his glass. "A toast, then. To Diana's Regiment."

When they had drunk, Kit swept the coins Mick and Ned Tyler had left on the bar and gave them to Alex. "A down payment, old thing. We'll come back with the rest if I have to sell Crawley's corpse to the knackers."

Alex followed his brothers from the dim taproom, watching them move purposefully through the crush of people and vanish around a corner. For a moment he was wild to go after them. He had missed too many last battles, fighting nearly to the end only to be elsewhere when the decisive action played out. It was the battles he hadn't fought that haunted him. He was never where he was supposed to be when it counted.

"Were a good fight!" Jemmy declared, appearing at his side. "I sneaked in to watch. When the black-haired bloke pulled out the steel, I thunk fer sure Mister Kit were a gonner. Right handy, he be. You never got much inter it, though."

"I'm sorry to have disappointed you," Alex said, "but my opponent was disinclined to joust. I daresay you expect a reward, Jemmy, and you shall have it after you have guided me back to where I left my horse."

"Don't want no reward, sir. I owed this 'un to the lady. 'Sides, I'm doin' well enough." He reached into his coat and came out with two pocket watches and several coins. "Filched these while ever'body wuz gawkin' at the fight. I ain't even got started at the market square. Good pluckin's to be 'ad there, what with folks all packed together pushin' and shovin'."

Good Lord. Alex glared down at the filthy face beaming up at him. "You're a bloody pickpocket?"

"A fella's gotta eat, sir. What I gets t'day will keep me fer a month. C'n we go now? I be glad to take you back where I found you, but then I's work t'do."

Alex took hold of his hand, letting Jemmy tow him through the winding backstreets of Kendal. He ought to turn the cheeky little felon over to the authorities, he supposed, but it was really out of the question. So was letting him ply his trade. One day the boy was certain to be caught, and fairly soon if he couldn't resist boasting of his successes.

"How old are you, Jemmy?"

"Dunno. I sez I be fourteen, but it's more like 'leven or twelve."

"And where do you live when you're not come to town for the fair?"

"Oh, I allus live in Kendal or nearabouts. Sometimes in a barn when it be too cold to sleep unner a tree or a wagon. I run off from the foundlin' home mebbe three years ago. There be a man there what likes to cane folks just fer breathin'. Reckoned I'd do better on the streets, 'n so I 'ave." They came alongside the River Kent and followed it a short way. Soon Alex saw the blue and white tent directly ahead. Several men surrounded it, shoveling broken glass onto the back of a wagon. Kendal, always thorough, must have hired them to clean up the mess.

Alex came to a decision, although he expected to wind up regretting it. When they arrived at the tree where Thunder was tethered, he turned Jemmy to face him and gazed intently into the boy's surprised blue eyes. "I want you to come with me, young man. You will have a warm place to sleep, regular meals, and a job that will pay steady wages. I've no use for a pickpocket, and devil knows what else you are capable of doing, but we'll find something. My wife has a talent for putting people to work. Are you interested?"

Jemmy gaped at him.

"I'm not promising a life of ease," Alex warned. "You'll have to work hard, obey orders, and keep out of trouble. Can you do that?"

"Mebbe." He looked worried. "Will the lady 'ave me, sir? After what I said to 'er?"

Diana would sweep the boy into her arms in a heartbeat. "She has a great regard for courage," Alex assured him. "If you are brave enough to leave what you know and make a new life for yourself, you will be most welcome."

He might as well have been addressing himself, Alex thought with sudden, painful insight. He had failed to do what he was demanding of this child. Mired in the failures of the past, he had lacked the will to strike out and make a new life, even when one was practically handed to him. Diana was a gift he'd accepted without giving of himself in return.

Well, he had given what he was willing to spare. He gave his time. His work. He supported the regiment. He was more than willing to kill on her behalf. But he withheld what she had asked of him, knowing all the while how hard it was for her to ask.

"You changed yer mind, sir?"

Alex, hot with shame, had forgot the boy. He put his hand on Jemmy's shoulder, gazing past him to the bridge where fairgoers were making their way across the river. A bright mound of color drew his attention. Flowers piled on the back of a wagon.

He located a guinea. "We'll set out in a minute. But first, see that flower seller? Go buy the best she has to offer—roses if there are any. I mean to give them to my wife."

Chapter 19

On her knees in the kitchen garden, Diana wrenched a stubborn weed from the base of a rosemary bush and tossed it into the basket at her side.

The Candale gardens, all of them, were far too well tended to suit her mood. For the past two hours she had been at pains to search out the occasional stray weed, and it had become something of a challenge to find one. When she succeeded, she felt a special satisfaction at ripping it out.

She had just pulled something she expected ought not to have been pulled when she heard Alex call her name. He was coming across the lawn, his arms filled with flowers.

"*There* you are!" he said. "I've been looking everywhere for you. What the deuce are you doing in the kitchen garden?"

Rising, she brushed soil from her skirts and stripped off her gardening gloves. "Taking out my temper on hapless plants, I'm afraid."

"Well, here are some more of them." He put the flowers into her hands. "Tear them to pieces if you must."

"They're lovely, Alex. Thank you." He looked—well, it was impossible to know. But there was something in his eyes she had not seen before. "I should put them into water, I suppose."

"Aren't you going to ask me what happened?"

"Yes. Certainly." She wasn't sure she wanted to hear it. The news could not be good if he'd brought hothouse roses to soften the blow. "Shall we go inside? You can tell me while I arrange the flowers."

"They are meant to be a gift," he said, walking beside her to the house. "I brought you another, too, but you won't like it half

197

so well. Where the devil is everyone? It was all I could do to locate a servant."

"They've all been given a holiday to attend the fair, save for the babe's nursemaid and one or two others. Lady Kendal and Lucy have gone, too, and taken the regiment ladies with them. It was foolish for them to sit around here moping when they could be enjoying themselves. We have the house quite to ourselves."

"Excellent. I've had enough of crowds for one day." He opened the door for her. "Where does one go to arrange flowers?"

"If you will fetch some water, sir, I'll find a vase and scissors and meet you in the downstairs parlor."

He arrived a few minutes after she did, with water, two glasses, and a bottle of brandy. "Would you care for a drink?" he asked, still with that odd look in his eyes. When she declined, he poured one for himself and sat on a sofa near the table where she was clipping leaves from the bottoms of the rose stems. "May I tell you the news now? It's not all bad, I promise you."

"I have been afraid to hear it," she acknowledged. "Did you find the culprits?"

"Yes indeed. Jemmy led us straight to them. There was a bit of a scuffle, but no harm done except to a particularly loathsome specimen who once, or so I am informed, put a bullet in Kit."

She dropped the rose she had been holding and spun to look at him. "Sir Basil sent them? I should have guessed he was behind this."

"Ah. You know the fellow. Well, he is now in the hands of the magistrate, and we expect he'll be transported when next the assizes are held. As for his employer, my brothers have gone to deal with him. Kendal assures me that he will return this evening with full compensation for the regiment's losses."

She felt her blood drain to her toes. "It's all over, then? Sir Basil will not—"

"You are free of him, my dear. Destroying the booth was a petty act of vengeance by a desperate man. I would be very much surprised if Crawley spent another night in Westmoreland, and Kendal means to pursue him through the courts until he is hounded from England or thrown into Newgate. In either case, he'll make no more trouble for you. He knows that we'll kill him if he tries."

"Oh." Relief made her dizzy. She sank onto the sofa beside Alex, welcoming his arm when it went around her shoulders. "He was the spider," she murmured.

He drew her closer. "What spider?"

"The one in my dreams. The one that did this." She put her fingers to the scar. "It was my uncle who hit me, of course, but only because Sir Basil drove him past reason. And I have felt him lurking in every dark corner since first he set out to have me, waiting to strike."

"You must put him from your thoughts, Diana. And from your dreams as well, although I know how difficult that will be." He hesitated a moment. "I, too, have bad dreams."

She remembered watching him thrash about on her bed, tormented by nightmares, mumbling words she could not distinguish. He was a stranger then, but she had felt, during those long hours, a closeness to him that they had not shared since. Not even when they kissed at the picnic. His heart was open and raw that night, and at times she thought she could touch it. But morning came, and when next she saw him, he was wearing the armor that had kept him separate from her to this very moment. She nestled her head against his shoulder, accepting his comfort and wishing he would permit her to comfort him in return.

"The fair is over," he said after a while. "For us, in any case. And I promised you that when it was, we would take up again where we left off. I should like to do that now, Diana, if you are willing." His voice was strained. "And no, I don't mean that we should . . . that is, not right away. First I would like to explain, if I can, why it is I have been . . . why I *am* . . . well, what I am."

He took a drink of brandy. "Damn. I'm making even less sense than usual. But I'm no good at talking, Diana. You know that. Can you bear to hear me out?"

She lifted her head, breathless with astonishment. "Oh yes, Alex. Of course I will."

"Don't look at me, then. And don't say anything. Just let me get on about it as best I can. It's an ugly story, and one I am not proud of. Very much the contrary. But you must hear it, because you'll give me no peace until you do. And most like I'll have no peace until I tell it. Only the core of it today, though, because the whole of it would take too long."

"Whatever you wish to say, Alex." She leaned into him again and closed her eyes. "We have a lifetime for the rest."

"Thank you," he whispered against her hair. "The hope of that will see me through."

He spoke then, sometimes faltering, sometimes stopping for minutes at a time. Often she could not understand him. She knew nothing of military matters, and he used words she had never heard and described things she could not imagine.

Not battles, though . . . not at first. He said nothing of the war in Spain, beginning at the point when his regiment was ordered to America. It was clear he'd been reluctant to go, and had done so only because he would not abandon his men.

His disgust at the politicians who sent them there was bitterly apparent. "We were ordered to 'chastise the savages,' " he said at one point. "I could find no sense in it. Bonaparte was a tyrant, and we'd no choice but to put him down, but why the Americans? By running the blockades and keeping commerce open with the French, they had certainly made things more difficult for us. But the war didn't touch them. They were under no immediate threat, and failed to understand the consequences of what they were doing. I grant them foolish and shortsighted, even greedy to profit from the war, but never savages. Their actions did not merit the punishment we were directed to inflict on them."

He expelled a sigh. "I expect there were grievances on their part as well. And we certainly gave them more than enough reason to despise us in the months ahead."

He took up the story at the point they made land and set about a campaign of burning houses, farms—even whole towns—if the residents held out against them. He told of places she had never heard of—the Chesapeake Bay, the Potomac River, Bladensburg and Baltimore and Georgetown. He began describing battles then, in excruciating detail, and she felt perspiration running down his neck.

"In one Maryland township," he said, "a tiny, insignificant place, I disobeyed a direct order for the only time in my life. We had been sent to burn it to the ground. And so we did, torching even the chicken coops after making off with the birds for our suppers. It was the middle of the night, and all the occupants had fled long before we arrived. All but two, as it turned out. I was in company with a handful of men when we arrived at a pair of small houses standing side by side near to the church. A woman came out of one of them and leveled a rifle at me. Her name was Miss Kitty Knight. She said that with pride, and it is a name I shall never forget. Her neighbor in the other house was ill, she told us, too ill to be moved. If we fired her home down about her, we would first have to deal with Miss Knight. And she would shoot the first one of us to raise a torch.

"I've no doubt she was ready to put a bullet in me. But that wasn't the reason I ordered the men to move on, leaving both houses standing and the church as well. If we had come to making war on women, brave ones and sick ones alike, I wanted no part of it."

Diana pressed her nails into her palms, longing to assure him that he'd done the right thing. Perhaps he knew that he had. But it was nevertheless a violation of his duty, and it struck him to the heart.

Next he described the march into Washington and the burning of the president's house and the Capitol. His regiment had been left on the outskirts of the city to keep guard, but he had been summoned to join the officers who wandered through the buildings, sometimes taking souvenirs and even snatching food from President Madison's dinner table, which had been laid out for a meal just before word came that the British were almost at the door.

"When we had demolished the Capitol, even the Congressional Library, the decision was taken to go on to Baltimore. It was summer, hot and muggy. The Sickly Season, it was called. The whole area is one great marsh, and men were dropping by the hundreds with fever and dysentery. I went down, too, and was billeted in a farmhouse where an old lady and her daughter did all they could to keep me alive. It was a near-run thing. I'd little interest in making a recovery by that time, but they fought me like tigers, pushing food down my throat and cleaning up after me when I expelled it again."

201

He reached over and poured himself another drink. "Suffice it to say I had become useless to the army. Before heading on for Baltimore, my commanding officer advised me to take ship back to England as soon as I had recovered. But it was one thing to despise the war and another thing to flee it. I insisted on catching up with the regiment when I could, so General Ross gave me papers granting extended leave—no questions asked—for as long as I required it. That was an extraordinary gesture on his part. But I had chanced to spare his head from being lopped off by a saber some years earlier, and I suppose it was his way of repaying me. In any case, Diana, I am still on that leave. I have made no effort to take up my duties again."

She thought he was finished then, and almost spoke. But he must have sensed it, because he covered her hand with his.

"There's more," he said. "The worst is to come. I don't think I was malingering, but I have often wondered if that is true. It's certain that whenever I thought myself well enough to follow the army, I went down with another bout of fever. Two attempts were made to get me on ship for home, but I resisted them. For several months I remained in Maryland, but shortly before Christmas, I was well enough to travel. The army had gone south by then, in the direction of New Orleans, so I set out after them."

His hand tightened around hers. "Before I got there, word came that the battle was over. Jackson had routed our forces and driven them from Louisiana. But worst of all, to my mind, was that the Forty-fourth went down in shame. They had drawn the Forlorn Hope for the attack, and were assigned to march at the head of the column. The Americans had raised a parapet to hold them off, and the Forty-fourth was responsible for carrying the ladders and fascines needed to scale it. But the officer in charge mistook where they had been stored. He sent the men to the wrong place, and by the time they were redirected, it was too late. The column had been ordered to advance, and the Forty-fourth were coming up behind them. But they thought they were in front, you see, so when the shooting started, they shot back and took down the fellows in between, who were now being fired at from both sides. They panicked and broke ranks, as did the Forty-fourth, and the officers could not rally them."

He fell silent, his head thrown back against the sofa. "My brave lads," he murmured after a time. "For so many years they fought with honor, only to end in disgrace. And all because Mullins failed to do his duty. I should have been there. The fight may have been lost in any case, for it was ill planned from the first. But I'd damn well have known where to find those bloody ladders."

Diana felt tears streaming down her cheeks. He might not think she understood, but she did. He would rather have died in that battle than failed to be with his men when most they needed him. And the fact that it was in no way his fault changed nothing. He wasn't there. That was all that mattered to him.

"The greatest irony," he said, "was that a treaty had already been signed in Ghent and ratified in London. A ship was on its way to America with the news. Those men fought and died in a war that was over, Diana, and the ones that lived were left only with their shame. I felt it, too, need I tell you?

"Transports were departing from several ports, and when I had word of a convoy, I went to the docks with the intention of boarding the next vessel bound for England. I arrived too late. Of course, I might have sought out another port, and ought to have done. But there was a cargo ship about to depart for Cartagena, and for no reason I can explain to you, I bought passage and sailed with her. From Cartagena I went on to Rio de Janeiro and Buenos Aires, and from there around the horn to Chile and Peru."

Pursued by his ghosts, she had no doubt. The ones that haunted him still. She thought he was done now with his story, and thought it safe to open her eyes and look at him. He was staring into the distance at something she could not see.

"I didn't suppose it would signify to anyone," he said, "my futile, self-indulgent odyssey. With no more battles to be fought, who would miss one ineffectual half-pay officer? But I was wrong yet again. Bonaparte escaped Elba, and the most important battle of them all took place without me. Because I failed to ship home any one of the many times I had the chance, I was not at Waterloo."

"Where you might have found redemption," she said softly.

"Yes. Perhaps." His eyes came back into focus. He turned to her. "I believe that is all for now, Diana. You have been remarkably patient."

Not quite all, she thought, wondering if she dared to ask any of the questions burning on her tongue. She could not bear to leave the story where he'd left it, but neither did she wish to make him regret telling her by prodding him for more.

He put his handkerchief into her hand. "I have made you weep. You mustn't. Not on my account."

"Of course I must," she said, blotting her wet cheeks. "I am a weepy female, don't you know? Considering the buckets of tears I've shed for myself, I can certainly spare a few for my husband."

A smile flitted over his lips, faint but unmistakable. It gave her heart to continue. "Will you sell out now, Alex?"

"I suppose so. I've been putting it off because it means a trip to London. My separation from the army was somewhat out of the ordinary, and I expect I've got some explaining to do. One day I shall present myself at Horse Guards, hand over my orders from General Ross, and see what the officials can make of it all."

She tossed a mental coin, but heads or tails, she already knew what she must say to him. "Why not straightaway? You can settle things with the army and attend your friend's wedding as well. It's on for Saturday next, I believe."

His eyes darkened. "No."

"Tell me why, then. It was learning of it that sent you away from me. At the time, I could not imagine a reason for you to react as you did. But now I think it's to do with what you have said today. Was Lord Blair somehow involved with the battle in New Orleans? Or another incident in the American War?"

For a long time she thought he would not reply. But he shook his head with what looked like frustrated resignation.

"Will you ever leave me in peace, woman? But no, Blair was never in America. He was one of my particular friends on the Peninsula, as were the others he'll have roped in to play groomsmen. I cannot face them. Perhaps someday, but not yet. They will know, don't you see? They'll have heard what happened with the Forty-fourth, and that I wasn't there. Had I gone back when I should have done, things would be different. I might have stood with them at Waterloo and regained some small degree of the honor I had lost. But I took myself off to South America, no one advised of it, no reason for it, and stayed gone the better part of two years. There is no explaining that to them, Diana. I'll not even try."

She put a hand on his knee. "Honor can be won other places than on a battlefield, you know. And you have never lost yours, no matter what you think. It is so much a part of you that no one with the barest acquaintance could fail to recognize it. Your friends surely will not. But for your own sake, Alex, you must go to London and meet with them. And when you do, I believe with all my heart that you will be glad of it. Lord Blair would scarcely have invited you to his wedding, after all, if he shared the misguided opinion you have of yourself."

"Is there no mercy in you, Diana?" But his eyes were no longer so bleak. "Misguided, am I? Well, I shall need an escort then, to show me the way. Shall we strike a deal? I'll go to London, if you will come with me."

She hadn't expected that. The last thing in the world she wanted was to be paraded among strangers to be gawked at. Well, the second to last thing. What Alex needed was infinitely more important than her own sensibilities, and all he'd asked was that she accompany him to London. She needn't show herself, nor would he expect her to once they got there. Would he?

He was waiting for an answer, a challenge in his eyes. And a trace of fear, she thought, that she might let him down. "Yes, of course I'll go with you to London," she said, as if she had never questioned it. "Lancaster is the largest city I've ever set foot in until now, and I've always longed to travel."

"Well, then." He looked relieved, although he was trying hard not to show it. "You can purchase a fashionable new wardrobe while we're there, and I'll take you around to all the sights. We'll make a wedding trip of it, and go on to the seashore if you like, or anywhere else that takes your fancy. Perhaps we can look about for a property suitable to raising horses."

"Oh, yes! Let's do that, Alex. A new start for both of us." She

205

flung herself onto his lap and wrapped her arms around him. "We shall dispatch my spider and your ghosts to the devil and get on with things. Except," she added in strictest honesty, "I still wish to hear about South America. Two years is an exceedingly long time to be wandering about all by yourself. Or were you?"

"By myself?" He chuckled. "Are you imagining a flock of señoritas at my heels? I assure you, Diana, that I was very much alone. Never more so. A man has no need of company, nor does he wish any, when he has gone in search of his soul."

She sat back, gazing into the deep blue of his eyes. "And did you find it? Your soul?"

"Not there." He brushed a finger across her lips. "Turned out it was waiting for me in a dark room at Lakeview with a skillet in its hand."

"Oh." Her heart made great leaps in her chest.

"Yes, madam," he said, a hesitant smile curving his lips. "I'm afraid that *you* are my soul, or the part of it that had gone missing. I cannot do without you now. You will have to stay close by me, and whack me to my senses again whenever I run astray. Like it or not, my brave and beautiful wife, you have drawn the Forlorn Hope."

She was weeping again, this time for joy. "The Bright Hope, Alex. I have drawn the Bright Hope."

Next she knew, he had swept her up and was carrying her out of the room, pausing only to take a rose from the vase and put it in her hand. But as he mounted the stairs, his intentions clearly all that she wanted them to be, a piping voice called to him from the entrance hall.

"What I s'posed to be doin' now, sir?"

Diana looked down to see the boy who had made fun of her.

"That's your other gift," Alex said with a rueful smile. "I thought you might not like it. But he was on his way to pick pockets at the fair, so I brought him here instead. He might make a decent stableboy."

"Oh yes. What a good idea." And what a good man you are, she thought, afire with love for him.

"Kendal may not think so, if the scoundrel makes off with the silver."

"Sir?" The boy stamped his foot. "The cove what you left me with 'as gone to sleepin'. You got work fer me or no?"

"This is a holiday, Jemmy. Have yourself a nap or visit with the horses or raid the pantry. Just stay out of trouble. And if you want work, tell anyone who comes home in the next few hours that my wife and I are not to be disturbed. Understood?"

"Yessir." Jemmy vanished in the direction of the kitchen.

"Thank you yet again, Alex," she said as he carried her along the passageway. "Jemmy is a wonderful gift. The best gift ever."

He kicked open the door to his room and set her on her feet beside the bed. "Don't speak too soon," he said, reaching around her to undo her apron and tug it away. "I mean to give you a great many things." He sat her down and dropped to one knee to pull off her shoes. "I can afford it, since I'll be spending your money."

His hands reached under her skirts, sliding up her legs to where her stockings were tied. He took a deliciously long time removing the ribbons. "You have only to ask, Diana. Whatever you want, I will try to provide."

He had said the same words, she remembered, or words much like them, the night they were married. And he had kept to his promise, withholding only himself. Until today. Until now.

The scent of the rose she was still holding melted into the touch of his hands and the soft urgency of his voice as he made her new promises. And then she was naked in his arms, gone wild with desire for him, and he gave her the best gift of all.

Chapter 20

Diana was sitting precisely where he'd left her, cross-legged at the center of the bed, still wearing her dressing gown. Her disordered hair tumbled around her pale face and slumped shoulders.

Alex closed the door behind him, regarding her with concern. "Are you not feeling well?"

"You may say that I am ill, if you wish, although that is not the case." She raised her chin and regarded him steadily. "I'm not going with you, Alex."

"The devil you say!" His hand went to the hilt of his sword. "Dress yourself, madam."

She raised a brow. "Will you slice me to flinders if I refuse?"

"A reflex only," he said, dropping the offending hand to his side. "You took me aback. I cannot credit that you mean to dishonor your word."

"When you asked, I told you that I would come with you. And so I did, as far as London. We never specified that I was to attend the wedding."

"It was understood! What in blazes did you *think* I meant?"

"Oh, precisely that. And I hoped that I could. But I gave no explicit promise, and now I find myself unable to accompany you."

She looked markedly determined, he thought, but also despondent. Even ashamed. The scar was vivid on her cheek, as if she'd been rubbing at it.

"Then we'll neither of us go," he said, shrugging. "I didn't want to in the first place."

"But you must!" Her eyes pleaded with him. "When you meet with your friends, you will find that they have never given the slightest thought to what has obsessed you for so many years. They will deal with you as they always have, Alex, and hold you in the same esteem."

"So you have always said. Well, I am willing to take your word on it. No need to put it to the test." He stripped off his gloves. "And since we now have the day free, would you care to go sightseeing?"

She scrambled off the bed and charged at him like all seven of the Furies come together in one fierce young woman. He would have backed up, but his back was already to the door.

"You are going to that wedding!" she informed him, poking at his chest. "How am I to learn to be brave if *you* are not? This time I have failed you, and doubtless I shall fail you again, but one day you will be proud of me. I *will* do better. And think on it, Alex." She poked him again. "If I am with you, your friends will be excruciatingly polite. They will be so busy wondering why your wife is veiled that you'll learn nothing from them. And you'll be so busy worrying about me that we'll *all* be distracted. You will come away with nothing. Our long trip will have been wasted."

"Nonsense." He slipped away from her and unbuckled his sword belt, reflecting on the four long days alone in a comfortable carriage and the four long nights in the best rooms at the finest posthouses. They had not made up for all the celibate months of their marriage, but they'd had a considerable go at it. "Would you prefer that we had not taken this journey, madam?"

She ignored the question, although color rose in her face. "What's more, this day belongs entirely to the bride. She cannot wish a stranger in a veiled bonnet drawing attention from her."

"You are rationalizing, Diana. These are wretched excuses for your own faintheartedness."

"Undeniably. And I am ashamed of myself, although what I have said is nonetheless true. You won't be able to deal with your friends as you ought if I am with you."

"You refine too much on what you imagine will occur. Wear a damned veil if you must, but come with me. I will most certainly not go without you."

She met him eye for eye. "So it has come to a battle. Which

of us is the greater coward? Well, sir, I claim the prize. Hands down, I win. You will be at the wedding because you have the courage I lack. And because I cannot bear to show my face and am too proud to wear the veiled bonnet, I shall wait for you here at the hotel. So there you have it."

For all her defiance, her chin quivered. Tears had stolen into her eyes. He knew her well enough now to sense her hurt, although she was such a brave little thing that it never failed to astonish him when she let that damnable scar vanquish her.

It had done so this morning, precisely when he had meant to lean on her for support. He *needed* her with him. But she knew that. If she was sending him on his way alone, her need must be greater than his. And if he refused to go without her, he would only add to her hurt. To her guilt, because she trembled with guilt and sorrow for letting him down.

He would throw himself in front of a bullet before hurting Diana.

Taking her in his arms, he brushed a kiss against her scarred cheek. "You win indeed," he said. "I'll go. So long as you are here for me to come back to, I could face down the Imperial Guard."

He retrieved his sword and gloves, smiling at her over his shoulder. "But don't be surprised if I reappear within the hour, scampering for cover under your skirts."

"I very much doubt that you will," she said, returning his smile. "But you are always welcome under my skirts."

Alex held to that delicious thought while the carriage took him through the crowded London streets to St. George's, Hanover Square. The driver, calling back that the main thoroughfares were clogged, chose a circuitous route through backstreets, but they were soon stalled in a crowded intersection.

Alex stuck his head out the window. "How close are we?"

"You'll do better walking," the driver advised him. "Go two streets ahead and turn left. Can't miss it."

If the others were mired in traffic as well, perhaps he would arrive in time for the wedding after all. Alex jumped from the carriage, feeling conspicuous in scarlet regimentals with a ceremonial sword dangling from his hip. He noticed that passersby were careful to keep out of his way.

When he turned onto George Street, he saw Max Sevaric standing between two of the enormous portico columns, scanning the street with one hand held to his forehead as a shield against the bright morning sun. Behind him, clustered under the pediment, were four men. He could not make out their faces, but Alex recognized two uniforms of the 52nd— Sevaric's regiment—and an officer of the Coldstream Guards.

There was no mistaking the bridegroom. Major Lord Jordan Blair shamelessly confessed to buying colors in the 10th Hussars because he would look so well with a fur-edged overjacket slung across his shoulder.

Jordie had always put him in mind of Kit—outspoken, outrageous, and with enough self-confidence to boil water. Alex had been drawn into his circle of friends at the Officers' Mess, where Jordie held court like a princeling. He didn't admit just anyone, and Alex—a taciturn loner until he was inexplicably singled out—had felt flattered to be included in such company.

Now he had to face them again, these men he so respected, wearing the shame of his failures. There was no use hoping they didn't know. Soldiers gossiped as freely as women, and word quickly spread when a man had distinguished himself—or done otherwise.

He ordered his feet to move forward, and saw the moment when Sevaric spotted him on the pavement. And he kept moving, because he had committed himself. At worst, they would turn their backs to him. More likely they would be distantly polite. He didn't dare hope for the best.

But in a rush, all five men swept down the stairs and surrounded him, grabbing for his hand and clapping him on the back.

Stunned, he shook their hands and said their names in a gruff voice. "Blair. Trent. Sevaric. Corbett. Pageter."

"Bad enough that m'bride appears to have deserted me," Jordie said with a theatrical groan. "I was just thinking that if I had to spend tonight drowning my sorrows, I'd be wondering why the blazes you didn't show up either. Don't tell that to Emma, by the way. She'd rather I'd have been thinking about her. If she comes, of course, and if you ever meet her."

"We are drawing a crowd," Trent pointed out with his usual calm.

Sure enough, passersby were gathering around them, attracted—Alex reckoned—by all the swords and medals and regimental lace.

Sevaric walked beside him up the stairs and into the vestibule. "Blair is fit to be tied, so pay him no mind. He hasn't spoken a word of sense since we got here."

"I heard that," Jordie said, grasping Alex's arm. "Sevaric wouldn't know sense if it bit him on the arse. So where the devil have you been, Valliant? Last I heard, you were off to South America. Well, not quite last. Met up with your brother, which you know or you wouldn't have got m'message, and he said there were rumors you'd come home. Must be true, for here you are."

Sevaric gave Alex an I-told-you-so look.

"I was nearly two years in South America," Alex said stiffly. "The American War did not suit me. When it was done, I—"

"When it was *lost*, you mean." Jordie shook his head. "Tell you what, old man. You had the worst of it there. Take no offense, but I never could see the point dispatching good English soldiers across the Atlantic to fight for no reason. In your place, I'd have sold out."

"Not if your regiment had to go on without you."

"Right." Jordie grinned. "I'd have stayed with them and hated every minute of it. Bloody politicians ought to be taken out and shot, that's what. At least you'll be giving us some new stories to talk about at the club. We've rehashed Waterloo into the ground."

"I wish I'd been there," Alex said darkly.

"We could have used you. On the other hand, we managed to win without you, even if it was only by the skin of our teeth." He glanced over his shoulder. "Hah! What's this?"

A hackney had pulled to the curb directly in front of the church.

"Your bride must have arrived," Alex said. "Aren't you going down to meet her?"

Jordie turned back to him with a frown. "Can't be Emma.

212

She's coming in my carriage with Dori Sevaric and Allegra Trent. Unless she's jilted me and they've all gone shopping."

Alex watched over Jordie's shoulder as someone opened the hackney door and lowered the steps. For a considerable time, no one emerged. Finally a gloved hand wrapped itself around the panel and a foot came down on the top step. He saw honey-gold skirts, and then the crowd gathered around the hackney and blocked his view.

Of a sudden, they all went quiet.

Heart pounding, he shoved Jordie aside and went to the top of the stairs.

Diana, her auburn hair spilling over her shoulders, was standing helplessly on the pavement, surrounded by curious onlookers. She had used the two Spanish combs he'd given her to hold her hair back from her face. Her scar blazed in the morning sunlight.

With an oath, Alex cut through the crowd like a sword and seized her hand, bowing over it to brush a kiss on her wrist. "You came," he said, his voice breaking. "My brave, brave girl."

She gave him a tremulous smile. "I'm terrified, you know. My legs are shaking like reeds in the wind. But how did it go with you, Alex?"

"Just as you said, of course." He was so proud of her he thought his heart would shatter, just when she'd made it whole again. "Come meet the troops."

She took his arm, and he led her up the stairs to where his friends were waiting. "My wife, gentlemen. Diana Valliant."

Jordie was the first to make his bow. "Welcome, madam. I am honored to meet the only lady gracious enough to attend my wedding. Not excluding my would-be bride, I hasten to add, who appears to have dropped from the face of the earth."

"She'll not fail you," Diana assured him, clinging to Alex's arm as he introduced the men in turn. One by one they bowed, speaking words of welcome, absorbing her into their circle as if she'd always been among them.

Her eyes glowed with pleasure when Nick Trent trotted out a miniature of his son for her to examine. Max Sevaric advised her not to believe a word Dori told her about him. Jordie Blair promised to let her know what her husband had *really* been up to on the Peninsula. Before a few minutes had passed, she had loosed her death grip on Alex's arm and was laughing at one of Jordie's absurd stories.

Alex was the only one to notice that the carriage had arrived. "If you can tear yourself away from *my* wife, Blair, yours is waiting for you on the pavement."

"The devil you say!" His face splitting in a grin, he rushed down the stairs and caught her up and spun her round and round.

Trent and Sevaric followed, dodging the bride and groom to claim their own wives, and soon the bridal party was sweeping down the wide aisle toward the altar where the minister was waiting with an impatient look on his face.

Alex held Diana back from the others, taking refuge in the shadow of a marble column to kiss her thoroughly. Rather breathless when he was done, he brushed a tendril of hair behind her ear. She smiled up at him, her eyes shining like golden stars.

"Shall we wed each other again in our hearts?" he asked softly. "Say the words along with Jordie and Emma, say them to each other?"

"Please, yes. Let's do. I wasn't really attending last time, you know. I hadn't even decided to marry you." A single tear streaked down her scarred cheek. "But oh, Alex, I am so very glad that I did."

"Come then," he said, leading her down the aisle. "Let us take the vows once more. And this time, my soul, we will speak them with love."

Francesca's Rake

For Jill Limber

Chapter 1

It is impossible to please all the
world and one's father.
—*Jean de la Fontaine*

Galen Pender, Viscount Clayburn, reined in his
mount on the narrow bridge and seized a calming
breath. Just ahead, the massive limestone walls of
Montford House loomed over the Bedfordshire countryside, reflecting the pale winter sunlight like blocks
of ice.

Wind whipped at his capes as he stared at the home
he rarely visited, except to call on his mother when
his father, the earl, was certain to be elsewhere. For a
moment, scudding clouds cast the estate in shadows,
as if his dark mood had summoned them.

A storm was blowing in—in more ways than one.

Steeling himself for a battle long overdue, Clay
urged his bay to a gallop and rounded the circular
drive in a hail of gravel. Before he could change his
mind, he tossed the reins to a startled gardener, ran
up the marble steps, and pounded on the door.

Javits, butler at Montford House for thirty years,
stepped quickly out of the way as Clay charged into the
house. "Drawing room, milord," he directed. "Lady
Montford is with him."

Clay slowed a trifle. Damn. He did not want his
mother to witness this confrontation. But then, when
did the family ever come together without a brawl?

Montford must have heard the commotion in the

1

hallway. He was on his feet, one arm resting on the mantelpiece and a look of bored disdain on his face, when Clay erupted into the room.

"How dare you, sir?" Clay closed ground until he was inches from his father, staring straight into silvery eyes so like his own that he had to blink to remind himself he was not looking into a mirror.

The earl lifted a brow. "How dare *you*, Clayburn? To bumble here in all your dirt is inexcusable. Repair to your room, or to the horse trough if you must, and return when you are presentable. Your mother and I shall expect you to be properly announced."

"I d-don't mind, Montford," the countess said in a meek voice. "It is good to see you home, Cl—"

"Be silent!" Montford did not spare her a glance.

Clay turned to his mother and bowed, stricken to see her trembling after the earl's harsh words. "Forgive my poor manners, Mama, but this cannot wait. Perhaps you should leave us for a few minutes."

"She will stay," the earl decreed. "Better she have no illusions about your latest folly and what it has cost me to repair the damage. How could you think to buy colors, Clayburn? Were you intoxicated? But of course you were, to fancy yourself of use to the army, or capable of surviving so much as a week on the Peninsula."

Although his father had scored a direct hit, Clay managed an indifferent shrug. In truth, he'd little idea what was expected of a Light Infantry officer and marveled that the Fifty-second had accepted him in spite of his reputation. "England is at war," he said evenly. "I wished to play my part."

"Nonsense. You imagine yourself gaming and whoring as you do now, but wearing fancy regimentals and out of my reach." Montford smiled his cold smile. "Did you think to escape to Spain, boy? Did you suppose for a moment that I would allow it?"

"I am seven-and-twenty, sir. Old enough to decide for myself. And I bought the commission with my own money."

"Indeed? Since your allowance barely suffices for lodging and food, shall I assume you enjoyed a lucky streak at the hazard tables?"

Clay felt his skin go hot. "Whist, as it happens. And I won with skill, not luck."

"A talent for card-playing?" Montford lifted his quizzing glass. "You astonish me. I had not thought you to have any talent whatsoever. But I do not mean to be unkind. From all accounts the ladies find you irresistible, which will serve us both well when you resign yourself to the business at hand."

Whelping an heir. It always came back to that. Clay glanced at his mother, who gave him a nervous smile of encouragement. He couldn't tell if she meant him to defy the earl or back down.

"Do not hold me accountable for this unpleasant situation, Clayburn." Montford turned his quizzing glass to the countess. "Had this pitiful woman produced another son or two, I would cheerfully disinherit you and leave my fortune to a worthier man. But she failed me, and we all suffer for that."

Clay stripped off his gloves, meaning to fling them at the earl's face, but he heard a choking sound from his mother and looked over at her pale, anxious face. With effort, he curbed his first rash impulse. It would only make him look foolish, after all, and this time he was deadly serious.

"Insult me as you will, sir, but I'll not stand quietly by while you dishonor my mother." He slapped the gloves against his thigh. "Do so again, and I swear we shall come to blows."

3

Dismissing the threat with a wave of his hand, Montford crossed to a side table and lifted the stopper from a decanter. "As you know, I have directed that your commission be resold to some other young buck with more swagger than sense. It required a small gratuity to handle the transaction, so you will be unable to reclaim the full amount."

He poured claret into a glass, sniffed it, and took a long, slow drink. "In fact, I regret to inform you that the funds were misdirected to me. Some error of accounting, no doubt."

Stunned, Clay could only stare at his elegant, hateful father. Still slender and handsome in his late fifties, the earl kept fit by riding to hounds and fencing. He rarely went to London, but his power there was the stuff of legends. It would take only a word in the proper ear to appropriate three thousand pounds rightfully belonging to his son.

Heart pounding, Clay wondered why he still fumbled like a grubby schoolboy in the presence of a man he despised. At least he had trained himself to conceal his emotions, to the point he seldom felt anything deeply, and nothing for very long.

Already his rage had burned out, leaving only a hard knot of determination in his belly. "I accept that you have sliced me out of the army," he said in a calm voice. "But you have no right to steal from me."

"Steal? An absurd and disrespectful accusation, boy. Naturally I shall return the price of your commission, *when* you provide an incentive. And you will definitely need the money, ill begotten as it was, because I am cutting off your allowance."

That was no surprise. Montford had always kept him on a tight leash, financially and in every other way he could devise.

"But there is good news," the earl said with another

of his glacial smiles. "In spite of your rapscallion past, I am willing to give you one last chance to redeem yourself."

"Let me guess." Clay pretended to think it over. "Ah. It can only be the same tune you have sung these last three years. To win myself into that undiscovered country—your good graces—I must marry the Albatross."

For once, he had managed to startle his father. Montford set down his glass and clasped his hands behind his back. "Albatross? One of your obscure jests, no doubt. But yes, I remain convinced that you should wed the young woman I have chosen for you. She will bring to the settlement a large tract of land marching on our estate, along with an enormous dowry. Why you continue to shrink from this ideal marriage eludes me, Clayburn. Once you've got an heir and a spare on her, you may resume your dissipated ways with my blessing."

"Have you considered that she might not have me?"

"Oh, indeed. My contacts in London bring me word of all the reasons why no decent woman of fortune would welcome your addresses. Never doubt I am aware of everything you are up to, Clayburn. But I have some . . . shall we say, influence? If you make an offer, the heiress will surely accept. And you *will* make an offer, if you hope to see another guinea from me. I can make your life very difficult."

"You already have." Clay forced his taut muscles to relax as the glimmer of a plan lit the back of his mind. But he could not work out the details in his father's presence. The earl sucked all the air out of the room, making it hard to breathe.

Only the goal remained clear—freedom from Montford's iron-fisted control and a touch of revenge to seal his independence. This time he meant to defy his father and win.

And he must find a safe haven for his mother. That goal immediately shot to the top of his list. Until now, he had failed the only person he had ever loved, shaming her when he meant to shame the earl.

No more. While he rather enjoyed his notoriety as London's most profligate rake, he could change. He *would* change.

But to best the earl, he must be cold, deliberate, and unrelenting. He must learn to use his father's own weapons—cunning and deceit—against him.

"Well?" Montford made an impatient gesture. "Gone napping, Clayburn?"

"Merely devising a compromise, sir. What if—"

"I do not believe in compromise," Montford interrupted, scowling.

No, Clay thought angrily, his father expected capitulation. Unclenching his fists, Clay produced a smile like the ones his father had perfected—smiles that could freeze molten lead. "Hold off the allowance if you choose, sir, but give me the money from the commission. It is rightfully mine. In return, I swear to marry within the year."

"The heiress. I forget her name. Agree to marry *her*."

Unwilling to break his word, even to a man he loathed, Clay fumbled for a loophole. "I certainly agree to meet her when I return from London. Shall we say two months from now?"

"Why not immediately? What is the point of delay?"

"You have made it necessary with your interference. I must cancel orders for uniforms, horses, weapons, and the like. Or have you already seen to that?"

For the first time, Montford looked ill at ease. "I suppose you must give up your rooms and attend to business before resettling here. But do so in one month, not two. Otherwise, I'll not give you a penny."

How absurd to do battle over a few thousand pounds with so much else at stake. Clay wanted to tell his father, graphically, what he could do with the money. It would make a good exit line. But he was through with dramatic flourishes. And he truly required funds just to survive while he set his tentative plan in motion. At the moment, he had thirty guineas to his name and owed several times that amount to his landlord and assorted creditors.

Fortunately, the earl expected him to beg. With a bit of fake humility and a few vague promises, he could win seed money to finance his new plan. "Tailors and gunsmiths will expect something for their labor," he said, pasting a downcast look on his face. "And I have other debts. If only for the sake of your own reputation, they must be paid."

Montford released a heavy sigh. "Oh, very well. One thousand pounds, on your promise to marry within the year. Contact my solicitor when you reach London. But you will return here in four weeks, prepared to honor your vow, or I shall break you. Trust me on that."

Lacking ammunition for a battle of ultimatums, Clay choked down a few vulgar retorts and bowed curtly.

With a gesture of dismissal, the earl settled in his chair beside the hearth, put on his spectacles, and picked up the book he had been reading. In the firelight, his thick white hair shone like a halo.

Clay regarded his father's aloof profile with contempt. All of a year since he had been home, but to the earl he was of no more consequence than a tradesman. Their business completed, the arctic silence he remembered from childhood enveloped them again.

7

Forcing a warm smile to his cold lips, Clay turned to his mother and offered his arm.

"Surely you are not leaving so soon," she protested in a low voice when they reached the foyer. "Please, Galen," she said, using her favored name for Clay. "At least stay the night."

"I am too angry, Mama. Forgive me, but it is better that I depart immediately. Besides, Jerry and Bertie are in Thurleigh with the carriage, expecting me within the hour. We plan to be well on the road to London before nightfall."

She lowered her head. "You must not keep your friends waiting, of course."

"Ah, Mama." He raised her chin gently with his finger, remorse clutching at his heart. Her pale blue eyes shimmered with tears, but she had learned never to weep openly. Her husband despised weakness of any sort.

With a groan, Clay drew her into a tight embrace. "In a few weeks I shall be here again," he promised. "And very soon, you will have a daughter-in-law and grandchildren to cosset. I expect you to leave this mausoleum and come live with us, so do not think to make excuses. In this matter, neither you nor the earl will overrule me."

She understood, he knew, as she stood on tiptoe to kiss his cheek. Probably she understood more than he imagined. A wonder that she had never lost faith in him, despite his rackety life. While he rebelled against his father, she endured.

Her quiet courage fired his resolve. Somehow, he would make a new home for her. If all else failed, he would even wed the Albatross.

But for now, he must reach London with all possible speed. By reselling the commission and making no secret of it, Montford had publicly, and quite deliberately, disgraced his son. And in response, Clay meant to do the last thing his father expected of him. He would stay the course. For however long it took, he would deflect gossip with charm and wit, hold his head high, and ride out the scandal.

"Good-bye, Mama," he said, giving her one last hug. "When next we meet, I shall have good news for you."

Stepping back, she fixed him with a clear-eyed gaze. "Only tell me you are happy and in love, Galen. Nothing else will do."

Chapter 2

They drink and dance by their own light;
They drink and revel all the night.
                    —*Abraham Cowley*

"I wish this were over and done with, Papa." Francesca pulled a chair close to the enormous canopied bed and sat beside the frail man nestled against a bank of pillows.

Melchior Childe, Duke of Sotherton, stroked her cheek with a gnarled thumb. "You will return to plague me soon enough, Cesca. In spite of the disagreeable task that takes you there, London will do you a world of good."

For his sake, she rallied a show of enthusiasm. "I expect the booksellers to declare a holiday after I buy out half their stock. And I long to visit the Royal Gallery and the museums. Maria Beaton says in her letters that there are lectures about science and art nearly every day. She has even promised to secure an invitation to one of Lady Holland's dinners."

The duke frowned. "Never you mind the political debates and stuffy museums, little bluestocking. You must dance and make merry. I insist upon it."

"Scarcely *little*, Papa. But fear not. I shall be present at every rout and ball to which we are invited. Until the girls are betrothed, of course, at which time I'll gladly wash my hands of them and come home to pluck rare sirloin and buttered lobster from your greedy fingers."

10

He shuddered dramatically. "I have so few pleasures these days, and you scheme to deprive me of every one. Even so, I shall miss you dreadfully while you are gone. My brother has exceeded all bounds this time, snatching you away to chaperone his daughters and hounding me to pay for their come-out."

"What a clanker!" Francesca broke out laughing. "As if Bromley Childe ever rubbed two thoughts together in a single hour. I know very well you engineered this absurd plan as an excuse to propel me into Society."

"True enough, I put the flea in Bromley's ear. But how else was I to rid myself of the tyrant who feeds me pap and hides my cigars? For the next several months, you can apply that iron will to my nieces." He poked her on the shoulder. "Be careful of the bird-wit, Cesca. Runs ahead of the fox, that one."

Francesca nodded ruefully. "If only Bromley were not coming with us. He permits Livvy to do whatever she wishes, and I dare not overrule him."

"You can, and you must. Only remember who holds the purse strings. Bromley cannot afford to present his daughters without my support, and I have put you in charge. Buy expensive wardrobes for yourself and the girls, stage the most lavish ball of the Season, and do me proud. Not a farthing to my brother, though, under any circumstances. He will only game it away."

"I promise. And I shall apply to you constantly for advice, which you will send by return post or—"

"Yes, yes, I shall write, if only to assure you there is no need to come flying home. But tell me happy stories in your letters, *carina*. I wish to hear of your beaux and how you have taken the ton by storm." He took her hand and pressed it to his heart. "Most of all, I want to hear that you have fallen in love."

Beneath the soft nightshirt, she felt his sunken

chest and the erratic throb of his pulse. *Oh, Papa.*
She blinked against a sudden wash of tears. *How can
I leave you?*

But how could she deny him, especially after he
had so cleverly backed her into a corner?

Papa cared not a whit for what became of the
Sotherton dynasty after his death, so long as his precious library survived. It was willed to her, and she
knew every volume and manuscript as if they were
her brothers and sisters.

He had compiled a list of books for her to find and
purchase in London, but that was only another
excuse to send her away. In truth, Papa did not want
her here to watch him die.

But the doctor felt certain he would survive at
least another year or more, and she fully intended to
return within a few weeks.

Moreover, she had a special reason of her own to go
to London. Ever since she could remember, Papa had
searched high and low for a book he longed to possess.
And just last month, Maria Beaton had written with ex-
citing news. The slender volume of Petrarch's sonnets,
illustrated by a nameless artist who might have known
the poet, had appeared in a list of items up for auction.

Francesca intended to buy it for her stepfather, to
thank him for all he had given her—a home, security
for the future, and, most of all, his unfailing love. The
book was trivial in comparison, a gesture only, but
he would understand.

She also meant to see that the Sotherton title survived the scapegrace brother who stood to inherit.
Bromley was already beyond hope, but his son, safely
installed at Oxford, might yet become a worthy Duke
of Sotherton.

And, too, Bromley's daughters deserved a chance
to marry well. Unless she escorted them to London

for the Season, Ann and Livvy would eventually dwindle into spinsterhood. No eligible man had ever shown his face in Rutlandshire, so far as she knew.

For herself, Francesca had no illusions. She was one-and-thirty, taller than most men, and better educated. If all that failed to spook a potential suitor, her illegitimate birth to an Italian commoner would turn the trick.

Even so, she would most likely be courted by a fortune hunter or two. One bidder had already applied for her hand, but only because it happened to be attached to a parcel of land he wanted. And he refused to take no for an answer.

Letters arrived regularly, but they were not even written by the man she was expected to marry. Instead, the Earl of Montford conducted negotiations with the Duke of Sotherton, as if the bride and groom had nothing whatever to say in the matter.

What kind of man would allow his father to sell him off in a business transaction? she wondered. Lord Clayburn must be thoroughly spineless.

Not that she cared in the least, because she'd no intention of accepting a marriage of convenience. Why would she want a man ordering her about and spending her money? With financial independence, a consuming love of books, and a wide circle of pen-friends, what more could she need?

Still, there were those pesky dreams, in the cold hours before dawn, when she fretted alone in her bed. Perfectly understandable, she supposed, but most annoying.

"Italian women are passionate," her mother had warned when she began her monthly bleeding. After explaining how a female body changed and why, she had spoken with an urgency that forever sealed her words in Francesca's mind.

"I shall never regret yielding to the Englishman," Renalda had said in her honeyed Italian accent. "Because of him, I have my precious daughter. But passion without love nearly always ends in disaster. Had Melchior not rescued us from the streets, we would surely be dead by now. So take care, beloved. When a man tempts you, and when your body longs for his touch, trust only your mind and your heart."

At the time, Francesca had had no earthly idea what her mother had meant, although her understanding had improved since. Most of her information was derived from books, though, because she knew better than to place confidence in anything her body had to say—even when it was practically shouting.

Never mind that it squirmed on the sheets at night, wanting what a healthy female body was bound to want. That same body also sniffled with colds and got rashes when she ate shellfish. Who could account for what a body did?

"My dear?" The duke tugged at her long braid. "Did all this talk of love cause you to go mute?"

"In fact, it set me to air-dreaming about London." Mustering a smile, she told him what he wanted to hear. "I shall dazzle all the eligible bachelors and break hearts by the score, until I find the man of my dreams. Then I shall bring him here for the most lavish wedding celebration in Rutlandshire history, and the Duke of Sotherton will lead me down the aisle."

He squeezed her hand. "You are humoring me again, Cesca. Do not think I fail to mark your stratagems. Although my body is failing bit by bit, my brain still functions perfectly well."

"Of course it does. You are the wisest man I have ever known."

"Faint praise, since I am virtually the only man

you know. But make yourself useful one more time and pour me a glass of brandy. One for you, too."

"Papa—"

"Go!"

Unable to quarrel with him during these last few minutes together, she went to the sideboard and measured a bare half inch of brandy into a pair of glasses. One driblet would do no harm. Besides, he kept a flask under his pillow, to use when the pain assailed him at night. They both pretended she didn't know.

The duke had pulled himself straighter on the pillows. Accepting his glass with courtly grace, he patted the spot on the bed near his waist where he wanted her to sit. "I never look at you without thinking of your mother, *carina*. You are so much like her—beautiful, intelligent, and blessed with her loving spirit."

"Don't forget her temper."

His eyes grew misty, and Francesca knew he was about to launch into a familiar tale. She leaned into the circle of his arm, trying as always to remember what he described. But she had been three years old at the time, half-starved, and probably terrified. She recalled nothing of how he had met her mother. Indeed, if not for the duke's stories and for her mama's vague descriptions of their hardscrabble life in Italy, she would swear she had been born here at Sotherton Manor.

Her real father was British, a navy lieutenant whose name Mama took to her grave ten years ago. She had said he died of cholera before they could marry, but more likely he had seduced and then abandoned her.

Perhaps he was dead, or perhaps he now had a family of his own. Francesca didn't care one way or the other. With all her heart, she loved the man who had adopted her and raised her as if she were his natural child.

The duke had come to his favorite part of the tale, which Francesca could almost recite with him word for word. "I nearly tripped over her there in the street. Just another beggar, I thought. Naples was full of them. I tossed her a coin and tried to move on, but you jumped up and kicked me on the shin. I still don't know why."

"Nor do I," she said on cue. "Except that I was born a brat."

"Poor Renalda. She was so embarrassed, pulling you away and apologizing in Italian. I understood little of what she said, but when I looked into her clear dark eyes, I fell head over tail in love. Only imagine, pumpkin. I was lost, trying to get somewhere or t'other, and God led me into the alley where I met my wife and daughter."

"God was watching out for us all," she affirmed dutifully.

She wanted to believe that. Could a mere coincidence change so many lives? And yet, the cynic in her refused to accept the possibility of divine intervention in everyday human affairs. The occasional miracle, perhaps, when the Lord saw fit. But in general, people were expected to struggle on as best they could.

"Again you humor an old man's folly," he said gently. "Thank you for listening, and forgive me for prosing on. I relive my past and plot your future, which must surely grate on your nerves." He lifted his glass. "Shall we make a toast?"

"Aye, sir. To what shall we drink?"

"Why, to love. What else matters?" He swallowed his brandy in a single gulp, coughed, and took the handkerchief she pulled from her sleeve, pressing it against his mouth.

Then she touched her glass to her lips, preserving the moment for his sake. "To love."

"But I don't *wish* to stop!" Livvy kicked her foot against the leather squabs, barely missing Francesca's knee. "Father, tell her we must go on."

Francesca ignored Bromley's muttered protest and spoke to the shivering footman peering at her through the carriage window. His eyelashes were crusted with ice.

"Tell the driver to pull in at the next posthouse," she said firmly. "And watch for the baggage coach. I fear it may have got stuck. If it fails to catch up, we must send help."

The footman disappeared into the swirling snow, and soon the carriage resumed its slow progress, swaying against the buffeting winds.

"We'll never get to London at this rate," Livvy whined. "Move over, Ann. You are taking up more than half the seat."

"I'm sorry." Ann scrunched even closer to the paneled door and smiled at Francesca. "Livvy is a restless traveler."

Francesca swallowed a scorching reply. She was fond of sweet, conciliatory Ann, although the girl really ought to find her backbone. As for Livvy, Francesca already wanted to strangle the wretched chit.

It was Livvy who had insisted they set out that morning despite the snow flurries that had already begun when the Sotherton coaches arrived at Lord Bromley's house. They should have waited until the weather cleared before proceeding to London, but Livvy had thrown a tantrum right there in the driveway.

Now, because Francesca had given in, the carriage would likely be mired in the drifting snow before they could reach the safety of an inn. The hot bricks under her feet had long since gone cold, and her fingers and toes felt like slivers of ice. What must the driver and footman be suffering?

Next to her, Bromley wrapped himself in a heavy blanket and soon began to snore. Just as well, Francesca thought. Awake, he was only slightly less irritating than Livvy.

The wan winter light slowly faded, and when the sun disappeared altogether, even the body heat of four passengers could not warm the carriage. Ann and Livvy forgot their quarrel and huddled together, faces invisible under fur-lined cloaks.

Francesca tried to sleep, but her mind whirled with visions of disaster. This nightmare journey was all her fault. Papa had advised her to ignore Bromley's wishes, but already she had let him overrule her judgment. It would not happen again, she resolved. From now on, she would make the decisions.

Pulling out her watch, she looked at the time and grimaced. Nearly midnight. Where the devil were they? She rubbed frost from the window and peered outside, but windblown snow had frozen in a thick sheet on the glass. She could see nothing.

Moments later, the coach shuddered to a halt.

Dear God! Swallowing a rush of panic, she waited for word from the footman.

After an endless minute, she heard him stabbing at the encrusted ice on the carriage door. When he broke through and raised the latch, icy wind screamed into the compartment.

"P-posthouse," he shouted through chattering teeth.

Gathering her cloak around her, Francesca accepted his arm and stepped into snow up to her knees.

Light streamed from the posthouse windows, and she saw a long line of coaches parked in a row. Most wore a thick mantle of white. A pair of ostlers had just detatched horses from another carriage, the latest to arrive, and were leading them toward the stable.

"I can make it from here," she told the footman. "See to the others."

Livvy jumped out next to her. "Why are we stopping again?"

Francesca whirled around. "Help your father and Ann to the door while I go ahead to make arrangements. And if you question why we are stopping, here is the answer." Scooping up a handful of snow, she mashed it into Livvy's startled face.

Laughter and music blared from the taproom, louder than the screeching wind. Through the window, Francesca saw a man playing a fiddle. She tramped to the door and let herself in.

Three travelers stood in the passageway, facing away from her, their caped greatcoats dusted with fresh snow. She could not see the man who was addressing them.

" . . . reserved for families with children, you understand. Can't have 'em running underfoot, what with all this crowd."

"A private parlor, then?" said a low baritone voice.

"Got three, but they ain't private tonight. Not even for Quality, milord. The one in front is for the ladies, and the middle room for anyone who cares to use it. I expect you gentlemen will prefer the rear parlor, where I've set up tables with cards and dice to help you pass the time. A servant will bring you a meal there, unless you prefer to eat in the dining hall."

"We'll take supper in the parlor, thank you, along with several bottles of your best claret."

"I'll see to it immediately. Straight ahead, then. Last door to the left." As the men walked away, stripping off their coats and gloves, the proprietor caught sight of Francesca by the door and gave her a welcoming smile. "Traveling alone, ma'am? Wait just a moment, please. I'll be right back to attend you."

"B-but ... " Her voice faded off. Time enough to correct him when the others arrived.

One of the men turned then, acknowledging her with a slight bow.

At first she pretended not to see him run his gaze slowly from the toes of her wet half-boots to the brim of her drooping bonnet. *Diàvolo!* No man had ever looked at her that way, as if he could see right through her sable-lined cape and woolen dress.

All too aware of a flush rising to her cold cheeks, she planted her feet solidly and gave him back eye for eye.

Within seconds, she regretted her boldness. No man ought to be that handsome, or make it clear he knew that she had noticed. But try as she might, she could not look away from his eyes.

Until now, she had not imagined that eyes came in that color. Blue, hazel, gray, brown, even black. But pure silver? She wrenched her gaze to his dark hair, sleek and wet from the snow, took swift note of smiling lips over a firm chin, and finally realized she was actually looking *up* at a man.

He stood nearly a head taller, and seemed to fill the narrow passageway with his broad shoulders and long legs. "You should not have been left here alone," he said affably. "Shall I keep you company until the innkeeper returns? Better yet, why not join me for supper?"

Stunned, Francesca gaped at him for a moment before snapping her mouth shut. Join him for supper indeed! No gentleman would make such an offer to a lady he had never met.

But then, he was clearly *not* a gentleman, and she could only imagine what he thought of her. "Thank you," she said curtly, "but I do not require your assistance."

"Are you certain?" His smile widened. "It will be a long night, I fear, and my friends will be glad of someone new to converse with. After too many hours together in a coach, we are heartily sick of one another."

"I'm not surprised."

He laughed. "*Touché*. We would be dull company indeed for a goddess."

Goddess? A silver tongue to match his silver eyes, she thought, wishing she had not let him bait her. Mortified, Francesca deliberately gave him her back, which left her staring foolishly at the closed posthouse door.

After a moment, still laughing, he headed in the other direction, the heels of his boots clicking on the oak-wood floor. She could not resist looking around. He must have been expecting it. Turning, he grinned at her before disappearing into the parlor.

Arrogant coxcomb! He was precisely the sort of man her mother had warned her about—a glib charmer with good looks and bad intentions. Thank heavens she would never see him again.

The proprietor emerged from the taproom as Livvy burst into the foyer, followed by her father. Ann limped beside him, clinging to Bromley's arm.

"I twisted my ankle when I jumped from the coach," she explained, "but it hurts only a little."

"Have you secured our rooms?" Bromley stomped snow from his boots. "Who's in charge here? I want a hot bath and a bottle of brandy."

The proprietor moved forward, ignoring Bromley to take Ann's other arm. "This way, ladies. When you are nestled right and tight by the fire, I'll send Mrs. Hoyt to look at the young miss's injury. M'name's

Josiah Hoyt, and you are welcome to the Rose and Thistle."

He led them to a small room already crowded with women, some of them stretched on mattresses that had been laid out on the floor. Two wing chairs were angled by the fireplace, and Mr. Hoyt quickly offered a free meal if the ladies who occupied them cared to adjourn to the dining room. They were gone in a flash.

Francesca gave him a grateful smile. "Thank you. I shall pay for their dinners, of course."

"Oh, I'll be makin' plenty of blunt tonight, this bein' the only posthouse for ten miles either direction. You just settle back and let old Josiah take care of you."

Old Josiah was a marvel. In the next hour, Francesca watched him handle fretful customers with bluff good humor while his staff served up bowls of spicy beef stew, chunks of crusty bread, and wedges of cheese.

Mrs. Hoyt brought a pot of steaming water for Ann to soak her ankle and gave her a pillow to support her foot. The ankle was slightly swollen, but after dinner Ann was able to walk down the hall to use the commode.

Livvy, still in a huff, had long since disappeared with her father into the taproom. Francesca suspected she ought to go after her, but it was nearly midnight and the ladies' parlor had gone quiet except for a few murmured conversations and soft snoring from the corner. Dragging a recalcitrant Livvy there would disturb everyone's rest.

Francesca leaned back in the chair, smoke from the fireplace stinging her eyes. She let them drift shut. In a few minutes she would go check on Livvy. Really she would.

* * *

"Cesca!" Ann tugged at her arm. "Wake up."

The first thing she saw was the mantel clock. Good heavens! It had gone past three. How had she slept so long? Francesca sat up and looked at Ann's worried face. "What is wrong? Does your ankle—"

"It's fine. I went looking for Livvy, but I cannot find her. Or Father. They aren't in the taproom."

"You shouldn't be wandering about on your own," Francesca chided gently, "especially on that sore foot. Sit, please, and wait here while I track them down."

Except for the rowdy taproom, the Rose and Thistle was filled with sleeping travelers. Servants had curled up on the floor, and she saw her own driver and footman snoozing in a corner of the dining hall.

Tiptoeing around the prone bodies, she returned to the passageway. Josiah had said there were three private parlors, so she tried the second door and scanned the crowded room. A few people turned in her direction, scowling at the disturbance. Softly, she closed the door and swore under her breath.

She should have guessed immediately. The last parlor was reserved for gentlemen, "with dice and cards to pass the time." Naturally her uncle would find his way there, with Livvy in tow if she insisted. As she would. Dear Lord, at this rate the child would be ruined before they even got to London.

Guilt soured Francesca's tongue. She had allowed Livvy to slip the leash, and now there would be the devil to pay.

Steeling herself, she went to the last door on the left and cracked it open. The stench of cigars, stale wine, and sweat hit her like a fist. *Còrpo di Bacco!* How could anyone remain in that room? A blanket of smoke hung over the tables, and she could scarcely see to the opposite wall.

"Come on in, precious!" called a voice to her right. "Don't be shy." A loud chorus approved the invitation.

Francesca drew herself to her full height and stepped inside, looking over the crowd until she spotted Bromley huddled at a table with three other men. Pretending she did not hear the catcalls and insults aimed at her, she strode calmly across the room.

Livvy was wedged between her father and the silver-eyed man, her knee pressed against his thigh. She held a glass of wine.

"Hullo, Cesca," she said, her voice slurred. "I'm learnin' to play whist."

Francesca took a deep breath and glanced at a long-fingered hand resting on the table next to a large stack of guineas and banknotes. The man had removed his coat and untied his cravat. In the light from a chandelier directly overhead, his white shirtsleeves and silver-threaded waistcoat shimmered through the cloud of smoke.

What effrontery, to dally with Olivia right in front of her father! Even now he made no move to withdraw his leg. The sight of his muscular thigh against Livvy's knee made Francesca want to throttle him with a blunt object.

She moved to Livvy's side and leaned over to whisper in her ear. "Come with me now, in silence, or we shall not continue on to London."

"Ah," the man said, his voice amused. "The ladies have a secret. Shall we compel them to share it with us?"

Compel? Francesca lifted her chin and glared directly into his silver-mirror eyes.

"Whoever the devil you are, sir, I suggest you mind your own blasted business!"

Chapter 3

Therefore who her will conquer ought to be
At least as full of love and wit as she.
                                    —*Charles Cotton*

Clay sat back in his chair, laughing.

What a termagant! But not at all a garden-variety shrew. Immediately after swearing at him, she had blushed a delicious shade of pink. Enchanted, he watched her bend again to whisper in the tipsy girl's ear and take the wineglass from her hand.

Clearly she was not traveling alone, as he had thought when he spoke to her in the passageway. Flirted with her, truth be told, but more from habit than attraction. Wet and bedraggled under her heavy cape and sagging bonnet, she had appealed only to his deepest male instincts.

But those instincts had been right on target, as usual. Now he could see what the cape and hat had concealed—a ripe, full-breasted figure under her drab woolen dress, a smooth complexion, and a magnificent pair of flashing black eyes. Clay ran one finger under his collar. The room had gone a great deal warmer in the last few minutes.

For all her startling beauty, he suspected she was employed as governess or chaperone to the chit who had plagued him for the last three hours. Since there was no wedding ring on her finger, she could not be Bromley Childe's wife. Another of his children, perhaps?

But those exotic eyes and the long black hair escaping the single braid down her back set her apart from the vapid gamester and his annoying blond daughter. A mystery, this vastly seductive woman.

And he loved mysteries, especially when they came packaged in soft female flesh.

At last the goddess managed to pry Miss Childe from the table, and loud protests from the besotted men rang out as she hauled her young charge from the room. Clay tried to catch her eye, but she never looked back.

Unfortunate. But she had been aware of him when they met in the passageway. Deliciously aware.

He understood women, having made a study of them since his voice changed, and this one was a banked fire. Or an explosion waiting for the right man to light her fuse. Were he not too squiffy from the claret, and the inn so crowded, he would strike that flame this very night.

The card game had long since grown dull, so he gathered his winnings and stood. "Deal me out, gentlemen. I require a breath of fresh air."

"You can't quit now," Childe protested. "My luck is bound to turn."

"Then you must recoup your losses from someone else, sir." Clay pulled on his coat. "May I suggest you try another game? You have no skill at whist."

With relief, he stepped into the dim passageway and closed the door behind him, pausing to enjoy his first smoke-free breath in several hours. Two bottles of claret had turned his legs to noodles. Leaning against the wall for support, he waited for his head to stop spinning.

Decadence would be a great deal more pleasurable if it could be indulged in cleaner surroundings with more agreeable companions than Bromley Childe. And without the inevitable hangover.

Mostly without the self-disgust that usually haunted him until he drank enough to stop caring. Lately, though, even liquor and a succession of delightful bedmates could not still the inner voice that nagged for his attention.

Fool! You are throwing away your life.

Drawing himself erect, he took a few tentative steps down the long hall and stopped again. Just ahead, the termagant had the widgeon plastered against the wall. He slipped into a dark spot between two bronze candelabra to watch.

The widgeon stamped her foot. "Father didn't mind. And he is almost a duke."

"Not *yet!*" The air fairly sizzled. "How dare you, Olivia?"

Her voice lowered then, and Clay had to settle for looking at her. Gilded by the flickering light, she was altogether splendid. An earthbound goddess, tall and regal and imperious, with a body shaped for pleasure.

"One more trick like this one," she said in a loud hiss, "and the only offer you can expect from a man will not include a wedding ring. If you are determined to scandalize your family, confine yourself to the farmhands in Rutlandshire. I shall whisk you there in an instant if you shame the duke again, as you have done this night."

"That means you'll have to go back, too," the chit said defiantly.

"My greatest wish is to return home this very moment. Pray remember that, whenever you are tempted to misbehave. I agreed to be your chaperone against my will, and I shall seize any excuse to end this nightmare."

"That's because you are old and dried up and not

likely to have any fun! Do you even know *how* to have fun? Tonight a handsome viscount paid me considerable attention. You are jealous, Francesca, because that will never happen to you."

Francesca? A lovely name. If only he knew the rest of it. But did that little blond witch mistake his tolerance of her outrageous behavior for genuine interest? Clay had not meant to interfere, but Francesca's stunned silence after the bruising attack rang in his ears. A soundless cry of pain, he realized, surprised that he had heard it.

Angry for her sake, he lifted his shoulders away from the wall and strode down the passageway, feigning a look of surprise when he reached the two women. "Ah, we meet again. Forgive me if I have interrupted a private coze."

Livvy gave him a cheeky grin. "You are most welcome, sir. I am being read a lecture."

"Indeed?" He lifted a brow. "Perhaps you have earned it. The gaming tables are no place for a young lady, Miss Childe, but of course, you know that. Fortunately, no one will remark that you joined your father this night. The inn was crowded with stranded travelers, and we all took refuge where we could find a shred of space."

"Y-yes." Even Olivia could not mistake the censure in his voice. "Excuse me, please. I must find my sister." With a swift curtsy, she fled down the hall.

And good riddance! Now he had the goddess all to himself. Clay opened his mouth to say something charming, one of the practiced compliments that never failed to beguile a woman, but his tongue stuck to the roof of his mouth.

Francesca was regarding him with curious astonishment, as if she had just seen a pig stand on its hind legs and recite a sonnet.

To be sure, she could expect no good of him after what she had observed in the gaming room. In fact, she had caught him in one of his better moments— partly sober, no woman on his lap—which spoke volumes about his general behavior.

"Truly, I am not so b-bad as you think." Damn! Could he possibly have said that more awkwardly?

Her eyes narrowed.

"Be sure I have no carnal designs on the young lady," he continued like a stampeded mule. "Whatever her misapprehensions, or yours, Miss Childe is perfectly safe."

"I shall see to that," Francesca replied sharply. "But when gentlemen—and I use that term with no certainty it applies to you—are in their cups, impetuous young ladies are easily led to mistake their intentions. You are older and wiser than Olivia, sir. In future, pray recall how easily a woman's reputation is damaged beyond repair."

This particular woman might have taken lessons in intimidation from his father. Impressed, Clay lifted his arms in a gesture of surrender. "I was careless and irresponsible. In truth, I paid no attention whatever to the girl. But I should have sent her away."

To his relief, Francesca melted slightly. "She is a handful, to be sure, and I am at fault for letting her escape my protection. Thank you for setting her straight a few minutes ago. She got a bit above herself in the gaming room, but you brought her down to earth."

"I hope so." Clay grinned. "If I never see her again, she will not be missed. I cannot say the same for you, however. Your name is Francesca?"

With a startled look, she backed up a step. "Did Brom—Lord Bromley tell you that? Or were you listening to my conversation with Livvy?"

"Does it matter? I wish to make your acquaintance, and I would do so in proper fashion were there anyone to introduce us. But we are both snowbound and alone together, so perhaps we can dispense with the formalities." He bowed. "I am Galen Pender, Viscount Clayburn."

He had rather hoped she would be impressed. How many chaperones won the attention of a viscount, after all?

The more fool he. Francesca's eyes went round as moons, as if the devil himself had sprung up in front of her. Before he could react, she spun around and vanished into the ladies' parlor.

What was *that* about? He stared at the empty passageway, unable to credit that the mere sound of his name had sent her scampering. Surely reports of his unsavory reputation had not reached all the way to Rutlandshire. He'd never set foot in the tiny rural county, and had the impression no one lived there but cows and sheep.

Another mystery to solve, when he sobered up.

Clay aimed himself at the main door and wobbled on shaky legs into the cold air. The storm had passed, and someone had shoveled the path to the stable. Overhead, Orion blazed in the clear black sky.

After finding a dark place at the side of the inn to relieve himself, he trudged through the knee-deep snow toward a copse of oak. The leafless branches, crusted with ice, glittered in the starlight.

The silence and the stark beauty made him feel painfully alive. Achingly alone.

He wanted so many things that eluded his reach. Or he assumed they did. He wanted, but he didn't know what he wanted most, so he never tried for anything important. Only good times and irresponsibility, which left him unsatisfied and useless. Above all, useless.

Even now, with a goal in mind, he scarcely knew where to begin. Clay picked up a handful of snow and let it sift through his fingers. There would be no easy escape from his father's tyranny, so he might as well resign himself to the inevitable.

Marriage.

Not to the Albatross, God forbid. Damned if he would marry solely to bring a few acres of land into the Montford holdings. All he knew about the heiress was her age, which the earl had let slip in an unguarded moment.

One-and-thirty, for pity's sake. Four years older than he. An heiress unwed at that advanced age could only be an antidote of the first order. Besides, she was his father's choice, which made her the last woman in the universe he would take to wife.

But if he married someone else . . .

The ill-formed plan at the back of his mind began to take shape. The earl had the influence to buy back his son's commission in the army, but surely he could not annul a consummated marriage. And if the bride were of no consequence, a cit or a foreigner, so much the better.

Clay rubbed his hands together, feeling an unfamiliar surge of excitement. He imagined himself drawing up in a coach at Montford House with a wholly unsuitable wife and thumbing his nose at the earl.

Money would be no problem once he married, even when Montford inevitably deprived him of everything that was not entailed to the legitimate heir. His grandmother had settled a fortune on him, currently managed by the earl, which would revert to Clay when he produced a son or daughter. Blessedly, women were not so fussy as men about the gender of children when they made out their wills.

It wasn't as though he had the option of marrying

for love, if such a thing existed. Now and again he tried to picture a happy home with a wife he adored and a gaggle of children clinging to his legs, but the vision never formed clearly enough for him to believe in it.

Reality was the trap his father had set for him, and his plan was to escape it. All he needed was a bride.

And tonight, by sheerest luck, he had stumbled upon the perfect woman. Francesca. A hot-tempered beauty for his own pleasure, and a wife without fortune or lineage to gall his father. True, she had a poor opinion of him at the moment, but what spinster chaperone would not leap at the chance to marry into the aristocracy?

The nagging voice at the back of his head said, *This one.*

Ah, well. He relished the challenge of bringing a goddess to earth. And he wanted to bed her. The intensity of his desire astounded him. He had felt lust . . . he often felt lust . . . but never an overwhelming attraction to a specific woman. How ironic to feel his body grow hard just thinking of the most straitlaced female he had ever met.

On fire with more enthusiasm than he had felt in years, Clay went to the stable and instructed a sleepy ostler to make his carriage ready to depart at first hint of daylight. Even with a blanket of snow covering the road, he would make faster time than the travelers slogging through grimy slush later in the day.

In high spirits, he returned to the inn and rallied his friends. The Quest was under way!

Feet propped on hot bricks, steaming pork pies in their hands, Bertram and Jeremy Porter stared blankly when Clay outlined his plan.

"You can't mean it," Bertie said.

"Are you queer in the attic?" Jerry fell forward and then back against the squabs as the carriage made its halting way through the drifted snow. "Marry a nobody? The earl will hang you up by your nether parts."

"He'll want to," Clay agreed. "Which is the whole point. Or a good part of it," he added with strict honesty. The Porter brothers had been his boon companions since his early days at Eton, and he rarely lied to them. But this time he meant to keep a few secrets, including his peculiar obsession with the goddess. They would not understand. For that matter, neither did he.

"If I don't marry someone else, Montford will legshackle me to the Albatross. Better a wife of my own choosing, and best if she is the last woman he would welcome into the family. No money, no rank, no property, nothing but a certificate of marriage to put an end to all his plots."

Bertie frowned. "Albatross? What the devil is an albatross?"

"A large bird," Clay explained slowly. Bertie was none too bright, even when not in his cups, but his sweet nature made him a favorite in Society. "In a poem by Mister Coleridge, a dead albatross is suspended around the neck of the sailor who killed it, as punishment for his sin."

"Aha!" Bertie waved his pork pie. "See what comes of reading about birds who cock up their toes. Claws. Whatever birds cock up. The earl is trying to marry you off to an heiress, which is no bad thing in my opinion. But you figure she is an albatross before you even meet her." He took a bite of pie and spoke through a mouthful of thick crust. "Me, I know a female from a dead bird. Prob'ly because I never read poems."

Clay grinned at Jerry. Amiable Bertie had survived

Oxford only because his brother had written all his papers and exams. And they were both spared expulsion because Clay took full blame for the pranks they devised and pulled off together. Only he had been rusticated after they herded a flock of sheep into Christchurch Chapel, precisely when the dean was addressing a congregation of wealthy benefactors.

"What's the difference between marrying an albatross and a servant?" Jerry asked reasonably. "Either way, you are shackled to a wife you don't want. Why not bite the bullet and make peace with the earl? He will hound you forever if you continue to defy him, and it's not likely you will ever win."

When Clay frowned, Jerry gave him back an innocent smile. "I say take the albatross, sire an heir on her, and come back to London with us. That's the sensible thing. Your life can proceed as it has always done, once you give up this benighted notion of trumping your father."

Clay opened his flask and took a swig of brandy. Jerry meant well, but he didn't know how the earl treated his wife. "I cannot give it up," he said softly. "And any marriage is better than the one he plans for me."

"Are you sure?" Bertie wagged a finger at him. "Sounds to me like you're cutting off your nose to smite your face."

"Spite," Jerry said. "To *spite* his face. But you are spot on, Bertie. It is spite that drives him now. Am I right, Clay?"

"To an extent." Clay remembered his wild ride from Montford House to Thurleigh after the confrontation with his father. Had he chanced to encounter a whore or a toothless hag selling rags, he'd have swept her off to London, acquired a special license, and made vows. He had been that angry.

Luckily, the roads had been deserted. And a new passion had since replaced his impulse to punish Montford any way he could. "As a matter of fact," he said, "I am *after* rather more than either of you know, and I'll need your help when we get to London. Will you stand with me?"

Bertie swallowed the last of his pie and belched. "Always with you, Clay. We stick together."

Jerry folded his arms. "No one gets hurt?"

Clay looked at him with surprise. That was not a question that ever arose when the three of them began an adventure. "Only the earl, I trust. Surely you cannot object to that. I doubt the Albatross knows of my existence, so she will be unaffected. As for the chaperone, you may safely leave her to me." He chuckled softly. "She has a will of her own, and a strong one at that. If I cannot win her over, so be it."

"You intend to play fair?" Jerry looked doubtful. "We are no longer schoolboys, and females are easily hurt. Their feelings and reputations ought not to be trifled with."

"Do you mean I should not seduce her?" Clay couldn't help but imagine the scene. His gentle, compelling summons. Her retreat. The suggestive words and the sly touches. Her slow, reluctant capitulation. Finally, her eager—

"Are you listening?" Jerry demanded. "Bed her if you must, and if she agrees, but that's no way to begin a marriage."

"I beg to disagree. Half the marriages in England produce children within a few months of the ceremony." Clay swiped his fingers through his hair. "But no, I'll not drag her to the altar because she is increasing. Most likely she will jump at my offer for even more practical reasons—money, a life of leisure, and the chance to escape Bromley Childe's household.

Good Lord, she stands to be Countess of Montford one day. How can she possibly turn me down?"

"You have a heart of ice, my friend. I wonder you have not dispatched an accountant to your prospective bride, with a ledger book listing the pros and cons of wedding a disgraced viscount and acquiring a tyrannical father-in-law."

"Only because the cons would far outweigh the benefits. Nevertheless, I shall pursue the governess until she consents to be my wife. A friendly wager, Jerry? Five hundred guineas that I succeed."

Bertie, snoring loudly, had slumped against his brother's shoulder. With a sigh, Jerry pushed him away. "He drinks too much, and I cannot stop him. We need some occupation beyond revelry, Clay. All three of us."

"I did try," Clay reminded him.

"Yes. But your heart wasn't with the army or you'd have found a way to outwit the earl, even if it meant taking the king's shilling. You haven't asked, but I'll tell you what I think. Stop reacting to your father and go in search of what you want for yourself."

Good advice, except that everything he wanted was tangled up with his father. Even Francesca, although he would have wanted her anyway.

But Jerry was right about one thing. She must not be hurt. "Forget the bet," he said. "Neither of us has fifty guineas, let alone five hundred. I'll not begin my courtship of Miss Francesca Nobody by making her the object of a wager."

"A wise decision. Women have a way of finding out about these things. Her name is Francesca? Sounds foreign."

"I suspect she's Italian. Maybe Spanish or Portuguese, but it doesn't matter where she came from. I intend to marry her, and I require your assistance."

"Not for a reference, I trust?"

"Perish the thought. Even without your accounting of my sins, she is convinced I am Satan in a waistcoat. I merely want you and Bertie to draw the Childe girls away, giving me time alone with their chaperone. We saw only the tart in the gaming room, but apparently there are two of them."

"Twins," Jerry said laconically. "I encountered the other one in the taproom when she was looking for her father. Ann. Quiet and shy, nothing like her sister."

Clay regarded his friend with interest. "Something new here?"

"Let us say I am willing to keep her occupied while you make sheep eyes at the dragon. So what is the plan?"

Devil if he knew. "By the time we reach London, I'll have one. Certainly we must be present wherever young girls go to find husbands. Polish up your dancing shoes, Jerry. We may be forced to do the pretty at Almack's."

"Bertie will have to pull off a miracle to get us admitted there. Especially after—" He shrugged. "Well, you know what to expect."

Clay tipped his hat over his eyes and folded his arms, ending the conversation. Yes, he knew precisely what to expect in London. Gossip. Titters behind gloved hands. Pointing fingers. Humiliation.

Francesca was bound to hear of his disgrace, reinforcing her low opinion of Lord Clayburn and making his courtship all the more unwelcome. But failure was out of the question. Within a month he would woo and win his reluctant goddess, rescue his mother, and consign his father to the devil.

The Fates must have a sense of humor, Clay reflected. He had wanted to go to war. And now, in a backward sort of way, he'd got his wish.

Chapter 4

Clere be thy virgyns, lusty underkellis:
London, thou art the flour of Cities all.
                    —*William Dunbar*

"Such a waste," Francesca said, stepping away from the ballroom door to let a carpenter pass with an armful of wooden moldings. "All this turmoil and expense, just to give a ball."

Maria Beaton brushed sawdust from her skirt. "How tiresome it must be, listening to the ceaseless clatter. And when they begin to paint, the smell of fumes will be positively unendurable. You should consider relocating to the Crillon for a few days, my dear."

"Set Livvy loose in a hotel? Oh, I think not. Although it *would* detach her from the young carpenter she has been hounding for the past two weeks."

"How came you to lease this monstrosity?" Maria asked on their way downstairs. "The location is excellent, to be sure, and the public rooms are in tolerable condition—"

"*Now* they are!" Francesca laughed. "When we arrived, the Holland covers had yet to be removed, and with every step on the carpets, we kicked up a cloud of dust. I'm afraid the owner withheld a few details. He assured our agent that the house was fully staffed but failed to add that the servants were unacquainted with the concept of work. As for the ballroom, he gave only the dimensions. You must admit it is a very *large* ballroom. Regrettably, only mice and spiders have danced there for several decades."

"Deplorable! Someone must answer for this."

"I assure you, someone is. Papa's agent has renegotiated the lease, and now the owner is virtually paying us to stay here."

When they arrived in the foyer, Francesca led her friend down a wide passageway and opened a heavy oak door at the far end. "The library. Notice there are precisely seven volumes on the shelves—the ones I brought with me. Do you suppose we shall have time to visit a bookshop this afternoon?"

"I can always find time for books, my dear. And, of course, we must also see to your wardrobe."

Francesca glanced down at her blue kerseymere walking dress. "But it is already seen to, except for a few items that have not been delivered. Livvy insisted that we set out for the mantua-maker the very day we arrived in London. Indeed, outfitting the three of us is the only task I have managed to complete."

"Perhaps not altogether. That dress is marginally fashionable, but pale colors do not suit you. When we have done with our calls, I shall put you in the capable hands of Madame Flambeau."

Francesca abruptly closed the library door and marched in the direction of the foyer, leaving her guest to follow. How dare Maria Beaton criticize her gown! It was the outside of enough to fall into bed exhausted after wrangling with servants and leasing agents and carpenters and Livvy—always Livvy!—only to toss and turn all the night, fretting over the mountain of tasks still awaiting her attention.

She worried about Papa, whose letters were invariably cheerful so that she would not worry. Which only made her worry all the more.

Bromley rarely came to the house now, after she'd

made it clear the duke had forbidden her to give him so much as a shilling. She was pleased not to have him underfoot, certainly, but his long disappearances made her uneasy. So far as she knew, he had no acquaintances in the city, and even a here-and-thereian required a place to sleep.

After a fortnight in London, she had yet to find time for a visit to the galleries and museums. All her dreams of mingling with people who shared her intellectual interests had been replaced with nightmares about recalcitrant maids, dull-witted cooks, and greedy dressmakers.

Finally, two days ago, she'd stolen an hour to call on the woman with whom she had corresponded for more than a decade. Maria Beaton, noted bluestocking and advocate of women's rights, had always encouraged her meager pretensions to learning. Francesca often spent hours, sometimes days, researching and drafting her replies to Maria's letters.

Now she understood what a trial it must have been for Maria to indulge the Rutlandshire yokel. Even this brief time in London had proven she lacked the experience and sophistication to deal with simple tradesmen, let alone with the beau monde.

Francesca realized she had come to a stop in the foyer, with her hand clutching a carved newel for support.

Maria tapped her briskly on the shoulder. "Are you done with the fidgets, young woman? We must be on our way."

"I cannot go with you." Francesca tightened her grip on the newel. "I simply cannot."

"Nonsense. Stand up straight, turn yourself around, and look at me."

Fairly sure Bonaparte would obey an order delivered in that tone of voice, Francesca straightened and turned. With effort, she looked directly into Maria's calm brown eyes.

"I haven't the merest idea how to go on in Society," she confessed, relieved to say out loud what she had been thinking since Papa first proposed this scheme. "They will laugh at me, all the hoity-toity ladies you mean for me to meet today. Not while I am in their company, certainly, for they are far too well mannered. But afterward, I shall be talked about like a two-headed pig at the county fair."

"Only if you oink, my dear. And should you do so, it may well start a fashion for oinking. Recollect that you are the daughter of a duke."

"Only the adopted daughter. And I'm half-Italian, by birth an illegitimate commoner. Also a country bumpkin."

"And thereby all the more fascinating." When Francesca began to object, Maria waved a hand dismissively. "Needless to say, we shall never discuss the circumstances of your birth. Sotherton accepted you, and that is all anyone needs to know. Moreover, you must recall that *I* am sponsoring you. A mixed blessing, what with a few doors closed to me, but the stiff-backed snobs behind them are of no account. I expect you to become the Toast of the Season."

"And I expect the high sticklers will have me for toast."

"Oh, Lud, do postpone this attack of megrims until a later time. We are expected at Lady Sefton's within the half hour. Where is your wrap, child? My horses have been kept waiting too long as it is." Maria clapped her hands. "Hop to it!"

Francesca practically leaped for the bell-rope.

After several minutes, Maria pacing restlessly all the while, the sour-faced butler shuffled into the foyer, still pulling on his coat.

Maria examined him with searing displeasure. "Watch and learn, my dear," she murmured to Francesca before advancing on the butler with the force of a bullet. "Miss Childe has just informed me that you are to be dismissed. What is your name?"

"P-Peters, ma'am." He took a quick step back, and then another, until Maria had forced him to the wall.

"I have asked that she reconsider, Peters. But henceforth you are on trial, as is each and every servant in the household. Miss Childe naturally expected a period of adjustment, but her patience has now run out. Do we understand each other?"

"Yes, ma'am. Completely."

Maria moved aside, allowing him room to bow to Francesca. "What do you wish, Miss Childe?" he asked with amazing deference. "I am at your service."

Torn between awe and a fit of the giggles, Francesca lifted her chin. "Have the maid fetch down my pelisse, bonnet, gloves, and reticule. Also an umbrella. Send a footman to inform Mrs. Beaton's driver that we are on our way out. And I rely on you, Peters, to make sure Miss Olivia does not leave this house while I am gone."

As the butler hurried off, Francesca turned to Maria. "How was that?"

"A good beginning, my dear. Next time be more haughty, as if you expect a task to be done before you think to order it. Servants in a leased house have not a grain of loyalty, and they will be just as lazy and insolent as you permit."

The peevish lady's maid Francesca had inherited with the other servants, bony arms full of a woolen fur-collared pelisse, bonnet, and gloves, was nearly trampled as Livvy charged down the staircase directly behind her.

"Where are you going, Cesca?" Livvy demanded, shoving the maid aside. "I want to go with you."

"Not today," Francesca said, aware of Maria watching her attentively. Servants were not the only recalcitrant dependents she must learn to handle. "Have you forgot, Livvy? There is to be another dancing lesson at one o'clock."

"Pah! Monsieur barely manages to waddle through the steps, and his stays creak so that I can scarce hear the music. If I must have a teacher, can we not find one who is young and slim and tall?"

Francesca slipped into her pelisse. "Sadly, all the desirable dance masters have already run off with silly girls. You must settle for Monsieur Peltier and his wife, who plays the pianoforte well, don't you think? And while we are on the subject of wives, the carpenter you've been tormenting has one of his own. Let him alone, Livvy."

"Oh, very well." She nibbled her lip. "He's told me the same thing. But I'm *bored*, Cesca. You cannot close me up in this mausoleum for the rest of my life!"

The image of Livvy laid out on a marble slab, silenced forever, made Francesca's fingers curl. Sometimes she truly longed to strangle the girl. "Today Mrs. Beaton . . . the same Mrs. Beaton you have so rudely ignored . . . will present me to five fashionable ladies. And we are paying these calls for the sole purpose of securing invitations to their routs and balls. For *you*, Livvy. And Ann, of course. I personally have no interest in balls and routs. What is more, you will be barred from every door unless you deport yourself like a gently bred young lady. Do you understand?"

"Yes, Francesca." She made her curtsy to Maria. "Pleased to meet you, Mrs. Beaton. Forgive my poor manners. I have lived all my life in the country and am still learning how to go on."

From the militant gleam in her eyes, Francesca

knew Livvy had learned nothing at all, except when to cut her losses and beat a retreat.

It was a relief to be settled in Maria's carriage a few minutes later, even though they were on their way to meet the crème de la crème of London Society. "You must think me a self-pitying, whiny ninny-hammer," Francesca said by way of apology. "Truly, in the general way I am nothing of the sort. My faults run more toward a flashpan temper and a lamentable tendency to act without thought."

"I have noticed," Maria said dryly. "Had you stopped a moment to consider in the last few weeks, you would have sought help instead of shouldering every burden alone."

"Add pride to my list of flaws. I find it difficult to ask for assistance and often refuse help when it is freely offered. Ludicrous, is it not, since I am the veriest child of charity? If not for Papa's benevolence, I would be scrounging an existence on the streets of Naples. More likely, I would be dead."

"And now you are determined to prove that you can make your way unassisted. Perfectly understandable. As a champion of female independence, I hesitate to dissuade you." Maria smiled. "But we all require help to achieve our goals, and we help others in return, to keep the river flowing. Ask and give, Francesca. That is my lesson for today. Now compose yourself, for here is our first stop."

Two hours and five calls later, Francesca emerged from Lady Jersey's mansion with the promise of vouchers to Almack's ringing in her ears. The wind promptly upturned her umbrella, but even the cold rain pelting her bonnet and pelisse could not dampen her excitement.

"We did it!" she exclaimed as the footman closed the carriage door. "Maria, you are a treasure. How did you manage to bring me through this ordeal? I was absolutely terrified at each and every visit. And when that cucumber slice flew out of my sandwich and onto Lady Jersey's lap, I just knew that I was ruined forever. Whatever did you say to make her laugh? I was so busy trying not to faint that I failed to hear you."

Maria placidly adjusted her sable-lined cloak. "Nor have you heard the last of that cucumber. She will enjoy recounting the tale, as I quickly pointed out."

"Oh dear."

" 'Tis nothing to worry about. In fact, providing Sally that tidbit of gossip was your greatest accomplishment. Now she will be your staunchest ally, and see to it that you and the twins are welcomed everywhere."

A lump settled in Francesca's throat. "How can I ever thank you, Maria? Or repay you?"

"Pish-posh! As a rule, I find London Society tedious. But I need to preserve my influence with these people, and you give me a delightful excuse to set aside my books and lectures for a few weeks. Shall we agree to be mutually indebted?"

Only if I can keep Livvy from shaming us both, Francesca thought. She glanced up at Maria, who was regarding her with concern. "Mutually? No. I absolutely reserve the right to be indebted. Shall we go to the bookshop now?"

"Oh no, young woman." Maria's expression grew stern. "First I mean to hand you over to Madame Flambeau. Unlike your former mantua-maker, who dressed you like the pale English beauty you are not, she will fit you in the simple styles and vibrant colors that suit you."

"But what does it matter how I look? I shall attend balls only to chaperone Ann and Livvy."

"If you wish to repay me for introducing you to the

ton," Maria said firmly, "begin by making me proud of your appearance. Madame is a most annoying woman, as you will soon discover, but Hatchard's Book Shop will be your reward for patience."

Chapter 5

He is stark mad, whoever says
That he has been in love an hour.
　　　　　　　　　—John Donne

It was a typical winter afternoon at White's, with fires crackling at each end of the reading room, the occasional rustle of newspapers, and the low rumble of male voices. Slumped on a wing-back chair in one corner, Sir Harvey Felterpell snored in rhythm with the rain beating against the windows.

Clay passed a coin to the young footman who had remembered to keep his coffee cup filled for the past two hours. "Any luck yet?"

"I checked all the rooms again, milord, but they have not come in." He added a log to the fire. "The doorman will direct them here when they arrive."

Alone again, Clay stretched his legs toward the hearth and stared moodily into the flames. He'd always considered patience his chief virtue, and he carefully nurtured his supply because a gamester who made his living at the tables required a great deal of it.

But the past two weeks would have tried the endurance of a saint. As gossip about his aborted army commission swirled around him, he could do little but grip the edges of his dignity and hang on. At the clubs and other haunts of fashionable gentlemen, he replied to lifted brows and sly gibes from his fellows with careless humor. The young men could scarcely accuse him of cowardice, after all, since not a one of them was off fighting Napoleon either. And the older men, who knew the Earl of Montford and the power he wielded, had some degree of sympathy for his besieged son.

But Clay knew the worst was yet to come. He had received no invitations, not even from hostesses who generally welcomed a titled rake. Not that he would give a twig, in the usual course of things, since balls, routs, and musicales bored him senseless. But those were the sorts of places at which Francesca would be found, so he must contrive to be there, too.

He sipped at his coffee, mentally lining up targets. Sally Jersey would surely restore him to her list, if he offered up a morsel of tittle-tattle about the scandal, and her rivals would jump just as eagerly to the bait. The idea of approaching them hat in hand made his stomach turn, but it might well come to that. Jerry and Bertie had dutifully made an appearance at all the important pre-Season parties without catching a glimpse of his quarry.

It seemed that Francesca, along with Bromley Childe and his twin vixens, had gone to ground somewhere in London. Or returned from whence they had come, wherever that was. How little he knew of the woman he planned to marry! More peculiar still, he could practically feel her in his arms whenever he thought about her, which was most of the time.

Everything in him that was male had sprung to attention the first time he'd seen her. But he'd also divined any number of logical reasons to woo and wed the beautiful Francesca. She was a woman of inconsequential birth and questionable breeding, which served his purposes exactly. When presented with his new daughter-in-law, Montford would understand immediately what she represented—a final avowal of independence by his son. Moreover, once she gave him a child, he could secure the inheritance from his grandmother and provide a new home for his mother.

Rational, perfectly acceptable reasons to find and marry the elusive goddess. He could almost believe them himself.

But where his reason stopped and the rest of him began, he was utterly obsessed with her.

"Pardon me if I am de trop," a voice said near his shoulder. "I'll take m'self off if you prefer. Or maybe you don't remember me at all. Most people don't."

Startled, Clay looked up at the round, pleasant face of Lord Mumblethorpe. He was in no mood for company, but good manners forced him to his feet. "A pleasure to see you again, Mumblethorpe. Etonians always remember their schoolfellows."

"The Brotherhood," Mumblethorpe said. "More in theory than in fact, but you were kind when I followed you about like a puppy the whole first term. Certainly I shall not repay you by intruding on your privacy yet again. Thing is, I am just returned from paying a call on Lady Sefton. Your name came up in the conversation."

"Unsurprising, since my latest fall from grace is on everyone's lips."

"For the moment." Obviously nervous, Mumblethorpe cleared his throat. "Once the Season is in full swing, new gossip will replace this rather dull tale. No offense, but the buying and selling of a military commission is of little concern to those who dance and make merry while England is at war. Should you choose to create a genuine scandal, preferably involving a woman or a duel, we shall all happily natter about it over tea and cakes." He flushed from his neckcloth to his receding hairline. "Fact is, some of us never do anything of note, so we busy ourselves passing judgment on the people we envy."

Clay was astonished to think of anyone envying him. What had he ever accomplished, beyond surviving a virulent hangover or winning enough at the gaming tables to pay off his creditors? On the whole, he had lived a remarkably useless life.

"Well, I don't mean to make a nuisance of m'self," Mumblethorpe said when Clay failed to speak. "Thing is, Lady Sefton asked me if she ought to send you an invitation, and I put her off because I didn't know what to say. Her ball will be the first of significance since Parliament convened, but perhaps you do not wish to appear in Society. Under the circumstances, that is. Thought I'd ask you, before I gave her an answer."

His words faded off at the end, to the point where Clay barely heard them. A shy man, Clay thought. With his plain looks and timid manners, Mumblethorpe probably drew as little attention now as he had done at Eton. "You think she'll send me a card on your say-so?"

Mumblethorpe gave a diffident shrug. "Perhaps. She is unaccountably fond of me."

"Then I applaud her taste. And if she is kind enough to admit me, I shall attend the ball with great pleasure. You may assure her that I'll behave myself."

Mumblethorpe accepted Clay's extended hand with a surprisingly strong grip. "As to that, she may well prefer that you do not. The whole point of giving a ball is to have everyone talk about it for weeks. I'll be off now. Good to see you again, Clayburn."

Bemused, Clay resettled on his chair. How odd that a youngster he'd scarcely acknowledged at Eton had resurfaced just in time to do him a favor. To be sure, there was no certainty Lady Sefton's invitation would materialize, but it didn't signify. He liked Mumblethorpe. One day, when Lord Clayburn was a respectably married pattern card of propriety, perhaps they could be friends.

"There you are!" Jerry clapped him on the shoulder. "Thought for sure you'd be tossing dice. The doorman tried to lead us here, but we had to poke our noses in the gaming room first."

"I am a reformed man," Clay advised him cordially.

"Don't look it." Bertie tugged a chair closer to the fire. "Missed a spot by the ear when you shaved. Bloodshot eyes. Disposition like a bear."

"Devil it, I've spent the last fortnight prowling through every gaming hell in London. What do you expect?"

"You've spent half your life in those very same hells," Jerry pointed out. "Never bothered you before. So, any word of Bromley Childe?"

"Nothing of use. Last night I found one man who remembered him from a club in Manchester and another who once tossed dice with him in York. From what I can tell, this may be his first trip to London. Who knows where he'll turn up?"

"Bad luck, that, what with gamesters being easier to root out than obscure young ladies from the provinces." Jerry propped an arm on the mantelpiece. "No sign of the chits so far, although we've spent all week paying calls on the tabbies. Even went to a musicale last night. Bertie was evicted for snoring. It would be a lot easier, y'know, if we could ask a few direct questions."

"Well, you cannot." Clay rubbed his forehead. "I won't compromise their reputations before they have even made their come-out. Francesca would never forgive me."

"Can't matter," Bertie observed, "if you don't ever see her again."

"Oh, I'll find her." Clay drained the last of the coffee from his cup. "And it's just occurred to me how to go about it. Why did I fail to think of this earlier? The Tongue will know."

"The Tongue knows everything," Bertie said reverently.

"But I thought she was dead," Jerry put in. "Wasn't there a funeral? Everybody went but me. I had a cold."

"The corpse was her last husband. Or maybe not her last. She may have remarried by now." Clay grimaced. "She'll ring a peal over me for neglecting to call, and another for popping in uninvited today. Want to come along?"

"Not me!" Jerry and Bertie replied in unison.

Clay stood and bowed. "I am in your debt, gentlemen, and forgive me for wasting your time to no purpose. The Tongue will have the answers we've all been looking for."

He was waiting in the foyer for his coat, hat, and gloves when the door swung open, a blast of cold air preceding two grumbling men who had apparently been caught in the rainstorm.

Without pleasure, Clay recognized Lord Rupert Heston and Clarence Briggs, a pair of weasels who had set out to make his life miserable from the day he first set foot at Eton. It was tradition for the older boys to persecute newcomers, of course, but Heston had taken a personal, inexplicable dislike to the eight-year-old viscount, one that had grown stronger over the years. Briggs, without a single opinion to call his own, followed Heston like a shadow and echoed his every word.

True to form, Heston no sooner spotted his old adversary than he raised the sword. "I say, Clayburn, why lurk you here in the foyer? Taken employment as a footman?" He removed his wet curly-brimmed beaver and held it out. "Make sure to brush this carefully."

"Here's m'gloves," Briggs said, tossing them in Clay's direction.

Clay ignored Heston's hat and the gloves that landed at his feet, but he was very much aware of the men gathering in the passageway, sniffing a quarrel like hounds on the scent.

Heston's lips narrowed. Whipcord-lean and graceful in the manner of an experienced fencer, he always relished an audience for the scenes he created. This one, Clay knew from the glint in his mocking eyes, would be particularly ugly.

"Snap to it!" Heston ordered when Clay failed to acknowledge him. "My hat requires cleaning. Should you fail to do your duty, I shall complain to the management and have you turned off." He added maliciously, "How then will you earn your bread . . . since the army won't have you?"

"He don't even qualify as a mess sergeant," Briggs chimed in, preening when a few onlookers chuckled. "Good thing the likes of him ain't standing between England and Bonaparte We'd all wind up speaking Frenchie."

"Not you," Clay said to Briggs with a smile. "You have yet to master English."

When that quiet observation elicited a smattering of applause, Briggs sidled into a corner, leaving Clay and Heston to confront each other directly. The small space where they stood was charged with mutual antagonism.

Clay, with the impassive expression of a gambler holding bad cards, waited for Heston to make the next play.

"Where's your papa?" Heston inquired silkily. "I had thought he always kept close by, to hold your leading strings. But after buying back your army commission and making you the laughingstock of

53

London, he seems to have vaporized. How unfortunate. Who will protect you now, I wonder?"

Clay examined Heston slowly from boots to scalp. "Protect me from what?"

He shrugged dramatically. "The rain? Who can tell what will spook a coward?"

The audience sucked in a collective breath.

Coward. The word had been said, to his face and in front of witnesses. "Not you," Clay said with a quelling look. "Rupert Heston couldn't spook a kitten. But if you are of a mind to fight, sir, I am more than ready to oblige you."

"Are you calling me out then?"

"If you require a challenge, I might consider producing one. But then, a formal duel would mean rising at dawn, which neither of us has done in recent memory. Not to mention appointing seconds who are honor-bound to negotiate a peaceful settlement if one is to be had." He gestured to Clarence Briggs. "Do you really want that nincompoop speaking on your behalf? I believe he is your only friend."

"I can negotiate for myself," Heston snarled. "Name your weapon!"

"Ah, I seem to have misunderstood. You are calling *me* out. Very well, then, but I'll not give you the advantage by choosing swords. A bullet between your eyes will save us both a great deal of time. Assuming I have correctly interpreted the situation, of course. Precisely who is challenging whom?"

Laughter erupted from the bystanders, and during the brief lapse of tension, the servant holding Clay's incidentals managed to shoulder through the crowd.

Not altogether pleased at the interruption, Clay took his greatcoat and pulled it on, watching Heston closely. After two weeks of public humiliation, he was spoiling for a fight, and who better to exterminate than the man he had loathed for twenty years. Hell, if not for Francesca, he would long since have picked up one of Briggs's gloves and slapped it in Heston's face.

To his disappointment, Heston backed off with a languid wave of his hand. "If Montford will not permit his son to fight Bonaparte, I daresay he'd throw himself between the two of us if we came to blows. To spare an old man the trouble, and for that reason only, I bid you good day."

"Thank heavens for that. I had thought you meant to bore me to death." Clay drew on his gloves, set his hat on his head, and nodded to the footman, who hurried to open the door.

Spikes of wind-driven rain pounded his face as he slogged through ankle-deep puddles toward Pall Mall, where hacks were lined up waiting to be hired. He climbed into the first coach after shouting Eudora's address several times to the jarvey, who wore a heavy set of earmuffs against the cold.

Clay settled on the lumpy squabs and folded his arms. Just as well it had come to nothing, he supposed. A duel would have forced him to leave England for a year or two, and that was no longer possible.

He had to find Francesca.

Chapter 6

Why should we defer our joys?
Fame and rumor are but toys.
—Ben Jonson

"Well, well. Long past time you deigned to call, rascal!"

Clay gave Lady Eudora Swann the flamboyant, old-fashioned bow she expected. "Your servant, ma'am."

She snorted. "Oh, Lud, you sweet-talking men! Vows of servitude at every turn, with not the least intention of following through. Where are you, Felicia? Push me into the light, gel."

While Eudora's ancient companion shuffled to her feet and guided her employer's Bath chair to the center of the room, Clay smiled fondly at the most intriguing creature he had ever known.

She had changed little since last year. Sleek ebony hair, dyed with boot-blacking, he suspected, formed a helmet over her wrinkled, rice-powdered face. Her thin lips were stained berry-red, as were her cheekbones and, probably, her nipples. But for all the flamboyant jewelry and garish cosmetics, it was her pair of canny blue eyes that held his attention.

At four-and-eighty, Eudora retained her sharp wits and even sharper tongue. She had married and buried five or six husbands that he knew of, including two earls and a viscount, but now she played the game of love for vicarious amusement. Or so he assumed. For all he really knew, she had a lover waiting upstairs in her bedchamber. He rather hoped she did.

"Come closer, boy," she commanded, raising her lorgnette. "Sit here on the divan where I can see you. Closer. No, closer than that. Open the curtains, Felicia. Cast some light on this devilish handsome lordling."

Clay blinked as daylight flooded into the stuffy room. "You are the true beauty, my dear."

"And you are in trouble again," she shot back. "I am so glad of it. These last few weeks have been prodigiously dull. Felicia, ring for tea. No, go below-stairs and bring it up yourself. But be slow about it, for I wish to be private with Clayburn."

"Not proper," Felicia muttered as she shambled to the door. "Not proper."

"These old women!" Eudora put a gnarled hand on Clay's thigh. "No heart under their saggy breasts. They die to life so long before they're planted in the ground."

"While you remain ever young," Clay replied, sincerely. "If I should make an offer, Lady Grace, would you marry me?"

"In a heartbeat, sir." She slid her fingers up his leg. "Are you asking?"

"Ah, left to my own devices, I would happily do so. But there remains the pernicious matter of siring an heir."

"Titles do come equipped with obligations," she agreed with a disappointed sigh. "And for all the considerable prowess of my several husbands, I never managed to pop out a babe. No reason to expect that will change now."

"A pity," Clay said. "The world would be richer with your children in it."

"More interesting, certainly." Her wandering fingers moved closer to his privates. "Consider this.

Once you are wed and have got a son on your wife, you will require a mistress." She grinned over pointy yellow teeth. "I'd not turn you away, Clayburn."

Just before her fingertips reached their target, he slipped a hand gently under her wrist and lifted it for a kiss. "I am rehearsing fidelity, my sweet. And as that is scarcely a role I am accustomed to, I must implore you not to tempt me beyond my strength."

"Fidelity? *You?*" She sat back in her chair, clearly astounded.

The very idea of it amazed him, too, and he could hardly explain to her what he did not understand. For the moment he put the astounding notion aside. He had more pressing business to attend to. "While I am naturally delighted to see you again," he said, "I have, in fact, come to you for information."

"Most everyone does, sooner or later. But you know the rules, Clayburn. Tit for tat. No offense, but I must take in more gossip than I give out, or I'll soon run dry." She folded her arms. "You may proceed."

"Let me see. Recently I bought a commission in the army, whereupon my father pulled strings to seize it back without consulting me."

"Stale news. I heard this paltry tale weeks ago. Montford intrigues me, self-righteous looby that he is, and I am up on his every move. Do you know, I expect I am better acquainted with his enterprises than you are."

"Almost certainly. He is of no concern whatever to me, until he interferes with my life. And apparently his latest attempt to meddle will not buy me so much as the answer to a question."

"True enough," Eudora said without mercy. "You'll have to do better."

Clay loosened his neckcloth. "This you cannot possibly have heard, as it occurred less than an hour

58

ago. Lord Heston made an ass of himself at White's, and I almost called him out."

"Almost? I give you no credit for *almost*, Clayburn. Someone should have put a bullet between his eyes long since. In my experience, his transgressions are seldom of any consequence. Worse, they are never amusing."

Laughing, Clay stood and crossed to the window overlooking Upper Brook Street. "Alas, poor Eudora. The only gossip I can place on your altar relates to a tedious villain and a reformed rake."

"Reformed!" She wheeled in his direction so quickly that he had to grab the chair before she propelled herself through the window glass. "Tell me more."

"Got your attention, did I?" He squeezed her thin shoulder with affection. "Perhaps this will loose your tongue. I am soon to be married."

The stunned silence following that pronouncement gave him enormous satisfaction, and enough time to regret what he had just disclosed. "Please understand this information is for your ears only," he added hastily. "Until I inform the bride of my intentions—"

"Who is she?" Eudora demanded.

"Have I your word to keep the secret until I release you?"

"Yes, yes. Excluding hints. Do not forbid me a few hints."

He dropped to one knee beside her chair and gazed directly into her eyes. "You'll say nothing to the point, Eudora. I need your help and will beg for it if need be. But I won't have the woman I mean to wed become the object of speculation and scandal."

Eudora chewed on her lower lip. "Oh, very well, you irritating boy."

"Thank you." He brushed his lips across her papery

cheek. "Now tell me everything you know about Francesca Childe."

"Never heard of her. Wait. Childe. The name is familiar."

Clay lowered his other knee, leaning both hands against Eudora's chair as she closed her eyes. She was casting back, he knew, through her remarkable store of memories. Eudora Swann was a veritable repository of the past, the song-singer of nearly a century of aristocratic history. Like Homer, she could recount whole epics about the lords and ladies who had caught her interest, and most did.

She emerged from her recollections with a start. "Ah yes, I have it now. Melchior Childe. The Duke of Sotherton. 'Lord Least-in-Sight,' we called him in the old days. But he's not set foot in London since the Great Scandal. How came you to know him?"

"I don't," he said, wondering if the Great Scandal involved Francesca. "More to the point, what do *you* know of him?"

Eudora tapped her fingers on the arm of her chair. "Little enough, I fear. He married Lord Glenchester's youngest, a sweet-faced, vapid chit who died shortly after. He fled to the Continent then, and no more was heard of him for several years. But all this took place before you were born. Why should you care— Oh!" She prodded Clay on the chest. "What a slowpoke I am! You must be sniffing after the mysterious daughter. Am I right? If Montford gets wind of this, he will chain you in the attics."

"I'll deal with my father when the time comes," Clay said evenly. "Tell me about the daughter. And the scandal."

" 'Twas most savory, while it lasted. All the hopeful mamas were longing for Sotherton's return, rich eligible dukes being thin on the ground. Then word came he had married abroad and resettled on his estate with an Italian wife of dubious lineage. Renalda was her name, as I recall. She had a child, possibly by a previous marriage. Nobody knows for certain. Sotherton immediately set his lawyers to arrange an adoption, so the child cannot have been his own."

Eudora frowned. "Someone, probably one of the disappointed mamas, took to calling this negligible business the Great Scandal. But as Sotherton never again appeared in Society, there were no fresh rumors to fan the fires and they soon died down. Nothing more was heard of him until a decade ago, when notice of his wife's death appeared in the *Times*."

Clay stood and brushed carpet lint from his breeches. "He must not have had a son by his Italian wife, because I understand his brother is to inherit the title. Lord Bromley Childe."

"A flea-wit if ever there was one! Last I heard, he was staging cockfights in Yorkshire. So he has come to London, you say? Here to fire off the twins, no doubt, but I'd thought him pockets-to-let. How is he to finance their come-out?"

"Perhaps His Grace is paying for it. Sotherton's daughter has come along as chaperone, or did you already know?"

Eudora picked at her shawl. "As I cannot leave this house without considerable difficulty, I must wait for news to come to me. And Bromley Childe is of less significance than a climbing boy. Who would think to mention him or his whelps?"

Clay grinned. "Your reputation stands, my sweet. If not for a chance encounter at a posthouse, I would not be aware of their existence either. Nor would I have met the duke's mysterious daughter."

"So we arrive at the point," Eudora said slyly. "Francesca. The bride who does not yet know of your intention to marry her. What exactly happened at that posthouse, wicked man? Did you seduce her?"

"Lord, no. Well, under the circumstances, I could not. Miss Childe and I spent no more than a few minutes together, never privately."

Eudora clapped her hands. "How delicious! It was the same with me and my second husband. No, my third. I forget precisely which man was involved, but the *feeling* was unmistakable. Love at first sight, yes?"

"No indeed, you atrocious wench. For my part, it was sheer lust at first sight. And as for her reaction to me—"

He rubbed the back of his neck, which grew tight as he recalled their first meeting. "Truth be told, she took me into immediate dislike. *Loathing* is probably a more accurate term. But I must add that she did not see me at my best."

"Drinking and gaming, were you? I daresay she could come across you doing the same at any time or place." Eudora wheeled closer to where he stood, her eyes alight with curiosity. "Why do you want the foreign girl, Clayburn? Lust soon flames out, leaving ashes and heartbreak. Believe me on this point, for I know all there is to know about lust. Or is it the money? Sotherton may will his considerable fortune to his brother, you know."

She nudged the wheel of her chair against his leg. "Never tell me you mean to punish your father by marrying a wife he cannot approve? Montford is too much the snob to accept a woman of mixed ancestry."

"It is fortunate, then, that he will not be the one taking her to wife. As for the Sotherton inheritance, I care not if Francesca comes to me barefoot and in rags."

Eudora patted him on the backside. "Excellent. There is hope for you yet. But I wish to take the girl's measure, Clayburn. You must bring her here as soon as may be."

"Gladly. But first I must find her again. Like 'Lord Least-in-Sight,' she has a knack for disappearing." He went to the secretaire and wrote his address on the back of a calling card. "Should anything more about the duke and his family come to mind, please send word."

Eudora accepted the card and slid it down the lacy bodice of her gown. "Sotherton was ever a bookish fellow," she reflected. "Even in his youth he haunted the auction houses, buying collections for his library. Seems to me he was especially fond of poetry."

"You think she inherited a taste for literature?" he asked, welcoming any clue that might lead him to Francesca's heart, if not her location.

"Well, how could she inherit anything at all, being another man's daughter? But he doubtless encouraged her to share his interests, and what else is there to do in the wild northlands but read?" She chuckled. "Or have a tumble with a well-hung farmhand. That would certainly be my choice."

Clay dropped onto a chair. "By the stars, Eudora, compared to you I am the veriest choirboy. But since I have called on your memories, may I now draw upon your experience? Once she is found, how am I to proceed with Miss Stiff-and-Proper Childe?"

Through her lorgnette, Eudora ran an intent blue-eyed gaze from the crown of his head to the toes of his Hessian boots. "Find a way to be alone with her," she said tartly. "Then remove your clothes."

"I beg your pardon?"

"That would turn the trick with any woman of spirit. Never mind that I've been unable to walk these last three years. If you stripped to your skin here and now, I'd be out of my chair and on top of you in the blink of an eye. Or under you, if you preferred."

He doubled over with laughter.

" 'Tis no joke, Clayburn. By the grace of God you are a splendid-looking man, and charming to boot. Play to your strengths. Besides, if Miss Childe fails to appreciate your magnificent body, what is the hope for your future together? You cannot mean to spend your life with a cold bedmate." Her eyes narrowed. "Especially if you intend to remain faithful."

He sobered instantly. "I do. Not by choice, you understand. But likely she will demand it."

"She has Italian blood," Eudora reminded him. "Beneath the starchy propriety that holds you at bay, she is Mediterranean sun and drizzles of olive oil over ripe peppers. Never forget that. Nick away at her defenses with proper British wooing and you'll make no progress whatever. But assault her with passion, and she is yours. And if she isn't, you didn't want her anyway!"

"I expect this wooing to be a bit more complicated," he said thoughtfully. "Francesca is something out of the ordinary. And remember, she already detests me. I made a lamentable first impression."

Just then, Felicia staggered into the room, listing from side to side under the shifting weight of crockery and food atop an enormous silver tray. Clay jumped up to take the tray from her hands before she collapsed.

"Very good, Felicia," Eudora said. "Now disappear again until I call for you, and turn away all visitors. It seems that Lord Clayburn requires an education."

Cheeks burning, Clay poured the tea and set thin ham sandwiches and an Eccles cake on a plate for his hostess.

"Are you prepared to heed my advice?" Eudora asked sharply. "As you are unwilling to take the direct approach, and stand convinced that the lady will not be moved by it, let us consider the alternatives."

"By all means," he said numbly.

"When next you meet, you will naturally be the perfect gentleman, to counter the impression she has already formed. At the same time, you must be relentless and romantic. A delicate balance, to be sure, but a woman needs to know that she is desired. The combination of restraint and determination will wear her down."

"Relentless," he said. "Romantic. Restrained."

"Precisely. But meantime, you must prepare for the second phase of this campaign. You will not like it," she warned. "This is the most difficult stage of all. It resides, for Francesca, between mild attraction and sleepless nights."

Whatever that means, Clay thought. Women were damnably complex creatures. "I shall do whatever you say, Eudora."

"I can only wish," she said with a saucy grin that subtracted fifty years from her age. "In any case, you must write her a love poem."

"Bloody hell!"

"It will be, I expect, unless you have a talent for composing verse. But consider. She has only to look at you to know that women leap into your bed if you so much as point the way. As a consequence, you must exert effort to prove that she is extraordinary and that your intentions are sincere."

"So I'll send flowers. Lots of them."

"A trifling matter of passing coins to a flower seller." Eudora wagged a scolding finger. "Pathetic, Clayburn! And could you afford to drape her head to toe in diamonds, which I very much doubt, she would conclude that you wished to set her up as a mistress. Only a poem will do it, lad. Not the careless words a rake uses to bait his hook, but words from your heart."

"Why can't I just write her a letter?" he asked desperately.

"Oh, far too easy. Your avowal of love must present itself in rhyme and meter, however excruciating the process, because she is so very different from all the other women you've wanted and bedded before meeting her."

"She is," he affirmed softly. "But it would be a far sight easier to slay her a dragon than cobble a couplet, let alone an entire poem."

"And she will know it! You begin, at last, to get the point of this exercise. Mind you, stand ready to slay any dragon that crosses her path, and be alert to any favor you can do her, however insignificant. Preferably before she asks. In my experience, men require a kick on the arse to notice when a woman stands in need of help. You must do better."

The Tongue lectured him for another hour before sending him on his way, mildly befuddled and certain only that he had first to write a pestilential poem. God help him. Her other advice would apply only after the wedding, and his ear tips burned to imagine the things Eudora suggested he do with Francesca.

Until this afternoon, he had thought himself an imaginative, considerate lover, but females apparently had a whole different perspective on lovemaking. He was relieved to know that he served up the main course to advantage, but mortified to learn that women were equally partial to the hors d'oeuvres and the dessert.

Well, first things first. He actually liked poetry, so long as it came equipped with a story like the *Odyssey* or "The Rime of the Ancient Mariner." Lyrical jabbering bored him senseless. But if he was going to write a love poem, he probably ought to read a few for inspiration.

The rain had let up, he saw when he reached the street, and luckily, a hackney came by at the same moment. "Hatchard's," he told the driver.

Chapter 7

Lost is our freedom,
When we submit to women so.
                    —*Thomas Campion*

When the bow windows of Hatchard's came into view, Francesca's weariness vanished straightaway. Books!

The driving rain had stopped sometime during her long ordeal with Madame Flambeau, where she had been measured for gowns no decent woman ought to wear in public. It was the style, Madame insisted, to expose a great deal of bosom. And Francesca had lots of it.

Not that she was pleased to be so lavishly endowed. In her opinion, breasts served no purpose whatever for a female who did not mean to marry and nurse babies. They only got in the way and bounced when she was walking. But there they were, a legacy from her voluptuous mother, and Madame Flambeau had decreed they must be displayed to all and sundry.

Men were partial to women's breasts, Maria explained patiently. They enjoyed looking at them. But what had any of that to do with a woman of one-and-thirty, long past the age to attract a suitor even if she happened to want one? And since she did not, why dress herself to be ogled?

Another of London Society's vast mysteries, she thought as a footman opened the carriage door and lowered the steps.

Walking into the large, well-appointed bookshop felt very much like coming home. To her nostrils, the smell of leather bindings and glue was sweeter than any perfume, and she took a deep, happy breath of musty air.

The shop was crowded with patrons, most busier socializing than buying books. On chairs drawn up to the large fireplace, several men and women leafed through newspapers and periodicals, while clerks wearing aprons moved silently through the lines of standing shelves, locating books the shoppers had requested.

"I see a few people I wish to greet," Maria said, "but you have made enough new acquaintances for one day. Wander about as long as you like, my dear."

"Don't speak too soon," Francesca warned. "When surrounded by books, I generally forget that time exists."

"As do I." Maria gave her a warm smile. "Do you wish directions to particular sorts of—? No, of course not. You'd rather discover them for yourself. Off with you, then."

Francesca headed immediately for the back of the shop, which was all but deserted, and spent a desultory half hour in paradise. Rather than carry the many books she wanted to purchase, she marked their location and took with her only Miss Sydney Owens's new historical novel for fear someone else would snatch the only copy.

"May I disturb you for a moment, Francesca?"

She looked up to see Maria standing a few yards away, in an open space between two blocks of shelves. Beside her was a quietly dressed, somber-looking man about forty years old. He bowed politely when she joined them.

"Francesca, this is Mr. Hatchard, my friend of many

years. John, Miss Childe is likely to be your very best customer while she remains in London, even though you come to her with bad news. Perhaps you should tell her what you have just told me."

His cheeks reddened slightly, but his voice was calm and to the point. "I am pleased to make your acquaintance, ma'am. My news relates to the collection of Petrarch's sonnets you wish to acquire. At one time, I thought we had found it. A book matching your description turned up on a list of items to be auctioned at Christie's, pending valuation."

He glanced at Maria, who gestured for him to proceed. "This morning I learned that the auction has been canceled. That comes as little surprise, to be sure, since the Marquess of Fallon is nothing if not unreliable."

"I'm not sure I understand," Francesca said. "The marquess is the owner of the book, and he has decided to keep it for himself?"

"Not precisely. When the representative of Christie's went to examine the lot up for sale, half the heirlooms on the preliminary list were missing. According to his report, they may well be in the house, which is enormous, cluttered, and closed off except for a few rooms. But the sale commission is not worth Christie's effort to ferret them out, and they figure the most valuable items have already been used to settle Fallon's gaming debts."

"The family has an infamous history," Maria said, "and Percival is the worst of a bad lot. He is so ravaged by an unmentionable disease that he cannot appear in public, so he invites other heathens for weeklong bouts of gambling and . . . well, never you mind the rest. From what I understand, he is nearly gone mad from his illness, and his repellent guests have probably carried off everything of value."

"Oh." Francesca tried to absorb all these fascinating revelations. "So it's possible the book may still be there, hidden under the clutter. It is quite valuable and ought to fetch a decent sum at auction, but I would pay far more. If he knew of my interest, would the marquess conduct a search or tell us who owns it now?"

"Naturally I paid a call on your behalf," Hatchard said, "but Fallon was rather too inebriated for coherent discussion. Our best hope is that he did, in fact, use the book in payment of a debt. Unless the new owner has a particular fondness for Petrarch's sonnets, it will eventually come up for sale again."

But will Papa be alive by then? Francesca thought with a shot of pain. Will there be time for him to hold it in his hands, remembering how Mama used to read to him, in her musical Italian, the sonnets Petrarch addressed to his Laura?

One year, as a birthday surprise, Papa set out to write a love sonnet for Renalda. Every night after supper, he shut himself in the library, remaining there for hours on end. Francesca, eight at the time, had been exceedingly curious about this odd behavior. Most evenings she crept to the door and listened in, using a trick involving a drinking glass that one of the maids had taught her. But all she ever heard was a great deal of stomping about and unfamiliar words like *dammit*.

Papa never actually produced a poem.

No secret could be kept from Renalda, though. Each morning she removed the scraps of paper from his trash basket and read the ink-smudged, crossed-out lines. Francesca had discovered those papers after her mother died, bundled together under the pillow on her sickbed. Now they were her own most treasured possession. While Papa's images and rhymes were beyond dreadful, his love shone through like stars on a clear, bright night.

Maria plucked at her sleeve, and Francesca wrenched her attention back to Mr. Hatchard.

". . . marquess turned me away the second time I called," he was saying, "and refused to spare another second for a mere tradesman. His language cannot be repeated, but I'll not be welcomed there again. He opens his doors only to gamesters."

"Has he family you can deal with?" she asked with a sinking heart.

"Only a son, who departed years ago for India. Or the Indies. I cannot recall which. But be assured that I have not abandoned hope, Miss Childe. If the book is no longer in Fallon's possession, there is an excellent chance I will find it."

"Thank you. It's to be a gift for my father, who is not in good health. Be assured that I shall cover any expenditure required for a speedy and thorough search." She mustered a smile. "What a splendid shop, Mr. Hatchard! Pardon me while I collect the books I have already decided to buy and select a few more, too."

With a knowing look at her face, Maria quickly drew Mr. Hatchard away, leaving Francesca to find a place to be alone in the crowded store.

How infuriating! Her precious Petrarch was in the hands of the Marquess of Fallon or one of his abominable friends, not a one of whom would recognize its value. On a cold night, the current owner might well feed it to the fire. What gamester ever cared a fig for books?

Eyes burning, Francesca reached for her handkerchief and dove into a narrow space between two shelving cases before the tears began to fall.

She nearly collided with a born gamester.

He had a book in his hands.

* * *

Clay, lurking in a dim aisle while he eavesdropped on Francesca's conversation, barely had the presence of mind to grab a book from the shelf when she suddenly turned in his direction. He flipped it open, pretending to be absorbed in the text as she came to a halt inches from where he stood.

Even in the shadow of the tall bookcases, he could see through his lashes that tears were welling in her eyes. Oh, damn.

A heartbeat later, her chin went up. "You!"

He raised his head, trying to look surprised, but the first real sight of her in a fortnight sent all his senses reeling. Unaccountably, his boots felt too tight. So did his neckcloth. And his breeches, which made more sense. Francesca Childe had been ruling his every waking thought and most of his dreams, but she was a million times more beautiful than he remembered.

Slowly, as if their meeting were taking place underwater, he watched her draw herself up to full, glorious height and level a blistering gaze at him. He waited for her to speak, so that he could summon a charming reply, but she only glared at him as if sheer scorn would make him go away.

Stampeding wildebeests could not have moved him from that spot. He bowed, awkwardly, over the book now clutched to his chest and forced polite words from a constricted throat. "How fortunate we should meet again, Miss Childe. I have wondered how you fared after the snowstorm, but obviously you made it to London in fine fettle."

"Whatever are you doing in a bookshop?" she fired back.

"Why, I wish to buy a book, of course." Mildly insulted, he raised the impressively large tome as evidence.

A light scent, like rainwater and lilac, registered on his senses as she moved closer to examine it. He traced the source to her thick black hair, which was barely contained under a rain-wilted bonnet. Such beautiful hair, he thought, imagining it spread out on a satin pillowcase.

"You read Italian?" she asked in surprise.

He glanced down at the text, seeing the words for the first time. Immediately the blood that had begun to gather below his waist shot to his head. He was fairly sure his ears had gone on fire.

"I've not yet decided if this will suit my purposes," he said evasively. "But I must confess that I was momentarily distracted, Miss Childe, when I chanced to overhear some of your conversation with John Hatchard. Mind you, I caught only a few words, relating to a book you wish to find, but you seemed distressed by what he told you."

"Which relates to the book you are holding—?"

"In no way whatsoever." He put it back on the shelf. "I do apologize for my poor manners, Miss Childe. And I confess to snatching the nearest book to hand when you came in my direction, for use as a shield. To no effect, I gather."

"None. But I still wonder why you are here at all." She frowned. "Have you been following me?"

His pulse raced. "Whyever would I do such a thing?"

"No reason," she said after giving it some thought. "I, too, apologize. The news Mr. Hatchard conveyed has overset me, and I am not thinking clearly. Of course you have every right to be in a bookshop. Please continue to browse." She made a slight curtsy. "I must find Mrs. Beaton. Good day, my lord."

Without thinking, Clay reached out for her arm. "Is there anything I can do to help?" he blurted. "Perhaps I can find what you are looking for. It happens I know

74

the Marquess of Fallon, and I have spent time at his estate."

"No doubt." She pulled away and brushed her sleeve where his hand had been. "A favored haunt for drunkards and gamblers, or so I understand. But unless you have won or carted off books from his library, you cannot assist me. Do you now own any of Fallon's books?"

"I'm afraid not. But please reconsider my offer, Miss Childe. While I no longer frequent Fallon's house parties, I have fr . . . acquaintances who do. There is a good chance I can trace the book, so long as you provide a description."

She regarded him with new interest. "Perhaps you are right. Since the marquess appears unwilling to conduct business through normal channels, unusual measures may be called for. Perhaps I should recruit a libertine to handle the negotiations."

"Exactly!"

"Some *other* libertine," she specified. "You will not do, Lord Clayburn."

"But why?" If Francesca required a rakehell, what was wrong with the one standing in front of her? Finding the book she wanted would give him an excuse to see her again. And let him prove that he was, in fact, a *reformed* libertine. Well, to be strictly accurate, on his way to reformation. But surely that counted for something. "I truly wish to be of service to you," he said earnestly.

Her eyes widened. And then her lips turned up at the corners, as if she were enjoying a private joke at his expense. "Because your father has commanded it?" she inquired too sweetly.

Clay nearly swore aloud. She knew. Well, how could she not? All London had been talking about the repurchased army commission for weeks. "Whatever you have heard," he said between his teeth, "it is unlikely to be the truth. And in any case, Montford has nothing whatever to do with us."

"If you say so, Lord Clayburn. And should I ever require the services of a coxcomb, you will definitely be on my list of candidates." She examined the book he'd returned to the shelf. "Oh my. Machiavelli's *Discourses*. You might learn something, were you able to read it."

Clay watched her walk away with an imperious, purely feminine flounce. So tall and proud and confident, his goddess. His beautiful, desirable goddess. The blood in his flushed cheeks and neck began a southward journey back to his loins.

He reckoned that his blood had better get used to these round trips between humiliation and lust, since Francesca seemed to inspire both in equal measure.

She felt a strong response to him, too, he was fairly certain, although she tried to pretend it didn't exist. Something hot and bright, like heat lightning, had ignited the air around them.

It frightened her. He wanted to think so, anyway. It sure as the devil scared *him*. So much that he was willing to change his life for her.

Not a great sacrifice, certainly. And he'd set out to change before he even met her, hoping a few years in Wellington's army would give some purpose to his existence. More likely, the first battle would have put an end to it.

Despite the scandal, he was no longer sorry Montford had squelched his impulsive plan. Had he taken his place with the Fifty-second, he would never have met Francesca.

Now to discover where she lived. He peered around the bookshelf and saw her standing at the counter next to Maria Beaton, watching a clerk wrap the book she had been carrying.

While her back was turned, he swiftly exited the shop and swung left on Piccadilly, spotting a hack in front of the Egyptian Museum just a few doors away. The slumping driver perked up when Clay tossed him a coin.

"In the next few minutes," Clay directed, "two ladies will emerge from Hatchard's. One is wearing a blue pelisse. I'll let you know when I see them. Most likely they are traveling in a private carriage, but they may summon a hackney. In any case, I want you to follow them."

The jarvey spat on the pavement. "Sounds havey-cavey to me, guv. I don't want no trouble."

"Nothing of the sort. I merely wish to send flowers to a beautiful woman who was kind enough to advise me about a book." Clay passed up another coin. "Help me discover where she lives, and I'll double your fee. But be discreet. I don't want to alarm her."

"She won't ever know we is on her trail," the driver promised. "Rap on the panel when you spot 'er. I'll take it from there."

Clay swung into the cab and sat by the window, which gave him a good view of Hatchard's. Soon Maria Beaton appeared and spoke to a servant waiting on the benches in front of the shop, presumably dispatching him to have her carriage brought around. Francesca joined her on the pavement to wait.

When the coach drew up a few minutes later, Clay rapped on the panel and the chase began. But very soon the jarvey drew up curbside and leaned down to speak to him.

"They're just ahead, stopped in front of a house on Grosvenor Square. What next, guv?"

"Good man! Drive past, slowly enough so I can see the address. Then take me back to Hatchard's."

When the hackney lumbered by, Francesca was standing at the top of the stairs leading to a large town house, waving good-bye to her friend. Clay tilted his hat over his face, drinking in what little he could see of her without drawing her attention.

Then she was out of sight, until the next time. It would be soon, he promised himself, leaning back against the squabs and folding his arms. He required an excuse to call, but surely he could devise something to get him through the door. He would think on it tonight.

And begin his poem, of course. Of a sudden, images flooded into his mind, all color and light, so ephemeral he could not begin to capture them in words. Not yet.

But he knew then, of a sudden and without question, why he needed her. Why she was the woman he had never imagined wanting . . . until he met her.

He had grown up in a house of ice, and she was fire. The only woman he had ever loved, his mother, had always been weak and compliant, but Francesca was strong and confident. And although she despised him now, it was only for the same reasons he despised himself.

A painful laugh rumbled in his chest. On the subject of his flaws, if nothing else, they were in accord.

Chapter 8

Bid her come forth,
Suffer her self to be desir'd.
—*Edmund Waller*

"Oh, Bromley!" Francesca followed her uncle down the passageway to the entrance hall. "I wish you would not."

"No harm in it," he said, pulling on his gloves. "What's more, can't say I blame the chit for wanting to escape this madhouse. All that banging and shouting gives me the headache."

Not to mention his daily consumption of wine and brandy, she thought crossly. Bromley's arrival last night had been unexpected and disconcerting, mainly because he was looking altogether too pleased with himself. That never boded well. "Where have you been staying, Uncle?" she asked bluntly.

"Here and there, m'dear, here and there. More to the point, where in blazes is that girl?"

Just then Livvy pelted down the stairs, her flimsy muslin skirt plastered to her legs.

Francesca could scarcely believe her eyes. The goosecap had actually dampened the fabric, in the middle of winter, for an afternoon excursion with her father!

Bromley scowled. "Whatever are you thinking, widgeon? 'Tis devilish cold outside. Go put on something with a bit of substance, and be quick about it."

Grumbling loudly, Livvy slogged back up the staircase.

Arrested by this uncharacteristic show of paternal discipline, Francesca felt a spark of hope. Perhaps this excursion would not, after all, turn into the disaster she feared. "Where have you in mind to take her?" she asked.

"Oh, the Tower, I expect. After that, who can say? At some point I shall have a nip from my flask, and when 'tis emptied, I'll not be so particular where I land. Give the brat a little money, Cesca. She may be required to make her way home without me."

The spark flamed out. "Please don't let that happen, Bromley. At the very least, take Ann along as company for Livvy if your own plans change."

"Won't go," he said. "I did ask her, by the by, but I knew what she'd say. Ann's a good child, quiet and proper like her mama. I expect she'll wed a vicar or some polite stay-at-home fellow and raise a passel of brats. You find Ann a nice young gentleman, Francesca, and one for yourself, but never you mind about Livvy. She will go her own way."

Francesca, who had rarely seen Bromley sober or heard him speak sensibly, was astonished when he seized her hand and gazed steadily into her eyes.

"Livvy takes after me," he said, "to her great misfortune. She is quite as rattle-pated and even more self-willed, with no thought beyond the pleasure of the moment. You cannot change her, m'dear. You cannot even help her."

"But surely I must guard her reputation whilst we are in London. She is my responsibility."

"Ah, there you are quite wrong, Cesca. Whatever you are thinking, I assure you that Sotherton never meant you to salvage the unredeemable branch of the family. The angel Gabriel could not do that. We are merely an excuse to pry you from his sickroom long enough to find a husband."

She nodded with ill grace. Papa saw her through the distortion of a father's love, wanting for her what he'd found for himself. But the whimsical vision of a love match for his tall, ungainly daughter would never materialize. She was at her last prayers, for pity's sake.

"Do cease grinding your teeth," Bromley complained. "If it eases your mind, I've an invitation that will take me out of London the day after tomorrow. Lord Heston tells me that our host possesses an excellent wine cellar and invariably loses at cards and dice, so I expect to be gone for a considerable time." He winked. "And return considerably plumper in the pockets."

That would be a change, Francesca thought as Livvy arrived in her usual flurry, wearing her new claret-colored pelisse. The fur collar framed her pretty, stubborn face to advantage, and her blue eyes shone with the prospect of an adventure.

Since there was nothing else to be done, Francesca smiled. "You look exceptionally lovely, my dear. Wait here a moment longer, please. I have something for you."

She rushed to the library, which she had been using as an office, and unlocked the desk drawer that held a few guineas and banknotes. But by the time she arrived again in the foyer, Livvy and Bromley had departed.

Not altogether surprised, she returned to the library, where the morning post waited unopened on her desk. Bromley had interrupted her just as she was beginning to sort through an impressive stack of invitations.

Word spread fast in London, she thought. Only

two days ago, no one knew she existed. Now, after the calls she had made in Maria Beaton's company, her only problem was deciding which balls and routs to attend.

Discovering a letter from Papa buried near the bottom of the pile, she slipped it into her pocket for a later reward and broke the seal on the first invitation. Was Lady Drummond-Burrell anyone of importance? she wondered. And what would she make of Livvy Childe?

Half an hour later, Francesca threw up her hands in dismay. Except for the five women she had already met, she failed to recognize a single name among her would-be hostesses. How could she be in four places at once on Friday next, for heaven's sake? And which three of the four ladies would be most insulted by a refusal?

"Miss Childe?" The butler appeared at the door, which she had failed to close. "Three gentlemen have come to call. I put them in the Green Salon."

"I beg your pardon? We are not receiving guests, Peters."

"Perhaps they failed to notice that the knocker is not fixed upon the door. In any case, there are *three* of them and only one of me. They were most persistent."

"Remind me to acquire a large, nasty dog," she muttered, pushing away from the writing table. "Very well, I shall speak with them. Did they give you their names?"

"As to that, ma'am, I offered the tray for their cards, but they allowed as how they forgot to bring them. Then I asked their names, and they looked me up and down as if I'd been impertinent. Otherwise, they appear to be proper gentlemen."

No expert on men, proper or otherwise, she decided that the shabby brown dress she'd worn to inspect the carpenters' progress in the ballroom would do for a trio of uninvited, anonymous callers.

When Peters opened the door to the Green Salon, two young men immediately stepped forward and bowed. Although they looked vaguely familiar, she was unable to recall where she had seen them before. Then she spotted the tall, broad-shouldered figure standing near the bay window, hands clasped behind his back.

Clayburn. Her own personal Nemesis.

His father must have some dreadful hold over him, she thought disdainfully, a grip so compelling it had forced a proud man to pursue a woman who wanted no part of him.

Still, some parts of him were rather appealing. Very well, they were spectacular. When she'd ninety years on her plate and her spoon all but stuck in the wall, she would doubtless remember him as the most beautiful man she had ever seen. And perhaps wonder how it might have been to do unmentionable things with him.

Not that she would, of course. Her mother had done those things with a man who soon abandoned her to the streets, leaving Francesca with a good idea what to expect from heedless, immoral rakes.

Unfortunately, Renalda's hot blood ran in her veins. The Italian Inheritance, she'd named it years ago, a pepper-broth of temper and love of music, poetry and devotion to family, and, inevitably, the lusts of the flesh. But so far, those had only tormented her in her dreams.

She fully meant to keep it that way, in spite of Lord Clayburn's unspoken intentions. Sooner or later, she knew, he would ask her to marry him. And apparently he meant to do so in person this time, not by way of his father's letters to her father.

Clayburn was not at all what she'd imagined when Papa read her the earl's starchy communications, which were more in the way of legal briefs than letters. She had always pictured the heir as a skinny, spotty young man, the top of whose head barely reached her shoulders, a fellow who spoke with a decided lisp. The sort who could only secure a marriage of convenience, and only if the bride never saw him beforehand.

Now, confronted with this tall, splendidly muscled body, perfectly outlined by tight doeskin breeches and a well-fitted dark blue frock coat, she wondered why he let himself be manipulated in such a way by his father.

Francesca suddenly realized that she had been staring at him for God only knew how long ... with her mouth hanging open. Snapping it shut, she cleared her throat to get his attention, rather sure he had been well aware of her from the moment she entered the room.

"Miss Childe," he said, turning slowly to face her. "How kind of you to receive us."

While she had been air-dreaming, his two friends must have moved closer. She was now all but surrounded by men.

"You already know me," Clayburn continued with a wry grin. "May I present the Honorable Jeremy Porter and the Honorable Bertram Porter? Although they happen to be my friends, I assure you they are in general more discriminating."

"Gentlemen," she murmured with a curtsy, scheming how to be rid of them in the shortest possible time.

"Is Miss Ann Childe at home?" Jeremy Porter inquired politely. "We chanced to meet a few weeks ago, when taking refuge from a storm at the Rose and Thistle, and I wish to pay my regards."

Ah! So *that's* where she had seen him before. These jackals must travel in a pack.

Clayburn feigned a cough, staring meaningfully at Bertram.

"What?" Bertram asked, flushing.

"Didn't you tell me on the way here of your eagerness to see Miss Olivia Childe again?"

"Oh. Yes. Sorry." Bertram turned to Francesca. "If she is available, I am supposed to ask her for a dance."

"At Lady Sefton's ball," Clay reminded him.

"Right. I'll dance with Miss Ann Childe, too, if she likes. And you, Miss Francesca. Miss Childe. Drat it all. I can't keep the names straight." He glared at Clay. "This was your idea. *You* do the pretty."

Deliberately turning her back to Clayburn, Francesca smiled at Jeremy and Bertram. "Excuse me for a moment, gentlemen. Livvy is not home at present, but I shall go find Ann and see to refreshments."

After dispatching a servant for tea and sherry, she located Ann in the upstairs parlor, embroidering a pillowcase. Ann's face lit up when she heard that Jeremy Porter was downstairs, wishing to renew their acquaintance.

Francesca blocked her precipitous rush to the salon. "I do not fancy stirring up trouble," she said, "but the young man obviously consorts with reprobates. Exactly how did you meet him, Ann? What passed between you?"

"Must you spy an ogre around every corner, Cesca? Not all men are like my father, you know. I chanced to encounter Jerry at the inn while you were asleep, when I went in search of Livvy. He was most considerate."

Jerry? One meeting and she called him by a nickname! Oh my. Francesca decided to leave that alone for now. "Considerate he may have been. But he failed to tell you where Livvy could be found, although he knew very well that she was in the gaming room with Lord Clayburn. A man who begins by deceiving will continue to deceive, Ann. You must not trust him."

"He might have lied to me, I suppose, or simply withheld information out of loyalty to his friend. I shall keep it in mind. But truly, I would like to see him again. May I?"

For all the alarms sounding in her head, Francesca could not bring herself to disappoint Ann. "Of course you may. Go ahead of me and dish up the tea, will you? I'll be down shortly."

Propelled by a disconcerting rush of vanity, Francesca fled to her bedchamber and spent a frantic few minutes washing her face and rebraiding her hair. She longed to change her dress, but knew that would give Clayburn entirely the wrong impression.

When she reentered the Green Saloon, Bertram and Jeremy were propped like bookends on the divan with Ann seated primly between them, smiling at something one of them had said. Then she made a reply, and both young men broke out laughing.

Francesca paused, considering this wonder. Shy Ann, who had never said boo to a goose, seemed perfectly at ease with all this unaccustomed male attention.

Unwilling to disturb them, she looked around for Lord Clayburn. He was standing by the bay window, gazing out over the winter-brown garden at the back of the house. His dark hair shone in the pale sunlight, and she took an extra moment to enjoy the slight lift of his tailed coat as it curved around his taut buttocks.

She could have this man.

Stop it, Francesca! Such foolishness. Lord Clayburn might be an especially magnificent incarnation of the devil, but he was a demon nonetheless. And demons must be exorcised.

But how? He'd been clever, even coaching his friends to draw Ann into the room and keep her there. Under the circumstances, she could not precisely order him from the house.

But she might be able to freeze him out. "Shall I pour you some tea, my lord?" she inquired, hoping she sounded a hundred degrees colder than she felt.

He turned, his silver eyes gleaming with amusement. "Thank you, madam, but no. Appearances to the contrary, I do understand that you are not receiving. And that even if you were, I should not be welcome here."

"But here you are," she observed incontrovertibly. "And I daresay you hear the clatter from upstairs. Between the carpenters and the painters, the household is all at sixes and sevens."

"Point taken, Miss Childe. But since I have already intruded, allow me to present my excuses for doing so." He lifted a quizzical brow. "Or would you prefer to know the *real* reason I have come?"

"Oh, do begin with the excuses," she said, trilling a laugh that must have come from somebody else. Livvy trilled in just that fashion. Francesca steadied her voice. "As it happens, I adore fiction."

"Very well, then, we shall start at the bottom and work our way toward the light. Transparent and shabby though they certainly are, I devised reasonable pretexts for dragging my friends along with me. Oh, and I confess to intimidating your butler when he tried to turn us away. You must forgive all three of them, Miss Childe. Only *I* am responsible for cutting up your peace."

"I never doubted that for a moment, sir." She was

finding it difficult to repress a laugh. Such feigned charm and fake sincerity, from a master of both! "May I hear the reasonable pretexts?"

"To be sure." He held up a pair of fingers. "Item one has already been mentioned by Bertie, who is, by the way, more sensible than he sounds and extremely good ton. Figuring that the twins would make their first appearance at Lady Sefton's ball, I set myself to ensure they would not lack for partners. Jerry and Bertie wish to claim the first two dances, which will give the young ladies a bit of confidence when they find themselves among strangers." He lowered his index finger. "Are you impressed?"

"Mildly." In fact, she had worried herself to a nub imagining Ann and Livvy among the wallflowers all evening. "It was kind of you to make this effort on their behalf," she admitted, "although I expect you have ulterior motives."

"Oh, I do," he said without a trace of remorse. "But back to the pretexts." He waved his middle finger. "Item two. You are attempting to locate a book, and I still very much want to help you find it."

"Can you possibly have mistaken me, Lord Clayburn? I declined your assistance."

"Indeed. But should you ever require anything at all of me, send word to this address." He retrieved a slim golden case from his pocket and pulled out an engraved card. "Whatever you ask, I will do . . . with one notable exception. Which leads me to the primary reason for this unwelcome call."

She accepted his card and stared at the address he'd inscribed on the back in bold, slashing strokes. "And that would be . . . ?"

"I wanted above all things to see you again," he said simply.

Had she not known the truth of the matter, she

might well have believed that flattering declaration. His eyes, before she forced herself to look away, had held just the right touch of earnest conviction. Oh dear. Safer by far to move quickly on, she decided, sliding the card into her pocket. "And if I wish a favor, Lord Clayburn, what is the one thing you will not grant me?"

"The thing you most want, I fear. But do not ask me to keep my distance, Miss Childe, for you may be sure I'll not obey."

Oh dear, she thought again with the minuscule part of her brain that was still functioning. *Hallelujah,* the rest of her sang to Handel's music. *Hallelujah!*

Clayburn obviously recognized a good exit line when he spoke it. Rather like a border collie herding sheep, he expeditiously separated his friends from Ann and steered them out the door.

It all happened so unexpectedly that Francesca had no chance to give Clayburn the sharp setdown he deserved. The last thing she saw was Jeremy Porter casting sheep's eyes at Ann, who gazed back with disgusting adoration.

Oh, surely not Jeremy! Today he'd let himself be used as a pawn in Clayburn's game. He consorted with reprobates.

But Ann was wise enough to take the measure of his character and entitled to have some fun. Francesca reluctantly decided to let their flirtation run its course without meddling.

As for Clayburn . . . Well, what harm could it do to lead him on for a short time? It would be amusing to observe a master of seduction at work. Dangerous, to be sure, but there was no chance whatever that he would succeed. She knew full well he was acting on his father's behalf, wooing a parcel of land while pretending to court the woman who came with it.

A man like that deserved to be made to jump through hoops. Besides, he was the one who'd sworn to seek her out again, so what happened thereafter was his own fault. Why not allow Clayburn to imagine she found him irresistible? He assumed that she would. And then, when he thought the prize within his grasp, she would send him packing.

Oh, for shame, Francesca! How can you even *think* anything so mean-spirited? Gathering her skirts, she fled upstairs to distract herself by wrangling with the carpenters.

But all the while, she could not help anticipating her next encounter with Lord Rakehell. It was certain to come. And in a battle of wits, she was certain to win.

Ah, but what would she do if he carried the battle to lower ground? she wondered with a thrill of fear. What if he set upon her treasonous body, or laid siege to her lonely heart?

Dare she risk all to experience, however briefly, those hot, prickly, utterly baffling feelings he conjured with the slightest glance in her direction?

No!

Well, possibly. Even probably.

She sighed. Why lie to herself?

Yes.

Chapter 9

When the bonny blade carouses,
Pockets full, and spirits high.
                    —*Samuel Johnson*

Bright, early-spring sunlight streamed into the parlor where Francesca and Ann sat, listening for a knock at the door. Conversation had all but died out hours ago, and the only sound was the scratching of needles through the linen stretched on their embroidery frames.

It was a way to pass the time, Francesca supposed, wincing as the needle dug again into her forefinger. She could easier walk a high wire than embroider Papa's initials without leaving the handkerchief stained with her blood.

"You mustn't worry," Ann said for the twentieth time that day. "Young gentlemen prefer to be out and about. I expect he was not at home to receive the message."

"Indeed. It is foolish to sit here waiting for him, I know. But there is nothing else to be done."

Most likely he would see her note tomorrow morning, Francesca thought sourly, when he staggered home after a night of carousing. But she had, without reason, assumed he would materialize immediately. Wasn't there a saying to that effect? "Summon the devil and he will appear."

Apparently the devil had other plans for the day.

With a sigh, she examined the lopsided *S* she had created and began to pull out the thread for another try.

The standing clock had just chimed three when Peters entered the drawing room, a calling card on the salver in his hand and Lord Clayburn close on his heels.

Francesca stood, relief whipping through her like a March wind. "Thank you, Peters. That will be all. Please see that we are not disturbed."

Clayburn stepped forward and bowed. "Pardon my deplorable manners, Miss Childe. I should have waited to be announced, of course. And forgive me for the delay. Your message was delivered hours ago, the landlord informed me, but I only just returned home."

"Pray do not apologize, my lord. You are most kind to have come at all. Please be seated. Would you care for tea or a glass of sherry? You remember Ann Childe, I presume." Francesca bit her tongue to stop from babbling on.

Now that he was finally there, she perversely wished him elsewhere. Wished she hadn't sent for him at all. She had sworn never to do so. Contrarily, he looked very much like the answer to her prayers, strong and calm and capable of handling even this hopeless situation.

You are delusional, she told herself as he greeted Ann with a smile. Any tall man wearing a caped greatcoat looks imposing. Under all that wool, Clayburn is the same irresponsible rakehell he has always been.

But under desperate circumstances, even a rake could prove himself useful. She required only a few answers, after all, perhaps a little advice, and certainly a promise of silence. Any one of the three would be more than she expected from him.

Realizing that he was gazing at her with a puzzled expression, she gestured to a chair.

"No, thank you," he said, stripping off his gloves. "This must be something out of the ordinary, or you'd not have called for my assistance. How can I help you, Miss Childe?"

Grateful for his straightforward manner, she set herself to match it. "This morning we learned that Livvy has once again gone out in company with Lord Bromley. I hoped you might have some idea where they could be."

"I'm afraid not." He frowned. "Surely an afternoon excursion under her father's protection is harmless enough. Have you reason to be concerned?"

She retrieved a sheet of paper from her pocket. "Perhaps you should read this."

He skimmed the brief note, which was signed with a large *L*.

By now, Francesca had Livvy's words by heart. "I am off to a big estate with Father. We might be there a few days or maybe all week. Tell everyone I am sick. I don't need to appear at balls any longer. You must not go into a tizzy, Cesca. I'm perfectly safe, and Father says we will have lots of fun."

"I see," Clayburn said.

He gave her a smile that was meant to be reassuring, but she had seen his hands tighten when he read the note. He understood the implications as well as she did.

"It is inexcusable," he continued in an unruffled voice, "for Lord Bromley to take the girl away without consulting you or leaving notice of their direction. But this may be nothing more than an impulsive departure for a perfectly innocuous house party. In the weeks before Easter, many fine families prefer to entertain at their country estates."

Did Clayburn think her such a slowtop, to be mollified with absurd explanations? "And precisely which of these fine families would know of Bromley Childe?" she inquired tartly. "You have taken his measure. Is he like to be a welcome guest at a fashionable country estate?"

"Hardly." Clayburn gave her a faint smile of apology. "I suspect, as you do, that he has gone to a place no father should take his daughter. Lord knows he gave no thought to Livvy's reputation at the inn where we first met. Nor did I," he added quickly, as if expecting Francesca to leap in with a reminder.

This would all be a great deal simpler, she thought as he read the letter again, if it were possible to ignore the unspoken matters that lay between them. But she must, so long as she required his help.

"What does she mean about not needing to go to any more balls?" he asked, dropping the letter onto a side table.

"I have no idea. She's only been to one, last night at Lady Sefton's, and she never lacked for partners. But now that I think of it, she said little on the way home. That is strikingly out of character. In general, Livvy is forever rabbiting on."

"I thought it odd, too," Ann said in a quiet voice. "She had a strange, rather dreamy look on her face. I tried to talk with her about the ball while we were dressing for bed, but she seemed to be off in a world of her own."

Livvy has met a man, Francesca thought immediately. But *which* man? Only young Bertram Porter had danced twice with her, probably because Clayburn had ordered him to. And his duty done, he'd hastily taken his leave.

Francesca liked Bertram, but he was not the sort of man to put stars in the eyes of a young, excitable female. Only someone edgy and a bit dangerous, like Clayburn, would appeal to Livvy.

"I think we should focus on Bromley," Clayburn said. "Did he mention plans to leave town?"

"Yes, but mind you, he's been gadding about since we arrived in London. He reappeared a few days ago and assured me he would soon be off again. There was something about dice and an excellent wine cellar. Since reading Livvy's note, I've gone over his words again and again, but I'm sure he never said who owned that wine cellar. It is my impression he was invited secondhand, by someone whose name I cannot recall."

"It was mentioned?"

"In passing, but I never imagined it would be of importance. I'm fairly certain it started with an *H*, though, and that it had two syllables. Hickox? Halbert? Hilton?"

Clayburn, who had been pacing the room, suddenly froze. "Heston?"

"Yes! That was it. Heston. Do you know him?"

"As it happens, I do. We—"

"Livvy danced with Lord Heston last night," Ann interrupted. "I remember because he asked me first, but there was something about him that was not quite pleasing, so I told him I was on my way to the retiring room. I had to go there, of course, once I'd made the excuse. But on my way, I looked back and saw him take the floor with Livvy."

Francesca's heart sank. "This isn't good, is it?" she asked Clayburn.

"No," he said after a moment. "Whatever your opinion of me, Miss Childe, you would find Heston even more detestable. Still, he has little to gain by seducing Livvy, and he never exerts himself unless there is profit to be had. I expect he told Bromley about the gaming party, recognizing a pigeon ripe for the plucking."

"But Bromley hasn't any money."

95

"Not at the moment, perhaps. But he has prospects. His vowels are accepted because he stands to inherit the Sotherton title and fortune."

Francesca swallowed her response. Anyone holding Bromley's vowels would be vastly disappointed, since the Sotherton fortune was willed to her. And she'd no intention of using a groat of it to pay off any man's debts of honor. Was ever a term so ridiculous as that? What could be remotely honorable about gaming away a family inheritance or the bread from a child's mouth on the turn of a card?

Perhaps she ought to have made Bromley's exact situation known in London, if only to keep the River Tick from swallowing him up. But even thinking about her future inheritance, let alone speaking of it, was utterly repugnant. If she had her way about it, Papa would live forever.

"It's possible I may be able to learn where Heston has gone," Clayburn said reflectively. "Ought we to assume Bromley has landed in the same place, or should I mount a search for him elsewhere? That will be more difficult, I expect. He is not admitted to the clubs or known to most of my acquaintances."

"He often veers off in the most unlikely directions," she replied, "but I'm fairly certain he aimed first at the place Heston invited him."

"Very well. Give me a couple of hours, then. I understand your concern for Livvy's reputation, so be assured that the Childe name will not be mentioned in my inquiries. Have you a carriage at your disposal?"

She nodded, aware his mind had leaped several leagues ahead of hers.

"Then tell your driver to be prepared to leave on a few minutes' notice. I suggest you gather up a few things, since you may be obliged to spend the night at an inn. Doubtless you'll wish to come along."

"Oh, yes," she managed from a dry throat.

"And I!" Ann said, jumping to her feet.

"Certainly." Clayburn smiled. "I already have a fairly good idea where they can be found, but allow me to verify my hunch before we set out."

"Is it very far?" Francesca asked. "And how are we to extricate Livvy without creating a scene?"

"If the weather holds, we can be there within two hours. As for the rest, you may safely leave it to me." He bowed. "I shall return as soon as possible, Miss Childe. Try not to worry."

A few hours before midnight, Clay set out on horseback for the two-mile ride from the Black Dove Inn to Wolvercote, country seat of the Marquess of Fallon.

Lord Heston was already there, a pair of his cronies had confirmed, along with Clarence Briggs and several other die-hard gamesters. Unsurprisingly, Bromley Childe's name had not been mentioned, nor had Clay been free to bring it up. But he was confident of finding Livvy and her feckless sire within the hour.

Although there was no moon to light the road, Clay had little trouble finding his way to Wolvercote. He had spent a score of dissipated weekends there, back when the Marquess of Fallon entertained in royal fashion. Fallon had squandered much of his fortune providing vintage wines and beautiful women to the men who traveled from London to indulge his addiction for gaming.

He'd lost even more at the tables, and now his house parties attracted only hardened punters out to glean what little remained. Clay had not joined them since the parties stopped being fun, but he had a good idea what to expect.

Gaining admission to the house would be simple enough. Extricating himself, Livvy in tow, would not.

His thoughts turned to Francesca, now ensconced at the small inn a few miles back with Ann and Jerry for company. After discovering Heston's whereabouts, he had located Jerry and brought him along, not wanting to leave the women without protection.

As it happened, it wasn't the ladies who required protection. He had barely escaped with his skin intact.

When Francesca learned he meant to go alone to Wolvercote, her immediate reaction had all but set the Black Dove ablaze. Their quarrel lasted more than an hour, and he doubted she'd let him finish a sentence the entire time.

Such a firebrand, he thought, still a bit awestruck. Eventually she had calmed, fractionally, and sent him on his way, her eyes shooting darts of flame into his back.

What a lover she would be, all that rage transformed into passion. When at last he took her into his arms and his bed, he would be the luckiest man in the universe.

But first he must pluck the recalcitrant Livvy from Fallon's private gaming hell, and possibly even from Heston's bed. He profoundly hoped things had not yet progressed to that point. When he met Heston, which was inevitable, he bloody well did not want to be fighting a duel over the likes of Livvy Childe.

Clay reined to a halt on a knoll overlooking the rambling patchwork mansion, assembled by five centuries of Fallon marquesses with wildly differing notions of architecture. Nearly the whole house was shrouded in darkness, but light streamed from the windows of the large saloon where Fallon usually set up his tables. By now, the gaming would be in full swing.

After considering several plans, he decided on the simplest approach—walk directly in, determine

Livvy's whereabouts, and improvise some way to make off with her.

Before leaving London, he had gone to his rooms long enough to change clothes and pocket the last of his funds. Four hundred pounds would buy him into the game, but the stake would last only a short time unless he got very lucky. Fallon played deep and expected his guests to do likewise.

Within a few minutes, Clay had stabled his mount and gained access to the house. A bored servant admitted him without question and escorted him down the long, meandering passageway to the gaming parlor.

"You'll be needing a bedchamber, milord," he advised by rote. "When you are ready, ask whoever is on duty to show you to the Peacock Suite. I'll see a fire is made up for you."

Clay passed him a coin and stepped through the door, blinking against the cloud of cigar smoke that all but obscured a large round table in the center of the room. He counted eight men, recognizing most of them. Sure enough, Bromley was there, seated close to Heston. Between them, a disgruntled look on her face, Livvy fidgeted on her chair.

So far so good. He sauntered to the table, bowing when a few of the gamblers glanced up from their cards to acknowledge his arrival.

Heston was the first to speak, grinning sourly. "Too hot for you in London, Clayburn?"

"Just so," he replied in an amiable voice. "For my sins, I am compelled to slum with the likes of you." Clay turned to Fallon, immediately repelled by his drink-glazed amber eyes and the narrow face pocked with open sores. "Good evening," he said with another polite bow. "May I join you?"

Fallon waved a skinny hand toward an empty chair.

"Sit down, sit down. Your money is always good here. Got any?"

"Never enough, I'm afraid."

While the men played out the current deal, he leaned back in his chair to study the situation. Bromley was already having trouble focusing on his cards. Another hour of drinking and he wouldn't notice if a horde of Mongols swept into the room and made off with his daughter. No problems from that source.

Heston was another matter. No telling if he meant to bed Livvy tonight, but from sheer perversity he would object if Clayburn showed a speck of interest in the chit.

Without question, he would have to finesse her away before anyone guessed what he was about. He drew half his small bankroll from his pocket. Everyone assumed he'd come to gamble, so for the next few hours his main concern would be to stay in the game.

Livvy waved her fan in his direction. "Hullo, Lord Clayburn. We keep meeting in the oddest places. This time I'm learning how to play macao, but they—"

A chorus of shushes interrupted her. Pouting, she leaned forward and set a possessive hand on Heston's shoulder. He batted it away as he would an insect, and she lapsed back on her chair with an audible sigh.

Clay ignored her, still evaluating his options. Too bad that Fallon had chosen macao for the evening's entertainment. A game of luck, it offered almost no chance for him to apply skill against the random fall of the cards. Not that he meant to win heavily, of course. Indeed, his half-formed plan required him to lose . . . eventually. No winner could leave the table without rousing immediate protest, and attention was the last thing he wanted.

But he required an edge, to manipulate the action, and macao didn't suit his purposes. He managed to hang even the first hour, contriving to look almost as bored as Livvy. Fortunately, the marquess had been losing steadily.

"I say, Fallon," Clay drawled when it came his turn to hold the bank. "How about if we liven things up by changing the game? Vingt-et-un, perhaps?"

Fallon jumped at the chance to reverse his run of bad luck. "Vingt-et-un it is. Agreed, gentlemen?"

Everyone knew better than to object, so Clay dealt the first hand of a game wherein he could seize an advantage by counting the cards already played and wagering accordingly. Most of the others were too drunk by now to do the same.

Another hour passed with money changing hands at rapid speed. Then Livvy spoke up in a whiny voice. "Why won't you let *me* play? This is an easy game. I've already figured it out. And I'm *bored*."

"Quiet!" Fallon glared at her. "Or take yourself off. This is no place for a squirrel-brained female."

Clay hoped she would give up and retire to her bedchamber, where he could easily find her later. But she stayed in place, squirming and fiddling with her fan.

Play grew more intense. And when the heavy drinkers began to slide out of control, upping the stakes and betting at random, Clay was hard put to keep from losing everything. At one point, only ten guineas remained on the table in front of him.

Heston gave him a malicious smile. "About plucked dry, old sod? Pity you couldn't stay with us longer, but your vowels are no good here. Everyone knows Montford has cut you off."

Clay reached into his pocket and pulled out a sheaf of banknotes. Over his objections, Francesca had pressed the money into his hand just before he left the Black Dove. He'd never meant to use it.

Still, instinct told him it was too soon to leave the

room. And when he did, the men had to figure he was planning to return. "There is more where this came from," he said, slurring his voice. "I need a drink. Where's the bottle? Somebody deal."

He refilled his glass with an unsteady hand and contrived to pour most of the brandy on the floor while the players were busy studying their cards. The brandy joined a pool of liquid under his boots, where all but one or two earlier drinks had been deposited. This one night, he had to appear drunk and remain starkly sober.

Even Heston began to play carelessly after a while. Clay managed to win a considerable amount from him and Briggs while losing to Fallon and the others. Now and again he slipped notes back into his pocket, because he would need them later. Soon he'd recovered all of Francesca's money, along with half his own stake. That amount he kept on the table, visible to everyone.

Always, he watched Livvy closely. The chit had an overabundance of stamina, he thought with admiration. Although she drank almost as steadily as the men, it didn't seem to faze her in the slightest.

But at long last she began to raise the fan to conceal her yawns. Clay played two more hands, winning heavily on the first and losing a bit on the second. By now, a decent number of guineas were stacked on the table in front of him.

It was time.

He lurched to his feet. "Gentl'men, deal me out a li'l while. Gotta do what a man's gotta do. Call of nature, what? Better clear m'head, too. Can't tell a ten from a deuce." He swayed and put both hands on the table as if trying to regain his balance.

Livvy was sitting directly across from him, and he stared at her for a long time. Then he jabbed a finger in her direction. "Izzat a female? What's she doin' here? Thought you had better sense, Fallon. Ought to be somewhere else, I say. But if you want her here, well, so be it."

"I don't," Fallon said with a snarl. "She's been a damned nuisance all night. Take her with you, Clayburn. Have a servant put her in a room and turn the key. Make sure she don't come back."

"If you say so, m'lord." Clay pushed himself upright and staggered around in a complete circle. "Where's the bloody door? C'mon, female. Show me the way out."

For a tense moment, Clay thought Livvy would toss a fit. Then she leaned toward Heston and whispered something in his ear.

"Not now," he grumbled. "I'm playing cards."

She gave him a scorching look, bolted from her chair, and stomped to the door. "This way, Lord Clayburn. I'd rather come with you than stay here with these boors."

To his relief, Heston failed to react to her challenge. Clay waved at the guineas he was leaving behind on the table. "You wait here," he told them. " 'Bye for now. I'll see you later."

He lurched toward the door and let Livvy escort him down the passageway until they arrived in the foyer. Luckily, there was no servant in sight. "Wanna see m'horse," he said. "Nobody with any sense works for Fallon, and I don't trust that ostler."

"But it's cold outside." To his astonishment, she rubbed up against him, making sure he noticed the swell of her breasts under her thin, low-cut gown. "I'm sure the horse is fine. Perhaps we should go to bed now."

"H-horse," he insisted. This time his stammer was genuine. Did the girl mean to seduce him? Hell, if she was that eager to put her back to a mattress, he might as well leave her here with Heston.

But Olivia's virtue was none of his concern, he reminded himself. He was doing this for Francesca. Stripping off his coat, he placed it over the girl's bare shoulders and led her outside.

"Oh!" she said when they arrived at the stable. "Can that huge black be your horse? He hasn't even been unsaddled."

"How convenient." All business now, Clay slipped the ostler a half crown. "There will be another on my return. Meanwhile, you have seen nothing."

The old man bit the coin with his few remaining teeth. "Feels solid, m'lord. Can't see it 'cuz I 'appen to be blind."

Laughing, Clay swung onto the saddle and held out his arms. "Up you come, young lady."

She took a step back. "Where are we going?"

"For a ride under the stars." He gestured to the ostler, who moved behind Livvy in case she tried to bolt. "Just the two of us. I've been planning this since first I saw you in Fallon's gaming room. Perhaps before that," he added in strictest honesty. "Where would you rather be? In that smoky room where nobody pays attention to you, or up here with my arms wrapped around your waist?"

Within seconds, Livvy was settled in front of him, giggling like a schoolgirl. "I knew you liked me," she said as he guided the horse onto the road. "And you are much more handsome than Rupert, although he is very attractive, too. He said we would have a good time together if I convinced Father to bring me to Wolvercote. So I did. Supper was fun. Everybody laughed and told amusing stories. But when they all started playing cards, I might as well have been invisible."

In spite of the dark road, Clay urged his mount to a trot, in a hurry to rid himself of this chatterbox, and damnably cold in shirtsleeves and waistcoat. As further proof he meant to return, he'd thought it best to leave his greatcoat, hat, and gloves at Wolvercote.

"They kept telling me to be quiet," she continued relentlessly. "Even Rupert was beastly. He was much nicer when we danced at Lady Sefton's ball. I'm glad you came, actually. I'd much rather be with you. Even though you didn't ask me to dance at the ball last night. Why?"

"Because I didn't want to," he said between his teeth. "Shut up, Livvy. I need to concentrate on the road."

"Of course," she said.

"Where are we going?" she asked a few moments later. "This is vastly romantic, to be sure. But if we wind up back at Wolvercote, Rupert might take offense that we were alone together. He will probably call you out."

From her wriggling against his thighs, Clay reckoned she found the notion of men dueling for her favors an appealing one. "Heston and I are almost certain to face off with pistols some foggy morning," he said dryly. "But it won't be over you. Our quarrel dates back to school days, and if ever there was a reason for it, I cannot recall what it was."

"You might ask him," she suggested. "He is perfectly reasonable, unless he has cards in his hands. Then he is a positive sourpuss."

Clay was more than pleased to see light directly ahead. The Black Dove. He reined the horse to a walk as they came near the entrance.

"Oh!" Livvy leaned back against his chest. "An inn. You *do* mean to be alone with me. I am so glad.

Not that I expected anything else, since you are the very model of a rake."

He dismounted and barely managed to catch her when she jumped into his arms, rubbing against his body like a harlot. Fueled by all the wine she'd drunk, she had clearly abandoned what few inhibitions she ever possessed.

Setting her at arm's length, he tapped her on the nose with an excruciatingly cold finger. "Yes, but I am a most *discriminating* rake. Now, come along. I have a surprise for you."

Chapter 10

If of herself she will not love,
Nothing can make her.
     —*Sir John Suckling*

In a private parlor at the Black Dove Inn, Francesca was diligently wearing a circular track on the floorboards with her pacing.

Clayburn had been gone for hours. Aeons. She'd long since despaired of him, and only Jerry's calm objections prevented her from setting out for Wolvercote on her own.

She glanced at Jerry as she passed by the sofa where he'd sat quietly with Ann all evening, except when he left to secure fresh tea and more logs for the fire. How incongruous that such a nice young man should be Clayburn's friend.

It was past one in the morning when the door swung open with a bang.

Livvy, a man's coat draped over her shoulders, staggered into the room as if she'd been pushed. When she spotted Francesca, she emitted a loud squawk and whirled to face Lord Clayburn, who had come in behind her.

"The prodigal returneth," he said to Francesca. "Under some duress, I fear, and with a few preconceptions about my intentions in her regard. Those have just been demolished."

"Indeed they have, you brutal, lying fiend! Father will call you out for this. See if he doesn't!"

"I am quaking in my boots. Meantime, unless you relish the taste of my neckcloth stuffed in your mouth, I suggest you close it."

Francesca knew she ought to relieve Clayburn of his unwelcome charge, but the pleasure of watching Livvy being managed by an expert was too delicious.

He beckoned then to Ann and Jerry, who had risen from the sofa to observe the spectacle. "If you please, Ann, take this tiresome nitwit elsewhere and clean her up. I hope you've brought a spare gown or two, but if not, wrap her in a blanket. We were forced to leave her luggage behind, and she is wearing precious little at the moment." He whisked his coat from her shoulders. "I'll take this back now."

Francesca gasped. Livvy had been wearing *that* dress, what there was of it, in company with England's most notorious degenerates?

Livvy stomped her foot. "I demand to go back to Wolvercote! Now!"

From directly behind her, Clayburn clamped his hand over her mouth. "How unfortunate, since you will be on your way to London within the hour. Jerry, should she give you any trouble upstairs, do whatever you must to restrain her."

Ann approached her sister and brushed a windblown lock of hair from her forehead. "Come, Livvy. You are vastly outnumbered, you know. And I imagine you are excessively tired after such an eventful day. If Francesca promises not to ring a peal over you in the carriage, will you come along peaceably?"

In spite of Clayburn's tight grip over the bottom half of her face, Livvy managed a resentful nod.

Ann smiled over her shoulder at Francesca. "You do promise?"

"Oh, very well. We are all out of temper. I shall contain mine, if Livvy does the same."

"She will," Ann said confidently. "You may release her now, my lord."

Clayburn stepped away. "Miss Childe will let you know when it is time to leave, Ann. Meanwhile, we wish to be private."

With an insolent toss of her head, Livvy swept out of the room like a ship of the line under full canvas.

"Oh my," Francesca murmured as Jerry closed the door.

"She is fearless," Clayburn said. "I'll grant her that much. But Ann appears to have got all the brains in the family."

"All the heart, too." Even though the crisis seemed to be over, at least for now, her own heart was thumping at triple speed.

She had rarely been alone with a gentleman other than her father, and never with one who managed to look both elegant and disheveled at the same time. It must be damp outside, because the sleeves of his white shirt were molded to his shoulders and arms, outlining contours that suddenly fascinated her.

Under his buff-colored waistcoat, doeskin breeches clung explicitly to narrow flanks, powerful thighs, and other amazing sectors of male anatomy. For an indolent wastrel, he possessed a splendid array of muscles. With an act of will, she lifted her gaze to his face. And immediately wondered how it would feel to comb her fingers through that tousled dark hair.

Casting about for her scattered wits, Francesca realized that Lord Clayburn was staring at her with equal intensity. His coat, which had been dangling from one hand, now lay crumpled on the floor.

She thought to go pick it up but dared not go so close to him. *Say something*, she told herself, *preferably something comprehensible*. "What happened?" she asked.

He looked as though the sound of her voice had snapped him from a trance. "Ah, yes. Livvy. I had almost forgot." He strode to the fireplace and held his hands to the flames. "Forgive me for turning my back to you, madam, but it is devilish cold outside. I seem to have grown icicles where my fingers used to be."

Her tongue, which had been stuck in her throat like a log, suddenly broke loose with a vengeance. "Oh dear. I am so very sorry. And to think you permitted that vexatious girl to wear your coat. Please do thaw yourself. Shall I send for tea? Or do you prefer brandy?"

He chuckled. "I *always* prefer brandy. But nothing for now, thank you. I know you are anxious to learn what transpired at Wolvercote. It's not all good, of course. But so far as I can detect, Livvy came to no serious harm. She was in the gaming room when I arrived, watching the play and sulking because Fallon had ordered her to cease her prattling." He glanced over his shoulder. "I fear the chit has a prodigious capacity for wine. In fact, she could probably drink me under the table."

"Yet another dismal inheritance from Bromley," Francesca said with a sigh. "Did he object when you took her away?"

"*Nobody* objected. Indeed, they were all too pleased to see the back of her. Mind you, they assumed she was merely headed for her bedchamber."

"With you?"

"Hardly. Good Lord, Francesca, I hope they credit me with better taste than that!"

"Even Lord Heston?"

"Who knows what he thinks? But Livvy has him in her sights, that is certain. And anything she offers him, other than a leg-shackle, he will almost surely accept."

"Do you suppose they have already . . . ?"

His wide shoulders rose and fell as he took a deep breath. "As to that, you must ask Livvy. But I would presume not. They arrived at Wolvercote quite late in the afternoon, and she hasn't the look of a woman recently bedded."

Francesca wondered exactly how a recently bedded woman was supposed to look.

"Heston's intentions remain unclear," he said, all but straddling the fire in his effort to get warm again. "I chose not to put them to the test by making off with her in an obvious way. Not any one of those men would credit that I meant only to restore a silly girl to the bosom of her family, so a more devious strategy was in order."

"And clearly it succeeded," she said, impressed. "Will you explain it to me?"

"I'll not even try." He turned his back to the hearth and folded his arms, smiling at her. "I have some experience with sodden gamblers, having been one in my time, and that is all I mean to say on the subject."

"Was there a fight?" she couldn't help asking. "Was anyone hurt?"

Laughing, he shook his head. "Leave it alone, my dear. If there is to be trouble, which I seriously doubt, it will take place when I return to Wolvercote."

"But why would you do such a thing? Especially if there might be trouble."

"Well, to begin with, Childe must be told what has become of his daughter. At the moment he has no idea she is gone, but he's bound to notice in a day or two. Also, I lost rather a good deal of money and mean to recover it. Which reminds me . . ."

He crossed to pick up his coat and drew something

from the pocket. "A portion of this is yours. A hundred pounds, as I recall."

"Keep it!" she insisted as he began to peel off banknotes. "Heaven knows you have earned that pittance, and a great deal more besides."

His head shot up. "Do you imagine I did this for *money*?"

"N-no. But you would not have been in that game if not for me. And by your own account, you . . . Well, the very least I can do is cover your losses."

"Confound you, Francesca!"

He advanced on her, backing her up until her shoulders hit the wall. She gazed helplessly at his cravat as he planted his hands against the wall just behind her head, imprisoning her with his large body.

"There is much I want from you," he said stonily. "Far more than you can imagine. But money is no part of it. And you will never, *ever*, be in debt to me."

She could not mistake the anger radiating from him. And she knew the exact moment when he realized what he was doing. Seconds later, he stepped away, both hands lifted in a gesture of apology.

"There is no need," she told him when he began to speak. "I already understand. As it happens, I have somewhat of a temper myself."

"I had noticed." He lowered his arms. "But as a rule, I do *not* have a temper. Not one I've been unable to control, at any rate, until the last few moments."

It disturbed him, she realized, that loss of self-control. And at the same time, she was reassured to find him capable of a temper that matched her own. When they had quarreled about his solo venture to Wolvercote, she had raged at him to no purpose whatsoever. It had been like pounding her head against a glacier.

"Do you mean to rake me over the coals?" he asked

lightly. "If so, please get on about it. Waiting for punishment, I have learned, is far more painful than the actual whipping."

"Which is why I keep you waiting, of course. But in truth, I much prefer to deal with people who speak their minds, which you have done. Now I shall speak mine. Whatever you choose to believe, Lord Clayburn, I am indebted to you. Not because you demand repayment or expect it, but because I feel an obligation to return the favor you have generously performed."

"Then you feel what does not exist. There is no obligation."

"Yes, you have said so, and my mind accepts it. But I *feel*, quite inexorably, an obligation you must allow me to satisfy. Perhaps only another woman could understand."

"But then, a woman would not be distracted by wondering at the precise nature of your inexorable feelings." He moved closer, until the fabric of his waistcoat brushed against her suddenly sensitive breasts. "Let it not be said I have ever refused a lady, madam. If you demand satisfaction, then naturally I must oblige you."

It was impossible to order her thoughts with him standing so close, gazing at her in just that way. "How?" she asked feebly.

"Not with money," he said, his voice husky and suggestive. "It's quite simple what I want from you."

There was an endless, breathless pause.

And then he grinned. "The next time I ask you to dance with me, Miss Childe, you must say yes."

"B-but I cannot," she sputtered. "Dance, I mean. I told you so last night at the ball."

"Would you have danced with me if you knew the steps?"

"Probably not," she had to admit. She might have

113

wanted to. No, she *had* wanted to. But matronly chaperones of one-and-thirty did not take the floor with handsome young bucks. Everyone would have remarked upon it.

"May I ask why?" he inquired gently. "Or do I already know?"

No longer sure what *she* knew, Francesca could not begin to guess what went through his intricate mind. "I have never danced. I cannot perform the steps. All else is moot, Lord Clayburn, so name another favor I can perform."

He wagged his elegant eyebrows. "Now, let me see—"

"Never mind!" she interrupted hastily. "Perhaps in the future something will arise. Then you can tell me about it."

"Oh, something has risen long since," he said with a wicked glint in his eyes. "But I fear that will have to wait. Meantime, may I suggest a gamble on the futures market?"

Francesca had no idea what he was talking about. Flailing, she said the only thing that made its way intact from her brain to her tongue. "I have no idea what you are talking about."

"Speculation," he informed her. "This night's mission is done with, and that you called on me when you needed help was more than sufficient reward. Joined with the pleasure of your company, there remains some question about which of us is in debt to the other."

Apparently this was how rakes went about getting their way, she thought with annoyance. They threw handfuls of words, so fast any normal person's mind would lose track of the subject. And they stood close and looked so virile that any woman with a breath in her body wanted only to be kissed.

But wanting was not the same as doing. She squared her shoulders. "I hope you will one day come to the point, my lord."

He laughed. "Very well, if you'll stop my-lording me. Should it happen I have the good fortune to perform for you another service, one that makes you feel *inexorably obligated*, you will allow me to teach you to dance."

"Dance? Good heavens. Whatever for? I shall soon return to the provinces, where such a skill is singularly useless. And with my great height, few men would choose to partner me in any case."

"I am glad to hear it. Now have done with arguments, or I'll be forced to remind you who it was who began this absurd negotiation. The circumstance may never come to pass, you know. And if it should, I'll not take undue advantage." He gave her a coaxing smile. "Say *yes*."

"I'll say *perhaps*," she conceded reluctantly. "At the moment, I mistrust the both of us."

"Excellent. Not a great accomplishment on my part, but progress of a sort." He fingered a tendril of hair that had escaped her braid. "Last night, when I came into the ballroom, I looked everywhere for you. It was nearly an hour before I found you hiding in an obscure corner with the chaperones."

He leaned forward until his mouth was no more than an inch from hers. She thought he meant to kiss her then and shivered with anticipation.

But he only brushed her cheek with his lips. "When I saw you, shining like a torch in your red-gold gown, my heart stopped. And I wasn't at all certain it ever meant to start again."

"It must have d-done," she mumbled, unaccountably disappointed when he moved to a safer distance.

"No doubt you think I'm giving you Spanish coin,"

he said after a moment. "Even when I say words to you I truly mean, they sound false to my own ears because I've said them before, to other women, when I didn't mean them."

"I daresay."

"Well, I see you have already judged and sentenced me. And when I am gone, you'll soon convince yourself there was some self-serving motive behind everything I said and did tonight."

"There was not? People generally act in their own self-interest, I believe."

"Ah." He retrieved his coat and shoved his arms into the sleeves. "What a cynical creature you are, Francesca Childe. I wonder why. Hardened, worldly rakes like me are *supposed* to be cynical, but here I am, brimming with hope and high expectations."

And on your way to another night of debauchery, she thought irritably. "Then I must certainly take lessons in character and spiritual growth from you, Lord Clayburn."

"Shrew," he said, grinning. "I'd like to begin your education this very moment, but it's late and I must be off. Jerry will see you home safely."

A minute later, Francesca came to her senses. She rushed into the passageway and finally caught up with him in the taproom, negotiating with a farmer for a shabby pair of work gloves. Both men looked up at her in surprise.

Cheeks flaming with embarrassment, she curtsied. "Forgive me, my lord. It's just that . . . I mean . . . I never thanked you."

The farmer winked and prodded Clayburn in the ribs with his elbow. "Good goin' there, laddie. Always leave 'em happy and wantin' more, I sez."

"You sez right," Clayburn replied, handing him several coins and accepting the gloves. "There's extra there for a round of drinks." Still in no great hurry, he moved to Francesca and led her into the passageway.

"What was he talking about?" she asked with a frown.

"Oh, you'll figure it out on the way back to London." He smiled warmly. "Come to thank me, did you? There is no need, but I confess to enjoying the experience."

"Yes, well, it seems I also require a lesson in manners. I am truly grateful, you know. But—" Catching herself, she fumbled for a turn of subject. "Nice gloves."

He used them to lift her chin, gazing steadily into her eyes. "But what, Francesca?"

She owed him the truth, she supposed. Or part of it. "I'm sure it is not deliberate, sir, but you bring out all the most detestable aspects of my nature. I scarcely see you but that I feel my temper hotting up. And then, of course, I am insufferably rude to you."

"So you are." He didn't seem the least bit disturbed by her revelations. "But I don't mind. It's when you go cold and insufferably polite on me that I'll begin to worry. As for now, why don't you thank me in proper fashion?"

"And how is that?" she asked suspiciously.

Immediately he swept her into his arms. "Like this," he whispered into her ear. "Nothing more. Only a touch of your fire, to warm me on the ride back to Wolvercote. Something to dream about, until I see you again."

Francesca felt that embrace long after he was gone. All the way to London, she felt it. And she dreamed about him, too.

Chapter 11

The lunatic, the lover, and the poet.
                              —*Shakespeare*

Well after noon the next day, a slovenly house-keeper led Clay along a dim passageway lined with bare peeling walls, stopping before a pair of massive oak doors. "This be it, milord. Nobody uses this part of the 'ouse anymore, and I 'spect the chimneys is clogged. Ye'll have to make do without a fire."

"Thank you for escorting me," he said, passing her a coin. Fallon rarely paid his staff, and Clay knew he must offer vails if he expected any service. "This place is a veritable rabbit warren."

"Aye. But only rats come 'ere these days." After a look that cast him firmly in the role of demented rodent, she shambled back toward the moderately habitable portion of Wolvercote.

As he pushed open the heavy doors, Clay heard the unmistakable rustle of small animals scurrying for cover. The dark, cavernous library smelled of mold and animal droppings.

Oh yes, this will be jolly good fun, he thought, crossing to the curtains at the far end of the room. The drawcord had been eaten away by something desperate for a meal, so he grabbed a fistful of heavy velvet and attempted to open the curtains by hand.

Immediately a voluminous swath of decayed fabric broke loose and enveloped him, stinking like a shroud

118

unearthed from a mummy's tomb. He threw it off, choking as clouds of dust billowed around him.

When he finally controlled his fit of sneezing, Clay realized that eliminating the curtains made precious little difference. The grimy windows allowed only the barest trace of sunlight to filter through.

At least he could see the bookcases now. They lined both sides of the library from floor to ceiling, with a pair of worm-ridden ladders set nearby to provide access to the higher shelves.

There looked to be several thousand books there, all coated with a heavy layer of dust. Clay whooshed a breath and chose the left side of the library to begin his search. He wasn't exactly looking forward to the job, but he'd already been put to a great deal of trouble for this opportunity and meant to waste not a moment of it.

By the time he reentered Fallon's gaming room last night—well, this morning, not to put too fine a point on it—only five players remained at the table. Heston and Briggs had gone off to bed, and Bromley Childe, his head resting on his folded arms, snored away while play continued around him.

Clay had immediately set out to put Fallon in his debt, which became child's play when the company dwindled further and he was able to turn the game to whist. Finally, well past dawn, after the others headed for their rooms and Bromley slid bonelessly to the floor, Clay and Fallon discussed payment.

"Books?" The marquess regarded him as if he'd grown a second nose. "You'll accept books instead of cash? Well, by all means, take any damned book you want. Take the whole bloody lot of 'em. But when you leave here, we stand even."

"Agreed. I require only permission to examine every book you own before making my final selection."

"Yes, yes. Agathy will show you around. She's the housekeeper. Look wherever you like, except my personal rooms. No books in there." Fallon barked a laugh. "I only read the Devil's Books. Playing cards. Amusing, what?"

Clay had dutifully chuckled and gone to catch a quick nap atop the counterpane in his musty bedchamber. He woke up scratching and knew he must have provided breakfast for a host of starving insects.

At least he now had free run of Wolvercote, for as long as required to locate Francesca's book. Of course, it might not be there at all, in which case he could assure her that someone else now owned it. From what John Hatchard said, that meant it would likely come up for auction soon.

But Clay did not want another owner in the picture. He profoundly wanted to find that book himself and be the one who put it into her hands. He wanted to see her smile when she recognized what she held.

Would *he* recognize it? he wondered. He could not be sure of anything except that the book contained sonnets by Petrarch, and those were easily come by. There were even some in the anthologies he'd bought for himself at Hatchard's. The book Francesca wanted must be unique in some way, but precisely how? Perhaps it had once belonged to a famous personage who inscribed his name inside.

Well, no point worrying about it. He'd carry off every volume of Petrarch's poems he found and let Francesca sort through them herself.

By late afternoon, three dusty volumes that even he knew to be valueless lay on the table where he devoured the stale sandwiches Agathy had brought him on a tray. Absorbed by the search, he ate quickly and was soon hard at work again.

An hour or so later, he was balanced precariously on a chair, his back to the door, when he heard an unwelcome voice.

"Hullo," Rupert Heston remarked cheerfully. "Dare I ask why you are rummaging about in this catacomb?"

"Just catching up on my reading," Clay replied, the chair teetering ominously as he made a half turn in Heston's direction. "What of it?"

"Why, nothing at all. You were ever attics to let." Pressing his handkerchief to his nose, Heston gingerly stepped into the filthy room. "However do you bear this stench?"

"I detected none, until you arrived. Here's an idea. Take the odor, and yourself, away."

"In a bad mood, are we?" Heston tilted his head. "I know that I am, since you appear to have made off with Olivia Childe. Where, may I inquire, did you deposit her?"

"With her family. The reputable branch, which has some care for her reputation."

"Unlike her great looby of a father." Heston sneezed into his handkerchief. "Even I was astonished that he brought her to Wolvercote. Not altogether displeased, you understand. She is remarkably engaging when her mouth is closed, and a man in possession of a firm gag might consider pursuing the acquaintance. Not to mention that one day soon, she will be a duke's daughter. Rather boggles the mind, does it not? Bromley Childe a duke of the realm. Whatever is England coming to?"

"More relevant, is there some point to your nattering?" Clay asked impatiently.

"Probably not. I had thought, briefly, that we two were fixed on the same target. But as you are flopping about on a chair instead of romping in bed with said target, I was clearly mistaken. Or do you mean to go for the quiet twin instead? How droll. Think on it, Clayburn. Should you marry Ann and I Livvy, we would become brothers-in-law!"

"Don't count on it." Clay jumped to the floor. "Olivia has already returned to London, and you'll not find it so easy to approach her again."

"Oh, but she will come for me," Heston said confidently. "If you doubt that, you fail to understand women. The only question is, will I take her? I have not decided."

"Well, when you make up your mind, don't bother to tell me. I am profoundly uninterested in the both of you."

"How devastating. But you might be interested in my other snippet of news. Lord Philby has just arrived to join Fallon's games, bringing with him the latest *on dits* from the city. Steel yourself, old sod. Montford is in London. And he is looking for you."

Clay absorbed that blow with an indifferent shrug, although his stomach began to churn. The earl had not set foot in London for years. Why now, if not to drag his son home and shackle him to the Albatross?

"No doubt you'll wish to set out immediately," Heston said caustically. "Mustn't keep papakins waiting."

Oh, but he must, for the rest of his life if he had his way about it. He would certainly remain at Wolvercote until he'd found Francesca's book, Montford be damned.

"I understand you'd like to eliminate me from the gaming," he said, moving the chair a few feet along the bookshelves and climbing atop it again. "But I'll most certainly be there tonight, and for so long as I enjoy myself. Not easy to do in this rathole, I confess, but I'm having a good time pocketing your money."

"Ah, yes. Well, you have profited from my recent turn of bad luck, nothing more than that. And who can blame you for hiding out at Fallon's sponging house while your formidable sire waits in London to pounce?" With a mocking bow, Heston turned for the door. "Until later, then? We shall contrive to keep you entertained, if only to prevent your knees from knocking together under the table. Most distracting."

"Go to the devil," Clay said pleasantly.

Two days later, winning heavily from Heston had lost its appeal, as had the fruitless search for Francesca's book. After tedious nights at Fallon's table, Clay snatched a few hours of sleep and resumed his relentless appraisal of every book in the Library from Hell. He had even ventured to the high shelves atop those rickety ladders.

But for all his efforts, only seven books containing poems by Petrarch, not a one of them unique or valuable, had been located. By now, he smelled as putrid as the library itself, since he'd been living in the shirt, breeches, and coat he rode in wearing.

On his third afternoon in the library, as Agathy departed after plunking a tray of sandwiches on the table, she paused at the door and scratched her chin. "I dunno what you're lookin' fer," she said, "but some other gentlemen been through this room, mebbe six months ago. They took out some books and put 'em inter boxes. Said they was goin' to be sold off to auction at Christmas. Never was, though. Them boxes got put in another room with some paintings and the like. Happen you want to see 'em?"

Happen he did!

Mentally translating "Christmas" to "Christie's," Clay followed the housekeeper to an upper floor and

123

a small room crammed with antique furniture, statuary, ornate silver epergnes, and suits of armor. Canvases were stacked against the walls, and every spare inch of floor held wooden boxes piled one on top of another, reaching almost to the low ceiling.

The room was even colder than the library, but Clay understood that a fire was out of the question. He gave Agathy another coin and asked her to fetch his greatcoat and gloves.

He had managed to clear the top of a marquetry table and a foot or so of space beside it when she returned, in company with a wiry boy about ten years of age. The urchin immediately scrambled over the barricade of furniture and boxes to open the curtains, and then perched atop a large sideboard, propping his bony elbows on his knees.

"I reckoned you could use some 'elp gettin' to the back spots," Agathy said, "you bein' a man of size." She passed Clay his greatcoat and accepted a half crown in return. "Send 'im off iffen he plagues you."

"I works cheap," the boy piped eagerly after watching the coin change hands.

"Behave yerself," Agathy warned, trundling out the door.

"Have you a name?" Clay inquired as he opened the closest box and set it on the table.

"Don't ever'body got 'un?" he replied pertly. "Mine's Jedediah," he added when Clay shot him a look of reproval. "I generally answers to Jed."

"And I generally answers to my lord or your lordship," Clay said, disappointed when the first box turned up full of saltcellars and other knickknacks. He returned it to the floor and reached for another box. "But since we are to be informal, you may call me sir."

As the day wore on, he came to be glad of the boy's

company. It was Jed who thought of moving the paintings into the passageway, clearing more space for them to work, and Jed who made frequent trips to the kitchen for mugs of hot, strong tea.

Jed also chattered incessantly, when he wasn't gulping down the biscuits Agathy sent with the tea, and Clay learned rather more than he needed to know about the life of a kitchen scouring boy. But he was interested to learn that belowstairs rivalries and *affaires de coeur* bore a striking similarity to the scandalous doings of the Haut Ton.

Eudora Swann and Jed would get along famously, Clay decided, wishing he could introduce them. And were the halfling a few years older, he would make an ideal match for Livvy Childe. The pair of them could talk each other insensible.

There were a few books among the other items in the boxes he had searched, and Clay suspected most of them were enormously valuable. He'd uncovered leather-bound manuscripts in Latin, gloriously illuminated by monks long centuries ago, and a small quarto of *Hamlet* that surely dated from Shakespeare's time. Perhaps one of the Bard's own company, the King's Men, had scribbled those stage directions in the margins.

In all fairness, he could take the *Hamlet* and an armload of other treasures, sell them, and live like a gentleman for several years. The temptation to do so began to put down roots in his imagination. A fashionable house, his own carriage instead of hired job-coaches, a valet . . .

But in the end, he left the books where he'd found them. He wasn't altogether certain why, except that personal profit somehow cheapened his quest for Francesca's Book.

A collection of poetry was not precisely the Holy Grail, and the man seeking it was at best a knight in dented armor, but he was nonetheless bound on a Quest. He meant to conduct it with purity of heart.

On the other hand, should he fail to locate the Petrarch, he would certainly go back and retrieve that *Hamlet*.

Clay did set aside one large book, filled with drawings and descriptions of exotic plants and flowers discovered on a sixteenth-century voyage around the world, intending it as a gift for his mother. She had always loved flowers and spent most days cultivating her gardens or experimenting with plants in the conservatory.

By late afternoon, the pale winter light fading swiftly and no sign of Petrarch, he dispatched Jed for a brace of candles and cleared a wide space in the drafty room to set it. Then, wearily, he lifted an especially heavy box onto the table, pleased to find it crammed with books.

Most were mathematical treatises of some sort, but there were also gilt-edged volumes written in something he supposed was Arabic, and, at the very bottom, Bibles. A great many Bibles. At least one Marquess of Fallon must have had a spiritual bent.

He'd started to replace the books he'd removed when his eye caught a few gold-stamped letters on the spine of a slender volume trapped sideways between the Bibles and the box.

FRANCESC . . .

Stripping off his glove, he unwedged the book and held it to the light. FRANCESCO PETRARCA. CANZONIERE.

Hands shaking, Clay gently opened the cover and turned the pages to a delicate, beautifully colored illustration of a woman with blond hair standing near the Communion rail of a church. On the opposite page, in the lovely script of a gifted calligrapher, were lines written in Italian.

Era 'l giorno ch'al sol si scoloraro.

Clay had no earthly idea what that meant. As he turned the pages, he found more intricate, breathtaking pictures set opposite more groupings of fourteen lines.

If his faltering efforts at poesy had taught him nothing else, he knew that fourteen lines that rhymed in a pattern meant *sonnet*!

He was whirling around in the narrow space, chortling like the village idiot and clutching the small book to his chest, when Jed reappeared in the doorway with the brace of candles.

"I s-say, milord. You gone queer in the brain box?"

In fact, Clay was happy right down to the marrow in his bones. He felt a joy so unaccustomed that he might have flown, had the ceiling been higher or the windows open.

Pleasure and happiness are wholly different things, he realized with sudden clarity of vision. He'd experienced a great deal of the former, and little if any of the latter, until this very moment. He was also damnably dizzy from spinning around in tight circles.

The room stopped whirling a minute or two after he did. And when his gaze fell on the boxes yet to be searched, he experienced an acute shot of panic.

What if this *wasn't* Francesca's Book? What if the real thing still lay hidden under a clutter of porcelain cow creamers and Latin sermons?

Clay resolved to see his Quest through to the very end, just in case. By candlelight he opened every last box and searched all the furniture drawers before turning to Jed with an exhausted smile. "We are done," he said.

Since the grinning, spinning episode, the boy had

kept a careful distance. But he ventured closer when Clay held out a golden guinea.

"This is yours," Clay said, "after you tell the stableman to saddle my horse, and on your promise to return the paintings to this room and see it is left in good order. Agreed?"

Eyes rounder than dinner plates, Jed nodded and scurried off.

Clay reclaimed the books he'd selected in the library, scrawled a note to Fallon sealing the settlement of the gaming debt, and tossed the guinea to Jed when they met in the foyer.

The youngster produced a creditable bow. "You ain't like the others what come here, sir. I hopes you comes back soon."

Clay found another guinea and handed it over. "Thank you for your help, Master Jed. But if all goes well, I won't ever set foot at Wolvercote, or any place like it, again. Wish me luck."

"You bet, guv!" Jed called as Clay headed for the stable. "I means to pray fer you, too."

At midnight, so fatigued he could scarcely turn the key in the lock, Clay opened the door to his London flat and saw that Jed's prayers had fallen on the ears of a deaf deity.

Directly in front of him, lounging in the chair behind his writing table, was the Earl of Montford.

"You live like a pig," he said affably.

Clay closed the door behind him and leaned against it for support. "Greetings, Father. Welcome to the sty. Dare I ask how you got in?"

"A foolish question. By now you should realize I am invariably admitted wherever I choose to go. Have you been sleeping in those clothes?"

"As it happens, yes. On the rare occasions I slept

at all. And before you point it out, I have not shaved for three—or is it four?—days."

"Fallon would not provide you so much as a razor?"

Clay was unsurprised his father knew where he had been. If he wished, Montford could probably ferret out how often and in what locations Prinny had used a chamber pot this past week.

"A man with care to his health touches few things at Wolvercote," he said, figuring Montford would come to the point eventually.

"As it happens," Montford said, "I was called to London on a matter of some urgency by the Foreign Office. But the business was concluded more quickly than expected, freeing me to set off for home tomorrow morning. I stopped by to leave you a message, but how fortunate you chanced to arrive while I am here to tell you the news in person."

"Yes indeed," Clay said between his teeth.

"While searching through the rubble on this table," the earl remarked placidly, "I couldn't help noticing that you have been trying your hand at a sonnet." He lifted a scrap of paper. " 'Black-haired lady, wondrous fair—' "

"Enough!" Clay stalked to the desk and snatched the paper from his hand. "This is none of your concern."

"You relieve my mind. There is far too much bad poetry floating about without you adding to the flotsam and jetsam. But scribble away if you must. Perhaps it will keep you out of trouble for a few hours." He focused on the books Clay held against his chest. "Ah, I apprehend that you are *reading*, too. And they say the world holds no surprises. May I see which authors have wrought this miraculous transformation?"

Since Francesca's Book was nestled snugly in the breast pocket of his coat, Clay willingly dropped the others on the table.

Montford briefly examined each one. "Hmmm. Petrarch. Petrarch. More Petrarch. Petrarch yet again. And what have we here. Plants?"

"A gift for Mother," Clay said levelly. "Would you consider delivering it for me?"

"Certainly." He turned a few pages. "I suppose this will please her. Of late, Lady Montford exists only to grub about in the dirt."

Because she prefers the company of snails and slugs to her husband, Clay wanted to say. But he only shrugged and began to pull off his greatcoat.

Montford made a sweeping gesture. "Speaking of dirt, how came you to move from Jermyn Street into this squalid flat? The landlord assures me you have resided here for several months. Since long before I cut off your allowance."

"Have you forgot?" Clay gave him a chilly smile. "I meant to buy into the army, and the money saved on rent was put aside for uniforms and equipment. It was never my intention to remain here beyond a few weeks. By rights, I should even now be on the Peninsula."

"Buried somewhere *in* the Peninsula, more likely. Be sure that Wellington has little use for aristocratic cannon fodder. But let us not pluck that crow again." Montford stood, the book of plants in his hand, and crossed to the door. "I shall remove myself before your body odor causes me to lose my supper. And on the way out, I'll direct your landlord to send up a bath . . . at my expense."

Clay rubbed the back of his neck. "You still haven't told me why you came here in the first place."

"My lamentable memory. Naturally I wished to convey my paternal regards and advise you of my return to Montford House. You were bound to learn I'd come to London. But the coast, as they say, is now clear again."

Just before entering the passageway, Montford paused. "One more thing, Clayburn. I have advised my solicitor to release the rest of your commission money, which you may claim at your convenience."

Minutes later, Clay was still staring at the closed door, trying to make sense of what had just occurred. Something of significance, he was fairly certain, although his brain functioned with the precision of a stomped-on watch.

While he disrobed, and all through the hot soaking bath, he worried at the mystery. By usual standards, Montford had been almost friendly. His gibes seemed more habitual than malicious. And for no discernible reason, he had returned the commission money!

Clay knew better than to assume this unexpected largesse sprang from the goodness of his father's heart. Nor was it sudden remorse after noting the lowly state in which his son was forced to live. Reducing him to penury had been Montford's intention from the start, after all, another ploy to force a marriage with the Albatross.

Had he suddenly changed tactics? Set himself to win by other means what he had failed to achieve by tyranny? Clay rubbed soap through his matted hair. Well, whatever the earl had in mind, it would come to nothing.

His son was no longer the aimless, unsettled man he had been. By the grace of God, Clay thought with a soundless prayer of gratitude, he had met Francesca. He had fallen in love and set a new course for his life. Not a smooth one, for the goddess would not easily be convinced to accept him. To the contrary. But for once, he knew where he was going and what he had to do. Montford was now wholly irrelevant.

Even so, Clay had an eerie sensation that he was missing something vital. That his father, and even

Francesca, harbored a secret he ought to know. Nonsensical, of course, since the two of them had never met.

But as he rinsed his hair in the lukewarm water, he felt very much like the only actor in a play who had not read the entire script.

Chapter 12

Therefore, when flint and iron wear away,
Verse is immortal and shall ne'er decay.
—*Christopher Marlowe*

Whistling cheerfully, Clay guided his horse in and out of the bustling traffic on Piccadilly, on his way at last to Grosvenor Square.

He spotted a flower seller just ahead and pulled over to the curb, but the bouquets, all set in rusty buckets, were unworthy of his goddess. Better to stop off at a reputable florist and order up an elaborate display of hothouse blooms, he decided. Tipping his hat to the disappointed woman, he shook his head. "Perhaps another time, ma'am."

"Well, what der you 'spect, Mr. High 'n' Mighty?" She spat on the pavement. "It's bloody *winter*!"

"So it is." He changed his mind about the fashionable florist. A man in love with the world ought to share his joy with those who most needed it. "I'll have your finest," he said, pressing a guinea into her extended palm.

"For this, you kin take 'em all." She gave him a coy smile. "And me besides, you bein' such a fine-lookin' cove."

He laughed. "You flatter me, my dear. But as I am on my way to meet the lady of my heart, your flowers will have to do."

She passed up a bunch of slightly wilted blossoms

wrapped in a sheet of wet newspaper, which immediately began to drip on his pristine breeches. Well, what were handkerchiefs for but to mop up, he thought, proceeding to do so. Today, nothing could spoil his good mood. With a wave at the flower seller, the bouquet held at arm's length over the street, he continued toward his destination.

Francesca was beginning to thaw, he was reasonably certain, although he'd only his instincts to go on. Naturally she felt compelled to hold him at bay, even when he returned to the inn with her precious Livvy in tow. Her pride demanded resistance. A woman who began so very much set against him would not quickly admit that she had changed her mind.

Fortunately, he was a patient man. And for such a prize he would climb mountains, swim cold rivers, and even restrain his increasingly painful desire for her until she was ready to match it. Did a woman's body actually hurt for a man, he wondered, the way his body ached to make love to Francesca? He should have asked Eudora that question.

The slim volume of Petrarch, nestled securely in the breast pocket of his coat, burned against his heart like a glowing coal. He could scarcely wait to put it in Francesca's hands. Her dark, liquid eyes would shine with pleasure, and perhaps she would thank him with another hug. Maybe even a kiss this time.

Lord, he had been fantasizing about this moment since first clapping eyes on the book. After falling exhausted into his bed last night, he had dreamed of all the ways she would thank him.

What would she think if he asked her to marry him?

He wanted to. He'd rehearsed a proposal on his ride from Wolvercote to London. But now he couldn't remember the words, and besides, she was a long way from ready to accept his offer. Beginning to thaw was not the same as melting. He must be patient awhile more.

And, too, his poem was nowhere near finished. So far he had little more than a mishmash of badly mangled rhymes and a title—"Sonnet to a Goddess." "Ode to a Goddess" sounded better, but he wasn't precisely sure what an ode was. Better stick to a plain old sonnet, he told himself. Odes were probably a devilish sight longer.

Clay dismounted in front of Francesca's town house and tossed the reins to one of the boys who darted from the shrubbery of the Grosvenor Square garden. His heart overflowing with goodwill, he found coins for each of the other boys, too.

Later, he meant to visit Montford's solicitor and pocket the rest of his commission money, after which he would dispense a large portion of it to flower sellers, street urchins, and church poor boxes. A lucky man should spread his good fortune around.

But moments later, his luck screeched to a halt. Firmly blocking the door, Francesca's peevish butler announced that she was not at home.

At first, Clay didn't believe him. Then a more appalling possibility iced down his spine. Could she have given instructions that he was not to be admitted? Until that instant, it had not occurred to him that she would turn him away. But the more he thought on it, the more likely it seemed.

She feared him. Or rather, she feared the way she responded to him. He'd enough experience to recognize physical attraction when he saw it in a woman's eyes and in the small female gestures that expressed more clearly than words what she was feeling.

Francesca wanted him. She might not wholly realize it yet, or she might be unready to admit it, but she wanted him. And either way, her first reaction would be to throw up defenses.

That's what he figured anyway, as the butler stared at him with disdain. At bottom, he hadn't a clue to Francesca's thoughts or feelings, which only meant he had to persist long enough to decipher them. For certain, he would not easily be turned from her door.

"Naturally, I wish to leave a message," he said with all the aristocratic hauteur bred into him through six centuries of Montford earls. "You may show me into a parlor and supply paper, pen, and ink."

The butler retreated a step, his hand still firmly clamped on the door. From his belligerent scowl, he was more than ready to slam it in Clay's face, but something distracted him. He glanced over his shoulder.

"Who is it, Peters?"

Clay recognized Ann's voice. "It's Clayburn," he said loudly enough to be heard over Peters's mumbled response. "There appears to be some misunderstanding."

"Oh, dear. Please come in, my lord."

Stalking past the butler, he bowed to Ann. "I see you have made your way home from the Black Dove without coming to harm."

"My, yes. Jer—Mr. Porter was most solicitous. He took care of everything. And we are all very grateful to you, too, my lord." A faint smile curved her lips. "Well, perhaps Livvy is not."

"I daresay." He grinned back. "Is Miss Francesca Childe at home this morning? I wish to pay my regards."

"She will be sorry to have missed you. But Mrs. Beaton swept her off nearly two hours ago, and I understand they will be gone for most of the day." She glanced at the flowers he was holding. "May I take those from you and have them put in water?"

"Oh, your butler can see to that." He shoved the dripping wad of newspaper and stems into the outraged servant's hand.

At the same time, a young man thundered down the stairs. "*There* you are, Peters. I've been ringing for you forever! We need you to summon a hack." Belatedly he noticed the other two people standing in the foyer. "Sorry, Ann. And you, sir. We're in something of a hurry."

"We?" Ann inquired with unaccustomed sternness. "If *we* includes Livvy, think again. You know she is forbidden to leave the house without Cesca's permission."

"But Cesca's not here! And we meant to ask her this morning, but she was gone before we even woke up."

Bemused, Clay took the boy's measure. Blond and slender, he was obviously another whelp of Bromley Childe, perhaps a year or two older than the twins. And clearly he had lamentable ambitions to join the dandy set. Over a vile yellow waistcoat, those high shirt-points and overwrought cravat would have strangled any but the most determined young man trying to make a splash in London.

"Nevertheless," Ann replied, "Livvy cannot go with you."

"And who are *you* to say?" the boy demanded. "In Father's absence, *I* am the man of the family. And what harm can she come to in my company? Even Cesca would agree with that."

Not likely, Clay thought, wondering what they had planned for the afternoon. He suspected Livvy had cozened her brother into another of her disreputable schemes to go where proper young ladies never went.

"Arthur, do be quiet for a moment and recall your manners. Have you failed to notice we have a guest?" Ann gave Clay an apologetic smile. "My lord, may I introduce my brother, Arthur Childe? He has just come down from Oxford to stay with us. Arthur, make your bow to Lord Clayburn."

"Clayburn?" The boy's mouth dropped. "The *famous* Lord Clayburn? I say, what a stroke of luck. Pleased to meet you!" After a moment, he remembered to bow. "I'm at Magdalen, too, my lord. Everybody still talks of you there. Practically a legend you are, what with the sheep in the chapel and the two dox—er, ladies you smuggled into the don's room, and—"

"Never mind," Clay broke in. "Your sister will not care to hear of my youthful transgressions." He extended his hand, which was pumped vigorously by the enthusiastic Arthur. "A pleasure to meet you, too, Mr. Childe. I hope you don't mean to wrench my arm from the socket so early in our acquaintance."

Flushing brightly, the boy let go and clasped his hands behind his back. "Sorry, my lord. And please call me Arthur."

"Very well, Arthur." With dismay, Clay recognized a woeful case of hero worship. For all the wrong reasons, of course, not that there were any right reasons to venerate a rakehell. "I am not partial to formality either," he said, unsure how to deal with Francesca's cousin. One day soon, he hoped, they would be related. But for now, given Arthur's awestruck regard, he was loath to encourage familiarity. "Should we chance to meet again," he temporized, "address me as Clayburn. Or sir."

"I shall indeed, Clayburn. Sir."

"*Oh!* It's *you!*"

Everyone's attention turned to Livvy, whose precipitous rush down the staircase had come to a halt when she spied Clayburn.

He almost laughed at the look of frustration on her pretty face. Poor Livvy. The Fates were cruel indeed to have led him there minutes before she made her escape.

Gathering her cloak around her, she completed her descent to the foyer with a show of imperious disdain. Even Clay was impressed. Willful girl. Like ignited flash powder, she would not be contained.

"We are going to a balloon ascent," she proclaimed as if issuing an edict. "Arthur, have you secured a hackney? Do so at once, or we'll be late to arrive."

"And who has been waiting an eternity for you to trick yourself out?" Arthur responded with indignation. "I'm not the one who's been primping in front of a mirror since the world was created."

"Then why is your dressing-room floor littered with neckcloths?" she retorted. "I went there first in search of you. Obviously a typhoon swept through. That, or you were making a futile effort to—"

Clay closed his ears to their squabble, wondering if he dared intervene. Any protest Ann might make would be ineffectual, he knew. If Livvy were to be stopped, he would have to do it. But how? Short of wrestling her to the floor, what *could* he do?

Most important, what would Francesca want him to do?

"A balloon ascent?" he asked just as Livvy lunged, hands extended, for her brother's throat. "How diverting. It's been years since I saw one. Do you mind if I accompany you, Arthur?"

Shoving Livvy away, Arthur turned to him with shining eyes. "Oh, please do, sir. It's to be a race, you know. And Lord Heston has promised to take us up in his carriage. We'll follow the balloons and try to get to the first one that lands before any of the other—"

"Shut up, you ninny!" Livvy snapped. "Lord Clayburn has better things to do than chase a balloon."

She was right about that, he thought. But now

that he knew Heston was tangled up in this, he had no choice.

"What could be more fun?" Arthur insisted. "Besides, he's already said he wants to come with us. And I should like that above all things."

"I wouldn't!" Livvy shot back.

"But then," Clay told her implacably, "I would be compelled to remain here for the afternoon and make sure you did the same. Ann has said that you are forbidden to leave the house without supervision, Livvy. And for all that he is your older brother and a man of obvious savoir faire, Arthur is new to London. He does not know his way around so well as I." He turned to the wide-eyed youngster. "Am I mistaken?"

"Oh, no, sir. Fact is, I don't even know the way to Hyde Park."

"The hackney driver will get us there!" Livvy glared at Clay. "We'll do well enough on our own."

"No doubt," he agreed. "But even so, I'll trail along on my horse to keep you company. Ann, if Miss Francesca returns before we do, please assure her the situation is well in hand. Or do you wish to come with us?"

"I—no," she replied, a blush stealing over her cheeks. "Mr. Porter has promised to call, you see."

"Excellent." He smiled at her, and then at Arthur. "Shall we be off?"

Chapter 13

The passion you pretended
was only to obtain.

—*John Dryden*

Seated at a table in the dining room of the Crillon Hotel, Francesca absently rendered a scone to crumbs between her fingers while Maria Beaton, ignoring her companion's lack of attention, summarized the accomplishments of their frenzied morning together.

A lost cause, Francesca thought at the corners of her mind. What did it all matter?

At least she had been honest about her feelings. When they set out four hours ago, she had stated quite frankly that she'd rather mount a charge against Boney's Imperial Guard than contend with the arrangements for a lavish ball. And it didn't help that Ann and Livvy displayed even less interest in what was supposed to be their evening of triumph. Along the way, they had lost their initial enthusiasm for the ball or directed it elsewhere.

But Maria had been determined to proceed. "*I* shall handle all the details," she'd insisted. "You have only to make decisions and cease worrying about the girls. They are certain to come about."

The morning had passed in a blur of flowers and cards and print styles, while Francesca's thoughts perversely wandered to the man she had vowed not to think about. What in blazes had become of him?

It seemed an eternity since Clayburn had left her at

the Black Dove. Could he still be at Wolvercote after all this time, tossing dice with the other reprobates? Some of them had already returned to London, she knew, for she'd caught Livvy flirting with Lord Heston at Lady Potsworth's rout last night.

Finally, after hours of consulting with printers for the invitations, an agency to supply extra staff, several obsequious florists, and the manager of a small orchestra currently favored by Society hostesses, she had declared herself unable to continue without an infusion of strong tea.

And still Lord Clayburn haunted her, as if he had taken up residence in her head. Sometimes she felt him moving about her body, exploring, evaluating, leaving his mark.

"Francesca?" Maria tapped her spoon against the teapot. "Where have you gone?"

Her head shot up. "I'm so sorry. What were you saying?"

"Nothing of importance. But I sense you have something on your mind. Do you wish to discuss it with me?"

"No. Thank you. That is, I could not." Nervously, Francesca rolled a currant from the scone between her thumb and forefinger. "Have you ever taken a lover?" she blurted, to her own considerable astonishment.

"Oh, certainly," Maria replied easily. "Several, in fact, Mr. Beaton having considerately cocked up his toes within two years of our ill-advised marriage. Why do you ask?"

Heat stung Francesca's cheeks. "Oh my. I beg you to pardon me, Maria. That was an insufferably rude question."

"Not at all. I am convinced you inquire for reasons of your own, and not from curiosity about my personal affairs. Are you by chance considering a lover for yourself? Clayburn, perhaps?"

Francesca longed to slide under the table. Or better, into the Thames. However had Maria guessed? "Of course not. I s-scarcely know him." The lies felt like hot coals in her throat. "The very idea would be insupportable, given my circumstances and inclinations. But . . . I just wondered . . ." Her voice burned away.

Maria made a *tsk*ing noise. "All that Italian passion coursing through your veins, and you a virgin at one-and-thirty! It is positively unnatural, my dear." She spooned honey into her tea. "May I offer a bit of unsolicited advice? Clayburn is a gentleman, for all his scandalous reputation, and I've never known him to seduce an innocent. If you want him for yourself—and I suspect you do—you must make your interest very clear."

"I have *never* said I want him," Francesca returned defensively. "Nor any other man, for that matter. And if ever I thought to fancy Lord Clayburn, I would soon think better of it. He is a degenerate goat." The much-maligned currant was squashed messily between her fingers.

"Oh, never a *goat*!" Maria laughed. "More like an unbroken stallion, and what a pity 'twould be to clap a bit in his mouth. Clayburn is much more fascinating as he is, sulky, defiant, and unpredictable. The woman who draws him to her bed and keeps him there past a fortnight will be fortunate indeed."

Licking crumbs from her fingers, Francesca wondered how all that could be accomplished.

"He is not my sort, of course," Maria continued reflectively. "My present lover is almost his exact age, although not nearly so handsome. But then, few men are." She took a sip of tea. "I speak out of turn, Francesca, and you must not take lessons from me.

As a widow of independent means, I am able to do as I like, so long as I remain discreet. And because I care most for my writing, my female friends, and my causes, the men I select are compelled to remain in the background of my affections."

"Toys," Francesca said, repressing her disgust.

"By their choice, you may be sure. I am far too preoccupied with other matters to seek a man or cater to him. Men come to me for reasons of their own and generally stay for a considerable time." She reached for a jam tart. "You will, and should, expect more from your lovers, in the event you decide not to marry. But I believe you ought to set your sights high and demand the very best. You can have it, my dear, with a snap of your fingers."

Wishing she had never embarked on this conversation, Francesca could not stop herself from continuing it. "What precisely *is* the very best?" she asked curiously.

"Why, a love match with a handsome, intelligent, faithful husband. He must have a sense of humor, for that is essential if you are to live together for very long. And he must equal you in passion, which will be a considerable challenge for any man. Naturally he must possess a tolerant nature, if he is to endure your frequent bouts of temper."

"And I can have all that with a snap of my fingers?" Francesca erupted in laughter, snapping away to no avail. "As you see, this paragon has failed to appear. But never mind, for I cannot believe that such a man exists. And if he does, he is even now courting a younger, more pliable bride."

"Well, perhaps you are right to be skeptical, my dear. Such a love as I would hope for you is rare indeed."

"Yes, it is, and I'll not waste a single moment indulging implausible fantasies. But even a passing affair is out of the question, should I have such a notion. Anything I do must reflect on Ann and Livvy, and I am in London solely on their behalf." She released a small sigh. "And you know, Maria, my father is very ill. Above all things, I wish to return home as soon as possible."

"It does credit to you." Maria took her hand. "For now, you are pushed and pulled from all directions. But circumstances will change, as they always do, so you must not burn any proverbial bridges just yet."

"Oh my." Francesca folded her napkin and set it on the table. "This is a decidedly improper conversation, and we are scandalizing the good ladies at the table next to us. But I promise not to ignite a single bridge I may later wish to cross."

"What think you of a brisk walk?" Maria asked, standing with a groan. "I must do something to counter those three cream-filled pastries, not to mention that enormous jam tart."

After settling the bill, they strolled at a snail's pace toward Hyde Park. The pavement was clogged with pedestrians, and a veritable parade of vehicles crammed the street, every one of them aimed in the same direction.

"How odd," Maria said. " 'Tis only two o'clock. Not at all the fashionable hour to promenade."

Francesca stumbled as a young buck brushed against her shoulder on the way past, obviously in a hurry. Finally they turned onto Park Lane and saw people rushing from every direction toward a large crowd that had gathered in a wide circle on the open field. From this distance, she could not make out what had caught their attention.

Carriages and gigs lined Park Lane on both sides, forcing any traffic proceeding elsewhere to weave in and out with a great deal of shouting and cursing from the drivers.

Maria plucked at her sleeve. "Shall we make our escape while we can, or do you wish to see what this commotion is about?"

"The commotion, please." In all her years, Francesca had never seen so many people in one place. She doubted the entire county of Rutlandshire could assemble a congregation of this size.

"Very well, then. Stay close by and we'll go around the long way. I know a spot where we may have an excellent view."

Ten minutes later, they came to a small rise midway between the line of carriages and the noisy mob. A few others had also discovered the vantage point, but Francesca and Maria found a clear patch beneath the bare branches of a tree.

"I wish I'd thought to bring my opera glasses," Maria said, opening her parasol. "Can you see anything, my dear?"

A full seven inches taller than her friend, Francesca stood on tiptoe and made out two splotches of bright color against the brown grass in the center of the crowd. "I'm not altogether certain, but I think we are to witness a balloon ascent. How wonderful! I have longed to see one."

Maria was less enthralled. "In my experience, it means a long period of tedium followed by a few moments of breathtaking beauty. Then the balloon is gone from sight, and one is like to be trampled by the multitudes leaving the park."

Francesca remembered her manners. "Perhaps we should go, then, before the stampede."

"Nonsense. I shall occupy myself with the essay I mean to write this evening, and you will advise me when the balloons are aloft. Enjoy yourself, my dear, but do not wander away."

For half an hour Francesca delighted in the colorful spectacle. Jugglers and organ-grinders with monkeys entertained at the edges of the crowd. Children laughed and squealed. The cries of hawkers flogging oranges, gingerbread, and cheese pies rose above the general clamor.

No balloons rose, however. She was fairly certain there were two of them, both giving the aeronauts difficulty of some sort. Now and again, a raucous voice demanded they get on about it.

She wondered how the balloons were to be inflated, but Maria's eyes had the slightly glazed look of intense concentration, and Francesca knew better than to interrupt. Instead, she turned her attention to the vehicles lined up along Park Lane.

Only men occupied the carriages or strode among them to greet friends. Strange, that. On the field below her, there was no shortage of female observers. One more thing about London Society she failed to understand, she reflected with a sigh.

Just then, amid the dark blue and brown coats, she caught a glimpse of pink. Shading her eyes with a hand, she tried to find it again. Sure enough, a lone female in a straw bonnet tied with a wide pink ribbon was perched on the driver's bench of an open barouche, seated next to a gentleman wearing a tall hat. Behind them, four or five men crowded the passenger squabs.

Curious, she watched the small party for a time, wondering why only one woman had been admitted to such exclusively male company. Something about the way she moved seemed familiar, although the barouche was too far away for Francesca to identify her.

Suddenly the woman pulled off her bonnet with a

flourish, revealing short blond curls. And when she tossed her head, Francesca knew there could be no mistake.

"Livvy." The word came out in a growl.

"I beg your pardon?" Maria said.

Francesca was almost too furious to respond. She jabbed her finger toward the barouche. "Look there."

"Oh. I see," Maria acknowledged after a moment. "That is Lord Heston beside her, and Clarence Briggs is among the passengers, along with a pair of other wastrels. I do not recognize the fifth man."

With a fairly good idea who that fifth man was, Francesca charged across the grass with Maria at her heels.

Despite her shorter legs, Maria caught up and seized her elbow, yanking her to a halt. "Take a deep breath, young woman, and calm yourself. You do not wish to make a scene."

Homicide was more what she had in mind. But Francesca obediently drew in several long, soothing drafts of air and counted from one to ten. The hot blaze of her temper settled into a jittery fire.

"How am I to detach that insufferable girl *without* a scene?" she asked as they proceeded more sedately toward Park Lane. For the first time, she noticed an enormous black gelding tied up behind the barouche. She was almost certain she had seen that horse before.

Arthur spotted her then, jumping up so quickly he made the carriage rock. "Cesca!" he called, waving his hat. "Over here. It's me."

And you are a dead man, she thought, carving a grim smile on her face as she glanced up at Livvy.

Eyes rounder than blue Wedgwood saucers, the miscreant slid closer to Lord Heston and lifted her pert chin defiantly.

It would take heavy artillery to dislodge her, Francesca knew, still smiling as she came up to Arthur. "How serendipitous to find you in all this crowd," she said, watching him struggle to decipher *serendipitous*.

He soon gave up. "I call it lucky," he said. "Maybe that means my luck will hold for the race. No telling which way the balloons will go, but we'll beat the others to where they land. Heston is a prime whip."

It was Francesca's turn to decipher. "The balloons are racing?"

"Didn't I just say so? First one to touch ground twenty miles from here in any direction wins. But nobody cares about that. We are wagering which driver arrives ahead of the others and shakes hands with a balloonist. That's why all these coaches are lined up here, silly. When the balloons take off, so do we."

"Rather like a fox hunt," said a deep baritone voice just behind her, "the fox being irrelevant. All the fun is in the chase."

Francesca spun around to face Lord Clayburn. *His* horse! The one he had ridden when they set out for Wolvercote. She ought to have recognized it immediately. And guessed he would be at the bottom of this quagmire. "How dare you?" she whispered savagely.

Before she could object, he slipped a firm hand around her elbow and steered her away from the barouche. "In private," he warned. "The street is no place to have one of your temper tantrums." Drawing her to a stop within sight of the crowd, but distant enough to permit conversation without fear of an audience, he let go of her and bowed. "You may proceed now."

"How dare you?" she repeated, wanting to pummel him. "This is monstrous! I cannot fathom your intentions, Clayburn. You exert yourself to save Livvy from utter ruin, only to throw her back to the wolves."

"Are you quite finished?" he inquired when she ran out of breath.

"No!" Defiantly she loaded up another barrage of insults and fired them off. "You are beyond contempt. A devious, manipulative, self-serving beast. Pond scum. A snake in the woods."

"Grass." He looked amused. "A snake in the *grass*."

"A viper is a viper, wherever it slithers. And do not think to dupe me again with pitiful excuses for your behavior, because I know better than to believe a single word you say. Be sure of that, sir. I know precisely why you lie to me and to what ends you will go, though why you persist defies all reason."

His eyes glittered in the sunlight. "Except that you are speaking precious little sense, Miss Childe, I have never in my life been so enchanted. And although you fling bolts of lightning at my head, I believe I would sell my soul to the devil at this very moment for one kiss. From *you*, I hasten to add. Not a kiss from the devil."

"Poppycock! You *are* the devil, Clayburn."

"On occasion. But in the last two hours I have become something far more terrifying to my own sensibilities—a hovering nursemaid. Do you care to hear how that came about, or would you prefer to continue scolding me?"

"Oh, the former, please. I promise to remain civil and mute." After all, she could throttle him later.

His teasing grin warmed into a smile. "Ah, I have missed you, termagant. My recent incarceration at Wolvercote may have lasted only a few days, but it felt very much like eternal damnation."

"You ought to know."

"Witch. When I called on you this morning, only to learn that you had already gone out, I chanced to encounter Livvy and Master Arthur. They were in a considerable hurry to leave, but Arthur recognized my name when we were introduced and stopped long enough to make my acquaintance. Who would have thought I'd become something of a legend among the Oxford underclassmen? He thinks me a regular out-and-outer and a great gun, you will be astonished to hear."

"Not at all. You are notorious on several continents, and he is a nodcock."

Clayburn laughed. "Although Livvy tried her best to shut him off, Arthur could not resist blathering their plans for the afternoon. He is, as you observed, in high spirits about this race. It was when he confided that the dashing Lord Heston had invited them into his carriage that I was thrust willy-nilly into the role of chaperon."

"Hah!"

"Yes, I do understand. A woeful example of miscasting. But needs must when the devil drives, and what with Lord Heston playing the devil in this particular farce, I *very* reluctantly took on the part of bear-leader."

"Why did you not stop them from leaving the house at all?" she demanded. Irrationally, she knew, for how could he do so short of tackling them in the foyer and locking them in the cellars?

Clayburn looked pained. "Arthur believes his father is to join the party, although I rather doubt that will come to pass. Haring about the countryside in an open carriage is scarcely Bromley's notion of a good time."

"So you mean to hare in his place? Oh, that will certainly help!" Francesca shook her head vigorously. "How can adding yet another blackguard to this scandalbroth serve any purpose?"

"I quite agree. But you needn't imagine I have the

slightest influence in this matter, for good *or* ill. Livvy drives daggers into my chest each time she looks at me, and I am the last man on earth Heston would oblige. Thus far, I have used young Arthur's misplaced hero worship as an excuse to hang about where I am otherwise de trop, in hopes the balloons fail to go up, which often happens."

"Well, I am not so chickenhearted as you," she declared. "Livvy and Arthur will come home with me if I am forced to drag them by the scruffs of their necks."

"A delightful picture, to be sure. Caricatures will be hung in every shop window—'Tigress and Her Cubs.'"

"Oh."

A wave of bewildered frustration, like the ones that had swept over her almost hourly since leaving Rutlandshire, left her speechless. She put a wrong foot wherever she stepped, and London outwitted her at every turn. She had even ripped into Lord Clayburn, who had stood her friend once and seemed ready to do so again.

She ought to be grateful. Assuredly she owed him an apology for her blast of temper. But she also understood his motives, which were wholly selfish and deplorable. Resentment clouded her every thought and feeling about this man. If she scorned the kindnesses he did for her, it was because she scorned the reasons for them.

And, truth be told, she feared her own vulnerability to his charm. When all that focused male sensuality was directed straight at her, her insides promptly turned to mush. Meantime, some other creature that looked like her on the outside went on fighting him.

A small shock raced from her fingertips all the way to her toes. Looking down, she realized he had taken hold of her hands. Through his heavy leather riding gloves and her butter-soft kidskin gloves, she felt the slight tension in his grip and the rhythmic pulse in his veins, slower than hers and far steadier.

"You must not worry so much," he said gently. "Some matters are beyond your control, specifically those to do with Livvy, who is beyond *anyone's* control."

"Bromley told me the same thing," she admitted, forcing her disordered mind from Clayburn to the problem at hand. "But I cannot believe she will toss away her entire future for a few reckless hours of excitement."

"At heart she is a gambler, you know. And gamesters must risk all to feel alive. They ruin themselves and their families to recapture the brief, mad rush they experienced at their first big win. The thrill nearly always eludes them thereafter, but they will not be stopped."

"How does this signify?" she protested weakly. "Livvy has never won so much as a farthing at cards or dice."

His thumbs began to make small circles in the palms of her hands. "Ah, but Livvy plays a different sort of game. Some men, and women, too, are addicted to sexual pleasure. Others pursue intoxication by eating opium. Power, fame, even artistic creativity, can enslave people beyond reason. And once chained by their own compulsions, few make the considerable effort it would require to escape. It is the way of the world."

Remember this, Francesca told herself stonily. The next time you imagine that Clayburn will ever become other than the rakehell he has always been, *remember*. This once, he is speaking the truth about himself.

"I understand," she said, removing her hands from his as a bone-numbing chill swept through her. All around her, colors faded to shades of black and gray. She looked past Clayburn, over a dingy field of shadow puppets to a charcoal-colored balloon that must have begun to inflate because it was clearly visible above the crowd. Then it collapsed, and the crowd groaned in chorus.

She forced her knees to straighten and willed a javelin into her spine. "Advise me, sir. Am I to simply abandon Arthur and Livvy to those spiders?"

"Be easy. I expect Maria Beaton has already devised a plan to separate Livvy from the coach, and we have only to take our cues from her. As for Arthur, you must calmly wave him good-bye, for he means to follow those balloons. The race presents no danger, I assure you. Heston is an excellent driver, and even that job-house vehicle is safe enough while he holds the reins."

"You fail to reassure me."

"Nor will I fob you off with equivocations. Truth be told, Arthur is in for a wild ride tonight." Clayburn moved to her side and took her arm, which she had forgotten to stiffen. "For now, shall we concentrate on Livvy? Please take no insult, but you can best help by saying nothing at all."

Offended, primarily because he was right, she allowed him to escort her back to the carriage.

Maria, engaged in a lively conversation with Lord Heston, must have possessed eyes in the back of her head. Without turning, she beckoned Francesca to her side. "Is it not grossly unfair, my dear? These gentlemen will soon chase the very wind itself, leaving us behind to choke on their dust."

Treason! Francesca's hands clenched and unclenched, but she smiled and nodded politely.

"I have offered to take you up, Mrs. Beaton," Heston

said, gesturing with his whip. "There is room for one more in the carriage."

"Oh, were it only possible!" Maria heaved a dramatic sigh. "But I have other commitments for this evening, and a lady must honor her commitments. I daresay Olivia regrets that she, too, must stay behind after the balloons are launched, having accepted an invitation to Lady Felterpell's party. Is that not correct, Francesca?"

Francesca nodded again, furious with herself for misjudging her friend's intentions. When would she ever stop leaping to false conclusions? From childhood, that had been her besetting sin.

"I'm not going to that silly party," Livvy declared, crinkling her nose at the very idea of Lady Felterpell. "Nobody will miss me. And all the men of consequence are joining the race."

"Perhaps I have mistaken the situation," Maria said thoughtfully. "Surely you can all return in time for Lady Felterpell's drum. Indeed, if Lord Heston promises to bring you back by seven o'clock, I see no reason for you not to enjoy this adventure."

No reason? Anger mounting inside her again, Francesca chewed at her tongue to keep it under control.

With a frown, Heston glanced at his companions, who looked horrified at the suggestion of a deadline. Clearly they anticipated quite a different sort of evening. "In fact," he said, "there is very little chance we'll make our way to London again before tomorrow's breakfast. I am sorry for it, Livvy, but without question you must return home in company with Miss Childe."

"I won't! You said I could go with you! You *promised*."

"Nothing of the sort," he said tightly. "You cozened your father to play escort, but he appears to have thought better of it. Without his company, you cannot—"

"My brother is here! Arthur can be my escort." Midstream, she changed tactics. "Don't you *want* me to come along, Rupert? We'll have such fun."

Francesca watched in disgust as Livvy rubbed her fingers along Heston's forearm. Then, to her astonishment, he seized the wandering hand and gazed sternly at Livvy's startled face.

"You will remain here," he said in a tone that brooked no opposition. "Tomorrow afternoon, or whenever it is convenient, I shall call on you at Grosvenor Square. And if you cease making a fuss now, perhaps I'll even take you up in my curricle. To date, no female has been permitted to drive with me when I put my bays to their paces."

Her mouth a round O, Livvy considered her options. "I want to follow the balloons," she decided.

Heston swung down from the barouche and held out his arms. "That is no longer a choice. *Out*, Olivia. *Now!*"

A few seconds later, Lord Heston handed Livvy over to Francesca. "All yours," he said. Then, turning to the pouting girl, he brushed back a drooping feather on her bonnet. "Wish me luck in the race, Livvy."

She made an indeterminate sound.

For a moment, his gaze caught Francesca's. She detected mutual understanding and a bit of sympathy on his part. How very odd. Yet another rakehell had just exhibited a thread of decency. Not that Lord Heston and Clayburn were remotely alike, beyond their attachment to vice.

She had no idea what to make of all this, except that Livvy had once again been saved from ruin by a man who generally considered any willing female fair game. And no question about it, Livvy was more than willing. She had made that clear in front of witnesses, including her temporary guardian and her own brother. Shameless!

Maria must have seen the fire in her eyes. "Come, my dear," she said to Livvy. "One balloon is already inflated, and the other nearly so. Soon the tether ropes will be loosed, and they'll be off. We'll have a much better view from the embankment." As she drew the girl away, she winked at Francesca.

"That was well done, don't you think?" Clayburn said, moving to her side. "I was certain Maria could deal with the situation."

"She made a good beginning," Francesca acknowledged. "But it was Lord Heston who brought Livvy to heel. I am still amazed at it. What is between them, do you suppose?"

He shrugged. "They are the last two individuals on the planet who concern me, unless they are causing you distress. For now, all is well, so may we forget them for the rest of the afternoon? I most especially wish to be alone with you, Fra—Miss Childe. Perhaps after the balloon ascension? I have something to give you, and—"

"But what of Arthur?" she broke in as her cousin's laugh brayed from the carriage, followed by an oath he ought not have known. "He is only a boy, and in exceedingly bad company. Can we rescue him, too, do you suppose?"

Clayburn's silvery eyes flashed with anger. "You are not the halfling's mother," he said between taut lips. "And should you humiliate him in front of men he is trying to impress, he will not soon forgive you. Trust me on that."

Why was Clayburn so furious of a sudden? All she'd done was show a little concern for Arthur. He was not in her charge, of course, but she could not help but care what became of him. Should he turn himself into another Bromley, the Sotherton title would pass through *two* generations of profligate lackwits. For Papa's sake, she had no choice but to interfere.

"I don't want Arthur to go with those men," she said rigidly. "They will corrupt him. What is worse, he badly wants them to."

"Yes, he does." Clayburn turned her to face him and put his hands on her shoulders. "Young men crave excitement. You have no idea how tedious Oxford can be, especially when every nerve in the body is vibrating with rather primitive urges. Not all of them have to do with women, by the way. And those that do not are the most difficult to explain."

"I quite understand," she said. "You speak of rebellion. I have often felt it in myself. But when a young man's perfectly natural rebellion leads him to drunken oblivion, or to wager which raindrop will first slide to the bottom of the casement, what is the point?"

"There is none, I have belatedly come to realize."

His fingers pressed into the muscles below her nape, rubbing away the tension that had gathered there. All the rest of it was balled up in her stomach. No. Only some. The part relating to Clayburn had formed tight bands around her heart.

When she began to relax, he brought one hand to cradle her chin. "If you happen to ask me, very nicely, I will agree to follow Heston's carriage on horseback and make sure that Arthur doesn't get in over his head."

Her gaze slid away. Once again, Clayburn sought to throw her off balance with an act of kindness. If only she had someone else, *anyone* else, to ask. But there was only this man, and the treacherous current beneath the surface of everything he said and did. She knew exactly where it would carry her, were she so foolish as to trust him for a single instant.

But so long as he stood willing, for transparently selfish reasons, to do her another service, what was the harm in accepting? Purely for Arthur's sake, of course. Swallowing a lump of pride, she tried to appear delighted. "Oh, please do go with him. Although I suppose this means I'll be forced to let you teach me to dance. Wasn't that the agreement? If you did me another favor—"

"Never mind about that. This good deed is free and clear. And truth be told, I so rarely attend balls that I've long since forgot how to dance. No more *deals* between us, Francesca. They are meaningless, like the raindrop wagers you abhor. But I warn you, Arthur has the bit between his teeth. While I probably can keep him out of trouble tonight, what he sees will only whet his appetite for more."

"Th-then what?"

"As it happens, I do have an idea." He brushed her nose with his gloved forefinger. "But it can wait until you call on me again for help, should you elect to do so. I advise you to exhaust all other recourses beforehand."

"That means, I suppose, that your idea is unlikely to meet with my approval."

"You'll downright loathe it," he said with a laugh. "Ah! There go the balloons! I must retrieve my poor horse before the barouche tows him away. Keep your chin up, sweetheart. Arthur will return intact, I promise, if a bit tattered about the edges."

Francesca watched Clayburn lope up the hill with his athletic stride and disappear into the throng of milling traffic. Then she turned her gaze skyward and saw the balloons pass directly over her head. When the men in the wicker gondolas leaned out to wave at the crowd, she found herself waving back excitedly.

All too soon, the enormous balloons were no more than dabs of red and yellow and green against the clear blue sky. How swiftly the breeze caught them up and swept them away, she thought with a pang of envy. And how glorious it would be to loose her hair to the wind and fly in just such a way, with no fetters of propriety or obligations to keep her earthbound.

But, as Bromley liked to say, a chap must play the cards he's dealt. And since women generally found themselves holding deuces and treys, they must play cautiously indeed.

Good heavens, she thought, looking around for Maria and Livvy. She was starting to think like a gamester!

Chapter 14

Doubts are more cruel than the
worst of truths.

—*Molière*

Wearing a dressing gown and a pair of slippers,
Francesca wandered to a window in her bedchamber
while servants removed the ceramic bathing tub and
lit candles against the winter twilight. As she gazed
outside, the sky slowly darkened to a deep, ashy blue.
Tendrils of mist began to curl around the chimney
pots on nearby roofs.

It would be a foggy night, she thought, wishing she
could curl up with a book and enjoy a few hours of solitude. But Ann was looking forward to Lady Cowper's
ball, because Jeremy Porter had promised to be there,
and Livvy had secret reasons of her own for wearing
her nicest gown.

Since the balloon race, Livvy had been unnaturally
biddable, which Francesca regarded as a sign of trouble
to come. An openly defiant Livvy was far easier to contend with than the sly creature she had become.

When the servants were gone, Francesca took her
brush from the dressing table and knelt on a cushion
by the fire to dry her hair. It would take nearly an
hour, she knew, followed by a long session with the
complaining maidservant. All the pins in England
could not contain her thick, freshly washed hair, and
she really ought to have it shorn.

But that would mean accepting the probability of a

long stay in the city, when she longed for the peace of Sotherton Manor. There, she dried her hair by the hearth in Papa's library while he read to her, and her stomach never roiled with dread of Livvy's next cut-up or Arthur's plunges into the cesspools of London.

Just now, the servants were prying her cousin from his bed, where he had spent nearly all the daylight hours of this past week. He would likely swill several cups of strong coffee, eat all the dry toast his liquor-soaked belly would accept, and apply himself to the matter of dressing for yet another night on the town with Lord Clayburn.

With a stern application of self-discipline, she had thus far refrained from interfering. But for the life of her, she could not make sense of Clayburn's benighted plan.

How could an excess of debauchery set Arthur straight again? The formula had certainly failed to work for Bromley and Clayburn, who'd exceeded every excess for many a year. Absolute proof, in her opinion, that men were more apt to embrace a rakehell life, once begun, than turn away in disgust.

But Clayburn insisted this was the only way to disillusion Arthur, and she had no better idea to offer. At times she even found herself wishing that she, too, could experience a week of unbridled revelry, although drinking and gaming were not among the wicked things she imagined herself doing.

Her hair crackled as she stroked the brush, and her face grew painfully warm. Not sure if that was due to the fire or her searing thoughts, she turned on the cushion and applied herself vigorously to the damp tangle curling down her back.

Into which den of iniquity would Clayburn lead her feckless cousin tonight? she wondered. By now the boy must be up to his shirt-points in debt, with no way in creation to honor them. Better if he'd been introduced to vice by his father, who added no tinge of glamour to a life of dissipation. But Bromley had apparently dropped off the face of the earth, leaving Arthur to model himself after the bedazzling Lord Clayburn.

A soft knock at the door brought her to her feet with a start.

"Lord Clayburn has arrived," the butler said, averting his eyes from her dishabille. "I have put him in the Red Saloon."

"Did he ask to speak with me?" she asked, her heart thumping simply because he was in the same house, almost directly under the spot where she now stood.

"I believe he is here for Mr. Childe, ma'am. But the young gentleman has only now begun to shave, so there will be some delay. I thought you should be informed."

"Thank you, Peters. Offer Lord Clayburn some refreshments while he waits and make sure the fire is built up."

When he was gone, she returned to the hearth and continued to brush her hair, trying to pretend that nothing had changed. She did *not* feel her skin tingling. He was the *last* man in the universe she wanted in her house. She profoundly wished him at Jericho.

Five minutes later, she rushed to the standing wardrobe and pulled out the first dress she found with no hooks or buttons in the back. All her niggling doubts about Clayburn's scheme to reform Arthur had suddenly become a tidal wave of mistrust. It was past time she confronted him and demanded that he explain what he was about.

That was her excuse, anyway.

Unwilling to question her motives further, she pried her unstockinged feet into a pair of sandals and raced downstairs.

When she stepped nervously into the Red Saloon, she thought at first that Peters must have misdirected her. Then she spied a tall, still figure slumped on a wing-backed chair near the fireplace. On the side table next to him, a full glass of wine sat untouched.

He was asleep, she realized, silently drawing closer. Long legs in tight biscuit-colored breeches stretched toward the flagstone hearth. One arm was curled in his lap, and the other dangled over the side of the chair. His head lay against the wing-back padding, a swatch of dark hair fallen over his brow. His mouth was slightly open.

She leaned against the wall near the fireplace and looked her fill of him.

Except for one brief nod, when they chanced to meet in the foyer before he led Arthur away, she had not seen Clayburn for more than a week. His skin was paler than before, she noted critically, and there were dark shadows under his eyes.

But he was beautiful still, even with those faint lines of dissipation near his temples and at the corners of his lips. His chest rose and fell with the steady rhythm of his breathing. In sleep, he seemed younger. Guileless, although she knew he was nothing of the sort.

The man was simply worn down by a weeklong marathon of debauchery. Suddenly infuriated at the waste of it all, she sprang forward and kicked him on the shin.

"Bloody hell!" He shot upright in the chair, rubbing his leg. "What the devil was *that* about?"

"Just trying to get your attention," she replied genially.

"Pretend I have stood and bowed and greeted you properly, you rag-mannered wench. Because I'm damned if I will." He smothered a yawn behind his hand. "If you mean to give me a rake-down, I assure you that I am in no mood to listen."

"Your moods, Lord Clayburn, do not concern me. I merely wish an accounting of Arthur's progress, or his decline, whichever applies. Until he bumbled in this morning, he had been gone more than forty hours in a row. Where have you been?"

Clayburn frowned, as if trying to remember. "An inn about thirty miles from here. I think. We went to a cockfight, and then to a mill. Or was it wrestling? Men fought, at any rate, and we wagered on the outcome. Later, a few young bucks commandeered a pair of mail coaches and set out to race them to High Wycombe. You will be glad to hear I plucked Arthur from the driver's bench before he took the reins. We rode inside. And won."

"Congratulations," she said. "How proud you must be."

"Not in the slightest. I meant him to come home with his pockets to let, but Arthur recouped a week of losses on that stupid race. Now I must see to it he loses every groat of it tonight at the hells." He yawned again. "Tell you what, Francesca. I am too old for this nonsense. If my plans for this evening fail, I wash my hands of the whole business. Enough is enough."

"Why not call it off now? What little faith I had that you would succeed is gone, and even you are ready to abandon hope."

"Not quite." He stood and shook his whole body like a wet dog. "When this is over, I plan to sleep for a month. Meantime, point me in Arthur's direction. We need to have a private talk before going out."

Francesca passed him to a footman and spent the next few minutes wrestling with her conscience.

Her conscience lost. Removing her sandals, she tiptoed upstairs and huddled against the wall next to

Arthur's room, ear pressed to the closed door. But she could hear nothing through the heavy oak and was about to turn away when a servant emerged, carrying a shaving basin.

A mad charade ensued, she trying to keep him quiet and waving wildly when he moved to close the door behind him, he gaping at her with an earnest effort to interpret her gyrations. At last, with a shrug, he left the door cracked open and went on his befuddled way.

With care, she positioned herself where she could see without being seen through the narrow slit, managing an excellent view of Arthur at his dressing table. Clayburn, invisible from all angles, was speaking.

". . . what you have been clamoring for."

"A brothel?" Arthur bounced with excitement. "That's famous, sir!"

Brothel? Oh, dear Lord!

"Sometimes essential," Clayburn said in a dry voice. "Especially after a week in company with foul-breathed, unwashed men."

"But there are women in the hells, too. Didn't you notice? Some of them have rooms upstairs. They told me so. Invited me there," he added, preening smugly.

"I'm not surprised. But they are not women you wish to consort with."

"No indeed," Arthur agreed hastily. After a moment, he swallowed, causing his prominent Adam's apple to bob up and down. "May I ask precisely why?"

"The whole point of this discussion," Clayburn said, "is for you to ask any question that comes to mind. I do not mean to stand in place of your father, who should have explained these matters long since, but I rather doubt he has been of much help."

"None at all. And besides, he probably can't remember what it's like. We are young, and he is old. I never want to be old."

Francesca heard Clayburn sigh.

"Truly? Well, I certainly do. Not right away, of course, but I anticipate a pleasurable dotage as pudding to my wild salad days."

"Not me!" Arthur buttoned his waistcoat. "I mean to live hard, burn bright, and flame out like a Congreve rocket."

"How very theatrical."

Francesca wanted to applaud. She wished she could see Clayburn's face, but she knew his expressions well enough by now to imagine them with some accuracy.

"One day," he said, "when you are wise enough to appreciate her, I shall introduce you to Eudora Swann. She is four-and-eighty, I believe, and has rollicked through each day of her long life with vigor, passion, and joy. I expect she'll do the same for many years to come. And when she dies, she will flame out more gloriously than any rocket. Or any foolish boy with more bottom than sense."

Arthur paled.

"Take no insult," Clayburn said kindly. "I myself have only just begun to realize that life must not be held cheaply."

"But you still drink and gamble, sir. You go to cockfights and mills."

"Not so often as I used to. Keeping you entertained has been rather a challenge, young man."

Arthur looked confused. "I had thought you but seven or eight years older than I. No more than that."

"Assuredly. But the constant infusion of spirits has begun to leave me with devilish headaches. That won't happen to you for some time, but there will come a day when you wake up wishing you'd never been born. The merest whisper will sound in your head like an artillery barrage."

"It never seems to bother Papa," Arthur said. "He still drinks prodigiously."

"Only because he cannot help himself. He gambles for the same reason. And if you are heir to his addictions as well as his name, you will eventually become what he is now." Clayburn clapped his hands together. "But never mind all that. You are down from Oxford to enjoy yourself, and I am of a mood to do the same. Tonight we shall teach the devil to dance."

Arthur looked a trifle less enthusiastic than before. "What does that mean, sir?"

"Why, a bit of everything this side of perversion. First off, a fine dinner accompanied by the best wines, followed by several hours of dice and cards. Then on to Madame Fifi's House of Delights."

Francesca stifled a groan.

"Which brings me back to where this conversation began," Clayburn added after a moment. "Women. If you tell me you pass a single waking hour ... make that ten minutes ... without imagining a naked woman under your heaving body, you will astonish me."

"I won't astonish you," Arthur confessed, his face the color of a ripe tomato.

"I'll not probe your sordid past," Clayburn assured him. "But on the chance my own experiences may be relevant, I will tell you what I have learned from them. You may be spared a few of my mistakes." He paused. "Or perhaps you never amuse yourself with the town strumpets."

Arthur made a strangled noise.

"I certainly did," Clayburn said in a reminiscent tone. "But luckily, I made a friend among the senior students. He knew where the more fastidious ladies were to be found and cautioned me to avoid the ones I had been eyeing surreptitiously. The ones who wait on street corners, ready to exchange a toss for a shilling or two."

Impossibly, Arthur's face graduated to a brighter red. "What if a fellow only *has* a shilling or two?"

"Why, he gives the ladies a polite, respectful smile and keeps walking. But of course, if you persist in wanting to die young, by all means spend your shillings on alleyway doxies. Only keep in mind that they are often afflicted with the sort of diseases that will cause you to shrivel up, not flame out."

"Oh."

As Francesca watched, Arthur went from scarlet to paper-white. Really, she ought to stomp in and drag her hapless young cousin from the clutches of this rakehell before any more bits of carnal knowledge were transferred.

But no parts of her body would move. All parts felt hot and quivery, some more than others. And each and every one stayed in place as she listened, more fascinated by Clayburn's revelations than Arthur could ever be.

"If you have money," Clayburn said, "you can afford to be more selective. Before setting out for an evening of pleasure, I make sure to have enough to buy the very best. Or I was used to, back when I found it necessary to pay for a bed partner."

Francesca went rigid.

"You don't pay?" Arthur asked incredulously. "I was told a man got married or he paid. Usually both."

"Not wholly inaccurate. But like most generalities, it excludes the more discerning options. For instance, some men wed happily and remain faithful to their wives. Others would like to, but until a love match is found, they must opt for celibacy. . . . I shudder at the thought . . . or the careful middle ground."

Which is? Francesca wondered.

"Which is?" Arthur asked.

"Ah, that's difficult to explain. But for the most part, it has to do with controlling oneself at all times, which is exceedingly troublesome. I know, because I have too often run amok when temptation overwhelmed me. We have run amok together for the last several nights. Great fun, eh?"

"Oh yes," Arthur responded fervently. Then he frowned. "You never explained about the women, sir. Why you can choose without paying. But I suppose it's because of how you look."

"To an extent," Clayburn agreed easily. "Widows and fashionable ladies of easy virtue flock to me, but I take no credit for that. My appearance is an accident of fate, and while it may attract the women, it cannot hold them beyond a quick infatuation. Nor should you rely on your own considerable physical attractions. May come a time when your hair thins, as has your father's. And if you spend all your time drinking and lazing about, you will soon grow a paunch. More important, if you fail to secure an education, the ladies will find you a tedious companion and cast you off."

Arthur raised his bony chin. "Is this meant to be a lecture, sir? I hear enough of those at chapel."

"And pay them no heed whatever, I collect." Clayburn laughed. "Nor did I. In fact, I took my degree at Oxford only because my father would have filleted me with a spoon if I failed to emerge with honors. Your father is not so demanding, to your great good fortune. Or perhaps he hopes you will abandon the university so that he'll not have to stand the fees."

"Oh, Sotherton does that. Sends pocket money, too."

Francesca swallowed a growl of protest. She had not been aware that Papa was subsidizing Arthur's education, although she ought to have guessed.

"You have been gaming with the duke's money? May I suggest you not mention this to Miss Childe? Or anything else she would be offended to hear?"

"I'm never so sap-skulled as to do that!" Arthur began to wrap a cravat around his neck. "A man of the world don't talk to females about matters of importance. Right, sir?"

Man of the world indeed! Francesca thought scornfully.

" 'The better part of valor is discretion,' " Clayburn agreed. "Finish dressing yourself, please, and waste no time experimenting with your neckcloth. You'll be removing it soon enough, or allowing a woman to perform the service for you."

While Francesca conjured up that repugnant image, a fatal few seconds went by. And by the time she realized that Clayburn was headed for the passageway, there was nothing for it but to draw herself up and pretend she had only just arrived.

He wasn't the least bit fooled. Without pausing, he seized her elbow as he strode past and led her relentlessly to the downstairs parlor.

"I was coming to see if you wished the carriage brought around," she said brightly.

"Humbug." His eyes flashed. "You were eavesdropping."

The tips of her ears ignited. "Very well, so I was. But I only learned such shambag behavior from you! Or have you forgot skulking among the bookshelves at Hatchard's to listen in on my—"

"You were talking about *books*, Francesca. And in

171

a public place, where any number of people might have overheard. This circumstance was altogether different, as you are well aware. Arthur and I were having a private, man-to-man conversation."

"More like rutting-beast-to-rutting-beast," she fired back. "It's a blessing I chanced to come by in time to put a stop to this. Fifi's House of Delights indeed! You will not take that innocent boy to a brothel, Clayburn. I forbid it!"

"As you wish," he said indifferently. "For myself, I'd greatly prefer a good night's sleep. But when you tell him of your decision, I strongly suggest you not use the term *boy*."

"I won't." Flustered, she wrung her skirt with both hands. "I mean, *you* are the one who must speak to him. Inform Arthur that you have changed your mind."

"Oh, no, my dear. You will play despot on your own. And endure the consequences, too, for I promise he will immediately set out to prove his manhood in ways you do not wish to know about. Think on it a moment. If he will not tolerate lectures or discipline from me, a man he is misguided enough to idolize, how will he react to coercion by a pestilential female?"

Sinking onto the nearest chair, she studied her fingernails intently. "Then what am I to do?"

He came to her, so close that his knees touched hers. "This row is my fault, I know, because I failed to discuss everything with you beforehand. But these are not matters a man can easily discuss with a woman, Francesca. I hoped you might simply trust me, just this once. Surely you cannot believe I have set myself to corrupt the boy?"

"I don't know what to believe," she said plaintively. "He is so young and so incredibly foolish. Even you call him a boy."

"Never to his face, I assure you. For the past week he has been my boon companion, bang up to the mark in every way. A fine fellow to broach a bottle with, although he has twice cast up his accounts on my boots. A clever gamester, despite the fact he has lost on every wager until that mail coach race. He is living the life he has always dreamed of, and it is slowly turning into a nightmare. But he will never admit that, don't you see? Male pride is a fearsome thing. Insult him now and he is lost forever."

She gazed up into a pair of remarkably sympathetic eyes. "But a *brothel*, Clayburn?"

"The coup de grâce," he said, lowering himself to one knee before her. "You should know that Arthur is not so innocent as you wish to think, nor so experienced as he likes to imagine. Unless Oxford has changed radically since I was there, he has experimented with a few of the town fillies. I would be greatly surprised if he'd failed to do the same during his last few years at Eton. He is nineteen, Francesca. Few males survive to that age in possession of their virginity."

She supposed he was right. But then, as a virgin of one-and-thirty, she knew precious little about the business. "I shall take your word for that," she said in a resigned voice. "But how can an evening with Madame Fifi's Barques of Frailty convince him to return to school? It's more likely to have the opposite effect, I would imagine."

"Ah, but this particular evening will not live up to his expectations," Clayburn said with a wry grin. "Nor will he. Must I go into detail?"

"Not *vivid* detail, I beg you. But give me some reason to approve this ramshackle strategy. At the moment, I am certain you and Arthur are a matched pair of swine."

His mouth tightened. "Suffice it to say that I have already made arrangements with the young woman who will entice Arthur to her bedchamber. By then he will be quite drunk, for I shall see to that at the gaming hells we mean to visit first. An excess of wine wreaks havoc with a man's ability to perform. And in the unlikely case his virility outpaces the wine and his current state of exhaustion, Miss Lily has been well paid to make sure he embarrasses himself."

"To what purpose?" she asked, wholly confused. And wildly curious, although she would never admit it.

"Never you mind," he said firmly. "He will boast to me of his prowess as we make our way home, and I shall pretend to believe him. Leave him alone tomorrow, Francesca. For God's sake, don't nag or question him. He has decisions to make, and they won't come easily. But I'll wager anything you like that he will give you, before suppertime, some face-saving excuse for returning to Oxford."

"And I, pretending to regret his departure, will provide funds to see him there. And a bit more, so that he can buy a few rounds while he regales his schoolfellows with the account of his adventures in company with London's most notorious rake. Have I got it right, my lord?"

"Something like that, yes," Clayburn said approvingly. "One more thing. Be generous when you open Sotherton's purse. If Arthur cuts a swash at Oxford, he'll be all the more eager to remain there. And with luck, he will heed some of the advice I was attempting to provide a few minutes ago. You heard most of it, but I doubt you understood the significance. 'Twas for his own good, I promise."

One swine telling another swine how to rut with a bit of discrimination, she thought crossly. How very charming. "I'm sure you meant well," she said.

Wincing, he came to his feet just as Arthur launched himself into the parlor.

"Hullo, Cesca. We're off now."

Francesca pinned a smile on her lips. "Enjoy your evening, gentlemen. And, Arthur, secure a house key from Peters before you leave. No telling what time you'll be home, and I don't wish to keep a servant posted at the door all night. By the way, that waistcoat suits you, and your neckcloth is a thing of wonder. How do you manage to dress so well without a valet?"

Arthur flushed with pleasure at the compliment. "Lord Clayburn is teaching me how to go on," he said with a bow to his mentor.

"Well done," Clayburn murmured in her ear as Arthur went off to find the butler. "Stay the course and he will soon be back where he belongs."

"He had better be," she warned. "Otherwise, I shall come at you with a poker and beat your brains out. Assuming you have any," she added waspishly.

"That's my girl." He ruffled her hair. "Obdurate to the last. Remind me, when this business with Arthur is done with, that I still have a gift for you. Perhaps two, although I begin to despair of the second."

Wasn't that just like a man? she thought as he bowed and went to join his protégé. He implied, but he never *said*. This was the second time he'd mentioned a gift, the first a whole week ago, but she'd yet to receive so much as a potted violet from him.

She ached to run after him and demand clarification. So what that Arthur was destined for failure with his light-skirt? Clayburn never spoke of how he planned to spend his own time at Madame Fifi's.

Which meant that she would probably spend *her* evening imagining him in bed with a doxy.

Chapter 15

Love's a boundless burning waste,
Where bliss's stream we seldom taste.
—*Thomas Campbell*

A cavalry regiment, mounted on elephants, stomped through Clay's restless dreams. The great beasts circled his bed, their huge hooves pounding. Pounding.

Clay rolled over and buried his head under the pillow, but the thumping persisted. A blacksmith must be beating his brains out on an anvil, he decided, not sorry for it. The sooner the job was done with, the better.

"Open the damn door, Clay!"

Jerry's shout hit him with the force of an explosion. He bolted upright, moaning as sunlight daggered through the slit in the curtains and stabbed his aching eyes.

"Go away," he moaned.

More thumping and shouting from the passageway. Damn! Lurching to his feet, he grabbed at the bedpost for support. Then, glancing down, he apprehended that he was naked, although he'd no recollection of removing his clothes. Or of arriving in his rooms, for that matter.

With a struggle, he contrived to stuff his legs into the breeches he'd discarded on the floor. Must have, he thought muddily, for there they lay.

"I know you're in there!" *Thump thump thump.*

Clay staggered across the room and wrestled with

the key as he vaguely plotted ways to murder his former friend. Stood to reason a *real* friend would shut the devil up and go away.

When the lock clicked, Jerry burst into the room, all but knocking Clay off his feet. "About time, you—" His mouth dropped. "My God! What in blue blazes happened last night? Madame Fifi beat the stuffing out of you?"

Clay shook his head, immediately regretting it. The slightest move ignited firecrackers where his brain used to reside. He stumbled to the bed and lowered himself gently at the edge. "She wanted me, I think. But I only meant to wait in the parlor for Arthur. She kept plying me with champagne. God, I'll never touch that devil's brew again as long as I live. Which won't be very much longer, if I'm lucky."

"So you've got a hangover," Jerry said unsympathetically. "Too bad. Now, pull yourself together, because we have a *real* problem. Livvy's scarpered with Heston. According to her note, they are on their way to Gretna."

"Good riddance to them both." Clay rubbed his forehead with a shaky hand. His mouth tasted of cotton and old fish, and a beachful of gritty sand had lodged under his eyelids. "Now they can torment each other instead of plaguing the rest of us."

"I care no more what becomes of them than you do. Or I would not, except that Ann is concerned for her sister. Twins are close, y'know, even when they are nothing alike."

"Then *you* go hunt them down. I've had it up to my eyebrows with that spawn of Satan. If the chit wants Heston, I say let her have him. A marriage made in hell."

Jerry poured water from a pitcher on the side table into a glass. "Drink this," he ordered. "And try to pay attention. Francesca means to set out after them."

"What?" A mouthful of water spewed across the floor. "She can't be so muttonheaded as that."

"Well, I'm not certain she intends to chase them all the way up the Great North Road. Hard to tell. She's in a fearsome temper right now."

"I can imagine." Clay sat straighter, trying to focus his eyes. "You had better fill me in."

"Finally!" Jerry found a pair of boots under a chair and launched them onto the bed. "Get dressed. When I arrived at the house an hour ago, meaning to pay a call on Ann, everyone was in a turmoil. Francesca had all the servants lined up for questioning, but apparently none of them saw Livvy go out."

"Give me times," Clay said, pulling on a boot. "We need to figure how much of a head start she's got."

"That's what Francesca was working on. They all returned from the ball about three o'clock, and Livvy told her maid not to disturb her until she rang. Said she meant to sleep well past noon. Arthur was the one found her room empty, about ten o'clock. He went in to say good-bye."

Thank God for that much, Clay thought. Arthur had seen the light. "Tell me he's on the way back to Oxford."

"He is. Mind you, he wanted to stay for all the excitement, but Francesca sent him packing. He looked almost as bad as you do, I must say."

"Thank you." Clay reeled to his dressing table and gazed at his reflection in the shaving mirror. Two red-rimmed, bloodshot eyes stared back. His hair stood out from his scalp like wagon spokes, and through the dark stubble of his beard, his skin was white as flour paste. "I see what you mean," he said with a groan.

"Go downstairs and order some hot water, will you? I need a shave."

"No time for that." Jerry picked up a shirt from the floor, sniffed at it, and threw it back in disgust. "Before I got there, Francesca had already dispatched footmen to find out where Heston has his rooms. Soon as she has the address, she'll go after him." He went to the stand of drawers and located a fresh shirt. Tossing it to Clay, he rummaged for a cravat. "Naturally I lied when she asked if I knew his direction. Said I would find out and came here."

Clay yanked on the shirt. "Good thinking. But if Heston plans a Scottish wedding, they'll be well on their way by now."

"Francesca thinks he don't mean to marry Livvy at all. She may be right. Heston's a blackguard, but he's no fool. Can you imagine being shackled to that goosecap for the rest of your life?" Jerry shuddered. "Anyway, she suspects this may be a plot to blackmail the Duke of Sotherton. He's in bad health, you know. Francesca is worried about the shock to his heart and will do anything to stop them. She also thinks they may still be in London or holed up somewhere close by."

For a moment Clay was tempted to let Francesca find Heston on her own. The man didn't stand a chance against that Italian virago. First she would scratch his eyes out. Then she'd do him *serious* harm.

Clay abandoned his efforts to tie a passable cravat and knotted the starched muslin loosely around his throat. "Did you come by hack or horse?" he asked as Jerry passed him a riding coat from the armoire.

"Nag. An urchin is holding him in the street."

"Good. Run down to the mews and bring Galahad around. With luck, we'll beat Francesca to Heston's flat. It's no more than a mile from here."

When Jerry was gone, Clay finished dressing, swiped a brush through his hair, and headed downstairs. On second thought, he went back to his rooms and located his sword stick. He'd itched to fight Heston for nearly two decades, and if anyone was to be transported for slitting his throat, it would not be Francesca Childe.

The journey to Heston's flat was accomplished within a few minutes, but they were already too late. Clay swore fervently when he recognized Francesca's carriage drawn up in front of the tall town house. Somehow, she had unearthed the address and arrived in record time.

"Not altogether bad," Jerry pointed out as they handed the reins to a pair of eager street boys. "She'd be on her way again if Heston weren't to home."

A surly landlord directed them to the second floor, wholly unnecessary since Francesca's voice could be heard by anyone in the building. Clay and Jerry followed the sound of her tirade and peered through a crack in the door. It was partly open and led to a small parlor.

Heston, one arm stretched on the mantelpiece and legs crossed in a languid posture, looked singularly bored. Ann and Livvy were seated together on a small divan, holding hands.

And in the center of the room, practically glowing with fury, Francesca raged at Heston, and then at Livvy, and back at Heston again.

For a time, Clay held Jerry in the passageway. His goddess was on a rampage. And glory be, it was not directed at him.

Unfortunately, Heston's sharp eyes caught them out. "Ah, do come in, gentlemen. So long as we are to have a circus here, clowns are more than welcome."

Jerry immediately rushed to Ann and stood behind

her with his hands on her shoulders. Clay stepped inside, taking time to close the door, and leaned against it with his arms folded.

Silenced for the moment, Francesca was staring at him as if he'd just emerged from a peat bog.

"You look like hell, Clayburn," Heston observed amiably. "Horse sit on your face?"

Francesca found her tongue again. "This is *not* a joking matter, Lord Heston. And you have yet to explain yourself."

"Only because you've not given me the opportunity to speak, Miss Childe. Since opening the door to you, which I've frankly come to regret, you have held the floor. And I had thought Livvy impossible to silence."

Clay saw Francesca's black eyes go even hotter and decided to intervene before she went for blood. "I suggest you talk to *me*, Heston. Exactly what is going on here?"

"Damned if I know. Perhaps you can sort it out, although to look at you, I'm inclined to doubt it. For that matter, how is this any of your business?"

"I choose to make it my business," Clay replied evenly.

"Oh, well, then. I must, perforce, confess all." He shot a glance at Livvy. "This bumblebroth was stirred up last evening when, much to my surprise, Miss Olivia Childe proposed marriage to me."

When Francesca erupted with a rush of Italian, Clay lifted a hand and shook his head. To his surprise, she clamped her lips together. Good girl, he thought, turning back to Heston. "Can you have mistaken the young lady's intentions?"

"Hardly. Livvy has no acquaintance with subtlety, as you must surely know. Naturally I was flattered and honored by her offer, and what is more, I accepted. But

I rather expected our nuptials would take place some-time in the distant future, when she had grown up and learned to conduct herself like a real lady instead of the rag-mannered brat she is."

He favored the brat with a cordial smile. "I'm not at all averse to wedding her, you understand. We share a mutual distaste for rules of any sort and cannot tolerate a bit in our mouths. In very many ways, we are well suited to each other."

"But neither of you has a feather to fly with," Francesca objected. "How are you to live?"

"On our wits?"

When Francesca glowered, his eyes hardened. "You needn't fear we'll cling to your purse strings, Miss Childe. Livvy has explained that you stand to inherit Sotherton's fortune, and what little Bromley receives along with the title will not outlast his forays at the gaming tables."

Flushing hotly, Francesca cast a swift look at Clay. She was gauging his reaction to the news, he collected. He struggled to maintain a passive expression on his face, as if the information were of no import to him. But his heart was turning great somersaults in his chest.

Oh, damn. Why must she be wealthy? He felt the ground cut out from under him. Anything that preserved her independence subtracted from his hopes. Now he understood that she had absolutely no reason to accept anything but a love match. And from all he could tell, she was a far sight from loving *him*.

"Why must you all interfere?" Livvy demanded shrilly. Bounding up, she rushed to Heston's side and seized his arm. "Except for Ann, not a one of you gives a fig what becomes of me. Father cares nothing for any of his children, even Arthur, because we are a nuisance to him. Cesca, you only wish me to stop making trouble long enough to find a husband, so that you can be rid of me, too. Well, just see, I have found a husband."

"Ah, but you continue making trouble," Heston pointed out.

"It's the only way I can ever get what I want," she retorted. "And if you'd spent even a week in Rutlandshire, not the lifetime I endured there, you would be a bit of a monster, too."

"I daresay." He smiled down at her. "But Miss Childe has your best interests at heart, you know."

"Yes, I'm sure of it. But her heart is vastly different than mine, Rupert. The only thing she truly wants is to go home." Livvy cast pleading eyes in Francesca's direction. "Don't you see? You can wash your hands of me now. And when Jerry rouses himself to make an offer, which I'm certain he means to do, Ann will surely accept. Isn't it famous? We are both fired off. You need not give the ball you've been dreading or shepherd us to any more tedious affairs. You ought to be pleased, Cesca. And happy for us!"

Unfair, you nasty little witch, Clay thought in the agonizing silence that followed. Ann's cheeks flamed with humiliation, and Jerry looked as if he were about to sink through the floorboards. Heston remained sardonically aloof, but the tight hand clamped on Livvy's shoulder was a clear reproach.

Alone in the center of the room, Francesca stood tall and splendidly regal, but her lips trembled with uncertainty. He could not mistake the hurt in her eyes. After all she had done and endured for Livvy, to be dismissed in such a fashion!

Clay knew better than to go to her now, although he ached to console her. But he could best help by drawing attention to himself until she recovered her composure, although later, he supposed, she would comb him down for meddling.

"An interesting summary of events," he said with a nod to Livvy. "But you neglected to include the scandal that will attach to Ann and all your family if you make a bolt for the border."

"To which I have not agreed," Heston observed mildly.

"A rare venture into the realm of good sense," Clay acknowledged. "But neither did you return Livvy to her family immediately after she appeared at your door. Quick action on your part would have spared everyone this scene."

"True enough. But, my dear Clayburn, have you not realized that Livvy is impossible to budge once she has set her mind on a thing? I might have hauled her kicking and screaming through the streets to Grosvenor Square, of course. But I chose to await reinforcements, and lo, you have come to my rescue. Among us, five against one, we may be able to subdue her."

"Infamous!" Livvy broke from Heston's grip and turned on him. "I have risked everything for you. Even the affection of my sister, and I do love Ann, although I use her badly. You will *not* send me back, Rupert. I won't have it!"

Heston's smile was uncommonly sweet. "But what choice have we, my love? Alienating what few friends and relations we can claim, odious creatures that we are, is a poor way to begin a life together. I'll not take you to Gretna."

Sobbing, she threw herself at his chest. And after a moment, rolling his eyes, he opened his arms and drew her into an embrace.

Clay was unsure what to make of this. He glanced at Francesca, who seemed equally confused. "Shall we come to the point?" he asked, jabbing a finger in Heston's direction. "Do you mean to wed her?"

"Oh, eventually. When she is of age. Perhaps on her birthday, if she conducts herself properly in the meantime."

"B-but that's eight m-months from now," Livvy wailed. "I cannot wait so long. Abominable man. If you really loved me, you would carry me off this very instant."

Francesca pressed her hands together. "Consider, Livvy. Only a man whose affections are casually engaged would demand immediate gratification. The man who is truly in love stays the course, however long and rocky it may be."

Livvy glanced over her shoulder, arrested by a revelation that had clearly never occurred to her. Then she frowned. "Perhaps so, for others. But in this case, I think it's better to seal the bond right away. Rupert is handsome, charming, and poor. A woman with a fortune is like to steal him from me. And then I'd murder her, which would be a greater scandal than elopement."

Sometimes, Clay reflected, even a widgeon made good sense. But Francesca had gone white.

"Do you want the sort of husband who could be won over by money?" she asked. "Or a miserable piece of land? Lord Heston has declared himself willing to accept an impoverished bride. He has, for your own good, promised to wait until you are of age. Is it not time you repay him with a sacrifice of your own?"

Livvy lifted a hand to Heston's cheek. "I suppose. But all I have to give is my whole self, and that is pitifully little. I am a horrid girl, just as everybody tells me. You think I don't know it, but I do. And I'm not likely to change very much. That scares me, Rupert."

"It frightens me, too," he said softly. "But we shall deal well enough together."

Jerry cleared his throat. "Not to interfere, but has anybody considered that they can marry right away? We only need Lord Bromley to give his consent."

Everyone looked to Heston for a response. Or that was Clay's impression, since he still suspected Heston meant to use any excuse to avoid wedding Livvy. Not once in all the years Clay had known the man had he exhibited the slightest trace of honor. This display of concerned affection for Livvy and her family could only be a sham.

Livvy plucked at his shoulders with both hands. "Rupert?"

Heston shrugged. "If Bromley steps forward with his approval, I'll purchase a special license and we can do the deed immediately. But I have not seen him about this last week or more. Anyone know where he can be found?"

Attention swung to Clay.

"What?" He held out his arms. *"I* haven't seen him either. Not since Wolvercote."

"But you could find him," Francesca said. Her enormous brown-black eyes blazed with hope. "You did so before. Will you at least try, my lord?"

Oh *hell*! Another shamble through the gin mills, flash houses, and back alleys of London in pursuit of Bromley Childe. Bloody, miserable, *hell hell hell!*

He bowed politely. "As you wish, Miss Childe."

Chapter 16

Good-bye, knight, go your way,
I hear my father calling me.
     —Provençal Song

After scouring every gaming hell, gin mill, cockpit, and lowlife establishment in London, Clay finally thought to hire a Bow Street Runner.

Second only to fixing his attentions on Francesca, it was the best idea he'd ever had. Mr. Worbel quickly learned that Bromley had taken a public coach in the direction of Brighton, and they set off together to look for him there.

When that lead flamed out, they worked their way back toward London, inquiring at every posthouse where the London-to-Brighton coaches changed horses. Every day Clay considered returning to London, leaving Mr. Worbel to complete the search on his own, but he could not bear to let Francesca down. So he plodded on, inn by inn, town by town, for more than a week.

Finally, thanks to a postboy with a good memory, Bromley was traced to, of all places, Tunbridge Wells.

A favorite watering place for dowagers, refined widows, and gentlemen not in the first blush of youth, it was the most unlikely spot for Bromley to land. But there he was, starkly sober and with a slightly bewildered expression engraved on his face, firmly in the clutches of one Mrs. Phemia Vertue.

The widow of a well-to-do tradesman, Mrs. Vertue

was happily parading his lordship at the local assemblies to impress her friends and, most especially, her enemies. Short but solidly built, with a voice like thunder, she put Clay forcibly in mind of a battering ram.

Bromley had no objection to ridding himself of the twins. Quite the contrary. But since a thug to whom he owed money had promised to break his knees unless he paid up, he meant to keep well away from London for the next fifty years. It seemed that Clay would have to settle for carrying back his written consent to the marriages.

But when Mrs. Vertue heard the tale, she immediately offered to cover her dear Bromley's debt and rig him out in fine style for the ceremony. For the chance to rub shoulders with the nobs at a Society wedding, she would probably have dragged him to London by his hair.

And now, at long last, Clay was on his way to pay court to his goddess, the Petrarch burning a hole in his coat pocket. He chuckled, wondering what Francesca was making of her surprise houseguest. The widow's coach-and-four must have arrived at Grosvenor Square late yesterday afternoon, followed by another carriage loaded with trunks and portmanteaus.

Of a certain, Francesca would be pleased with *him*. For the first time since meeting her, he felt very sure of himself. Everything she had asked of him, he had done. And when he wasn't chasing down Bromley and Livvy, or setting Arthur on the straight and narrow, he'd spent every waking moment working on his poem.

Yes indeed, he'd been a veritable saint, martyr, knight, and poet, all rolled into one. The goddess could find no fault with him now.

When he arrived at her town house, the butler greeted him with more than his usual disdain, waving him churlishly into a foyer stacked with trunks and boxes and leaving him there while he ascertained if Miss Childe was receiving company.

Puzzled, Clay watched two footmen carry another large trunk down the stairs and deposit it in the foyer with a groan of relief. He was about to ask them what was going on when the butler reappeared, beckoning him along the narrow passageway instead of leading him upstairs to one of the parlors. More confused than ever, he trailed a few paces behind to a door near the rear of the house.

"Miss Childe is in the library," the butler said curtly, his hand on the latch. "She instructed me to ask if you wish any refreshment."

"That will not be necessary," Clay replied, wondering what he had done in recent memory to set the man's back up. Or perhaps Peters's surly mood had something to do with all those boxes in the foyer.

Reminding himself that he, at least, was in a very good mood indeed, Clay stepped through the door Peters grudgingly opened, looking around for Francesca.

"My lord," she said with a formal curtsy.

He bowed in return, automatically, a sensation of dread creeping up his spine.

She stood behind a large oak desk, which was cluttered with papers from corner to corner. She wore a plain, dark green dress. Her hair, barely contained in a loose braid, reached nearly to her waist.

She gazed at him politely, as if greeting a stranger. "Do forgive the racket and disorder, Lord Clayburn. Except for the public rooms, we are preparing the house to be closed down."

"But why?" He felt as if he'd wandered onto the moon. "Surely you mean to stay in London for the Season?"

"No indeed, sir, I return to Rutlandshire the very day after the wedding. Weddings, to be precise."

"I see," he said, although he didn't see at all. Oh dear God. *How soon?* was his first thought. He had not meant to declare himself this very afternoon. On the contrary. He'd intended to arrange a romantic proposal, on a sunny afternoon by the River Thames, with flowers and champagne and perhaps a violinist. He would read his poem to her, and drop to one knee before her, and tell her what was in his heart.

But like every other fantasy in which he'd indulged since meeting his goddess, this one, the one he'd most longed to create for both of them, had suddenly become impossible. And he had no idea why.

Through stinging eyes, he saw Francesca sink onto her chair and gesture to him to seat himself across the desk from her. Instead, he began to pace the room, struggling to order his wits. "Has a wedding d-date been fixed?"

"Not quite yet. Lord Heston and Jerry secured special licenses a few days ago. Now they are scouring the parishes for a church and vicar. Only one church, thank heavens, since we are to have a single ceremony. With luck, they'll find a location for Saturday next."

"But that is only three days away!"

"Yes, well, you may recall that Livvy is a trifle impatient. She wants to get on about it, and quite honestly, so do the rest of us."

He stopped himself before tripping over a footstool. "You are aware, I presume, that everyone will suspect other reasons for the hurried marriages."

"They may think what they like," she replied calmly. "In any case, we will invite a great many prominent guests to our *hurried* wedding breakfast, where they may quiz the brides and grooms and judge for themselves. At the least, my lord, we will serve up two love matches in a single morning, which is wonder enough in this cynical town. And we will all be long gone before the gossips begin to dissect the whats and whys of it."

Well said, he approved silently, still unable to link his tongue to his brain. *Francesca is leaving!* And from everything he could tell so far, without a single thought for him.

She made a sweeping gesture over the desk. "As you can see, Lord Clayburn, I am busily compiling a list of guests, and will begin writing a hundred invitations or more when the wedding date is firmly fixed. Maria Beaton, bless her, is arranging flowers and catering, but even so, I have much to do this afternoon. Pray forgive me if I seem a bit distracted."

He cleared his throat. "Shall I assume, under the circumstances, that Bromley arrived with the paternal go-ahead?"

"Oh, yes." A smile curved her lips and quickly vanished. "Widow in tow. Rather the other way around, actually. A most fettlesome woman, don't you think?"

"There was no stopping her from accompanying Bromley," he said ruefully. "I did try."

"No matter. She will keep him on good behavior through the wedding and breakfast, which is my only concern. After that, he may go to Hades with my blessing. Although I rather suspect Mrs. Vertue has plans of her own for Bromley. But however it shakes out, Lord Clayburn, you may be sure that I will never again send you off to find my dear uncle."

"I am relieved to hear it." He propped his shoulders against a bare bookshelf and folded his arms. "Naturally I take great pleasure in performing services for you, Miss Childe, and will do so again at the next opportunity. But one does relish a bit of variety."

That was supposed to make her smile. Instead, he saw her mouth tighten. Her gaze darted from the desk to the windows to the door. Everywhere but to him. A hard lump settled in his chest. What the bloody hell had gone wrong in the last ten days?

For all practical purposes, he had been the very model of a virtuous gentleman since meeting her. Every venture into the places where he had once run wild—the gaming hells, Wolvercote, even that one innocent night at a brothel—had been taken on her behalf.

Now, her twin charges about to marry and all her goals achieved, she had gone cold on him. Francesca in a temper, he could deal with. He longed for her to rage at him, because there was always truth in her fury. But the vast distance between them was unspoken, and the barriers she had erected invisible. He could not think how to reach her.

It occurred to him this awful silence could have a simple explanation after all. He had devoted ten days and nights to tracking Bromley, and she could not have anticipated the difficulty of the task. Now she felt guilty. That must be it.

"If you are working yourself up to a speech of gratitude," he said, "please spare us both. It has been my greatest pleasure to be of assistance."

"I know. That is, I understand. It makes everything so much easier for you. And so much more difficult for me. I cannot think how to begin." She twisted the inkwell stopper around and around. " 'Thank you' is woefully inadequate in one way and ridiculous in the other, although I am certainly grateful. Without your help, Ann and Livvy would not be looking forward to the happiest day of their lives."

So why wouldn't Francesca look at him? He needed to see her eyes, because what she said made no sense

192

whatsoever. What was it she *understood*? Why was a plain "thank you" *ridiculous*, of all things?

She picked up a pen and began stripping feathers from the quill. "It is long past time, of course, to clear the air between us. I take full responsibility. But in the beginning you were all but impossible to get rid of. And after that . . . well, never mind. Suffice it to say that your web was splendidly woven."

Tongue firmly lodged behind his clenched teeth, he made a vague gesture. By now, feathers were strewn over the blotter in front of her. And when she spoke, her face still turned down, her breath lifted them. They swirled around the way his mind was swirling, directionless.

He resumed his pacing. "Miss Childe," he said from near the window, "obviously you are distressed. But for the life of me, I cannot make out what it is you are trying to say."

Her head shot up. "Only that we should get this over with here and now, Lord Clayburn. It is best all around, don't you think?"

"I might, if I'd any idea what you were talking about." His heart began to jump crazily in his chest. "Have I offended in some way?"

"Oh, to be sure. But I do not take it at all personally. You have only done what you were told, after all. Short of the final step, of course, the one that requires you to come out from Montford's shadow and ask me to marry you. Face-to-face," she added, plucking madly at the few remaining feathers on her pen.

How else but face-to-face? Did she expect him to have a footman deliver his proposal? Wholly confused, he grabbed at the only thing she'd said that he understood. "What the devil has my father to do with this?"

"Oh, *please*! If not for him, you would never have paid me the slightest attention. Can you deny it?"

His mouth opened to do exactly that, then closed again as he recalled how his instant desire for her had become entangled with his stupid plan to marry the first woman he clapped eyes on.

"No, I cannot," he admitted. "Not altogether. There is no question I was captivated from the moment I saw you, but it took me a while to sort things out. I was still enraged after a bitter quarrel with the earl and caught up in a damned fool notion of marrying to spite him. Suddenly, there you were."

She was regarding him as if he'd turned green. "Captivated? Pah! Not by me, sir. You were *his* prisoner from the start. And how could marrying *me* serve any purpose but his own? Will you not have the decency to be honest, just this once?"

He was sure as hell trying. But however did she guess that the Earl of Montford came into this? Except for a niggling remnant of guilt, he'd all but forgotten his mad impulse to flaunt her before Montford's stunned eyes. Jerry might have let something slip, he supposed. Jerry was in love, and a besotted man said a great many things he never meant to own up to. As Clay was learning all too well.

"Look. I never imagined you would hear of this before I explained. Which I always meant to do," he hastened to add. "Well, after we were married, most like, but I would have told you eventually. Indeed, I rather thought you would find it amusing."

"Oh yes. Even now, I can scarce contain my laughter."

He released a harsh breath. "Is it so bad, Francesca? So I wanted you from the first. What man would not? And while I determined to have you for every wrong reason there can be, all those reasons vanished before the sun came up again. So how are they of consequence? Even before I learned your full name and discovered that you were not a chaperone, I—"

"You thought I was a *chaperone*?" She banged a clenched hand on the desk, sending papers to the floor like confetti. "What nonsense. Even Bromley could devise a more convincing bouncer than that. Oh, I don't doubt for a moment you were astonished to encounter me at the inn, and I'm sure you didn't recognize me at first. How could you, since we had never met? But once you heard my name, you knew exactly who I was. And that you were supposed to marry me."

It finally began to dawn on Clay that they were speaking at cross-purposes altogether. She might as well have been addressing another man. He lunged for the one thing she'd said that truly mattered to him. For whatever reason, Francesca had expected him to propose marriage, and God knew he'd always meant to do so.

He drew himself up. "I had certainly hoped for a more fortuitous moment to say the words, but yes, I very much want you to be my wife. With all my heart."

"But of course," she said. "That was always clear, except that hearts have no place in a matter of business. Ironic, isn't it, that Montford went wrong from the start? Had he left the whole matter to you, he might well have succeeded."

Suddenly, Clay remembered his father's unexpected presence in London. The return of the commission money. The almost approving way Montford had spoken to him. Was it because he'd known that his son was courting Sotherton's daughter? Why the devil would he be glad of that?

Light dawned. Montford had somehow dug his talons into Francesca. He'd convinced her to turn his son away. What else could explain this nightmare? "Tell me," he said softly. "What has he done to you?"

"Oh, excellent!" She clapped her hands. "Were I not buried under with plans for a wedding, I'd draw this out if only to hear which clanker you'd next invent. But let us come to the point. I have read the letters, Lord Clayburn. One arrived every year, always in October, whereupon Papa and I had a good laugh. How could the earl, or you, imagine I'd be *grateful* for a husband willing to have me despite my mixed blood and illegitimate birth? Arrogant snobs! Montford would have done better to dispatch you with orders to seduce me. Sad to say, I'd probably have yielded without a struggle."

Letters? Oh God. Not this! He plastered one hand over his eyes. "Never tell me you are the bloody *Albatross*!"

"I beg your pardon?"

"I . . . no." He felt himself melting into his boots. "I never said that. It's just . . . I had no idea that you . . . Oh hell!"

"Truly, you belong on the stage, Lord Clayburn. Might I suggest you always play the Fool? You do it so well."

He felt like the Great King of All Fools. He hated his father more than he'd ever hated him before. He saw his dreams slipping away and the empty void that lay ahead, and he couldn't think how to snatch them back again.

Francesca was the wife his father had chosen for him? His precious, glorious, fiercest of goddesses was the Albatross? And worst of all, she'd known it all along? Well, she'd just said so, hadn't she?

Anger wrapped him up, winding around him until he could scarcely breathe. She had *known*! And played him along, probably laughing the way she'd done

196

when Montford's letters arrived. What a joke, on every count. When she required a lackey to do her bidding, call on Clayburn. By his father's command, he would do whatever she asked of him. Act nursemaid to Livvy. Chase after Bromley from here to kingdom come. A wonder she hadn't demanded he clean the chimneys.

Such a fool he'd been, and she had played him for one. He crossed to the desk in three long strides. She looked back at him, clutching the pen in one hand and her skirt in the other. He realized she wasn't laughing at him at all. But her body was taut as a bowstring, and her chin was raised in that defiant way she had of taking on the world.

There had to be a way to stop this. Save them both. Damn it all, he *loved* her.

Hated her at the same time, for deceiving him, but that would pass. He resented her, too, for being the woman he didn't want, but already he knew that it no longer mattered. She couldn't help being the Albatross, any more than he could have stopped Montford from turning her against him before they ever met. But where to go from here?

"I knew that my father was determined to arrange a marriage of convenience," he said, choosing his words carefully. "Montford did everything in his considerable power to bend me to his will in this matter, and I was equally hell-bent to defy him. You may be sure that the woman he chose for me was the last woman on earth I would agree to wed."

"The Albatross."

"Just so. But I had no idea who she was. *Is*," he corrected swiftly.

"Oh, certainly not. Over a period of five years or more, your father attempted to negotiate a marriage, and in all that time he never told you the name of your future wife. Perfectly understandable."

"He may have done so. I cannot recall." Sweat broke out on his forehead. "That is to say, I formed an impression of her. You. *Not* you, clearly, but what I surmised from what he said."

"And what was that?" she asked too sweetly. "What impression of her, meaning me, did you derive?"

"Lord, I can hardly remember. Older than I am by several years, dowry that included land my father wanted. But what does any of that signify? Keep in mind that the earl and I keep well apart, by mutual choice, and I have schooled myself to listen to nothing he says. Your name, if it was told me, never registered."

"I see. Then I am to believe you encountered me by chance that night and fell instantly in love with a wet, bedraggled creature who snubbed you one minute and railed at you the next."

"At least you remember," he put in, like a drowning man clawing at the water. "That must count for something."

"Make nothing of it, sir. I lived three years on the streets of Naples and another eight-and-twenty in Rutlandshire. Any handsome aristocrat, however disreputable, would have caught my attention. Had we not met again, I'd easily have forgotten you."

"You were never to have the chance. I spent the next two weeks looking for you. I meant to find you again, Francesca."

"And you knew I'd be at Hatchard's that very afternoon, that very hour? An amazing feat. You do impress me, Lord Clayburn. You always have. A well-crafted marionette can be appreciated even by one who sees the Earl of Montford pulling your strings."

"Francesca." He was pleading now. "Listen to me. I didn't know."

Abruptly she stood and crossed swiftly to the door. "Likely we'll not meet again, Lord Clayburn, unless you mean to come to the wedding. Jerry will expect you, I suppose. In any case, I have much to do this afternoon, so please excuse me. You can let yourself out."

And then she was gone, while he stayed rooted in place like a tree stump. It took several minutes before he could move again, although he wasn't sure where to go. Well, out of the house. She'd dismissed him in no uncertain terms. If he'd possessed a tail, she'd have put a tinder-stick to it.

He still could not believe that it was truly over. There must be *some* way to make her understand.

But what if he managed to convince her that he'd fallen in love when he had no idea of her identity? It didn't necessarily follow that she would love him in return. From the beginning, she'd made it clear that he was everything she abhorred.

Never once had she wanted to spend time with him, talk with him, come to know him. No, she'd only called on the talents of a rakehell to accomplish what a decent man could not.

Despair settled over him. There had never been any hope. He had lost her even before he had begun.

At least he would have the satisfaction of thumbing his nose at Montford, he thought. Cold comfort indeed. On the whole, he'd rather be coshed on the head with a mace.

On numb feet, he made his way to the door. And then he remembered.

The book he'd nearly killed himself trying to find. She might as well have the damned thing. He pulled it from his pocket and tossed it on top of her desk.

Here are the words of a real poet, Francesca. You would not have liked my own poem nearly so well.

Chapter 17

Once, I dreamed of light. And then you came
on wings of fire, to set my soul aflame.
—*Galen Pender, Lord Clayburn*

From a tall box pew in St. George's, Hanover
Square, Francesca watched Bromley Childe lead his
daughters to the altar and give them over to their
waiting bridegrooms.

Maria Beaton stood beside her, two handkerchiefs
in her hand, after confessing that she always cried at
weddings and rarely at funerals. That sounded reasonable enough to Francesca, for whom this day was
a bit of both.

Livvy had babbled all the way down the aisle and
found more to say at the altar. Finally the exasper-
ated rector advised her to hush so that he could get
on with business.

For once, Lord Heston had abandoned his usual sar-
donic pose. He gazed tenderly at his bride when she
promised to love, honor, and obey, choking slightly on
the last word. Ann wept with joy as she spoke her vows,
and Jerry made her laugh when he stumbled over his
own name.

Tears and laughter.

Francesca felt nothing at all.

She wanted to be happy, and knew she ought to be.
Everything she'd come to London to do, she had accomplished. Or rather, Clayburn had accomplished for

her. And certainly the brides and grooms had found happiness on their own, with no help from anyone.

All in all, she'd been pretty much useless. And she wanted to cry.

She had thought she would, bitterly and endlessly, after sending Clayburn on his way. But her eyes remained as arid as her heart. And really, she dared not let the pain come over her just yet. Perhaps she could weep tomorrow, alone in the carriage that would take her home. And try to think what to tell Papa of her adventures in London. Dear God, she would have to lie to him, too.

But she'd gotten very good at lying. And what could be more shameful than the lies she kept telling herself, after all? One day she might even convince herself that she was not in love with Clayburn.

Meantime, there was today to be endured. Only a few friends had been invited to the church, but more than a hundred guests were expected at the wedding breakfast to follow. This would be her sole opportunity to host the Fashionables who had welcomed her to their homes, and she meant to depart London on a note of triumph in that regard at least. Even the persnickety Lady Drummond-Burrell would find no fault with her lavish menu or the elegant decorations.

She had steeled herself for the ceremony, and she would make it through. She would *not* imagine standing at the altar with Clayburn while he took her hand to slip on the ring and made promises he could never keep. However much she wanted him, she had chosen not to settle for what little he would give her in return.

Thankfully, he'd not come to the wedding. Jerry, who had asked him to stand as groomsman because his brother had got the measles, was hurt when he declined with some vague excuse about a trip to

Brighton. To spare Jerry's feelings, she'd insisted that Prinny had long since commanded Clayburn's presence that particular weekend, although for all she knew, Prinny was firmly ensconced in London at this very moment.

But it was only one more lie, after all. She had told a lifetime's worth since meeting Clayburn.

Drat it! She *must* stop thinking about the man. Tomorrow I'll be gone, she reminded herself. Surely I can keep from falling to pieces for one more day.

While she was lost in her own thoughts, the wedding ceremony must have concluded. Lord Heston, with Livvy romping at his side, swept past the pew, followed more sedately by Jerry and Ann.

As she turned to watch them, Francesca saw a tall figure standing alone in the shadows at the back of the church. Her heart leaped to her throat.

"Can that be Clayburn?" Maria asked. "Isn't he supposed to be in Brighton?"

Francesca adjusted her cloak with numb fingers. "His plans must have changed at the last minute."

A pair of sharp brown eyes probed at her. Then Maria opened the pew door. "Very likely. Shall we join the others, my dear?"

Bromley, with the encroaching widow latched to his arm, intercepted them midway down the aisle. "Fine day, what? Popped 'em both off in one fell swoop. Hard to believe m'little girls are married ladies now."

Francesca couldn't help but smile. Bromley was positively beaming with pride, as if he had engineered this coup single-handedly. "I expect you'll soon have a grandchild or two to dandle on your knee," she said.

"Can't be a grandfather," he replied indignantly. "Too young."

Mrs. Vertue regarded him with fond forbearance. "Now, don't be tiresome, lovey. You're an old sot, but there's hope for you yet. And I'll be glad of grandbabies to coddle, so never you mind if those young bucks plant a seed or two this very night." She gave him a gap-toothed grin. "Not that you couldn't teach them a trick or two. There's lots to be said for experience."

With that, she bustled him off.

Maria broke out laughing. "My heavens, what an astonishing creature. 'Tis a wonder she didn't order the rector to preside over a third marriage while he was about it."

"She means to have him," Francesca agreed as they made their way to the vestibule. "But I cannot imagine why."

"I suspect she was planning to acquire a pet poodle when she met Bromley and set herself to housebreak a rackety aristocrat instead. He is all but nibbling out of her hand already."

"Which means she is like to become the next Duchess of Sotherton." Francesca shook her head. "Papa will think it all a great jest, of course."

Maria drew her to a halt. "You still mean to leave for home tomorrow, my dear? Is that a good idea?"

"Oh yes. Everything is arranged. I miss him, Maria, and he needs me. Except for the pleasure of your company, there is nothing to keep me in London now." She produced a quivery smile. "Well, except for that elusive dinner party at Lady Holland's. One day I may come back and hold you to your promise."

"I shall count on it. For now, I expect we had best hurry to Grosvenor Square. The caterers are generally reliable, but even a small wedding breakfast requires supervision."

In St. George's Street, passersby had stopped to cheer the nuptials. A pack of ragged children, always alert to a Quality wedding, scrambled for the coins Jerry and Lord Heston were tossing out for good luck.

Clayburn was nowhere in sight.

Francesca told herself she was glad of it. Even the brief glimpse of him in the church had turned her bones to jelly. If compelled to exchange pleasantries with him, she would surely dissolve altogether.

She couldn't help but scan the pavement in both directions, though. Three carriages had already pulled up, ready to convey the wedding party to Grosvenor Square, and she longed to slip around them to see if he might be standing across the street.

Perhaps he would appear at the breakfast. But in the deepest part of her heart, she knew he would not.

Suddenly, she could not bear the shrieks of the children and Livvy's shrill laughter. Surrounded by other people's joy, she felt a crushing blow of self-pity. This will never be mine, she thought. And when Papa is gone, I shall be truly and forever alone.

While Maria's attention was diverted, she slipped back inside the church to regain her composure.

Sunlight streamed through the stained-glass windows over the altar, casting patterns of color on the wide flagstone aisle. An elderly verger snuffed the last candle and tottered into the sacristy, closing the door behind him.

In the empty silence, she knelt on the icy floor and summoned a prayer for Papa's health. But it was a false, mechanical prayer, because her thoughts immediately flew to Clayburn again.

Had she been wrong to send him away? What was the use of pride, when choosing it above all other things left her so miserable?

Weak, silly, *stupid* woman!

And yet the pain she felt now, she would have felt eventually. Suppose you had married him? she asked herself. How soon before he would have left to resume his former life—months? Weeks? It's better this way, and you'll accept that, when it doesn't hurt quite so much. He never loved you, after all. You are losing nothing that you might have had.

And then she saw him.

Trailing one hand along the carved wooden rail, he appeared from the shadows under the overhanging gallery and moved to stand before the enormous painting of Christ's Last Supper suspended over the altar.

Stunned, she could only gaze openmouthed at his back. His arms hung at his sides, and in one hand she saw something white, like a sheet of paper. He might have been a groom, except that he did not turn to watch his bride walk down the aisle.

To her horror, she realized that she was on her feet and those same feet were moving toward the aisle. Haltingly, to be sure, but they would not be stopped. She drew closer to the tall, silent figure, scarcely daring to breathe.

His head lifted, and she stopped immediately, but he only made a low sound in his throat. It echoed in the quiet church. Then his hand, the one holding the paper, swung in front of him and his head bent. After a few moments, she heard the slight hiss of paper being torn apart.

When his hand dropped again, a few small scraps were clutched between his fingers.

Like a tiny book, she thought, the memory striking her a second later. She had never thanked him for the book! It gave her a perfectly reasonable excuse to speak to him one last time. Her feet must have agreed, because they were moving again.

He heard her, she realized when he glanced over his shoulder. And then only his eyes moved, every color in the rainbow reflected from the startled, silver-mirror gaze. She gazed back, vaguely aware that she had stopped once more, close enough to touch him had they both reached out their hands.

Vibrant light poured over him from every direction, through the faces of saints and prophets, through the wings of archangels and the smiles of cherubs etched in the stained-glass windows. It glistened off his thick dark hair and turned his white collar and neckcloth to red and blue and green.

He seemed poised before her at the instant just before being thrust into hell, she thought, a bright angel who had cast his lot with Lucifer. Until this moment, she had not truly understood what he might once have been or could have become.

Such a horrific waste. But perhaps one day he would find a Mrs. Vertue, as Bromley had done. He might then be desperate enough to grasp a lifeline, however tenuous, and cling to it.

If only she could be the one to pull him to shore.

He had turned and was bowing. "Miss Childe. I thought you long since on your way with the others."

Panic slammed her then, transforming her curtsy into a rubbery bounce. She had to speak to him as if they were the merest of acquaintances. *Book,* she thought, grasping at her own lifeline. Thank him. Simple words. Few syllables.

"The book," she ventured cautiously. "I found it. That is, I assumed you meant to leave it. Should I have returned it to you?"

"I've no use for poetry," he replied, his expression hardening. "Of course you must keep it."

"Well, 'tis my father who wanted it, of course. I mean to give it to him, if you have no objection."

"Why should I? The book is yours. Feed it to the fire if you wish."

Like a hard slap across the face, his words jolted her from panic to temper. But she pressed the anger into the hard ball of other emotions knotted up inside her. This was the last time they would meet. She absolutely must not give in to hysterics. "Even John Hatchard could not discover its whereabouts," she said, keeping her voice even. "However did you find it?"

"In my usual fashion," he replied with a touch of sarcasm. "Drinking and gaming with the other scoundrels at Wolvercote. You recall that I returned there after delivering Livvy to the inn. Fallon lost a sum of money to me and was delighted to settle his debt with books in lieu of cash." He shrugged. "Naturally, I could not be sure I'd discovered the one you were seeking."

"You've had it in your possession all these weeks?"

"I was waiting for the perfect moment to present it to you, with accompanying flourishes." With a faint smile, he gazed at a spot over her shoulder. "Now, of course, I realize that such a moment was never to be."

She ran her tongue over dry lips. "The Petrarch is quite valuable, Lord Clayburn. I have no idea what Fallon owed to you when you accepted the book in exchange, but I shall gladly pay that amount or the book's market price, whichever sum is greater."

"God. It needed only this!"

For a long moment, the air fairly crackled around him. He stared at her with acute loathing. But when he spoke again, his voice had no expression at all. "I am aware you hold me in contempt, Miss Childe. With some reason, for in all my life I have done little of value and a great many things I regret. But I have never been my father's lackey. I do not covet your land or your fortune. And though I sought to win your affections by being of service to you, how is that a crime? I am a stranger to love. I could think of no other way to prove my sincerity. Dammit, what did you expect from a besotted fool? Love poems?"

With that, he strode swiftly past her.

Paralyzed, she heard the hollow beat of his shoes against the floor, growing fainter until the sound disappeared. Still she could not move. After a long while, she remembered to start breathing again.

Her mind was as incapable of thought as her body was of motion. She felt only a deep, burning emptiness where her heart had been and an aching sense of loss.

"Francesca?"

Dimly she recognized Maria's voice calling from the vestibule. Life must go on, she supposed. The wedding feast awaited.

Legs rigid, she turned and made her way slowly down the aisle, gaze focused on the worn stone paving where countless brides had joyously walked. Where minutes ago Clayburn had walked out of her life.

A scrap of paper, torn at the edges, lay starkly white against the gray stones just in front of her. Without thought she bent to pick it up, meaning to discard it later in a trash basket, and continued to where Maria waited with a concerned look on her face.

"Is everything all right, my dear? Clayburn stormed by a few moments ago, failing to acknowledge me when I called to him. Did something happen between the two of you?"

"Nothing of consequence," she replied, glancing at the bit of paper in her hand to avoid meeting her friend's eyes. There was writing on one side, the side that had been turned down so that she failed to notice it. Now, one word practically jumped from the page. *Francesca.*

Clayburn must have dropped this. She remembered the sound of paper tearing and the remnants clutched in his hand as they spoke. A letter, perhaps? One he had decided not to send?

Heart pounding, she suggested that Maria proceed to the carriage. "I'll f-follow shortly," she promised.

Obviously worried, Maria nodded and left Francesca alone in the shadowy vestibule.

With trembling hands she lifted the fragment of paper to the light from the open door and read the few, broken lines.

Precious God. He had written her a poem!

She recognized the faltering rhymes, the commonplace images, the earnest struggle to wrench feelings into words. Papa had written poetry like this to Renalda, deplorable as literature but incandescent with love.

To think Clayburn had done the same. For *her*! In her wildest, most fantastical dreams, she could never have imagined that rakehell huddled over paper and an inkpot, composing verses to "beloved Francesca, goddess mine . . ."

Wings attached themselves to her feet. She all but flew outside, unsurprised to catch no sight of him. Only one carriage remained on the street, Maria standing beside the open door.

"Which way did he go?" she demanded.

Without hesitation, Maria pointed south.

Lifting her skirts, Francesca set off at a run, dodging pedestrians and veering into the gutter when necessary. For once glad of her height, she searched for a glimpse of his broad shoulders and dark hair over the stream of men and women about their Saturday morning errands. No sign of him.

She turned right at Conduit Street and shortly after dashed in front of a hackney to go left on Bond Street. Instinct drove her on. She had no rational idea where he was headed, but never doubted she would find him.

And sure enough, across the next street and mid-way down the block after that, she saw a tall man poised on the curbside, arm lifted to hail a hack. His hair shone in the sunlight as if on fire.

Summoning a new burst of speed, she darted across the intersection in defiance of the oncoming traffic, fractionally aware of a rider screaming oaths at her as his horse reared up. A brewer's dray careened into a streetlamp.

Ignoring the chaos in her wake, she ran even faster when a hackney pulled up in front of him. His hand went to the door latch.

Still a block to go! She could not reach him in time. "Clayburn! Wait!"

He must not have heard her. He already had one foot on the floorboard when she shoved herself between a large woman and her equally pudgy companion, all but knocking them to the ground.

"Clayburn!" she shrieked.

He turned, poised halfway between pavement and coach, an astonished look on his face.

She pelted the last few yards and hurled herself at his chest.

Just in time, he opened his arms to catch her. Only his strength held her upright. Her legs had cramped up, dangling uselessly from her body as she sucked huge mouthfuls of air into her burning lungs.

"I . . . found . . ." She panted. "Don't . . . go . . . please."

"I'm here," he said. "Breathe slowly, Francesca. That's good." His fingers massaged her back. "Relax. We have all the time in the world."

"No. Don't have . . . time. N-now! Here!"

"Whatever you say, my—"

"That's right, guv'nor," a voice shouted.

"Go on, dearie," said a woman from directly behind her. "You tell 'im. We won't let the bloke get away."

As the world stopped spinning in dizzy circles around her, she became aware of the fascinated crowd gathering to enjoy what promised to be an interesting spectacle.

She didn't care if everyone in England listened in, so long as Clay was among them. Nor could she stop the flood of tears pouring down her cheeks.

"I'm s-so s-sorry," she sobbed into his neckcloth. "I did everything all wr-wrong. You were so good. So very good to me. But I wouldn't *see*! I just c-couldn't believe, even though I wanted to. *Because* I wanted to."

"See what?" he asked softly. "Believe what?"

"That you might really l-love me."

A few onlookers hissed at Clayburn. "You blind?" one of them called. "She's a beauty!"

"I'll take 'er, iffen you don't want 'er," a male voice offered. There was a scuffle as someone objected to the man's impertinence, likely with a fist, from the thud and cry of pain that followed.

Francesca lifted her face, scarcely daring to look into Clayburn's eyes. He had indulged her fits of temper and emotional displays so many times. She feared he was doing the same now, no more than that, only until she was calm enough to be dismissed in a civilized manner.

But he gazed back at her with gentle curiosity. "Whyever did you think I could not love you?" he asked. "Is it because I lived a stupid life before we met? To be sure, falling in love with you is the only intelligent thing I've ever done. No wonder you are surprised."

"N-not your life before. That was the excuse. Your father was another excuse. I had thousands of excuses to hold you away, and fought you because it was easier

211

than fighting myself. But all the time, it's been *me!*" She clutched at his coat with both hands. "I'm too tall, and I don't know how to go on in London Society, and I'm a m-mongrel by birth. And worst of all, I'm o-ol-*older* than you!"

Mortified, she buried her face against his lapels and heard a low rumble from his chest. Good God. He was laughing!

"You omitted your hair-trigger temper," he reminded her fiendishly. "And your resolution to manage everyone who crosses your path, and your remarkable ability to flay a man with your tongue from thirty paces. But *older* than I? Perhaps when we began, before I became entangled with you and Bromley and Arthur and the fearsome Livvy. But I swear I've aged a decade in the last few weeks."

"Wretch," she scolded into his neckcloth. "Years of dissipation brought you down. We Childes only speeded the process."

"I say you marry her!" a woman exclaimed.

The crowd took up the chant. *"Marry her! Marry her!"*

"It seems we must humor the masses," he said, prying her gently from his chest and standing her back a few inches so that he could look into her eyes. His lips curved in a beautiful smile. "For no other reason than because we both want it, Francesca, will you be my wife?"

A hush fell over the street. Everyone leaned forward to hear her answer.

"Oh, yes," she whispered.

To loud cheers, he pulled her firmly into his arms and gave her a lingering kiss.

Then, breathless, she felt him lift her into the coach. A flower peddler stepped forward and pressed a bouquet of March daffodils into his hands.

"For the bride," she said with a toothless smile.

Clayburn spoke to the jarvey, jumped inside, and waved out the window as the carriage pulled away. Then he tossed the flowers onto the squabs, seized Francesca by the waist, and pulled her onto his lap. "We shall be the talk of the neighborhood over supper tonight."

"Where are we going now?" she asked, toying with a vagrant swatch of dark hair over his ear.

"Why, to Grosvenor Square, of course. Are you not the hostess for a wedding breakfast? Not ours, alas. But everyone will be concerned if you fail to appear."

"The devil with them all!" she declared, surprising another laugh from him. "But I suppose we must."

"Not to quibble with my great good fortune, love, but what exactly sent you chasing after me of a sudden? Certainly nothing I said to you in that church."

"You were beastly," she agreed, "which I roundly deserved. But it's what you wrote that opened my eyes at last. And my heart." She held out her right hand and realized it was empty. "Oh God. I've lost it! I must have dropped it in the street. We must go back and find it."

"We'll do nothing of the sort," he said tranquilly. "Whatever it was, I shall replace it. What precisely did you lose?"

"The poem! The one you wrote for me. The one you tore up by the altar. On your way out, one piece fell from your hand. I found it, and saw my name and read the words."

"A wonder you did not run in the other direction, then. I am no poet. Obviously."

"I don't care! I mean, I could hardly tell from the little that I found, but you must show me all of it."

"One day," he agreed, color washing over his cheeks.

"Not soon. As of now, I am three lines short of a sonnet and fourteen lines short of a decent one. But in a few years' time, when I've polished it up, perhaps I'll read it to you." He grinned. "You might have had the decency to be christened with a name I could rhyme."

"Lots of words rhyme with Francesca," she retorted. "But you'll need to learn Italian."

"Gladly. You can teach me." He untied the ribbons of her bonnet and sent it to join the daffodils. "Meantime, I'll not allow you the slightest opportunity to change your mind again. We are solemnly and very publicly betrothed to each other."

"I won't change my mind," she vowed. "I have only just found it, you know."

He gave her an uncertain smile. "Does your mind perchance tell you that you are in love with me?"

"Oh yes. My heart, too. And the rest of my body is shouting Amen."

She'd meant to make him laugh, but he only applied himself intently to the buttons of her pelisse, his expression unreadable. If she didn't know better, she would have thought her consummately sophisticated rake was having an attack of shyness. After a moment, she took his hands away and began to peel off his gloves. "You are supposed to be happy that I love you, Lord Clayburn."

His gaze met hers and held. "Never doubt it, Francesca. I'm a bit dazed is all. It suddenly hit me like a shot from a crossbow, you here with me, meaning to stay with me, *wanting* to. As many times as I dreamed this and told myself it would come to pass, I must not have believed it."

"Cupid has taken to firing a *crossbow*?"

That did make him smile. With gloves off, he made swift work of unbuttoning her pelisse and removing it. "I believe you should tell me a dozen times each day that you love me, if it's not too much trouble. And my first name is Galen, although only my mother has ever used it. I hope you will not."

"Do you prefer Clay? Unless I'm in a temper, of course, in which case there is no telling what I'll call you." She gave him an assessing look. "Are you altogether certain you wish to spend the rest of your life with a tinderbox?"

"Goddess of fire," he corrected softly. "And yes, I have been certain for a very long time. The question has always been, would you take a scoundrel to your heart?"

"Oh, you scoundrels have a way of pushing your way in, and a good thing, too." She brushed away another tear before it could fall. "Thank you, Clay, for not giving up on me."

He drew her into his arms and held her in a strong, silent embrace that told her more than words could explain. She felt him sealing her to himself with fierce possession and respect. And love. In those minutes, she thought as he gently set her back again, they had pledged themselves to each other. She looked into his eyes and knew he was thinking the same thing.

"It's done, then," she said.

"Yes." He smiled. "Long past time, if you ask me. There are the formalities to be got through, of course, and a few details to be settled. Most can wait, but is there anything you wish to discuss now, while we are alone?"

He knew her so well. "My father," she murmured, fumbling with the lapels of his greatcoat. "His letters say that his health is much improved, and he even enclosed a note from his physician to back him up, but I cannot leave him alone any longer. I'm all he has, you see."

"On the contrary, my love. He's about to be saddled

with a son-in-law. Perhaps a grandchild within the year. I certainly mean to do *my* part. You wish to live with him, yes?"

"Will you mind? We are talking about Rutland-shire, Clay. The back of beyond. It will be you and me and Papa and the sheep."

"Far better company than I've kept the last many years," he said with a laugh. "But there is one thing more, if you will. I should like to bring my mother into our home. She has lost all sense of herself under Montford's rule, and—"

"Most certainly she is welcome! As for your father, we'll not give up hope of him altogether. Maria Beaton advised me to burn no bridges, so let us leave one open for him to cross. Happiness has a way of disappearing if it is not shared."

"Well, then. So far as I am concerned, the whole world is invited to share with us. Meantime, I understand you have planned to leave for home tomorrow morning. We'll travel together, me riding outside the coach for propriety's sake. Separate rooms at the inn, for the same reason. I'd prefer to overnight at the Rose and Thistle where we first met, if you have no objection."

"N-none." She couldn't for the life of her put two coherent words together as he began to remove the pins from her hair.

"When we arrive at Sotherton Manor," he continued, "I shall quite properly ask the duke's permission to approach his daughter with an offer of marriage. I rely on you to convince him this is a good idea. Then I mean to go before you on bended knee with a well-rehearsed proposal, which I expect you to accept. After that, you may decide where, when, and with what ceremony we are to be legally wed. I vote for immediately."

His fingers combed through her hair. "God, how I've longed to do this." He lifted his hand. "Look, you. I am shaking like a rattle."

"No more than I," she said, seizing his hand and bringing it to her lips. "But how can you speak of propriety when I am sitting on your lap with my hair down and—" She squealed as his other hand began to roam up her leg, lifting her skirt as it went.

He took a moment to examine what his hand had uncovered. "Long, sleek, and bewitching. Exactly as I imagined."

"I th-thought we were going to the wedding break-fast, Clay."

"Why, so we are. And when we arrive, I mean to transform myself into a model gentleman. But I instructed the jarvey to take us the long way around. A *very* long way around."

"Oh my," she protested halfheartedly as he toyed with her garter. "But you can't mean to . . . here . . . in a *hackney*!"

"Well, perhaps not quite. We'll save the best for our wedding night." He brushed a kiss on her cheek, and another, moving closer and closer to her lips. "But for one brief hour more, beloved, I want to be a scoundrel and do wicked things with you."

"Yes, please," she murmured as his hand moved past her garter, heading north. "But why an hour? You may go on being wicked forever, Lord Rakehell, so long as it's only with me."

The invitations have gone out,
offering a select few the chance to
live in Paradise...

Dangerous Deceptions
by Lynn Kerstan

0-451-21248-7

One invitation is accepted by Jarrett, Lord Dering,
a family outcast who lives by his own rules.
Another invitation is accepted by Kate Falshaw, a
hot-tempered actress on the run
from a scandalous past.

The exclusive resort they travel to promises to fulfill
every desire, but beneath the glittering facade,
deadly games are in play.

Available wherever books are sold or at
penguin.com

S628

Now available from
REGENCY ROMANCE

Miss Clarkson's Classmate
by Sharon Sobel

Emily Clarkson arrives at her new teaching position
expecting her employer to be a gentleman, and she's
shocked to find a brute. He's expecting a somber old
maid. And neither is expecting the passion that soon
overtakes them both.

0-451-21718-7

Lady Emma's Dilemma
by Rhonda Woodward

Once lovers, Lady Emmaline and Baron Devreux have
different points of view concerning their long-ago
tryst. But in an unexpected encounter, the two simply
have too many questions and the answers only come
by moonlight—and with a little mischief.

0-451-21701-2

Now available from
REGENCY ROMANCE